baggage

baggage

A NOVEL

JILL SOOLEY

1 Stamp's Lane, St. John's, NL, Canada, A1E 3C9
WWW.BREAKWATERBOOKS.COM

Copyright © 2012 Jill Sooley
ISBN 978-1-55081-139-6

A CIP catalogue record for this book is available from Library and
Archives Canada.

We acknowledge the support of the Canada Council for the Arts which
last year invested $24.3 million in writing and publishing throughout
Canada. We acknowledge the Government of Canada through the
Canada Book Fund and the Government of Newfoundland and
Labrador through the Department of Tourism, Culture and Recreation
for our publishing activities.

PRINTED AND BOUND IN CANADA.

Canada Council
for the Arts
Conseil des Arts
du Canada

Canada

Newfoundland
Labrador

Breakwater Books is committed to choosing papers and materials for
our books that help to protect our environment. To this end, this book is
printed on a recycled paper that is certified by the Forest Stewardship
Council®.

RECYCLED
Paper made from
recycled material
FSC® C103567

Printed on Silva Enviro 100% post-consumer EcoLogo certified paper,
processed chlorine free and manufactured using biogas energy.

For Kristin, Jack, and Brooke

marie

I've always loved one of my girls more than the other. I don't think it makes me awful, just human. Floss was always mine—as sweet, airy, and transparent as her candy namesake. Floss was always eager to please, never once cursed at me or told me I had a face on me like a dog. How could she not be my favourite?

Lolly was never mine. She was hard like her own candy namesake, tough and unyielding with an impenetrable shell. I tried to uncover the sweetness in her, but she left me before I could find it. Eventually they all left me—first Ray, then Lolly, and then Floss, in such quick succession I could have blinked and they'd all have gone away. With each departure, I felt myself recede a little further until everything looked distant, even my own hands when I held them up in front of my face in bed at night just to make sure I was still there.

Lolly came back to me a few months ago. Floss comes home today. Last night I held my hands in front of me and noticed the fine lines and swirls of my own fingerprints.

lolly

M arie sits in the passenger seat of my father's car shivering either with cold or nerves, I'm not sure which. She reeks of wet wool mingled with musk—Jovan, the one that comes in the orange box, not the white one. I get it for her every Christmas and I imagine a stockpile of them somewhere in the house, stacks of orange boxes neatly piled on top of one another. And still she feigns surprise when she opens the telltale box wrapped with too much paper and too much Scotch tape on Christmas morning, making a fuss and exclaiming in delight that it was just what she needed, as if her proclamations were somehow meant to please me.

Marie fiddles with the heat, twisting both dials until they can't go any further. The sound drowns out the radio and I feel the blast of artificial heat blow from the vent into my face with such force my skin grows hot, then prickles, and I feel my stomach begin to turn. It's the heat, I assure myself, but in the back of my mind I know it's nerves too. I lower it and then turn it off completely, but after a minute Marie fidgets with the controls again until the air starts blowing back in our faces.

"Oh God, Marie. I'm sweating to death here," I snap, but that's not true. I am beyond sweating, the heat having sapped every droplet of moisture from my skin. I keep licking my lips but they dry almost instantly. I feel them begin to crack.

"Stop your bitching, Lolly," Marie snaps, but she is smiling when she says it. Nothing could dampen her mood, not even me.

"When you gets to be my age, it takes everything to keep a tiny bit of warmth in your bones." She leans her face closer toward the vent to emphasize her point. The air blows her hair back revealing more than an inch of grey roots. I stare guiltily at her and she makes a self-conscious effort to hide the growth, sitting up straighter now and smoothing a gloved hand over the back of her head.

"I'll do your hair the weekend, okay?"

Marie shrugs in response and her face and neck grow flushed. I've embarrassed her by drawing attention to her greys and yet she's always been the one to point out her aging body in the first place. Marie isn't really all that old, but she pretends to be downright decrepit when it's convenient. She claims to be too old to text, too old to sit on the floor and play dinkies with my son, too old to drive in the rain, or the snow, or the dark and it is all three right now.

The rain has changed over to wet snow and the drops hit the windshield with a hollow thud. Marie tsks in response, scolding the weather for having the audacity to worsen today of all days. My wipers squeak seemingly in agreement. She fidgets nervously with the zipper of her purse and looks to the sky like she's assessing the plane's ability to land in this weather. The fog looks thicker than it was even a few moments ago but it's probably because we're headed east, driving right towards it. I get an ominous feeling, consider turning around and heading back, trying again later when the fog lifts, but I also know the very notion is too absurd to entertain.

"Floss will get in just fine," I assure her. "Sure they can land in almost any kind of weather now." Marie nods although she furrows her brow and her lips tighten into a worrisome thin line.

Floss is coming home. "Three years out in Calgary is enough," she said over the phone. "I'm leaving Dave here." She said this casually, as if she were leaving behind a bedroom set or a coffee table or something too unwieldy to pack in a suitcase. "He said I was fucked up. Can you believe that?" There was indignation to her voice that suggested some sort of defence on my part was warranted. I could picture her eyes, bright green with tears, as she confessed the information. Of course I could believe it. How could either one of us not be messed up? I sat on the couch holding the telephone and stared at the floor as if I could avert my gaze from her stare. She was waiting for me to reciprocate, to reveal the details of my own breakup with Gabe. I knew she knew—knew Marie had already told her I'd moved back—but I didn't want to talk about it, not with Floss, not with anyone. "I'll tell your mom to call you," I said and then I hung up and scribbled a note for Marie next to the phone. *Call Floss.*

It's uncomfortably hot in the car now and I crack the window open just the slightest in an effort to get some fresh air. Marie responds by blowing first into her gloved hands and then rubbing the tops of her arms, both futile gestures in light of her thick wool coat and black leather gloves. She does this with such dramatic flair it's like she's in a play and trying to get the people in the back row to see. Dad would have told her not to get her piss hot. It feels like she's baiting me to assume my father's persona, but I don't possess the same kind of patience he had. Dad might have been amused by Marie's exaggerated gestures, but I'm only irritated by them. I respond by loosening my scarf, tossing it on the floor, and pulling at the neck of my coat like I'd just found myself out on the back deck of the

Hillier's cabin in Holyrood in the middle of summer.

Marie picks my scarf up off the floor and starts folding it expertly until it's a perfect square. I don't know if she needs to do something with her hands, or maybe it's just force of habit. She's spent nearly a lifetime picking up after me—hanging up coats, matching socks, changing sheets. She unfolds the scarf and begins the process anew, folding, smoothing. Marie could fold a fitted sheet as neatly as if it was just taken out of the plastic wrapper from Sears.

I have an image of Gabe on an overcast morning, sleep still in the corners of his hazel eyes, trying to roll the sleeping bag back into the sleeve it came in from Canadian Tire and then giving up in frustration. "This is fuckin' impossible. I'm gonna take a piss." Then he tossed the sleeve in the garbage can on top of an empty tin of beans and stepped into the woods. Was it Victoria Day weekend or was it Labour Day? I don't remember anymore. I do recall it was the first time we spent an entire night together and I didn't have to rush to get home. I felt very grown up having sex with my boyfriend in our very own tent, on our very own campsite. Only now does it strike me as the kind of carefree thing only kids could be capable of. Adults did not sneak away for the weekend with nothing but a cooler filled with beer and a tent. Adults worried about gas prices; they got up early, even on a foggy Sunday morning to pick their stepsister up from the airport.

It's still hot inside the car and I start to shed more layers, my gloves and my wool hat, the static from it making my hair stand on end. Eventually I shake my coat off, all with the same exaggerated flair Marie had shown moments earlier.

I hear it before I see it. The sound of the car horn makes me wince and is followed almost immediately by the screech of tires that drone out Marie's frantic shout of something I can't make out. I don't see my life flash in front of my eyes, but for a split second I picture my father in the passenger seat instead of Marie. The vision is so unexpected it leaves me breathless and disoriented until I am jolted back to reality by the impact.

Glass doesn't break. The metal buckles but only a little, and although I feel the seat belt tighten against my collarbone and thighs, I don't think it's anywhere near hard enough to leave a mark.

"Are you all right?"

Marie doesn't answer me right away. She crosses her arms over her face protectively like she was still waiting for the impact. I'm thankful that at least the airbag remains tucked tightly inside its compartment although, judging from my scarf in her lap with the perfect creases, I had confidence Marie was up to the challenge of putting it neatly back if she had to.

"Are you all right?" I ask again, although what I really want is to shout at her. *Now look what you made me do! You couldn't leave well enough alone with the goddamn heat?* Marie nods quietly, unfurls the scarf, and begins folding it again. She looks at her watch, her forehead lined with a worried expression that irks me.

"How long do you think this is going to take?" Marie asks me this as if I were in the habit of plowing into random cars on a daily basis and know just what to do. I can tell Marie is thinking about police and accident reports, and picturing a distraught Floss arriving at the airport with no one to greet her.

"Don't worry, we're not going to be late," I say, not bothering to mask my own annoyance with her. "It's just a little fender bender and we're almost there anyway." A manic radio announcer informs us it's expected to clear around mid-morning, that we should check out some great end-of-season sales on kerosene heaters and snowblowers at one of the big box stores on Stavanger Drive later today, and that the time is 6:13 a.m. Floss' plane is supposed to land in thirty-four minutes. Marie clucks her tongue like she always does when she's nervous and the sound grates on me almost as much as the reason for it in the first place. Floss is a full-fledged adult, older than me by two years, and quite capable of gathering up her own baggage and waiting in the middle of it.

The man driving the other car is already outside, inspecting the damage to his vehicle. His head is shaved completely and he sports a neatly trimmed goatee. His woolen overcoat does little to hide his broad shoulders and he's wearing a scowl across his face that causes me to shiver involuntarily.

"Lock the door will ya, for God's sake. He's probably drunk," Marie says disapprovingly, although he looks perfectly sober to me. His step is straight, assured, confident. He stands with his hands on his hips, peers at me through the windshield, seemingly annoyed that I haven't gotten out yet.

"What makes you think he's drunk?"

"What else is he doing on the road at this hour on a Sunday morning?"

"We're out on the road and we're not drunk."

"We're on our way to the airport," Marie shoots back defensively as if I had accused her of something.

"How do you know he's not on his way to the airport too?"

"Do you have to argue with me about everything?"

I've been arguing with Marie for years about everything and nothing. It's what we do, the foundation of our relationship, so I'm taken aback by the tone of exhaustion in her voice.

"What would you like me to do, Marie?" I am just as frustrated by the turn of events, but she is thinking only about how this is going to impact Floss, who is at this moment circling in the sky as oblivious to my current predicament as I am to her own problems. "We can sit here all day if you like, but if you want to get to the airport to pick up Floss, then I'm going to have to get out and talk to this guy."

I watch as the other driver bends down to inspect a dent in the bumper of his car, his gloved hand feeling the dent as if it were a child in need of comfort from a skinned knee. He stands up and looks expectantly at me once again, his facial expression a mixture of annoyance and impatience.

I've never been in a car accident before and I'm not sure of the protocol, so I simply follow his lead, busy myself with inspecting the damage to my own car. It's only a small dent so I turn my attention to his vehicle. I see my distorted reflection in his car door. I'm surprised there's an image at all. His car is shiny even in the dull light of dawn when every other car on the road in March, including my own, is covered in a thick layer of grey salt and slush. His driver-side mirror is on the ground in two jagged pieces amongst the sand and gravel left behind by the road-clearing crews. I see the sky reflected in the glass, see the snow falling above me, and the effect is disorienting. I place a hand on the hood of his car to steady myself.

"Are you all right?" His voice possesses a similar impatience as mine when I posed the same question to Marie a few moments earlier.

He continues to walk around the perimeter of both cars with a deliberateness that I find mildly annoying. I am about to say something to try and move the process along when he finally speaks.

"You'd think," he says to me, "that being the only other car on the road at this hour, you'd be able to avoid me."

"You're the one that ran into me," I point out uncertainly, since I'm not really sure what happened. I wonder if the crowd at the Hoyles Escasoni had seen anything. I look behind me at the old folks home, thinking I might see old people with their faces pressed against the glass, hungry for a little excitement, but there's nothing save for mini-blinds, closed up until the next shift comes.

"Yeah, except I didn't run a red light," he says sarcastically.

I am about to protest the accusation but realize with a sinking feeling that the light must have changed as I was preoccupied with shaking off my extra layers. I stand quietly in the street, silent while he continues to assess and examine the wreckage until I begin to feel the weight of the snow pile on my shoulders. I rub the tops of my arms in the same manner that Marie had done earlier and I regret having removed my winter coat. The snow lands in big drops along the man's bald head, melting immediately and then running in rivulets down his face. He wipes them away quickly as if they were tears or sweat. I am aware too of how cold I am now that I am standing outside in the dawn with nothing more than a T-shirt, grown damp with snow. My teeth begin to chatter and I don't trust myself to speak.

"Do you have a coat?"

I nod.

"You might want to put it on. Your lips are starting to turn blue," he says, producing a cellphone from an inside pocket of his wool overcoat. I get a sinking feeling that we will be here a long time on the side of the road, giving our own accounts of what happened. I will have to explain to the police how Marie distracted me, fidgeted with the heat, and tsked at the fog, but in the end it will still be my fault.

"Don't call the police." I'm surprised by the desperation in my own voice. "Please," I plead.

"And why is that?" he asks me, smiling at me as if I've somehow amused him, although I don't think I've said anything remotely funny.

Because, I think to myself, *I can't afford an increase in my car insurance. Because I don't want to be late to pick up Floss. Because I hate filling out forms.*

"I'll pay for your damages," I say instead, knowing full well I can ill afford to pay for my own damages. I think I have three dollars and eleven cents in my checking account and I'm not getting paid for another week. I've been living off Marie ever since Gabe and I broke up, and before that I had been living off

Gabe's parents. *It's just for a little while, until I get back on my feet* I promised Marie, but aside from buying a few groceries here and there, I haven't been able to contribute anything.

"I need to get to the airport to pick up my sister," I add when he doesn't respond to my offer of payment. He stares at his cellphone, debating whether or not to make the call. I sense he's on the fence, so I elaborate. "It's kind of an emergency. She's coming home from Calgary. She just broke up with her boyfriend and she's sort of fragile right now. I haven't seen her in three years."

I've never called Floss my sister before. Under normal circumstances I am quick to point out that Floss is not my real sister, as if it were an affront to my character to share the same bloodline. But right now I need her to be my sister, in part to appeal to his sympathies but also because I don't want him to make assumptions about me.

I sense Marie's nervous energy from inside the car. I don't have a watch on but I see the sun start to break, the sky goes from dark grey to light grey. "She's going to land soon, so maybe we could just exchange information for now and then deal with the insurance later on. I mean, both cars are drivable and I don't want my sister to think I'm after forgetting her. I'm sure you have somewhere you need to get to as well."

"I guess I need to get to a garage now," he deadpans.

I regard him curiously, wondering about his intended destination before this all happened. Anyone on the road before six on a Sunday morning must have a sense of purpose, a destination deemed important enough to get out of bed and brush your teeth before the sun rose. Or maybe it was the other way around. Maybe he's been up all night and is only now heading back to his bed. I don't know if it's curiosity, or if it's just that I'm uncomfortable when people know more about me than I know about them. "Were you coming or going?"

"What's the difference?"

I shrug in response, hear a plane circling overhead and look up, expecting to see Floss' face in the window looking down at me.

"Lolly?" I spin around quickly at the sound of Marie's voice. She pokes her head out through the window of the car. "What are you doing out there? Having a cup of tea? That's probably Floss' plane and you're standing out there with no coat on and not a care in the world."

"I'll be right there," I holler back, shooting her a pleading look. I turn back to him, my face red with embarrassment, although he looks amused at the exchange.

"You better not keep your mother waiting, or your sister for that matter." He thinks Marie is my mother and it's my fault this time, not hers. That's the way lies are, one leading to another. People used to mistake Marie for my mother all the time, at the grocery store, the doctor's office, a restaurant. She never corrected them not once, just smiled apologetically at me afterwards and said she didn't need to explain our family business to every single person she met in the run of a day.

He puts the phone back in his inside pocket, producing a pen instead. "Give me your hand," he motions and almost instantly I offer it to him, palm up like he was a fortune teller. He takes my hand in his and writes his name and telephone number in the lines of my palm. It tickles just the slightest but I resist the urge to pull it back and tuck it underneath my arms. He writes like my son, in all capital letters, as if the lower case ones were too small to bother with. His name is Carson Keane and he trusts me, even though he probably shouldn't.

"Call me after you catch up with your sister." He opens his mouth to say something else, the puff of hot air a visible cloud of smoke in the cold. It fills the space between us but then he stops, closes his mouth, and turns away from me. I watch his tail lights disappear into the fog, two red eyes staring back at me, before Marie starts honking the horn. He's gone and I'm still standing on a ditch by the side of the road, shivering like a lost dog.

"Lolly!" Marie shouts between blasts of the horn. "Are you planning on walking to the airport?"

"Don't get your piss hot," I mumble under my breath.

Floss' plane is late. Marie and I end up with an extra forty minutes to waste. We sit at a Tim Horton's table sprinkled with sugar from the previous occupant, and avoid looking at one another. Marie squints at an arrivals monitor that she can't read unless she's directly underneath it anyway. She keeps looking up at it waiting for it to change, to tell her Floss is here.

"I hates this airport," Marie says, her cheeks puffy with air as she blows into her paper cup. Marie said the same thing the last time we were here together, when we dropped Floss off. She followed her all the way up to the security line and then when she'd lost sight of her altogether she ran down to the bathroom and threw up. I waited for her outside, but I could hear her heaving.

"I don't know why they had to go changing it all around. It was so much friendlier before."

It didn't matter whether it was the old airport or the new airport, if you flew into St. John's you were going to be gawked at. You used to be gawked at on the main floor, where everyone jockeyed for position in front of the arrivals doors to mob some long gone but not forgotten family member. They could be making their first trip back to Newfoundland in forty years, could be coming home from working six months in Alberta, or even just coming back from two weeks in Florida. It didn't matter. There was always someone to greet you with a little bit of fanfare, enough to let you know you were missed. I used to feel bad for the four or five people that got off the plane without anyone to greet them. They'd get their bags and exit quietly by the taxi doors while everyone else around them was hugging and jumping with delight like overeager children, talking about how good everyone looked and how they couldn't wait to get a real feed of fish and chips, too absorbed in catching up to realize their bags had gone around the carousel three times already.

The way the new airport is laid out, you get gawked at coming down the escalator, which is even worse because it's like you're being examined in slow motion, all the faces looking up at you from the bottom, squinting and pointing like you had something stuck in your teeth. Not that I'd experienced that particular vantage point, the revered arrival. I'd only ever been one of the faces in the crowd.

My father brought me here to pick up my aunt after my mother died. *Oh Ray*, she sighed when she emerged from the crowd, and it sounded like she was scolding him but it wasn't his fault and I wanted to say something in his defence. He shrugged back at her, asked her how many bags she had and if she ate on the plane. Did anything but talk about my mother. When my father died, Gabe and I picked up the same aunt. *Oh Lolly*, she sighed, her voice thick with pity this time. I asked her how many bags she had, if she ate on the plane, my voice shrill and unsteady. I felt Gabe squeeze my hand, a reassuring tug that restored my voice and steadied my breath. I envied all of the happy reunions going on around me and found myself squinting up at the escalator in search of my parents.

"Are you all right?" Marie asks. "You looks awful far away."

She takes a dainty bite of a timbit coated in powdered sugar and chews slowly and deliberately. It will take my stepmother four bites and fifteen minutes to eat what my three-year-old can handle in a single bite. A coating of powdered sugar settles into the cracks of her lips along with the remnants of a frosted pink lipstick she must have applied in the dark before waking me.

"You seems upset," she adds when I don't answer right away. "Are you still rattled about this morning?"

"I feel bad about Dad's car. He was so particular about the car." I hear the slightest tremor in my voice as if I were afraid to tell my father I'd crashed his car, and I feel an emptiness at being denied this simple rite of passage.

"He wouldn't care about the car and you knows it. Besides, it's only a little dent. If Floss notices it we'll tell her someone hit you in the parking lot at the mall. She'll believe that because they're all mad over there."

In all likelihood Floss probably won't notice the scratch. She doesn't see the obvious. She won't notice the dent but will be able to tell from the inside of the car that Marie and I had a tense morning, the same way you could smell the lingering smoke from a cigarette.

"Is Floss excited about coming home?"

Marie sweeps the pile of sugar onto the floor in one quick motion as if it had only just gotten on her nerves although our coffee cups are nearly empty now.

"I don't know. I hope so. I'm relieved she's coming back."

I look at the spilled sugar, hidden amongst the pebbled tile. Relieved certainly wasn't Marie's reaction when I called to say I'd be coming back. She was hesitant on the phone, didn't quite believe me.

"You and Gabe must have just gotten into a fight. You'll work it out."

"We didn't get into a fight," I'd insisted, which sounded like the very thing someone would say if they did get in a fight, but I was telling the truth. We weren't the type of couple that fought and broke up. Gabe and I had never gotten into a fight, not even then. "We're just over."

Marie waited up for me, told me there were clean sheets on the bed and a spare key on the dresser. Kenny could stay in the small bedroom where all his toys were kept anyway. Then she looked at Kenny all bundled up in his snowsuit yawning and clutching his new Batman toy Gabe had just bought him. She tsked disapprovingly at me like I'd done something to offend her. "I hope you know what you're doing, Lolly."

When they announce the arrival of Floss' plane, Marie and I take our positions at the bottom of the escalator and watch the parade of passengers make their way down the slow-moving steps.

We notice Floss at the same time. Marie puts one hand over her mouth, maybe an attempt to hide her tears at seeing Floss, or maybe to hide her surprise. She looks different, Floss. She's gained weight. Her hips look wider, her chest fuller, but the extra weight looks good on her. It was like she left in the body of a girl and came home a woman. Her hair is almost as long as mine now, although it looks more unkempt than anything, like she'd just never gotten around to making that hair appointment. It's tangled, unruly, and uncombed and falls in her face. She wears no makeup save for a clear gloss that looks applied almost as an afterthought on the final descent. She hugs her sweater low on her belly and scans the crowd below for a glimpse of a familiar face. When she spots Marie, Floss bursts into tears and Marie takes her into her arms and pats her back, smoothes her hair, and whispers that everything is going to be fine. As I witness the scene, I am struck by the thought that you aren't supposed to cry at arrivals, only departures. And then I'm hit by a more shocking thought, one that makes me shiver. I wish Marie had held me the same way when Gabe and I broke up.

floss

"Do you think I have low self-esteem?" My mother looks irritated by the question, furrows her brows and looks at me like I'd just insulted her, said her shoes were ugly or she was after gaining weight.

"That's what Dave said," I say, already backtracking. "When we broke up he told me he thought I might have low self-esteem."

It wasn't exactly what he said. He said I was fucked up, but I'm pretty sure that's what he meant. He'd only asked me to squeeze a pimple in the middle of his back. If it was any other day, it would have been fine, but it was that day. He couldn't reach it and it was red and raised and filled with pus. I squeezed it hard, harder than I normally would. There was nothing gentle in my ministrations that day. I left fingernail marks in his skin and I heard him grunt. Eventually it ruptured and the more I squeezed, the more fluid came to the surface until eventually the tips of my fingers were white from the pressure.

"Ow! Jesus," he yelled, taking a wide step away from me. "You trying to fucking kill me?" He turned around to examine the red mound in the centre of his back in the bathroom mirror, his head twisting and craning awkwardly. My skin felt tender, like it was me who had the welt on my torso and I dug my nails into my palms. I felt everything come to the surface of my skin, the pus and blood mingled with my own insecurity. It covered my chest in a fine sheen of sweat and I had the worst feeling come over me, that sick feeling of dread when you know you'd lost something important. I had to leave. I'd left something precious behind and I was petrified I wouldn't be able to find it.

"I have to go back home to see my mother." My eyes filled up a little. I waited for him to ask me what was wrong but he kept staring at his back. A tiny dot of blood seeped from the centre of his back and dripped down at the same time a tear rolled down my face. I was frozen, unable to wipe either away.

"I feel empty here," I said. I thought maybe he might ask me to explain, or at the very least he might put his arms around me, offer me some source of comfort, and I could tell him about how I ran into my father that day, how it made me so confused.

"You're a complete fuck-up," he said instead.

I hadn't intended to pose the question to my mother while waiting for takeout fish and chips at Ches', the place where I could finally get the chips, dressing, and gravy I couldn't get in Calgary no matter how many other Newfoundlanders were there. I could still hear the hum of the plane's engines from this morning, or maybe it was the fryer in the back or the cooler filled with Pepsi and lemon meringue pie. I hadn't wanted to bring it up at all. I wanted to bury it like we bury everything else, cover it under six feet of dirt and rock and gravel alongside Ray.

It's Ray's fault we don't talk about our feelings anymore. Mom used to want to talk over everything. Feelings were important to her. She used to preface almost every sentence with *How do you feel about…? How do you feel about breakfast for dinner? How do you feel about wearing your red shirt to school instead of the purple one? How do you feel about living with Ray and Lolly?* Ray never wanted to talk about anything, but who could blame him, since talking with him always ended with someone either crying or fighting.

My mother doesn't respond right away to my question. She just continues to ferret away packets of salt and vinegar in a brown paper bag as if she didn't have the same bottle of vinegar in the fridge that she had when I left three years ago. She never used to be so cheap. It was Ray who made her that way, just like he turned her into someone who didn't want to talk things over anymore, made her the female version of himself. I feel a wave of resentment toward Ray bubble up inside me and I have to remind myself that Ray is dead. The anger feels like a waste, but it doesn't go away.

"Now what makes you say that?" my mother asks me dismissively, surveying a display of condiments as if she were picking out a piece of jewellery to wear to a party.

"Just because your boyfriend broke up with you, and you put on a few pounds? Sure that's nothing. You carry the weight good. At least it's not all in your hips." She grabs several packets of tartar sauce even though we haven't ordered any fish and shoves them in the paper bag and then goes back for ketchup.

"Kenny likes to squeeze his own ketchup packets," she offers by way of explanation. "He squeezes it all together in one big pile for dipping. I tells him it's better to spread it all around the fries so everyone gets a little bit, but he insists on doing it his own way. Stubborn like his mother, that one is."

I feel like we're having two different conversations, as we often do. She sits at a table where the scent of lemon cleaner wafts up and mingles with the smell of fish and grease. She looks expectantly at me, waiting for me to weigh in on the whole ketchup strategy, or perhaps make a lighthearted comment about Lolly's trademark stubbornness.

"I'm not fussy about ketchup," I mumble, but of course my mother knows that already. She is my mother after all and yet there are so many things about me that she doesn't know. She thinks I came home because I got into a spat with a boyfriend but it had nothing to do with Dave and everything to do with me. She'd be surprised to learn I saw my father in Calgary receiving chemo at the Foothills Hospital. She'd be happy to know that he's sick, I think—thrilled even—although she'd rather someone else ran into him besides me. It would be just the thing she'd call my Aunt Doris about, barely able to contain her excitement. *You'll never guess who has the cancer....*

I can still picture him bent over and heaving violently into the bowl. I wasn't supposed to be there but when I saw his name on a chart, among so many others, it startled me. I recognized the name the same way I remembered our old telephone number from before he left. It didn't mean anything to me anymore, but I could still recall it at will.

There was no one with him so I sat down next to him and watched in trepidation, fear, and fascination. He sneered at me when I sat down, his lips pulled away from his mouth, and I could see the remnants of vomit stuck to his teeth. I offered him a paper cup filled with water to rinse but he ignored me. He didn't smell as bad as I thought he would, just a faint sour odour that mingled with the pleasing scent of adhesive bandages.

"What the fuck are you looking at?" He spat out the words like it took all his energy. A wayward piece of vomit flew from his mouth and landed on my scrubs. He looked mildly apologetic and wiped the corner of his mouth with a plaid flannel sleeve. I customarily got worse on my scrubs on a day-to-day basis so I didn't flinch at that, but I did flinch at his words, which seemed to shoot right through me. I swear I could feel the exit wound at the back of my skull. They were Lolly's very first words to my mother and I laughed to myself at the irony. He looked perplexed by my presence. He could tell by my uniform that I worked at the hospital but I didn't check the equipment or look over his chart. I didn't do anything save for stare at him. He had no idea who I was although he kept staring back and squinting at me as if I were slowly coming into focus.

"I'm sorry you're sick," I said to him. It was sincere, although I doubt he perceived it that way. He was probably told the same thing by dozens of other medical professionals before me.

"Who the hell are you?" He might have thought he was hallucinating, a side effect of the drugs. Regardless, it emboldened me to tell him the truth. Either he wouldn't remember later, or he wouldn't believe it was true.

"Florence Donovan," I replied shrugging my shoulders as if I were insignificant. His eyes grew wide and we stared at one another. "Most people call me Floss now," I added since I wasn't sure if he knew that. I couldn't remember if I'd always had the nickname, or if it was a name that mom put on me later.

I didn't know if he was an ugly man or if the sickness had made him that way. He was frail, so thin he possessed the body of a prepubescent boy. His hair was just about gone, only a small strip remained along the back of his neck. There were lines and creases in his face so deep they could have been scars. He had an oval-shaped crater scar from chicken pox on his forehead, above the left eye. I had one just like it on my cheek. It might be the only thing we had in common. I felt my mother's shame at having been abandoned by the likes of him, and for once in my life I was grateful she'd had Ray.

His eyes welled up and I got up to walk away. It was too much to bear. He tried to say something, but I couldn't think of anything he could say that I'd be interested in hearing. There would be excuses, a whole lifetime of them. My pace quickened until I was practically running away from the oncology ward and back to my own floor.

My mother adds a handful of napkins and a few straws to her paper bag and lays it upright on a table. She's done collecting, at least for the time being.

"I got a job interview tomorrow at The Health Sciences," I say to her, changing the subject. "I'm probably not going to get it though. I don't have a lot of experience." I feel hot and my mouth is suddenly too dry to produce enough saliva despite the aroma of grease and onions that had my mouth watering in anticipation not five minutes earlier. I should have waited to get chips, dressing, and gravy, not run out as soon as it was open for lunch.

"That's wonderful!" She looks at me in happy surprise over a job I have yet to interview for. "Ray would be so proud of you."

"You don't even know what kind of job it is."

"It's a nursing job isn't it?"

"I'm not a nurse, I'm an LPN."

"Well what's the difference?" My mother waves her hand in the air dismissively. It's a rhetorical question, one that's been asked and answered several times without any understanding or desire for understanding on her part.

"No matter, so long as it's a union job with a good pension," she says. "No one thinks about that anymore, not since the oil came and there was all this money to be had. It used to be all you ever wanted was a steady union job, like Ray had at the phone company," she says shaking her head, as if it were a shame for people to have ambition. "Honestly I'm sick to death of hearing your Aunt Doris go on and on about Ted's job out on the rig. He may be making it hand over fist but he's gone all the time. You should hear her talk about him— *Ted this and Ted that.* He's got rainbows coming out of his arse that one does. But he is a good boy," she adds as if she felt badly for her jealousy infused tirade.

I feel as if I've disappointed my mother once again, for as much as she pretends to dismiss all of Ted's achievements, I know deep down she's been waiting for the opportunity to boast about mine and Lolly's achievements. I can picture her sitting in Aunt Doris' wingback chair with the blue floral pattern, listening to Doris go on and on about Ted's latest accomplishment. Mom will sip tea and think of something to say. Being a nurse's aide was all right, but I know she wanted more for me. Lolly wasn't much better either, a single mother who cut hair. Mom's taken to pinning all her hopes on the next generation. *Kenny eats all his vegetables. Kenny can write his name. Kenny knows his ABC's. Kenny can count to ten in French already.*

My mother peers inside the paper bag, surveying her haul. I can see a circle of white hair on the crown of her head where she's bent forward. I feel a burst of anger at Lolly for that growth of hair, along with inexplicable pity for my mother.

The girl behind the counter pretends to be busy even though there's no one else here. She wipes down the counter, the glass door of the cooler filled with soda cans, blows dust off the debit machine. She's heavy, wears a hairnet, and sports a waxy sheen of chapstick on the top of her upper lip. She watches us out of the corner of her eye and I sit up straight. I wonder if people can tell when you're feeling bad about yourself, if there's some sort of vibe you give off that makes people stare at you, or if people stare all the time, but you only notice them when you're feeling self-conscious. It was no wonder Lolly reacted to my mother's gaze on that first fateful meeting. I'm half-tempted myself to ask the girl what the fuck she's looking at.

In the car, Mom balances the bags of food on her lap, leaning over them and cradling her arms around them, although whether her posture is meant to prevent them from falling or to provide warmth, I'm not certain. The car will smell like fish and chips for a week now, and Lolly will be sure to remind me every day how much I stunk up her car. It didn't matter that it already smelled like sour milk, or that I had to wipe the cracker crumbs off the front seat when I got in.

She just didn't want me to drive it 'cause it was Ray's. She got like that over Ray's things, possessive, especially after he died. No one was allowed to touch his things, not even Mom. She took everything that belonged to him—his *Reader's Digest* books, his wallet, his decks of cards—and boxed them up for herself. Poor mom had nothing left of Ray except for his worn underwear, with the elastic showing around the waistband, and his wedding ring.

Mom stares out the window, craning her neck to the right to stare at the shops on Commonwealth Avenue, the dirty banks of snow where the sidewalk should be and the teenagers with their hoodies trying to walk along the side of the road, the bottoms of their jeans dragging through the slush. The fog and snow from earlier in the morning have cleared, but it's still grey and dreary.

"It's all my fault, I s'pose," Mom sighs.

"What's your fault?" I sigh wearily, already suspecting and wishing I had stuck to the mundane—Aunt Doris' new curtains, Kenny's dinosaur phase, even Lolly's car accident this morning.

"That you're all screwed up. That you think you have low self-esteem, or what have you."

"It's not your fault at all," I insist. "I didn't say I had low self-esteem. I was just asking you if you thought I did."

"It's always the mother's fault, Floss," she says defensively, crossing her arms and resting them on top of the food with more force than necessary. The bag crinkles under the weight and I imagine my chips all squashed up. She acts as if I'd outright accused her, blamed her for all my problems.

"Are you gonna bring up that time I sent you to school sick? You've never gotten over that."

"No," I protest, although it doesn't keep my mother from harping on it, giving me the sense that she's the one who never got over it.

"You forget you know. It was the same year you had the chicken pox. I used up all my sick days and all my vacation days to stay home and look after you."

"I know, I'm sorry." I say it like getting chicken pox was a selfish thing for me to do.

"You didn't have a fever that morning."

"I told you my stomach hurt," I remind her quietly.

"I thought it was just gas pains. You had cabbage the night before, remember?"

"Of course I remember, Mom. I threw it all back up in the cafeteria the next day, in front of the whole school. They gave me one of those cabbage patch dolls when I came back to school."

"If I didn't go in I'd get docked a day and I wouldn't be able to pay the bills. Besides, my stomach hurt going to work every day. I did the best I could at the time, Floss. It wasn't easy you know."

"I know," I nod.

"Ray was supposed to make everything better," she says, her voice considerably more subdued than a moment earlier. "I married him just as much for you as for me. He was good to you."

I swallow hard, have to bite my tongue to stop from arguing with her. I hate when she says she married Ray for me, like I begged her to do it. I can appreciate that she wanted a life of her own, someone to share the burden of responsibility with, but when she says things like that, it sounds like I forced her to do something she didn't want to do.

"I didn't mean to upset you, Mom. I'm sorry. I was just trying to confide in you." But my mom's lips are pinched and she won't look at me. She keeps her head turned out the window, lost in her own private thoughts.

marie

It wasn't snowing yet, but it felt like it was going to come down any minute. The sky was a dark grey, the clouds low and heavy with moisture. It was going to be a big storm. I could smell it in the cool air, breathed it all the way down to my lungs. I climbed aboard the Metrobus, annoyed that it hadn't started to storm yet. They'd been calling for it all day and the system acted like a stubborn child, refusing to come when it was called. I could have taken the car, but I didn't like driving in the snow, hated the feeling of the tires sliding around, the windows getting too fogged up to see, so I'd taken the bus to work, and here it was nearly dark at four thirty, and not a single flake had fallen yet.

The bus pulled in behind another bus at the Avalon Mall. I knew we'd be here idling for a while, waiting for transfers and schedules to be honoured. The thought left me with an anxious feeling. I wanted to get home. Floss would be there by now, hungry and looking for dinner. I had pork chops out on the counter and I hoped she wouldn't try to turn on the stove in my absence. It would be just the kind of thing Floss would do to try and surprise me. She made French toast the other day for breakfast and thought she was all grown up. I stared out the window at all the cars in the parking lot, their roofs and bonnets clean and waiting for the sleet and snow about to fall. Even the asphalt was mostly dry, save for a handful of tiny puddles collecting around the melting piles of hard brown snow.

A man and a young girl took a three-seater across from me, although they left the middle seat vacant as if they were saving it for someone else. They were both carrying shopping bags, him a TipTop suit bag, which he gripped by the hanger on his index finger, folding it in half and resting it on his lap. The girl tossed her shopping bag onto the seat next to her like it was a bag of trash. Her hair was stringy, long, and uncombed and hung in her face in a way that made me wish I had one of Floss' elastic ponytail holders to offer her. She chewed slowly on a lollipop stick that no longer held any candy. Dirt and lint adhered to a patch of skin on her cheek where the lollipop must have left a sticky residue. She was striking all the same, her features a marriage of perfect contrast. Her hair was so dark it was almost black, her eyes an almost aqua blue offset by a fair complexion. The two of them didn't speak to one another, didn't exchange any looks or glances, and if you didn't see them get on together you might think they were travelling separately.

The man had hair like hers, as black as tar and nearly the same consistency. He'd slicked it back with a pomade and I could see the evenly spaced grooves left from his comb. He had a moustache that I could tell he'd worn since he was capable of growing one, and now no one would recognize him without it. The whites of his eyes shone slick like the surface of a hockey rink, and I noticed them because they seemed to complement his light brown eyes, which put me in mind of toast done perfectly, with butter melting into the centre.

He was dressed inadequately in sneakers and a light jacket,

which was perfectly fine if all you were doing was shopping out to the mall where heavy winter coats and jackets could weigh you down. The bottom of his pant leg was wet, so he must have stepped in a puddle getting on the bus. Despite my appraisal, he seemed oblivious, stared ahead and gently rocked and bounced to the turns and bumps of the bus, along with the rest of the passengers.

I felt an instant attraction to him beyond the ordinary way in which I might notice someone who was handsome or fit, or someone who dressed well. This man stirred something in me that left me aching to know more. I knew he needed looking after and I wanted to be the one to do it.

It's not surprising that I would have such fast and strong feelings. I was approaching forty, young and attractive enough to enjoy the power of a man in my bed and to believe in some semblance of romance, even if maturity tempered my expectations. Floss was ten, more and more independent, and already she was favouring her friends over her mother. I caught glimpses of the future, sitting on a sofa in the evenings, alone, waiting for Floss to call, or watching the clock until I had to pick her up, or even worse, lying in bed alone while I worried if she was out drinking, smoking drugs, or having sex.

I wanted to know why the man was carrying a suit, where he was planning to wear it, why he was taking the bus, why he didn't have anything to say to his daughter. I wanted to tell him to take his wet pants off so I could run them through the dryer for him. I wanted to bring him a cup of tea after I cooked him dinner. I pictured him sitting at my kitchen table eating the pork chops and the mashed potatoes I was going to cook that evening. I wanted to hold his rough hands in mine. I wanted to trace my fingertip around his lips and feel his moustache tickle the space between my upper lip and my nose. I felt my face burn with heat at the thought.

"What the fuck are you looking at?"

It was the young girl who said it. It took me a moment to figure out that she was talking to me. My head jerked away to the window and my face burned. Other people on the bus looked at me, some of them sat with their mouths open and others snickered. *What a saucy little thing*, I thought. Like the savage, she was. I wanted to get up and smack the face off her. If Floss had dared utter such a thing to a perfect stranger, I would die with the embarrassment of it, but I would also publicly admonish her. I would make her apologize. But then Floss would never say such a thing.

The man kept his mouth shut. He didn't reprimand her, didn't yell at her, didn't even shoot her a disapproving look. He just stared at his wet sneaker and sighed, a heavy sounding breath that made the air inside thicker. I noticed the girl's lip quiver and I was glad about it.

"I'm sorry," he said finally. "She's not usually like this."

I nodded curtly. I suddenly couldn't wait to get home to see Floss, with her smiling face and her sweet attempts to please me. I stopped staring at him and his daughter and looked out the window. It was snowing now, big thick flakes that covered the sidewalks. There were only four more stops before mine.

"Her mother died today." I felt like the bus had hit a brick wall. I felt awful for judging him, worse for the rush of satisfaction I had at the girl's quivering lip.

"I'm so sorry for your loss." I turned from the window to look at him again.

"We were expecting it." He said it the way I might have said I expected snow, or I expected Doris to stop by for supper. "I thought we were all ready. But my suit was too tight on me and my daughter didn't have any good clothes. The muffler went on my car last week so it's in the shop. I was going to wait till the weekend to get it fixed. I thought I had time, but...you know." His voice trailed off, his thought unfinished. "I hope we don't get too much snow," he added when I failed to say anything else.

It had started to come down harder, a slick coating already covered the street, the cars, and the lawns. My stop was next and I yanked down on the wire overhead to signal I was about to get off. I didn't want to leave it like this. I didn't want it to be one of those interesting stories of two people who met in passing, the way most interactions were in life. I knew I would always wonder whatever happened to him, would search the faces in the crowd at the mall, on Water Street, at the Regatta, looking for him. I stood up slowly, my hand on the back of my seat for balance and he looked up at me. He was going to say something but then thought better of it.

"Have a good night then," he said, but the bus made a wide turn, skidded in the snow, and the sudden motion thrust me forward into his arms with such ferocity it was as if the hand of God had placed me there.

lolly

Gabe notices the dent in my car almost immediately, despite my effort to hide it from him. My intention was to park on the street with the good side visible instead of pulling into the driveway of his parents' house. But he's out on the front steps clearing off the snow. He stops shovelling the steps and rests his weight on the handle of the shovel, watching me reverse the car so that my intention to hide the dent becomes not only apparent, but obvious.

A prick of annoyance, first at Gabe and then at his mother, shoots out from the back of my neck and radiates down my spine. There's not near enough snow to shovel in the first place and it's changed over to rain. The snow will be all but gone again in a few hours. Gabe's mom sent him out to clear the walk I was sure, since Gabe would never volunteer to perform the task. She's afraid of slipping and breaking a hip. *That'll be the end of me then,* she likes to say, shaking her head. *Might as well take me out back and shoot me.* Mrs. Hillier hardly even went out anymore, except to the cabin.

"What the fuck happened to your dad's car, Loll?" My dad's

been dead for four years and yet Gabe's reaction is similar to mine—*What would Dad say?* He waits for my explanation but I don't answer him, just stand at the end of the driveway in front of the car, looking up at him on the top step. Gabe leans over the railing and spits into the snow-covered bushes for no apparent reason other than to melt a tiny circle of snow. He hops down the steps in his boots for a closer look; the laces are undone and drag through the wet snow, leaving a trail in his wake.

"What the fuck happened? Y'all right?"

I feel my face grow red under his stare. "I'm fine. It's just a little dent," I say dismissively. Gabe is giving it a thorough inspection, his brow furrowed in thought as he tries to piece together the cause. This was always part of Gabe's problem, trying to figure out the things that didn't matter and ignoring the things that did. He bites the corner of his lip now and rubs his hand along the car door, all for a dent that's barely worth talking about.

"What'd you hit?" Gabe looks at me, perplexed, waiting for me to tell him about the accident. His questions make me feel small, and part of me wonders if he knows this as well, if it's his intention to make me uncomfortable.

"Was it the drive-thru at that new Tim Horton's? There's that one really narrow spot." Gabe holds his hands parallel to one another to demonstrate a narrow curve. He's not wearing gloves and his fingers are red and raw with the cold. My silence keeps him guessing. "Did you hit another car trying to get into a tight spot? Cause you can't park for shit. Remember the time you tried to parallel park and went up over the curb?" He says it with a trace of amusement, an incident to be fondly remembered. At the time it happened there was very little amusement. He covered his head with his hands and bawled at me. "What the fuck are you doing?" like it was something I'd actually meant to do.

"Jesus, Gabe, shut up," I snap at him. I stand back, fold my arms with a mixture of exasperation and annoyance. Gabe won't understand because he's so competent and comfortable behind the wheel of a car. I always admired the way he drove, his ability to cruise along trafficked streets, making turns with nothing but an index finger while his other hand held mine. He could parallel park in the smallest of spaces on Water Street, using nothing but the palm of his hand on the steering wheel and a casual glance in the side mirror. He never got lost, never minded snowy or icy roads, never got frustrated in traffic. He never yelled or cursed at anyone because they cut him off or veered into his lane. He might make a quiet comment about how another driver was an asshole, sometimes even a cocksucker, but he said it in such a way that he might have felt sorry for them. I loved driving with Gabe, whether it was out on the Trans Canada Highway or just over to Shoppers because we ran out of diapers at ten o'clock at night. It made me think he was capable of anything. If you were to ask someone what quality they wanted in a man, good driver was probably not at the top of the list, but it made my heart swell with pride.

"I blew a red light," I confess. I expect him to be somewhat incredulous that I went through a red light—after all it's the type of thing Gabe would never do so he finds it inconceivable that anyone else could—but instead he looks amused at my explanation, bursts into laughter.

"I got something else you can blow." He grabs his crotch and thrusts his hips forward. Sometimes Gabe acts as if he's forgotten we broke up, forgotten that I'm the mother of his child, that he is not in the company of his guy friends, or even that he's not seventeen anymore. I sigh in annoyance and roll my eyes but I keep my comments to myself so he can't accuse me of not being fun anymore. We both remember a time when I might have laughed at such a crude comment.

"Where's Kenny?" I ask sharply, my patience wearing thinner. I told Gabe I'd pick Kenny up by three and I expected him to be ready, bundled up in his coat, Batman in his hands. I don't know why I should expect it. It always takes a half hour for Gabe to get him ready, locate Kenny's shoes, his coat, retrace his steps to find Batman.

"He's inside with Mom and Dad. Mom took him to Piper's and told him he could pick out something quiet to play with, so she bought him a colouring book and some crayons. Then she bawled at me to shovel the steps. I told her it was going to be gone in an hour but you knows what she's like. Want to come in?" Gabe tilts his head toward the front door in invitation. "Mom's got a roast on. I knows you don't get that over to Marie's anymore."

"No, I certainly don't," I whisper in agreement and Gabe looks for a second like he might apologize for bringing it up but then decides it's probably better to just drop it altogether. "I'm not hungry," I say, placing a hand over my stomach to indicate how full I am. "Floss flew in this morning and she got chips, dressing and gravy for lunch. She got some for Kenny but they're all cold now. I told her to wait for supper but she had to have 'em right then. You knows what it's like after you been away for a while." I say this with an air of authority but neither Gabe nor I know what it's like, probably never will. We only know what everyone else tells us.

I feel guilty using Floss' homecoming as an excuse not to go in and make small talk with Gabe's parents, but I can't bear to stand in the foyer while Gabe hunts down a missing boot and his mom and dad prattle on and on about the bad winter we're after having. Whenever they use words like bitter, cold, and icy, I can't help but think they're talking about me.

"What's she doing home this time of year?" Gabe looks perplexed when he asks the question. Hardly anyone comes home for a visit in March. They save their vacation time for summers and Christmas.

"She and her boyfriend broke up." I can't remember his name, although I know it was something common, like Paul or Ron or Steve. I try to think of it while an uncomfortable silence settles over us. I wonder how long before every reference to anyone breaking up won't make us think of our own.

"Bullshit," Gabe says finally, looking too upset for news that should mean nothing to him. It's the only word that pops into his head when something so bad happens it's almost too hard to believe, like that gas prices went up again, it snowed another thirty-two centimetres overnight, my father was dead.

It was the first thing Gabe said when the condom broke. I vividly recall that night in a rush of bittersweet memories. Would we be here right now, standing on a curb outside his parents' house, stiff and awkward, if I hadn't gotten pregnant?

It wasn't the first time we had sex, it wasn't even close. We'd been sleeping together for more than two years, stealing away at every opportunity, alone in the car, or in his parents' basement after everyone was asleep. That night Gabe's parents were up to their cabin in Holyrood and we could have just as easily stolen off to the living room, to his bedroom, even to his parents' king-sized bed if we wanted to, and yet still we snuck down into the dark, musty basement to have sex on the old brown sofa.

Gabe rolled off of me when he was done and I pulled my shirt back down over my breasts, which were coated in his sweat and a handful of loose chest hairs that had fallen off him. A fine sheen of sweat broke out on his upper lip and the euphoria he'd felt just moments earlier had been replaced with a pained expression. He stood up quickly and turned his back to me like he was trying to hide something. Repression was not one of Gabe's characteristics so I knew right away that something was wrong. He walked into the adjacent laundry room and flipped on the fluorescent light. There was a slight delay from the moment I heard the switch to the moment the light flooded the laundry room, but it felt like hours.

"Gabe?" My voice was panicked. He'd never acted like this before. He might have rushed to put his pants back on, but he always finished by kissing the side of my neck and tracing a heart on my wrist.

"Bullshit," I finally heard him whisper, a measure of panic and fear in his breath.

I took the test in the bathroom of McDonald's a month later and then ran out to the parking lot to tell him. I rested the bag of hamburgers and fries on my lap. It smelled greasy and salty and I wondered why it didn't make me want to retch. I wondered if I'd taken the test right—I might have gone back inside and done it all over again, except I didn't have to pee anymore. Gabe looked expectantly at me from the front seat, mustard in the corner of his mouth.

"Fucking bullshit," Gabe said when I told him about the two pink lines. He gripped the steering wheel tightly until his knuckles were white like he was driving along a high, winding road that required every ounce of concentration. "I got some money saved up, a few dollars put away."

I didn't know what he meant. Gabe was not usually ambiguous. I couldn't tell if he was offering to pay for an abortion, or if he was trying to tell me we could rent an apartment and get by. They were two completely different scenarios. I must have looked confused because he turned to me then and asked, "What do you want to do, Lolly? I'm okay with whatever you say."

I don't know why, but at that moment I thought of Marie's reaction instead of my father's. Surely they would speak in whispers at the kitchen table about how I'd screwed up my life, and Marie might even glean a tiny bit of satisfaction with the announcement. She'd be happy that for once my father would be in complete agreement.

But once the shock had passed, Marie would take care of things. She'd make doctor's appointments for me; she'd ask them questions about my cervix and my uterus and all the things neither Gabe nor my father would be able to discuss with me. Gabe probably didn't even know what those parts were since there were no slang words for them. Tits, balls, pussy, dick—that was as much reproductive terminology as he seemed to know, and he mostly used the latter two terms to refer more to people he didn't care much for.

Female anatomy was the one area where Marie took her motherly duty so seriously, she often overcompensated. Ever since I first got my period Marie was overeager to dispense advice of a female nature. Did I want some Midol for my cramps, did I want her to show me how to insert a tampon, why did I want the pads with wings when all they did was bunch up and stick to the hair down there?

"I think we should have it," I told Gabe and he sighed, nodded and then he smiled at me in a way that made my eyes fill up.

"I must have some fucking sperm." Gabe shook his head at the magnitude of his pronouncement, like he was in awe of his own power. "It broke right through the goddamn rubber, right through all your tubes and shit and boom, right in your fucking egg. Like a bullet it must have been," he said, his index finger and thumb making the shape of a gun. "I bet it's 'cause I drink a lot of milk," he said taking a sip of coke. "Some things are just meant to be, I guess."

Kenny sees me from the living room window of Gabe's parents' and jumps excitedly up and down. I smile and wave and see Mrs. Hillier stand behind Kenny to see what all the fuss is about. She scoops him up in her arms, tickling his belly and his neck.

"Sure you don't want to come in?"

"I can't," I say shaking my head and drawing loops in the snow with my sneaker. "Maybe another time, though." I didn't know when it was going to get easier, this dropping off and picking up of Kenny. A year later and it still felt forced. Gabe tries too hard, I think, sometimes pretending things were the way they used to be before Kenny was born and before Dad died and the distance between us became wider. Sometimes I think I might prefer it if he spoke to me in a tone that was clipped or biting.

"I'm just going to warm up the car," I announce, even though I'd only just turned off the engine a few minutes ago. "Bring him out when you're ready." For some reason I think this will make Gabe move more quickly than normal. It's easier to linger over the whereabouts of a sock when I'm standing in the foyer listening to Gabe's dad talk about oil prices than it is if he knows I'm sitting outside in the car.

It doesn't, and before long the car becomes unbearably hot. I lower the heat, turn on the radio and watch the minutes tick away. After ten minutes pass I debate charging up the front steps demanding to know what the holdup is. I peel off my gloves and stare at my hand, remembering the feel of the pen on my skin from this morning, seductive as it traced along my palm. The ink is smudged slightly from sweat and obscured by little black woolies from the inside of my knit gloves, but it doesn't matter, I've already committed everything to memory. His name is Carson Keane. I know his cellphone number. I know he keeps his car clean. I know he makes his sevens in the European style, with a line through the centre of them. These are the only things about him I know and still the minuscule information leaves me aching for more.

Gabe comes down the stairs with Kenny flung over his shoulder like a sack of potatoes. Kenny laughs at being bounced around and is laughing still as Gabe buckles him securely in his car seat before handing over his four-inch Batman action figure.

Gabe gives the dent a closer inspection and then crouches down by the driver side window so his head is level to mine and gestures for me to roll down the window.

"You going to get it fixed?" he asks through the open window.

"I guess."

"No you're not," he says shaking his head and laughing. "You don't have the first clue where to take it. I knows a guy who has a body shop over in Paradise. He'll probably give me a good deal. I can bring it over for you if you want."

"No thanks," I say dismissively, waving my hand in the air.

"What have you got on your hand?" Gabe reaches for my hand and I make a fist in response.

"Nothing." I resent his intrusion with an anger that surprises me. "It's none of your business," I snap unnecessarily since Gabe is already running up the front steps.

"Drive safely," I hear him mutter sarcastically.

marie

The house smelled like death and burnt soup. I knew as soon as I stepped into the foyer that something awful had happened. I may have even known it before then, on the way home. At a traffic light on Topsail Road, I had an anxious feeling overtake me. The turn lane was backed up and my stomach felt queasy. It's just the egg salad, I told myself. Doris put too much paprika in it and I wasn't one for spices. I thought if I went to the bathroom, everything would be fine, but as soon as I came through the door and smelled the acrid odour of something burnt, I knew I would never be the same again.

Ray was dead. He'd been dead a few hours already, slumped over the table like he'd been taking a rest, the same sort of position Floss used to take when she was a toddler and skipped her nap, too tired to sit and eat supper. His back was to me, his lifeless head rested on the quilted placemat like it was a pillow. All I could see was a mop of thick, black hair, not a single grey hiding amongst the dark ones. I walked around him to get a look at his face. The skin around his lips was tinged blue and everywhere else he was so pale it was like he didn't have any colour at all.

There was a bowl of soup on the table in front of him, and the pot on the stove was burnt. He wouldn't have turned it off after he took up his soup in case he wanted another bowl. Ray would eat just about anything so long as it was hot. The soup must have been simmering for hours now and the whole works was stuck onto the bottom of the pot. I'd have to throw the pot away. There was no amount of soaking going to clean it off. Ray would hate to have to throw it out. He didn't like to throw away anything. I turned off the burner, felt the heat on my face as I leaned over the stove. I tested the soup on the table. I heard the scrape of my own teeth on the metal spoon and the sound went right through me, gave me the shivers. It was ice cold, the spoon, the broth, the potato, Ray. I knew he would be just as cold but I couldn't bear to touch him.

"Get up Ray," I said as if he could hear me. At first I said it softly but then I started shouting at him. "Get up!" I felt the tears form from inside the corners of my eyes and slide down my cheeks. They weren't mournful tears, not then. They were the result of pure hysteria. "Get up!" I shouted louder and louder thinking if I yelled it loud enough he would stir.

It was nearly four o'clock and Ray had been dead for about four hours. I knew this because he ate lunch at 11:50 every day without fail. He'd heated up the turkey soup I dug out of the freezer for him that morning, picked out the parsnips because they were the only thing in the world he wouldn't eat, and shook a load of pepper on it. I felt something cold and wet seep into my sock and looked down. I was standing in a puddle of water that Ray must have spilled. His glass was on its side on the floor. It wasn't broken. There was enough give in the linoleum. I got out a paper towel and wiped it up.

I didn't know what to do next. Ray was already dead and it seemed a waste to call an ambulance with a full complement of life saving equipment and paramedics but no other number besides 9-1-1 came to mind.

"My husband's had a heart attack," I said woodenly into the telephone receiver. "He's dead already so you don't have to rush. I mean if someone is in a bad car accident then you should probably go there first." I knew there were cutbacks to the health care and I didn't want anyone to die because they sent the last ambulance for Ray. I called Gabe's mother next and asked her to keep Lolly there for supper. Floss got off work at six and I hoped Ray would be gone by then. I couldn't stand him sitting at the table any longer. I regretted telling the paramedics not to hurry, and I thought about calling them back to tell them to rush, things were urgent. He didn't even look like Ray anymore. While I waited, I cleaned up the kitchen, threw the burnt pot in a garbage bag and brought it outside in the backyard. I soaped up the bowl, the spoon and the empty glass in the kitchen sink, cleared away Ray's dishes for the last time.

An hour and a half later Ray was gone and my kitchen was spotless. I sprayed air freshener around to cover up the odour so now it smelled like a mixture of lemon cleaner and lilacs. I pretended Ray was at Kent Building Supplies, picking up lumber so he could fix the fence out back. That's what we were supposed to be doing today but then Doris had wanted me to come over and see her new chesterfield. She thought the pattern in the sofa clashed with her wallpaper and was thinking about returning it for a solid colour.

"We'll go to Kent tomorrow," Ray had assured me. He'd just retired and was afraid of not having enough to fill the days ahead. I'd suggested he go by himself but he insisted I was good at picking out things and asking the right questions. He couldn't do anything on his own, always asked for my opinion on things I didn't have any opinion about—lumber, latex paint, motor oil. What did I know about all that?

If he'd have gone on his own, he might still be alive. I pictured him clutching his chest in the lumber aisle at Kent, falling to his knees while somebody over in plumbing called 9-1-1. Maybe he'd have died all the same, but he might have had a chance. Instead, he was flopped over the kitchen table, all alone for nearly four hours while I was sipping tea at my sister's coffee table, convincing her that a floral pattern was good for hiding stains. I might have been laughing at the very moment Ray was gasping and I was wracked with guilt at the image.

Floss and Lolly sat on opposite ends of the couch, waiting for me to tell them something grave. I wished they could have sat closer together. Floss was still wearing her scrubs from the nursing home where she was doing her internship, and she carried the scent of bleach on her. It mixed with the lilac-scented Glade and the lemon cleaner. Still, I swore I could smell the burnt soup. I started to feel anxious.

"Your father...Ray..." My voice cracked. I was afraid I wasn't going to get it out so I blurted it as fast as I could. "Ray is dead. It was a heart attack, I think." He'd had a heart attack two years before and he'd grown lax in following his regimen. He'd started eating bacon again, sausage and fish and chips. His walks were shorter and he couldn't remember if he took his blood pressure pills or not. Sometimes he took them twice in a single night and other times he skipped his dosage altogether. I should have looked after him better, kept track of his medicine and steamed his food instead of putting it in the frying pan.

Floss gasped immediately, her mouth taking the shape of an O while her fingers covered it up as if it were somehow offensive to the rest of us. We both turned to Lolly for her reaction. She always went to Ray for comfort so I wasn't even sure how to gauge her reaction. Lolly was pale but she didn't cry. Of course, I hadn't yet either, not really.

"Where is he?" She said this like she didn't believe me that he was really dead, like we were playing a joke on her and he was just hiding behind the curtain or under the bed.

"The ambulance took him to the hospital," I said, realizing how foolish it sounded, to take a dead man to the hospital. "They said they had to do an autopsy."

"I'm pregnant." Lolly said it so softly I wasn't sure I heard her right in the first place but then Floss' eyes got so wide I knew I heard her right. "He was supposed to be mad at me."

This was all too much. My head hurt with everything that had happened. I looked at the clock. At lunchtime I'd argued with Doris about whether the flowers on her wallpaper were blue or black. It felt so long ago I couldn't believe it was the same day. None of this could really be happening. Ray was dead. Lolly was pregnant. She was going to be nineteen in a couple of months, still a child herself. Either one of those occurrences was bad enough but together they were unbearable. Ray was going to have a grandchild and he'd never know. He would have been a good grandfather. He would have taken the child to Bowring Park, taught him how to build things. I hoped it was a boy because Ray complained all the time of living in a house with too many women. *So much goddamn estrogen in this house, it's a wonder I still got a dick*, he'd say to me sometimes at night.

"I'm going to move in with Gabe," Lolly announced. "He said his parents could fix up the basement for us, turn it into an apartment. We haven't told them yet though, we were going to wait a couple weeks. They already have a bathroom downstairs so it's just a matter of putting in a kitchen."

I didn't know what to say. Congratulations? That I could fix up the basement to make an apartment for them too? I felt abandoned. Ray was gone. Lolly was going. It would just be me and Floss all over again. And maybe that was how it was supposed to be.

Lolly talked about the layout of her new apartment then, prattled on about putting an extra outlet in the bedroom because babies needed lots of things that plug in, bottle warmers, baby monitors. I stopped listening. She was only talking about it because she wasn't ready to face the fact that Ray was gone. It would hit her later, maybe at his wake, or at the burial when he went into the ground, or when she packed up his stuff to take to Gabe's with her.

For me the moment came the day after he died, when they called me from the hospital to tell me Ray had had a heart attack, that it was triggered by a blockage in his airway, a turkey bone.

lolly

Floss is after dreaming again. Every morning she asks Marie and I to interpret her dreams. Yesterday she was lost on the East Coast Trail after following a man off the marked route. The day before she was swept up in a rogue wave out to Cape Spear. This morning she's on a sinking boat.

She sits on the couch in her fleece bathrobe with her slippered feet resting on the coffee table on top of yesterday's paper. She cups her hands around her coffee cup to keep them warm, and shivers.

"I had some bad dream again last night," she announces, waiting for either Marie or myself to ask her to elaborate, although neither of us do. Marie continues to iron Kenny's clothes at the dining-room table while I kneel on the carpet and try and put away the blocks and the action figures scattered all over the living room floor. I'll do it at least three more times throughout the day but I don't mind. It gives me something to do, even though it's as futile as Marie ironing undershirts for a three-year-old.

"So I'm in this boat, right?" Floss speaks in such a serious tone, for a moment I forget that she's just relaying a dream. "It's one of them tiny fishing boats and the water starts to get rough. All of a sudden there's a leak in the bottom and water is rushing in all around my feet and I'm bailing as fast as I can but I'm not getting anywhere and the next thing you know…" she pauses for dramatic effect. "I jump out and start swimming to shore, only I'm not getting anywhere because the waves are too rough. Then I look over and there's someone else in the boat, but I can't see his face. I woke up sweating to death and my heart was racing. It was so real. What do you think it means?"

I've never had a dream anything remotely like Floss describes. I only feel that kind of helplessness when I'm fully awake. I dream of either silly things or mundane things I do every day, like going grocery shopping or cutting hair, or straightening up the living room. I once dreamed I stood in the checkout line with a cartful of groceries only to realize I forgot my purse in the car as soon as she tallied it up. I remember waking up thinking it was all bad enough I had these ridiculous problems in real life, but now I had to have them in my dreams too.

"It probably meant you had to go to the bathroom," Marie says flatly. Kenny's clothes sit in a neat pile on the table and Marie turns her attention to towels. "When you dream about water that's what it always means. Haven't you ever had to go to the bathroom in the middle of the night so bad you dreamed you actually sat on the toilet and relieved yourself, wiped and flushed, the whole nine yards, only to wake up a few minutes later with a bladder so full it hurts? You drank all that water last night so it's no wonder."

Floss sighs in defeat, gives up on the dream analysis and takes another sip of her coffee.

"I'm going to the doctor this afternoon," she says.

Marie puts down the iron, a heavy sounding thud on the

dining-room table. "What for? Are your sinuses acting up again?"

"No, I'm just getting a checkup," Floss replies.

"What do you need to get a checkup for?" It sounds absurd to someone like Marie, and frightening at the same time. Marie won't go get a checkup. She doesn't believe in preventative health care. She won't get mammograms or blood tests or colonoscopies. I think she's afraid of what they'll find, that she'll end up like my father always wondering if he took his pills or not, afraid they'll tell her she can't put salt on her potatoes, or that she'll have to watch her sugar. Maybe she's afraid they'll tell her she's old.

It's important to get checked out," Floss insists. "Do you know if cancer runs in the family?"

"Cancer?" Marie repeats the word as if she'd never heard of it before. "No, heart disease is more our thing," she says like it was something she and her ancestors opted for. "The heart disease is what got my grandfather. I suppose he might have gotten cancer if he didn't drop dead of a heart attack when he was sixty-two. And my father had the diabetes awful bad. You remember what a state he was near the end, don't you? Maybe that's why you were drinking all that water last night."

"What about on my father's side?"

In all the years I've known Marie and Floss, it's the first time either of them has mentioned Floss' father. He is slightly less of a ghost than my own mother, whose presence often lurked between my father and Marie, hanging over them with a watchful gaze. But Floss' father—it's like he never existed in the first place. Marie pretends like she didn't hear Floss and continues to iron, lining up crisp creases in pajama bottoms, sweatpants, and jeans, but I can tell that she heard by the way her tongue darts in the crease of her mouth and then curls around her upper lip like she's licking the remnants of salt after a bag of potato chips. Marie does that when she's concentrating on what to say because I've seen the look many times before, usually in the moments preceding a fight between her and my dad. She eases down into a wooden chair at the dining-room table as if she were suddenly too exhausted to continue standing. She folds a hand towel into a perfect square, unfolds it, and folds it again the same way she folded up my scarf in the car the other day. She looks tired and weary, frustrated even, with no idea what to make of Floss since she came home.

"I bet cancer runs on his side," Floss says more quietly.

"I wouldn't know," Marie whispers before getting up to put the clothes away.

"Well I would," I hear Floss whisper to Marie's retreating back before announcing she had to get ready for her doctor's appointment.

It's been a week since Floss came home, a week since I ran into Carson Keane on the slick roadway to the airport. I haven't called him yet. Every day I find an excuse not to. No one wants to be bothered on a Sunday. I didn't get a chance to call on my break because it was too busy. By the time I got Kenny to bed, it was too late. I don't know why, but the thought of calling him terrifies me.

I stare at the palm of my hand with the phone in my lap. My hand is clean, pink with curved lines, a life line, a love line, a line for health. I can't tell one from the other. There are no traces left of Carson Keane's neat letters, his French seven or the zero that looked identical to the O. I can still see it though, and I trace all the imaginary letters and numbers, even the dash, with the tip of my index finger. I feel the pressure and the tickle from the tip of the ballpoint pen when I do, and the warmth from his other hand as he held mine steady. I'd copied everything he'd written that day on a post-it note although I didn't need to. All I had to do was close my eyes and it was there, tattooed on my flesh.

"Keane," he states abruptly before the second ring is finished.

"Hello?" I answer uncertainly. I was going to ask for him by name. *Is Mr. Keane there, please? May I speak with Carson?* Since he's already answered by name, I'm not sure what to say. "Um, you ran into me the other day." It sounds like I was behind him in the checkout at Costco. "With your car," I clarify. "It was over by the Hoyles Escasoni." There's the slightest inflection to my voice, like I'm making it a question.

"Ahh, Laura Sullivan. I was beginning to question my judgment."

Laura. The last person to call me that was my father and he was angry with me when he said it. I'd been insisting Marie refer to me by my proper name after she once called me Lollipop, which was my mother and father's nickname for me.

"My name is Laura," I insisted to Marie, who kept on forgetting about it and ended up calling me Laurie or Lolla or else she'd string the two names together like they were hyphenated, Lolly-Laura. "Why can't you just get it right? It's not that hard," I yelled at her, which earned me a stern rebuke from my father.

"Laura!" His voice, a combination of disappointment, anger, and disgust, made it sound like a bad word.

"Just don't call me Lollipop again," I said.

"How do you know my name?" I never told him my name. In fact the only indication he might know my name was when Marie rolled down the window to ask me what the holdup was. I can't remember if she called me by name or not, but if she did, I was certain she never called me Laura, much less Laura Sullivan.

"I have special powers," he says evasively.

He must have reported it. He probably copied my license plate on the palm of his own hand before he drove away. I wonder what sort of trouble I could get in and I start to question my own judgment about him.

"So you reported it then?"

"No," he says after a pause. "I did not."

I expel a breath of air that I was unaware I was holding. "So did you get an estimate yet?"

"It's fixed."

"Already?"

"It was more than a week ago. Yours not fixed up yet?" He sounds a little incredulous. He's efficient, not at all the type of person who puts things off.

The car still has a dent and despite Gabe's offer to bring it to his body guy, I haven't done anything with it. "I'm getting an estimate," I lie. "How much damage did you have?" I brace myself for a figure that's going to be out of reach.

"It was just the mirror. It was nothing, don't worry about it." He sounds a little bit like my father the way he says it. Dad was always telling me not to worry about things. "That's for me to worry about, not you," he'd say so often I wondered how he could stand it with all the things he had to worry over.

"No, I should pay for it," I insist stubbornly, like it's nothing to me and my overflowing bank accounts. "I can write you a check," I offer. I have overdraft protection because my father once told me that was important.

"I said don't worry about it," he says, and there's something to his tone that makes me drop it immediately.

"Okay then." There's nothing left for me to say so I pause and wait for him to say goodbye. I wonder if this is how my father felt in that moment when Marie stood up on the bus just before she spilled into his arms, desperate to ignore convention but afraid of doing anything else.

"Were you on time at least? For your sister," he explains. "What's her name?" He asks like he's forgotten and is waiting for me to jog his memory.

"I thought you had special powers," I tease and he laughs. "Her name is Floss. It's short for Florence," I explain, "but no one ever calls her that." *No one ever calls me Laura either.*

"And how is Floss? You bought a tub of ice cream and talked about how all men are assholes? Or you went to a bar and drank all her troubles away?"

"No," I protest laughing, although less at his teasing nature but at the notion that Floss and I would ever get together in such a fashion. "She's fine," I say even as I know she's not. She's preoccupied by something. Floss never talked of bad dreams, or cancers, or even mentioned her real father before now.

"You have my number, Laura. You can call me if you ever need anything."

It seems like an odd thing to say, and I wonder what sort of thing I would call him for. He hangs up before I have a chance to ask. I'm listening to the dial tone when it occurs to me that I still don't know how he knows my name.

marie

It took Ray more than a month after our first meeting on the bus that day to call me. I was at work when the call finally came, on my lunch break eating a sandwich at my desk.

This is Ray Sullivan," he said. "We met on the bus about a month ago. You gave me your card. You probably don't remember me."

"Of course I remember. How are you?" I covered my mouth with my hands. I didn't want anyone in the office to see what I was saying.

"Pretty good," he answered in a way that I knew was far from good. "I had a question about car insurance."

"Oh," I said, disappointed. "I'm just a receptionist. I can transfer you to an agent if you want."

"No. Actually I didn't really have a question about insurance. I was just looking for an excuse to talk to you."

"You don't need an excuse for that."

"You're probably busy," he said. "I'm busy too. I'm just on my lunch break."

"Me too."

"Yeah?" He sounded pleasantly surprised by this information. "Maybe we could have lunch sometime. Together."

We met three days later at a Chinese restaurant on Kenmount Road. We had nine lunches together before we talked about going out for supper. He called to cancel just as I was blow-drying my hair.

"I don't have anyone to watch my daughter," he said apologetically. "My neighbour was going to sit with her for a few hours but something came up."

"Oh." I tried not to sound disappointed even though my heart felt like lead. I'd shaved my legs, used expensive shampoo and body lotions. I was wearing so many different scents, I smelled like the perfume counter at Sears. "Another time then." I would have to call Doris and tell her she was off the hook for watching Floss for the night.

"Another time," he echoed, but he didn't suggest another date and I had a feeling he was slipping away from me.

"You could come over. You could bring her." I told him Floss would love to make a new friend and it sounded more like we were setting up our kids instead of ourselves. I wanted to cook him something special, a nice roast beef or a *jigg's dinner* but he didn't want me to go to any trouble and insisted on getting takeout.

Ray came with a paper bag filled with styrofoam containers of chicken balls and fried rice, sweet and sour sauce, chow mein and eggrolls with little packets of plum sauce. He ordered the dinner for two, he said, since the kids probably wouldn't eat that much and he didn't want any of it to go to waste. He was right—it was just enough and the only thing left over was a bit of rice.

When we finished, Ray and I encouraged the girls to go and play in Floss' room and we both smiled at one another, thinking "the girls" had such a nice ring to it. *Can you pick up the girls, I'm running late? The girls need money to go to the movies. The girls went to the mall.* The girls, the girls, the girls. The phrase itself made me think of little angels running through green pastures and flower-filled meadows. I thought of my own sister, of Doris and I playing in the neighbourhood as little girls—tag, hopscotch, jump rope, evenings of spotlight, and later lying in our beds and whispering about boys and kissing and falling in love.

I was filled with such an overwhelming sense of relief that it left me breathless. Floss would have someone to walk her down the aisle someday. She would have a sister to share secrets with, and talk about boys in a way she couldn't with me. I had someone who could bring the groceries up over the stairs and clean off my car in the winter. Suddenly, I had a family.

I could tell Ray felt much the same way. He didn't have to live off pizza and toast. He didn't have to worry about matching socks or changing sheets. He wouldn't have to talk to Lolly about getting her period. I just had the talk with Floss a few months ago and I knew just what to say and how to answer all the questions. She would be able to ask me anything.

I might have been getting ahead of myself but these were the kinds of things I had to think about in my circumstances. I wasn't just falling in love with Ray, I was falling in love with the very idea of having a family, of taking vacations, putting on extra for supper every night instead of scaling back, doubling my load of laundry.

I could hear music coming faintly from down the hall in Floss' bedroom. I pictured the two of them painting fingernails and braiding one another's hair and then coming out later for a fashion show.

I turned to Ray on the sofa and put my feet in his lap. It was that easy between us, like we'd spent an entire lifetime together. He rubbed the soles of my feet, my calves and eventually his hands worked their way up to the tops of my thighs. I felt pressure in my pelvis, pushed myself against the palm of his hand. His breath became laboured and he laid on top of me, the weight of his whole body bore down on mine in a heady rush. I could taste the saltiness of the soy sauce on his lips, mingled with the sweetness from the Pepsi. We made out on the couch with abandon, like oversexed teenagers. I knew we'd have to stop soon before it got out of hand. One of us would have to push the other away, or whisper, *wait,* or *not like this* or something to that effect but I didn't want it to be me. It had been too long since I was with a man and I craved Ray's touch with an intensity that frightened me.

Ray had just slipped his hand up my T-shirt, his palm resting on my ribs when the girls ran out from Floss' room into the living room. Floss covered her eyes and looked to the floor as if the sight would turn her to stone. She gagged. She actually gagged like she was going to be sick. Lolly stood in the middle of the living room her mouth agape, unable to turn away if she tried.

"I want to go home," Lolly announced and she shot me a look of contempt that made me feel like a common tramp caught fornicating with her betters. My bra had unbuckled and my breasts sagged without the support. I contemplated putting it back on but I'd never get it fastened from behind and it would simply draw more attention than I wanted. I felt my face burning with humiliation, although I didn't know why I felt that way. I was an adult. Ray was an adult. We had every right to love one another if we wanted to and yet it seemed from the looks of the goddamn girls, that we'd done something awful. *The girls.* It didn't have the same singsong ring to it anymore. The expression was synonymous with cattiness, jealousy, manipulation. I smoothed my hair back in place, in part because I wanted to make myself look more presentable, but mostly so I would have something to do with my hands, which still longed to smooth over Ray's chest. I had only just begun my exploration.

Ray transitioned from passionate lover to concerned father with an ease I envied. "What's the matter, Lollipop?"

"I want to go home," she repeated.

"I have cookies," I offered with more enthusiasm than I felt. "Chocolate chip. Floss, go take out the cookies from the cupboard and get Lolly a glass of milk." I shouldn't have ordered her to wait on Lolly but I was still mad at the way she gagged at the sight of me loving a man. But Ray was already off the couch, his jacket on and digging in his pocket for keys. Without warning, Lolly burst into tears and Ray looked at her with his brows furrowed and the creases in his forehead thick. He looked confused and frustrated, but in that moment I understood Lolly more than he did. She possessed power over her father but she had no idea what to do with it. It frightened her, this willingness by her father to up and leave at her whim. Normal parents would say *Not yet*, or, *You'll leave when I'm ready to leave, young lady.* But Ray was lost and scared and overwhelmed by the situation he found himself in. He looked tired and defeated by all the tears, raised his palms in the air, either in defeat or in prayer, I couldn't tell.

"Maybe you could come back again soon," I said, tucking my shirt back inside my jeans. I tried to hug Ray goodbye but he was stiff as a board, wary of showing any more affection to me in front of Lolly.

After they left I turned on Floss. I knew it wasn't fair but I was frustrated. Everything had been going so well only to end so badly. "What are you after doing to her?" I shouted at Floss, but what I meant was, *What are you after doing to me?*

I didn't have any sort of life, hadn't had anything to look forward to in years. I'd never been on a single date since Danny left us. I worked and I sacrificed and I looked after my dad until he passed away last year and I was tired. I was so tired. I was tired in every way there was. Tired of hauling groceries up over two flights of stairs and down a hall, tired of working at the insurance company—copying, collating, stapling the same papers over and over again. I was tired of washing the same two plates and the same two cups every day.

"I didn't do anything to her!" Floss screeched and I felt guilty for blaming her for something she had no control over. "I don't even know why you invited them here. Is he your boyfriend now?"

"Oh Floss," I sighed. This would be the time when I was supposed to tell her that Ray was special to me and that I would like it if she made an effort but I couldn't make the words come out of my mouth. "If you don't want me to date him I won't," I said instead, and it was true. All she had to do was tell me she never wanted me to have a boyfriend ever again and I would have complied as easy as that. "I'll be bitter being all by myself and I'll be miserable too, but if that's what you want in a mother then fine. But if you want me to be happy then you'll try."

I'd made so many sacrifices. I gave up happy hours and turned down offers to go out to supper because I didn't have a babysitter. I turned down promotions at work because I would have had to go in earlier and get off later. I was sorry but it was time she needed to make sacrifices for me.

"Please, Floss," I begged her.

floss

I fall a little bit in love with Leo LeDrew the minute he walks into the waiting room and gives his name to the receptionist in a voice brimming with authority and not at all like the meek whispers of everyone else who gave their name before him. I don't know why everyone feels the need to speak in hushed tones when they walk into the doctor's office. They're only giving out their name, not announcing they have the flu, or a rash, or haven't gone to the bathroom in three days. Still, everyone seems embarrassed to be here in the first place.

Everyone except Leo LeDrew, who says his name so loud and clear, everyone in the packed waiting room stops what they're doing to look up at him. The receptionist reacts differently too. Instead of retrieving the folder with his name on it from the filing cabinet behind her and putting it in the pile with all the others, she wraps her cardigan tightly around her chest.

"Oh thank God," she says in relief. "We've been waiting since lunchtime for you."

"I came as fast as I could."

He doesn't look sick so I don't understand the sense of urgency that accompanies his arrival. A receptionist shuffles papers and writes something down on a notepad. She hands it to another girl behind the desk and asks her to give it to the doctor right away. And just like that, the frenzy stops and he's directed to the throng of faces hiding behind old magazines in the waiting room.

"Take a seat," the receptionist says. She hates it when people stand around and linger at her desk, steal glimpses at her computer monitor, shed their germs on her papers. I've been sitting here for the better part of an hour and I've seen her direct six other people to sit before Leo LeDrew. "We're just getting the keys to the room for you," she explains and then gestures to the row of seats.

Leo LeDrew takes a seat across from me, picks up a *Reader's Digest* and thumbs through it. He stops at the page with the jokes—Laughter, the Best Medicine, ironic when you consider we're in a doctor's office and if that were really true, none of us would be here. Ray used to get the *Reader's Digest* in the mail. He had a subscription. He'd read them in the bathroom when he came home from work and he'd tell us all the jokes and amusing stories during supper. I think it was so he'd have something to talk about with us instead of focusing on the sound of forks being pushed around plates, chair legs scraping against the floor, and napkins being crumpled up into a hard ball. *So I came across this funny story in the Reader's Digest....* They weren't funny but Mom laughed anyway. Maybe she thought it was funny, but I was pretty sure she just thought it was her wifely duty to laugh. *At least he's trying, Floss,* she'd say wearily if I complained about him when we cleaned up in the kitchen.

Leo looks around for a moment, assessing his surroundings for the first time. There are youngsters, miserable with coughs that sound like the barks of a seal, babies in blankets being bounced about on their mother's legs, lots of old people, more than I've seen in one place since I had that rotation in the nursing home. Most of them are accompanied by a middle-aged son or daughter who keeps stealing anxious glances at a watch or a phone. They're going to be late to pick up their kids from school. They're going to have to push the three o'clock meeting to four, the four to five. Supper will be late.

His eyes meet mine and stay there just long enough to feel deliberate and then he turns back to the pages of the *Reader's Digest*. I shiver involuntarily, which might be from his stare, but more likely is from the cold, or because I've been holding in my pee for more than forty-five minutes now. It is cold in the waiting room, freezing even, but no one complains. They sit shivering in their sweaters and winter parkas and think it's their fevers.

Leo LeDrew doesn't seem cold at all. He wears a shirt with short sleeves emblazoned with a logo for the Labatt 24-hour relay. It's a size too small for him and stretches across his stomach and chest, making the logo appear somewhat larger and distorted. It's an old shirt and Leo LeDrew must have been thinner and in better shape when he acquired it. There's not a single goosebump amongst the hairs on his arm.

His hair is just starting to thin but he conceals it by keeping it longer than is fashionable. It curls over the tops of his ears and around the back of his neck but I see glimpses of pink skin on the top of his head when he bends over to read his magazine. His jeans are stained with splatters of purple paint and black grease on the thighs from where he wiped his hands clean. The purple paint is embedded into his cuticles and settles into the cracks of his knuckles, which is how I know the paint is fresh. His beard covers most of his face and neck, and looks both coarse and soft at the same time. I unconsciously sit on my hands when I think about the feel of his stubble. I shiver again, and my knees start bouncing like all the other mothers in the waiting room who are trying to calm their fussy infants. The bounce grows faster and more erratic. If only it was warmer. If only there weren't so much pressure on my bladder. If only Leo LeDrew weren't sitting directly across from me.

"Are you okay?" he asks me, closing the magazine but keeping his page with a finger.

My knees immediately stop moving. "Yes," I respond once I realize he's speaking to me. "I just have to go to the bathroom."

"Then why don't you go?" He gestures to the hallway, to a door with a sign that says Restroom in brass letters.

"I have to give a urine sample and if I go now they're going to call me the minute I step out of the bathroom and then I won't be able to go."

He looks amused. "You're probably right," he says but then turns reflective, taking in his surroundings. "Are you okay?" It's the same question from a minute ago but it sounds different. Before there was a hint of irritability, my bouncing knees distracting, and now there is a slight hint of concern to his voice.

"Oh, yes," I say in a reassuring tone. "I'm just getting a physical. Cancer runs in my family. My father is dying from it right now." It sounds as if he's dying at this very moment, which could be true, but most likely isn't. He has some time, a few months maybe. I picture him, slight, weak with the tops of his hands bruised from where he had the IV. I wonder if there was anything else I should have said to him. I'd been cold and I feel a stirring of guilt.

"Oh shit. I'm sorry." He looks genuinely concerned.

"It's okay. We weren't close." I speak of him in the past tense, like he's already dead and gone but it's always felt like that.

"Shame," he shakes his head and tosses the magazine back on the table, over an old *Maclean's* and a *People*. I don't know if I've insulted him, or if he's just tired of waiting.

"So what were you painting?" He looks at me in confusion. "You have paint on your pants, and your hands," I offer by way of explanation. He looks at his fingers and self-consciously wipes them into his pants, although the paint has long since dried.

"My daughter's bedroom. She picked the colour out all by herself. She wanted a purple room. I tried to talk her into a lighter shade but she insisted on this one. It's pretty once you get used to it." There's a hint of pride in his voice that seems undeserved. A girl picking out purple paint doesn't seem all that extraordinary to me. If it wasn't purple, it would be pink. I would have been much more impressed had she picked out sapphire blue or maybe even topaz. "Faith, that's my daughter's name," he clarifies for me, "she's going through a purple phase right now. Everything is purple. Only drinks grape juice lately." His face changes at saying her name, the lines around his forehead soften and his lips smile in contentment.

I hate the name Faith almost as much as I hate my own name. I went to high school with a girl named Faith and the boys grabbed their crotches and thrust their hips out at her behind her back when she walked down the hallway on the way to Chemistry. *Have a little Faith. Who wants to spread the Faith?* I'll bet he hadn't thought of that when he named his child, but he doesn't seem like the type to have done something like that in high school.

"I love grape juice," I offer, but the truth is the very thought of it puts even more pressure on my full bladder.

"Do you have kids?" he asks me.

"I have a nephew." It sounds like it's a consolation. "I'm not married," I explain, but then Lolly isn't married either and she has a child.

"Me either. Well not anymore." Leo sighs. "I'm divorced."

"I'm sorry." I picture a plump woman who only wears pants

with an elastic waistband that leave a crisscross impression on her stomach when she takes them off at night. She has big breasts that get in the way, the upper half of her shirts are stained. She tells him not to track mud into the kitchen floor and bawls at him for leaving his socks at the bottom of the bed.

He shrugs. "Don't be. Life goes on, right?" He smiles, revealing a set of teeth that are straight and white and beautiful. I automatically run my tongue over my own teeth, every bit as straight and smooth as his. I wonder if Leo's father pointed out how much his braces cost him the way Ray did. He asked me once if I had any idea how much of his salary went to the orthodontist. I tried to pry them off that night with a butter knife but they wouldn't budge and I ended up cutting my lip.

"Well at least I have my daughter," Leo adds. "That's one good thing come out of it, right?" It's such an endearing sentiment I smile broadly back at him.

"Your daughter is very lucky."

"You're a sweetheart," he says softly and even though we are in a crowded waiting room it feels as if we are alone.

There's a sudden flurry of activity behind reception. A set of keys gets dropped on the receptionist's desk and she waves Leo over, says something to him in a hushed tone before handing him the keys and pointing to a hallway. I can't hear what they're saying. I can only hear the wails of a fussy infant. Another receptionist shuffles through manila folders and everyone stares at her expectantly, hoping to hear their names called or calculating how many people are ahead of them.

"Florence Donovan?" I jump at the sound of my own name, thankful to be out of the waiting room and following Leo down the carpeted hallway. I notice words written on the back of his shirt I hadn't noticed before. LeDrews Plumbing and Heating. Proud Sponsor. He's here to fix the heat. He twirls the keys around on his index finger. The sound of metal against metal mixes with the screech of the infant in the waiting room.

"Don't worry," Leo winks at me before he disappears inside the room at the end of the corridor, humming with fluorescent lights. "I'll have you all warmed up in no time." I feel the heat creep up my chest all the way to my ears and to my fingertips. I'm embarrassed, flustered as Mom would say, but the one thing I am not is cold.

marie

It happened in the middle of eating a ham and cheese sandwich. I lost my sense of taste. I didn't know if I had just lost it, or if I had just realized it. The ham tasted exactly the same as the egg salad sandwich and the tuna sandwich and even the cucumber sandwich that someone else brought over. It tasted the same as the pineapple glazed meatballs that a girl from the phone company made. I couldn't remember the last time I had tasted anything. Everything had the same flavour to me. Everything had the same texture.

Ray had been dead and buried for nearly three weeks and I kept going through the motions—eating, sleeping, showering, going to the bathroom—not because people told me I should, but because I wanted to. *You should eat something, Marie*, Doris said to me three times a day, but she didn't have to. I ate because I was hungry. Famished actually, which made it feel like I had somehow betrayed Ray. I wanted to be so mired in grief that the mere thought of food would make me sick to my stomach. If I could eat, then I didn't want to hold anything down. It didn't seem right that I could eat at a time like this but

I could. That I couldn't taste anything came as a relief so great I felt lightheaded, uplifted almost.

My stomach grumbled and I took another bite of the sandwich, chewing slowly to try and extract some taste from the ham. I waited for the flavour to kick in. I knew it should taste salty, smoky, even honeyed, but it tasted like nothing.

I deconstructed the sandwich, took the bread off first, slick with mayonnaise, then the cheese, which was a pale yellow and had a strong odour. Swiss maybe, but there were no holes. The ham was pink and smooth. I remembered coaxing Floss into eating ham sandwiches when she was a little girl by telling her it was pink. "Look how pretty it is, it even matches your nail polish." I thought of the animal, the blood and the bones and the fat and wondered how I could have done such a thing to her. I thought of the turkey carcass, how I boiled it for hours, waited for the meat to fall off and then picked out all the bones, all but one. I thought of Ray, the bone lodged in his throat, gasping for air, and wondered how I could have done such a thing to him.

I ran to the bathroom and threw up, heaved up the contents of everything I'd just eaten but it wasn't an unpleasant experience at all. If anything, I felt cleansed. I threw the rest of the sandwich in the trash and then I went down to the basement and opened up the freezer chest. There were chicken legs stacked neatly against one another in a yellow styrofoam tray like discarded body parts, steaks with fat running through them like a road map, roasts with droplets of blood frozen against the plastic wrap. There were packages of bacon with alternating red and white stripes of meat and fat, and pork chops packaged in pink styrofoam trays as if to colour coordinate. The sight of it all sickened me. I knew I'd never eat it ever again and I tossed them all in a huge green garbage bag and dragged it up the stairs. It was heavy and I was out of breath by the time I got to the front door. My palms were raw from pulling the bag, laden with frozen meat up over the stairs, and I scraped my forearm on a nail sticking out of the wall on the basement steps.

Floss intercepted me in the driveway. She'd been chatting with Mrs. Lush across the street. I could almost hear Mrs. Lush and her pitiful voice echo in my ears. *How's your mother doing? Oh, she must be in some state without Ray. I still can't get over it myself. I'd send over another bowl of beet salad, only you still got my salad bowl. You don't need to worry about washing it. You got enough on your mind, sure.*

"What are you doing, Mom?" Floss chewed the top of her thumbnail when she spied me dragging the garbage bag over to the curb.

"Taking out the garbage."

"I just took out the garbage."

"Well now there's more."

"What's in it?" Floss made a jump for the bag but I yanked it away from her. The bag was cheap though, the store brand ones Ray used to buy, and the meat spilled out on the front lawn, still frozen, although a light frost had formed on the plastic wrap as it had begun to slowly thaw.

"What is this, Mom?"

"Meat," I answered truthfully.

"I know it's meat, but why are you throwing it out? There must be hundreds of dollars worth of groceries here." Floss' voice was high pitched, incredulous and her eyes were as big as saucers. She couldn't believe I was capable of doing such a thing. We were too cheap, Ray and I. We didn't believe in wasting anything. We ate leftovers, things that were past expiration, and moldy cheese so long as the moldy part was sliced off. We shared the same teabag at breakfast. We used and re-used tinfoil until it was all crinkled and ripped. And here I was about to dispose of hundreds of dollars of meat, albeit mostly poorer cuts. Chicken legs and thighs, dark meat mostly still with the skin on it, bought in bulk at Costco, steaks and roasts that were tough and chewy along with a family pack of ground beef, seventy percent lean with a neon green sticker saying Manager's Special affixed to the plastic wrap.

I never used to be so cheap. Ray was the cheap one. He'd go to the grocery store with me and fill the cart with all the no-name brands, big yellow labels with bold black lettering— toasted oats cereal, macaroni and cheese dinner, tomato soup, creamy peanut butter, diet cola. I used to get embarrassed at the checkout with my shopping cart filled with so many no-name labels. Most of the other shopping carts had one or two of the store brands but ours had nothing but. I was always petrified I'd run into someone from work or another mother from Floss' school. *You're a cheap bastard,* I'd say to Ray and he'd smile like it was a compliment.

"I don't like meat anymore," I offered to Floss by way of explanation, and Floss looked at me pitifully. I saw a flicker of something cross her face, understanding, awareness, acceptance that our roles were slowly reversing. It was the first time she realized she was going to have to look after me. She'd have to remind me of the names of my grandchildren and remind me of their birthdays. She'd have to buy them presents from me because I wouldn't be any good with sizes much less fashion, and no matter how many times she told me the specific toy to buy I'd always get it wrong. I did the same thing for my father, and soon she'd have to do it for me. I hoped she'd have more patience than I did. Dad used to irritate me when he got confused. I kept having to explain why Danny wasn't around, and every time I had to tell him that Danny had left me, my father would look at me with such pity that the humiliation felt fresh, even though it had been years.

Floss looked a little horrified at this realization. I wanted to offer some comfort to her but I couldn't find the right words, and so I just stood in the middle of the driveway with a torn garbage bag full of thawing meat and a scrape on my arm. It would be just the thing I would call my sister Doris about if I caught Dad doing it. We would snicker at first and then grow sober while we discussed the ramifications of the act. I felt bad that Floss had no sister to bounce things off. She had Lolly, but Lolly had no interest in looking after me in my old age.

I sometimes imagined they might one day run into each other at the mall or at the bank and Lolly would ask after me. *How's your mother? She's hanging in,* Floss would say. *We had to put her in a home. That's too bad,* Lolly might say and maybe she'd actually mean it before saying something like, *Well, it was good to see you,* or *Tell your mom I said hi.* They would have this exchange just like they were casual acquaintances who grew up on the same block. It wasn't fair. I'd treated her like my own for years and she was going to leave Floss to do everything for me. Floss would feel the same way if it were Ray. This thought left me with an ache in my chest so bad I placed a hand over my breast and took an unsteady breath.

"Oh Mom, just put it back in the freezer and give it a few weeks before you decide," Floss pleaded with me.

"Did you even like Ray?" Floss didn't seem to grieve like me and Lolly, united for a short time in our love and loss for the same man. We stood together at the foot of Ray's grave and Lolly held my hand and whispered, "I'm sorry." But Floss, she didn't cry at all, not when she saw him laid out for the first time, not when they closed the casket at the funeral home to bring to the church, not when the pallbearers left their gloves on top of the casket and the priest gave each of us—me, Lolly, and Floss—a rose from the top of the casket. I accepted the rose and sobbed, Lolly cradled it in her arm like it was the baby she was carrying inside of her and wailed. Floss just stood there twirling the rose in her hand like it was a weed she plucked alongside Quidi Vidi Lake. She was probably just mad with him after what he'd done to me but I thought she could have shed a few tears.

Floss shrugged her shoulders. She was running out of patience with me. Mrs. Lush was pretending to check her mail but she was taking the scene in. "Of course I liked Ray."

It was hollow the way she said it, like she was trying to make me feel better or just wanted me to stop my foolishness. "Ray loved you, you know. He really did. He just didn't feel right being affectionate with you because you weren't a little kid when we first got together and he thought people would think he was some kind of pervert or something if he tried to hug you." It sounded inappropriate even to say it, which is why I never said it before, or why Ray had such a hard time trying to explain it in the first place. "He was always worried about that. That's why he never said you were pretty or beautiful like he used to say to Lolly, or why he never tried to rub the back of your neck like he did with her. But he did love you. He did."

"Jesus, Mom, shut up!" Floss spoke to me in a loud whisper and her eyes darted from side to side to see if anyone besides Mrs. Lush witnessed my breakdown. She was annoyed with me and I wasn't used to that. Floss was always eager to please me and I started to cry. I sat on the lawn and grabbed handfuls of grass, pulled them up from their roots and tossed them aside. Ray would roll over in his grave if he could see me tearing up his lawn like this. He was so precise with his mower and his seeds and his watering and weeding. The lawn would never be the same again. Nothing would ever be the same again.

lolly

Gabe comes into the salon just as I'm getting ready to close, a Dairy Queen Blizzard in his hand, which he holds awkwardly in the cuff of his sleeve so his hand won't get cold. Without looking, I know it's Smarties flavour, my favourite, because he used to do this all the time when I was pregnant and had cravings for the frozen treat. He presents it to me now, a peace offering flavoured with nostalgia.

"It's Smarties, your favourite." He says this like he's trying to convince me. I've seen him employ the same tone when trying to coax Kenny into eating his last chicken nugget. It's a mild night and the ice cream is half melted. I concentrate on sweeping the hairs from the floor until I've made a large pile of hair in all colours and textures. It makes me avoid eye contact with him.

"What are you doing here?" I mumble as I sweep the hairs onto the dustpan. "I knows you didn't come all the way over here to give me ice cream."

Gabe smiles. "Nothing gets past you, Loll. I'm giving you a ride home."

"I don't need a ride home."

"Yeah you do," he replies. I can tell he's smiling broadly when he says this even though I'm looking at the floor.

"Why?" He's up to something. He has that mischievous quality to his voice, which usually means I'm going to disagree with him and feel bad about it. He accuses me of being a killjoy all the time. It takes more effort than it should to carry the dustpan over to the garbage. They're only a pile of hairs, but for some reason my arm buckles with the weight of it and I have to grip the handle with both hands. I keep thinking about the last time Gabe picked me up from work.

"Because I brought your car in to be fixed. I told you I had a guy. And he's not going to charge us for labour."

There is no us, I want to say, but he looks so proud of himself I don't really have the heart. He wants my gratitude, I can tell by the way he's beaming at me and for a moment I think about acquiescing. It would be so easy and he would be so pleased, but for some reason I can't do it.

"So you stole my car," I say instead. I wonder what other keys he still has and I make a mental note to change my passwords and pin numbers. I don't know why it hasn't occurred to me to do that already.

"I didn't steal it, Jesus, Lolly. I was trying to do you a favour. Your dad would have had it fixed already and you know it." He's right of course. Dad was a stickler about keeping his car pristine. He got like that after Mom's funeral, like he wasn't going to get caught off-guard again. You weren't allowed in with food or drink and he made you kick the slush off your boots before you got in. He bawled at Marie once for leaving an empty tin of Pepsi and a crumpled brown paper bag on the passenger seat. I let Kenny eat Fruit Loops and Goldfish in the car seat and drink milk and apple juice out of the sippy cup. They're supposed to be spill proof but they still leak.

"I'll meet you in the car," I say tiredly. "I just have to put the towels in the dryer."

The last time Gabe picked me up from work I sat in the passenger seat of his car thinking it would be our last ride together. I knew I was going to leave him that night. Gabe didn't have any idea what I was thinking because he kept going on and on about a toy train Kenny wanted. Percy. "What kind of a fucking name is that for a toy train? He was bawling 'I want Percy,' in the middle of fucking Walmart. He may as well have kicked me right in the balls in front of everyone. So I got him a Batman instead. It only came to ten dollars and that was with the tax. Mudder bought it for him since she was the one who wanted to go to Walmart in the first place to get a new mat for the cabin. He loves it. Haven't put it down yet. You okay, Loll? You're awful quiet tonight. Look, I'm sorry about earlier. I had a shitty day. Maybe after Kenny goes to bed we can try again, unless you're too tired. I'm a little whipped myself. Are you not speaking to me now? Is that it? You're giving me the silent treatment now are you? Fuck, I just said I was sorry."

I had to leave him. He was lost to me. I didn't know if it was because I didn't love him anymore, or if I loved him too much. The lines were so blurred they were almost the same thing to me. The car smelled like WD-40 and I knew it was coming off him and not the actual car. I could see his fingerprints on the grey steering wheel, black smudges all over it. The ink was so far embedded into the fine grooves of his fingertips, it was like they were tattooed.

He left his fingerprints everywhere, on doorknobs, countertops, glasses of Pepsi, the bathroom mirror—all held traces of where Gabe had been. It was the saddest sight in the world to me, as if he were disappearing before my very eyes, nothing left of the boy I knew or the couple we were save for those ghostly fingerprints.

He'd stopped talking about the cabin he was going to build up in Holyrood on his parents' land, with the big deck and the stone fireplace. He'd stopped talking about the ski-doo he wanted with the one hundred and fifty horsepower engine, and the truck he was going to get. Instead, he talked about toners and cartridges and paper jams with the same passion he normally reserved for the cabin. He'd given up dreaming, Gabe had, settled into his work repairing office equipment. He talked about the phone bill, the car insurance, getting groceries. It was bad enough I'd given up, but I didn't think I could handle it if he'd given up as well.

Gabe worked days and I worked evenings so we wouldn't have to bother his mother too much to look after Kenny. Most times we passed one another, affording enough time to exchange information on whether Kenny ate or drank or napped or shit.

He had asked me for a quickie earlier that day. He'd just walked in the door when I was on my way out. "Come on, Loll," he'd pleaded with me. I reluctantly consented. "Just hurry up," I sighed and I followed him into the bedroom while Kenny sat in front of the television. Gabe tried to get the job done quickly. He didn't take off his shirt or his socks and even his pants and underwear stayed wrapped around one ankle. He bent me over the bed and hauled down my pants just enough. I remember glancing at my watch, sighing. He was taking too long. I was going to be late. I was going to run into afternoon traffic. I had a four-thirty appointment and I wasn't going to make it. Every second felt like an hour. "Jesus, Gabe, it's called a quickie for a reason," I snapped at him and it seemed to take the wind right out of him. He loosened his hold on my arms and his whole body went limp.

"Fuck you," he said, zipping the fly of his pants.

"Fuck you too," I echoed. "I can't believe I'm going to be late for work for that."

I was twenty minutes late and my four-thirty shot me a look of annoyance when I rushed into the salon. I apologized, hung my sweater on a hook and her expression changed from annoyance to pity. It was only when I sat her in front of the mirror that I saw why. Smudges of black ink, Gabe's ghostly fingerprints, were all over me, up and down the length of my arms from where he held me. The lady thought they were bruises. I wished they were. I ran to the bathroom and scrubbed them off with soap and brown paper I wetted under the tap, crying all the while, the kind of sobs that take your breath away. I cried for what Gabe had become, what I had become, and what we had become together.

Gabe's car is the only one left in the parking lot. I can hear the muffled sounds of a song on the radio reverberating from inside the car as I approach, but he shuts it off when he sees me. He makes another attempt to give me the ice cream and I accept it, reluctantly, but still manage to devour nearly all of it before we're half way to Marie's. I've pleased him in the way Kenny pleases Mrs. Hillier every time he eats a banana and has a glass of milk while she prattles on about his muscles and his bones.

I put the empty cup in a cup holder alongside an empty juice box Kenny must have drank earlier today. It feels strange to be with Gabe and not have Kenny with us the same way it still feels strange to be with Marie and not have my father with us. Some people only exist for us in the presence of someone else. The thought makes me shiver and Gabe turns up the heat in response.

I feel my face grow red with the heat and it reminds me of the morning Floss came home, when Marie and I fought over the temperature inside the car. I think about Carson Keane. I think about the way he caressed the chrome of his bumper and the way he wiped away the melted snow from his face like he had no patience for it. I think about Floss, the way she sunk into the back seat of the car in the airport parking lot like she was sitting on a cushion made of luxurious silk.

"How's Floss doing? Is she glad to be back or does she just want to get the fuck back out of here?" Gabe asks me the question as if he could read my thoughts.

"She's all right I s'pose. She's trying to get on at The Health Sciences. She has bad dreams too," I offer more casually than might be expected by such an announcement.

He shoots me an inquisitive look out of the corner of his eye. "You mean like the old hag?" I laugh a little. I've never had her visit me but lots of my customers talk about her, the way she sits on their chest in the night, steals their breath.

"No. I mean like being lost in the woods, drowning in the ocean."

"Shit. Does she actually drown, or does she wake up before she dies in the dream?"

"I don't know." I shrug my shoulders. "What difference does it make?"

"Have you ever died in a dream?"

"What kind of a question is that?"

"Have you?"

"No."

"That's cause you'd really die…if you saw yourself die in a dream, that is."

"That's not true, Gabe."

"Sure it is."

"How would you even know? I mean if you died in your sleep you couldn't tell anyone what happened."

If my father were alive, this is exactly the kind of thing I would tell him. *Gabe said if you see yourself die in a dream, you actually die.* Dad hated all the times I quoted Gabe's musings. *Gabe said that storm is mostly going to be freezing rain. Gabe said the Red Wings will probably win the cup this year. Gabe said that fella on trial for murdering his wife is guilty.*

Gabe said, Gabe said, my father would rant. *What is he Jesus fucking Christ now? That boy is more full of shit than St. John's harbour.* Marie would laugh at him then, say he was just jealous I wasn't saying *Dad said* anymore. Marie said it enough for the both of us anyway. *Your dad said you have to go to Doris' with me. Your dad said you have to come home right after school.* She figured I'd be more agreeable knowing the order came from my father instead of from her.

Gabe is silent for a minute, takes a breath that sounds like encouragement. "Do you ever dream they're alive?"

I feel my heart pound in my chest. I know who he's referring to, can't believe he's actually asked me. "No."

"I had a dream about your dad a few weeks ago. Nothing deep or anything. Just dreamed that he came to pick up Kenny. And it was totally normal in my dream. I was like, Hey Mr. Sullivan, I'll get him ready for you."

I feel a surge of resentment toward my father for appearing in Gabe's dreams and not mine.

"I was freaked out a bit the next morning 'cause, you know…" He swallows hard, can't verbalize it, although I know what he's thinking.

"Jesus, Gabe," I say harshly.

"But then I just figured it didn't mean that. It just meant that your dad was watching over him from heaven."

"That's bullshit," I say sounding more like Gabe now. "Dreams don't mean anything."

Gabe looks like he's about to argue with me but thinks better of it. "I s'pose," he nods in a way that sounds like he's placating me. He makes the turn to Marie's block, slows the car and says something indecipherable. "Whatthefuck?" He strings the words together the way he always does when he's nervous. It's the same way he first asked me out. "Goooutwithme?" I had to ask him three times before I understood what he was asking me. I'm aware of red and blue flashing lights inside the cab now. They highlight the sudden pallor to Gabe's face. It's a police car and it's in front of Marie's.

"Where's Kenny?" I don't recognize my voice. It's sharp, high-pitched, and belongs to someone else. I wait for him to tell me Kenny is at his parent's house, all tucked in and safely ensconced in his bed.

"Marie's," he says roughly. I don't recognize his voice either. My last thought is that I hope it's all a bad dream.

marie

The police officer was sympathetic, asked me if I needed anything after he delivered the news. I suspected this was an afterthought, having already fulfilled his job requirement, but he looked at me and then Floss, who was rocking her baby doll, with something that resembled pity.

"My daughter is about the same age," he said. "I can't imagine…" but then his voice trailed off, knowing he was veering into territory he wasn't supposed to wander. "Do you have adequate support? There are programs to get you over the hump."

I didn't know what that meant. Did I have enough money to make rent? Did I have someone I could call once he was gone? Someone who would rush over and help me get through the rest of the day. Doris. I could call Doris. I could call Dad too, but he would just keep saying I told you so. I figured the police officer was going to tell me about Social Services, but I couldn't stand to listen to it.

"Oh yes," I said more enthusiastically than was warranted for someone whose husband had up and left. I thought he was going to tell me Danny was dead, after getting into a fight and getting himself killed. That he wasn't dead at all, just gone, was more embarrassing than anything at that moment. I would feel the hurt later, but not yet. I stood with my hand on the doorknob, wishing the police officer would leave already. I felt the burn of humiliation travel from the roots of my hairline all the way down to my ankles. I wanted to cry but I would wait until I was alone, when the police officer was gone and Floss was settled away in bed. I could hang on. I knew I could. Floss once waited until I came home from work after dinner to cry about a scrape on her elbow she'd suffered at daycare. We were the same, Floss and I, patient, stalwart, and vulnerable all at the same time.

Danny had abandoned the both of us and it fell on the shoulders of a police constable to tell me. I should have known of course, but somewhere in the back of my mind I just couldn't fathom it. It wasn't unusual for Danny to come home late, but he always came home. I made all the requisite calls to friends and family and co-workers but no one had heard from him. It took me a long time to file a missing person's report. He was gone more than a week before desperation drove me to it. I explained how Danny had gotten into drugs and abused alcohol, knowing he would never forgive me for revealing such things to the police.

They put his picture in the paper, *Police Search for Missing St. John's Man*. Danny's face was on page A-3 of the *Telegram*. People hugged me, prayed for me, brought me casseroles like he was already dead. Now Danny would be back in the paper. *Missing St. John's Man Found Safe*. Some people will read the article and feel sorry for me at having been abandoned in such a public fashion. Mrs. Murphy from the apartment down the hallway will ask me if I enjoyed the tuna noodle casserole, and I'll tell her it was delicious even though it was only a box of tuna helper. She'll smile graciously at me and tell me how happy she is my husband is well, like he was getting over a bout of the flu.

"We have to alert the media that your husband turned up," the police officer said as he was getting ready to leave. "It's kind of standard procedure in any missing person's case."

I nodded, smiled stupidly at him like I was thrilled with this news, like I couldn't wait to tell everyone Danny was alive and well. "Of course."

"We won't give out any details," he said. "All we have to say is that he was found safe, thank the public for their assistance. Pretty standard stuff," he added as if it happened all the time. People went missing, left their families to wonder about them, and then turned up fine a few weeks later. When the paper came the following day, I read the headline out loud even though I was all alone, and then I read the rest of the article aloud, like I was a reporter on the CBC News. I tried to pretend it was someone else whom all this misery had befallen. I read all the headlines that way and then all the articles until I was finished with the whole paper.

I was thinking about what to tell Floss when the phone rang. She hadn't asked after her father once in the past week and I was wondering if I should say anything to her at all. Eventually she'd stop asking me where he was. It was Danny on the phone.

"I'm out west," he said, giving me information I'd already gleaned.

"I know," I answered with an air of confidence. "What are you doing out there, Danny?"

"I was trying to get clean. I'm a fucking mess, Marie." His voice cracked a little when he said it. I pictured him taking a shower, his hair flat to his head and his body covered in soapy bubbles. All the bad habits being sloughed off, going down the drain in a vortex.

"You couldn't tell me? I could help you."

"I needed to do it by myself. I was going to surprise you and Floss." He sounded so sincere I felt myself softening. Every muscle in my body had been strained and tense from the moment I heard his voice, but I relaxed them all at once, breathed through my mouth and felt the sweet taste of relief on the back on my tongue. He was trying to make a better life for all of us.

"I took out a missing person's report," I confessed. I giggled a bit at the silliness of it. He'd be mad about that but I didn't have much choice. "I thought you were dead," I whispered in explanation.

"Yeah, I heard." He sounded somewhat chagrined. "How is Floss?"

"She's good, but she misses you something awful," I lied.

"Kiss her for me."

"Come home and kiss her yourself." I pictured our reunion at the airport. He'd be sober, smell like soap instead of liquor. He might have a haircut. He'd squat to his knees and hold his arms out for Floss to run into them.

"I'm not coming home." I wished that his voice sounded far away, that it echoed or that we had a bad connection, but he sounded so clear it was like he was sitting next to me on the couch. "I'm not ready yet. I don't know if I ever will be. If I go back there I'll end up the same, maybe worse. You don't understand." I had to stop myself from blurting out that I understood him perfectly, but I didn't. Danny had always been an enigma to me. I waited for him to ask me to come to him, pack up Floss and start over, but there was nothing save for silence. I couldn't even hear his breath.

"Good luck then," I said to him in a clipped voice. I didn't want to hear any more so I hung up, thankful that he was across the country and seemed intent to stay there. He'd be homesick out there. He'd miss the little things, the smell of the ocean, the banks of fog, the radio announcers, the accents, even the hills. He'd miss them more than he'd miss me and Floss. This fact made me feel a little bit sorry for him, but more sorry for us.

As soon as I hung up the phone I walked into Floss' bedroom and sat on the edge of the bed. She was reading a storybook, making up her own words to go with the pictures. I wanted to make up my own story just like she was doing because I didn't know what to say to her.

"It's going to be just you and me from here on in," I said. "I promise."

lolly

Carson Keane is in the living room. It takes me a few moments to process this information because my first thought is Kenny, who thankfully has not swallowed any poisons or fallen out a window, but is lying sleepily on the arm of the sofa in his dinosaur pajamas. Kenny sits up at the sight of me and Gabe rushing towards him, each of us frantic and out of breath as we take turns inspecting him.

Carson looks different than I remember because he is Constable Keane. Of course. It makes perfect sense. It explains why he told me to go on that morning and explains how he knew my name. Laura, he called me. That's what's on my driver's licence, the name the car is registered to. I want to hear him say my name again.

He is an imposing figure in uniform, taller, straighter, and more assured if that's possible. His gaze falls on me and then on Gabe and then Kenny. I'm still wearing my apron from the salon, covered in splatters of dried up hair dye and with squares of crumpled foil sticking out of the front pocket. I rub my hands over the tops of my thighs. They're sticky from the ice cream and I end up with lint in the space between my thumb and index finger. He's piecing us all together, configuring our roles and making assumptions. His expression is unreadable, businesslike.

"What's going on?" I ask with some degree of trepidation. I'm half afraid he's going to arrest me for a hit and run. I start making my case in my mind. *I called. I offered to pay.*

It's Marie who answers the question. I hardly noticed her or Floss when I rushed in, I was so intent on making sure Kenny was safe. Marie sits with her arms folded in her lap, playing with the belt of her robe, twisting the terry around her fingers in a tight loop, and then repeating the same process with the other hand.

"Someone tried to break in," she says. She unravels a strand of terry cloth from the edges and she flicks it onto the carpet , in an uncharacteristic disregard for neatness. "I went out into the backyard to throw the empty bottles out in the shed and he was right there, trying to look in the back window. I was frightened to death but I must have surprised him because he ran off. I threw one of the bottles at him but I didn't hit him. It was only an empty plastic two-litre bottle. Sure the wind took it and blew it over the fence. I don't know why they don't make glass bottles anymore. You got to drink liquor to get a good glass bottle," she laments. "You remember Constable Keane don't you? From when we went to the airport to get Floss?" I don't need her to remind me.

"Yes of course I remember," I snap.

"This is the man Lolly got into the accident with the other morning when we went to pick up Floss from the airport," Marie explains to Gabe and Floss, as if she were letting them in on our private joke.

Gabe turns to me and laughs. "You hit a fucking cop?" He sounds incredulous and amused at the same time. "Holy shit, Loll. Why didn't you tell me? This is priceless."

"Because I didn't know," I say abruptly. I feel my face redden and I massage the spot in the centre of my palm where Carson had written his name that day. I tilt my head down and unconsciously rub the spot more vigorously like I was hoping the words might suddenly reappear.

Oddly, Floss is the one who appears distraught.

"Did you recognize him?" she asks Marie. "Was he thin, pale, sickly looking?"

"Like a drug addict you mean?"

"Something like that," Floss replies.

"They're all drug addicts," Marie contends, shaking her head. It's a sweeping generalization that suggests the whole population is an addict of some sort. Marie assumes every raucous band of teenagers that walks down the street is intent on breaking in and beating her to death for the four valium left over in her medicine cabinet from when the doctor prescribed it after Dad died. "I mean that's what they're always after. It's the prescription drugs that are all the rage now with the young people." Marie speaks directly to Carson when she says this, as if he were unaware of the problem. "Shocking ain't it, Constable? Never used to be like this I tell you. I didn't get a good look at him but he had on one of those big sweatshirts with the hood up, and a baseball cap. I mean it was dark out. I didn't see much else."

It didn't matter. She's described Gabe, although no one else seems to notice. I look at Gabe in his worn sneakers, his dark-grey hoodie, his Red Wings baseball cap with his long sandy hair sticking out from the sides. I feel a tinge of embarrassment—by his clothes, by his long hair, by the fact we have a child together. It will bond me to him for the rest of my life. I wish he would leave but he stands there holding Kenny upside down by his ankles and listening to Marie drone on about drugs and young people while Carson nods patiently.

"Put him down," I snap at Gabe. "It's going to be hard

enough to settle him in all this excitement without you holding him upside down." I don't sound like myself at all. There's a bitchy quality to my voice and yet I keep going. "Easy to tell you won't be putting him to bed tonight." Gabe flinches slightly but then complies, letting Kenny gently down on the couch.

"They got some set of balls on them," Gabe adds, nodding in agreement with Marie like he himself is an old man tired of chasing teenagers from his lawn. "Pricks aren't afraid of nothing these days. Sure they broke out a window up to the cabin. Mom was some upset too."

I didn't know this. Gabe hadn't mentioned anything about it. There was a time when I knew everything that happened at the Hillier household, when the newspaper got delivered, if the mail was late, what time Mr. Hillier's eye doctor appointment was. They'd been vandalized and no one had told me.

Kenny interrupts Gabe to ask for his Batman. He tugs at Gabe's leg and then at mine. I feel something akin to panic grip me as I remember when I'd seen it last. He had it when I buckled him in the car and the car was now in the garage and it was too late to do anything about it. I feel my heart rate quicken and my pulse soar as I scan the room frantically hoping Gabe remembered to take it out of the car. It's the only toy that Kenny insists travel with him, from here to Gabe's and back again. It's the last toy he got before his parents split up and he's never had a night without it. It's amazing to me that a missing eight-dollar toy that's mass produced in factories in China can generate such a physical response in me.

Kenny starts to wail for Batman and I shoot Gabe a look. "I s'pose you left it in the car when you stole it this evening."

"I'll get it tomorrow," Gabe says. "Relax already," Gabe shoots back defensively. "He's only bawling for it now cause you're flipping out." Gabe makes an effort to pick Kenny up to offer him some comfort for his missing toy but I scoop him up first and set him down on the opposite side of me.

Carson looks at Kenny, his face red from the exertion of crying, and crouches down to his level. "Batman is working with the police tonight. We need his help to get a couple of the bad guys, but he'll be back. Is that okay with you?"

Kenny shrugs first, then nods.

I wait for Gabe to leave but it's Carson who makes an exit. "I'll keep an eye on the place for you," he says.

The next morning Kenny is up at five thirty. He creeps into my room and flips the light switch on. He does the same thing every morning.

"God, Kenny, go back to sleep will you."

"I'm thirsty and I have to pee." It's part of our regular morning routine. Gabe says Kenny sleeps till seven when he stays over there but I don't believe him. He's just trying to one-up me by insisting Kenny sleeps better at his house than mine. I don't know when parenting became so competitive between us, but I can't resist the opportunity to tell Gabe that Kenny ate all his peas and carrots with supper, just like he can't resist telling me Kenny cleaned up all the blocks in his room. We share the information more to make one another feel inadequate than to delight in our child's accomplishments.

"Few more minutes," I mumble, bringing him under the covers with me. He smells like baby powder, which is how I know Marie must have given him a bath last night before she noticed the would-be robber and called the police.

"The policeman is back," Kenny whispers. "He's outside."

I bolt out of bed, fully awake now, and run to the living room window. Kenny is right. It's Carson, sitting in the same car I hit the morning I picked Floss up. I watch him through the sheers. He looks at his watch and then his gaze meets mine. He approaches the front door with a Shoppers Drug Mart bag in his hand, which he gives to me hesitantly after I open the door for him.

"Morning," he says. "I'm sorry to bother you so early."

"I was up. Kenny is up at the crack of dawn," I say, but that's not quite true. Dawn is still about an hour away.

"I had to get razor blades this morning," he says, rubbing his bald head. "You can get anything at Shoppers now you know. I saw this on the way out. It was one of those impulse buys and I'm not usually someone who does things on impulse, except for lately..." He shrugs like he's not certain what to make of his own behaviour before handing over the bag to me. "I was going to leave it in your mailbox but since you're up..."

There's a Batman action figure inside the bag. It's completely the wrong kind. The cape is blue instead of black, and there is no batarang tucked into the utility belt.

"It's perfect," I say. I feel the sting of tears at the pure sweetness of the gesture. I want to thank him, invite him inside for a cup of coffee and a slice of toast. "We're not together," I say instead. "Gabe is Kenny's father, but we're not together," I explain. I feel the need to clarify this, to make myself available to him. Carson steps closer to me in the foyer. He smells of coffee, extra cream and two sugars.

"Mommy?" Kenny's voice is muffled from behind the bathroom door. "I got some pee on the floor and a little bit on my pajamas."

Carson smiles at me. "Looks like you have your hands full then."

"Be right there," I shout over my shoulder, but when I turn around Carson has taken a step back, one hand on the doorknob.

"I should go," he says. "Let me know if you see anything suspicious. It doesn't hurt to be cautious."

marie

I was going to throw caution to the wind and see what happened. I was too old and too lonely to waste any more of my time.

There was nothing on the television even though I had sat watching it for hours on end. The news channels kept repeating the same stories over and over again like a record that couldn't stop skipping. There was a government official who owned a share in a company that had a government contract. There was a flood somewhere, a river crested and communities were forced to evacuate. I wasn't paying enough attention to figure out where it was. Although I had watched it so many times, I didn't feel anything anymore. There was no more shock value to the stop sign that was nearly submerged, and I couldn't conjure up any sympathy for the old woman who'd lost her wedding pictures. At least she'd had them, I thought, which was more than I had.

I would have went to bed, but it was only eight o'clock. Ray and I used to stay up till midnight most nights, until he retired. Then we couldn't make it past eleven and we'd laugh at that in a good natured way since he didn't have to get up in the morning. *We're getting old I s'pose*, he'd say, yawning and stretching out his arms almost the full length of the sofa. Since Ray died and the girls had gone I was going to bed at ten, then nine, only to be up before the sun. There were so many hours in the day to fill, it was exhausting to think about.

I picked up the phone and called Floss in Calgary. She'd been gone almost a year and I was certain when she left she'd have been back by now. She answered on the fourth ring, when I was just about to hang up.

"Hi Floss, it's Mom."

"Hi." Floss sounded out of breath. "What's up?"

"Do I need a reason to call my daughter?" I sounded defensive.

"No, I'm just making a bit of supper."

"Supper? At this hour?"

"It's only four thirty here, Mom."

"Right, I keeps forgetting about that." I think about it being four thirty again and shudder with the thought of having to re-live the past three and a half hours.

"So how is Calgary?"

"It's good," Floss said. If she were here she wouldn't give me an answer like that. She'd tell me what her apartment was like, the pattern of the curtains and the colour of the carpets and she'd tell me all about her neighbours. I hated talking on the phone. It was so awkward. I just wanted to sit across from her, watch her fold her legs underneath her and listen to her tell me everything. I wanted to tell her to come home, that she'd been out there long enough, but I knew she wasn't ready yet. She had to decide when it was time to come back.

"Why don't I call you later."

"I'm going to bed in a bit."

"Maybe tomorrow then?"

"Maybe," I replied and I hung up after a hurried goodbye,

knowing full well Floss wasn't going to call me tomorrow or the next day. She'd call me when she got the electric bill. I tried Lolly then, who sounded nearly as breathless as Floss.

"What's up, Marie?" Lolly sounded impatient, like I caught her in the middle of something too. It couldn't have been supper though since she was on the same time zone as I was.

"I was just wondering if you needed me to watch Kenny tomorrow."

"No thanks. Mrs. Hillier said she was around so you don't need to."

I resented Mrs. Hillier for taking Lolly away from me, and now my grandson. She'd swooped right in out of nowhere and stole them from me. She filled her days with pat-a-cakes and peek-a-boos and Lolly acted as if she were doing me a favour by keeping me from my own grandson.

"Maybe you and Gabe and Kenny want to come over for supper on Sunday?" I'd never invited them over before and Lolly hesitated. She wasn't sure what to make of the invitation.

"I don't know. I have to check with Gabe I guess." She was gesturing to Gabe now, shrugging her shoulders and trying not to giggle.

I envied them and their hectic lives. I used to be that way and I never appreciated it. I used to bitch and moan there weren't enough hours in the day. I went to work. I made supper and did the dishes. I ran out after dinner to buy a protractor because Floss couldn't find hers. I went to five stores looking for the outfit Floss needed for the Kiwanis Music Festival. *Who cared what colour her shoes were so long as she sang nice and remembered all the words*, I remembered thinking at the time when I couldn't find the black shoes in her size. I didn't realize how much of a blessing it was to have so many things to fill up the day. What I wouldn't give to have it all back. I'd sew the patches on the brownie uniform without complaint. I'd buy Floss' assigned item for the Thanksgiving food pantry with enthusiasm instead of being annoyed I had to make an extra trip to Dominion two days before the holiday for a tin of cranberry sauce because she forgot the notice in school.

I had the sudden urge for time to speed up until I was old and decrepit. My entire life had happened in a blur. I thought about how fast it had all gone and I felt the room move and spin around me. I swear I could see Floss and Lolly and Ray, out of the corner of my eye, dart across the hall and into the kitchen. I could almost hear their voices, the whispering and the laughter like a dull ache in my ear. I had to blink and bring myself back to the moment, where time slowed and crept along at a snail's pace, where I watched the same news stories all day long, followed the same predictable routine, counted the seconds along with the clock. Life had changed into slow motion.

I thought this was the worst age, the point where your youth was gone but you weren't considered old. If I was old, people would feel obligated to come by and check on me. See if I needed anything at the grocery store, if I needed my prescription for blood pressure picked up at Shoppers. Maybe they'd bring me raisin tea biscuits from Bidgoods and put the kettle on to keep me company. It would be their good deed for the day and I wouldn't mind being a charity case if it made the day go faster.

"Okay, what time Sunday?" Lolly's voice sounded so strange to me. I had the most overwhelming sense of joy. I could picture Ray then, up in heaven just like he always said he'd be. I didn't know who he was with, but he was happy me and Lolly hadn't given up yet.

floss

Kenny is so excited he can barely tell me his news. He's started the same sentence over five times. "The bad guys…they're going to the ocean…and a whale…the bad guys…they're going down in the water….the bad guy…he has on a green shirt…"

"Kenny, spit it out will you. What are you trying to tell me?" I'm minding him all day since Lolly got called in to work and she didn't want to bother the Hilliers. Mom offered to cancel her plans with Doris, so I volunteered. I didn't think it would be this hard. The child is exhausting. I entertained him the whole day, building towers and forts and fighting off bad guys, and the minute I sit down his tongue is wagging again.

I look for Ray in his features but save for the dark hair there isn't much. He has Lolly's blue eyes and Gabe's straight nose. But there's something about the way he stands in front of me jumping up and down that reminds me of Ray that I can't put my finger on. It's not like Ray was ever so animated, except for the time he won the fifty-fifty raffle at his work Christmas party. But then I see it so clearly I wonder why I never saw it sooner. It's the smile, mischievous, like he was up to something. Ray most often looked at Mom that way when they were stopped at a red light and there didn't seem to be anything else to do except look at one another. He used to smile at Lolly that way when she woke up late and came to the breakfast table with her hair all tousled looking for a cold piece of toast.

"Bad guys are gone," Kenny says again.

"Good," I nod. "I don't like bad guys."

"Down the toilet."

"Okay. Now go colour or something."

It's an hour later when I finally piece together what he'd been trying to tell me. The water in the toilet is so high it nearly reaches the underside of the seat. I try plunging it but it's useless and the water just sloshes over the side of the bowl and onto the bathmat. He flushed his toys down the toilet, the bad guys. I can't believe he actually did it. He never flushes the toilet. He's afraid of the noise, Lolly explained apologetically when I asked her to teach the child how to flush. Every time I have to go to the bathroom there's pee on the seat, pee on the floor. And it's not just pee. I've seen shit too, sunk to the bottom of the toilet and a perfectly unrumpled square of toilet paper floating in the bowl, and you'd think Lolly and Mom were after finding a pot of gold the way they make such a fuss over it.

"Kenny, did you do this? What a big boy you are using the big potty," they'd say, their voices filled with pride.

I don't know what I'm going to tell Mom. There's water all over the floor and I've used at least half a dozen towels to sop it up. There's no keeping it from her. She'll say I wasn't minding him properly. She'll be quick to point out all the things that could have happened while he was flushing toys down the toilet. He could have drunk the bleach. He could have fallen down the basement steps. He could have cracked his head on the countertop, burned himself on the stove. *It's a wonder they lets you look after sick people*, she'll say.

The image of Leo LeDrew winking at me pops into my head. I flip the phone book to the yellow pages under plumbing. It's a quarter page ad with a graphic of a van, with LeDrew's Plumbing & Heating written across the door. *Have Faith in LeDrews*, it proclaims in bold lettering, and I wonder which came first, the slogan or the child. All their technicians are fully licensed. They're on call seven days a week, they're prompt, they're courteous and professional.

I call the number and a woman answers. "LeDrew's Plumbing & Heating," she sings. I don't know why but I assumed Leo would answer the phone himself.

"Who's this?" I ask uncertainly. I chide myself for sounding like Ray. He'd call up from work around four o'clock every day and whenever I answered, he'd bark into the phone, *Who's this?* in a way that made me feel like I was in the wrong place. It could have only been Mom or Lolly or me, and I always felt I'd disappointed him when I answered.

"I mean, I was looking for Leo," I say. "Leo LeDrew. My toilet is backed up and I have to go to the bathroom." I actually did have to go the bathroom. I cross my legs now and squeeze my thighs but it only makes me have to go worse.

"He's out on a call right now but I can have another one of our technicians come right over."

"No, that's okay then, never mind. I'll try back later." I say it like I could live for weeks with a clogged toilet and a full bladder.

"Ma'am. If you really want Mr. LeDrew, I can have him there around five, but I can assure you that all of our employees are very competent."

"Five o'clock is perfect."

It's also supper time and I wonder if I should offer him something to eat, maybe put out a few crackers and cheese. There's nothing in the cupboards but peas and beans, pasta and rice. The fridge is stocked mostly with jarred or pickled condiments, ketchup, mustard, relish, cheez whiz, and beets. I imagine Leo is a meat and potatoes man, like Ray, like every other Newfoundland man.

Not for the first time, I bemoan what's happened to my mother, who used to cook turkey seven times a year, and made a roast beef every Sunday with potatoes and gravy. She used to love to cook for Ray. In the beginning she'd put so much effort into our suppers, ringing the bell for the butcher at Sobeys to request a specific cut of beef instead of picking out whatever was already packaged up in the cooler. I'd be in the kitchen helping her clean up after Ray devoured two platefuls and Mom would wink conspiratorially at me like we were in on something together, the two of us trying to woo him.

Leo is prompt, just like the ad said, ringing the doorbell at 4:58. He wears the same jeans with the lavender paint, although it's been scrubbed from his hands and underneath his fingernails. His shirt is different too, black with LeDrew's Plumbing &Heating written in white on his chest. He has a toolbox in one hand and a clipboard in the other. He smiles that bright perfect smile at me as soon as I open the door.

"Well hello again," he says like we are old friends.

"Hi," I smile back. Kenny emerges from behind my legs and gestures for me to carry him. He digs a foot into my belly when I lift him up and I grimace from the extra pressure on my bladder, a gesture not lost on Leo.

"Seems every time I run into you, you have to go to the bathroom."

"Yeah," I say, remembering our last encounter. "My nephew here flushed some bad guys down the toilet," I explain.

"Is that right? The next time you want to get rid of the bad guys you might want to try the washing machine." He crouches down and speaks directly to Kenny, high-fives him and fluffs the top of his head affectionately and Kenny responds with a huge grin. "You can be my helper if you want." He's good with kids and it seems like it's not just because he has one of his own.

"Let me take a look then," he says, following me into the bathroom where I show him the obvious problem, but then I afford him some privacy. It seems wrong to watch a man in the bathroom no matter what he's doing, except shaving maybe. The commercials always make it look so sexy. Leo has shaved since I last saw him. He still has his beard, but the growth from his neck is gone. He goes back and forth from the truck to the bathroom retrieving various tools and Kenny follows him obediently. It's nearly six thirty when I hear his cellphone ring, then hear his hushed conversation from down the hallway.

"I know I'm late. I got stuck at a job in Mount Pearl…just tell her I had to work and I'll get there as soon as I can. Look I'm sorry, what do you want me to do?" He shouts in a whisper. He's speaking to his ex-wife, I can tell. I can almost see her pointing her finger at him in an accusatory manner and I feel guilty for being the reason for his tardiness. The rest of the conversation is unintelligible but when Leo finally emerges from the bathroom, he looks tired and his customary good humour is gone. He presents the plastic toy to me in a Ziplock bag. I can make out the grotesque features of the joker through the plastic.

"This is your culprit," he says, sighing and shrugging his shoulders. He sits at the kitchen table to write up the charge, and hands me the pink copy. I'll have to retrieve Mom's checkbook from her bedroom. It's expensive. Ray would have had another heart attack. Small wonder he did all the work around the house by himself.

I pop into the bathroom on the way to Mom's room. The prints from his work boots are all over the floor tiles. I place my own foot inside them and marvel at how big his feet are. He must have just washed his hands in the bathroom sink because the porcelain is wet with bubbles and the hand towel is covered with dark smudges and is stuffed back onto the towel ring in a crumpled ball. I think of his ex-wife complaining at him for making a mess of the bathroom, but I like that he leaves traces of himself everywhere.

It's when I'm washing my own hands that I notice the blood in the sink. He's made an attempt to clean it, but it streaks over the countertop and trails on the linoleum and on the bath mat. I grab bandages, antiseptic and run back to him at the kitchen table where he's sitting with Kenny, debating the pros and cons of various superpowers. I see him rub the blood from his finger into his jeans under the table, the red mixing with the lavender paint and the grease stains.

"What happened?" I hold his hand in mine and assess the wound. It's small but deep and I feel somewhat responsible.

"It's nothing. I just caught it on one of my tools, that's all. I got a little distracted." He keeps repeating that it's fine, that he's done this sort of thing a hundred times. And he has. He has little scars in nearly each one of his fingers.

"I'm a nurse's aide. I fix people up all the time." I lead him to the kitchen sink, rinse it out and then apply pressure with a cloth. When the bleeding stops I rub Neosporin all around the cut. I do this sort of thing on a regular basis, but mostly to old, wrinkled people who look at their bedsores, frightened to death their bodies are decaying before their very eyes. This is different. It borders on the sensual as my hands linger over his. His hand, at first a tightly clenched fist, slowly opens and relaxes. I can feel his stare at the top of my head, his breath in my part, heavy and damp. I feel dizzy, wonder if it's the sensation of being this close to him, or the chemical odour coming from the bathroom.

"It feels better already," he says.

I look up at him, smile. "I feel bad for calling you out here at suppertime and I was just going to boil some water and make a little pasta. I mean, if you're hungry. We don't have any meat," I add apologetically. "We don't eat meat anymore. I eat some but my mom doesn't."

"I'm late already," he sighs.

Mom walks in on us just like that, the two of us standing in front of the kitchen sink with me still holding his hand, even though the wound has already been bandaged. I hope she didn't hear me rambling on about meat. She doesn't like for people to know all the particulars.

"What's going on?" Her voice is more confused than angry. She steps over Leo's toolbox by the front door. "What's that smell?"

"Sealant," Leo says. "I opened the window in the bathroom. You won't be able to notice it in an hour or so."

She looks to Leo's bandaged hand, the clipboard on the table, and the toolbox alongside the kitchen chair.

"Who are you?"

"Hi Mom, this is Leo," I say, finally finding my voice. "I called him because our toilet was backed up."

"Then what are the two of you doing standing over the sink? Is that broke too?"

Her tone is clipped, rude even, and it embarrasses me. "No, he cut his finger and I was cleaning it up."

Leo extends a bandaged hand to my mother, who takes it reluctantly. In that moment I understand the reasons for her behaviour. She's not used to having to call in people to fix things. Ray knew his way around a house and did everything. He installed a new showerhead, laid the tile in the kitchen, hung the chandelier in the dining room. There was no project he wouldn't tackle. It seemed that for as long as Ray had been gone, there were still some things that resonated with her.

Leo hoists his toolbox in his good hand. I walk him to the door where he places his bandaged hand on the screen door handle.

"Thanks for fixing me up so good." He swallows nervously, hesitates before pushing the door open. "Maybe I can take a raincheck on that supper."

marie

It was Ray's idea to take the girls to Bowring Park to feed the ducks, but we weren't there twenty minutes before he wanted to leave again. I'd just handed Lolly and Floss each a small bag of stale bread and buns from the bread tin. The buns were only a day past their best-before date, but I told Ray they'd been sitting there for more than a week. It was the first time since Ray and Lolly had moved in that we'd all agreed on something. It made me wonder why neither one of us thought of it earlier. It was a beautiful evening, crisp and cool but not a breath of wind, and I sat down on one of the benches waiting for Ray when I heard someone call out to him.

"Ray Sullivan, you old sonofabitch," the man shouted out and Ray turned quickly. His face broke out into a wide grin when he saw who it was calling out to him. I didn't recognize the man at all, but then again Ray hadn't introduced me to too many people. There was only Lolly.

"Darryl my son, good to see you buddy." They shook hands. I waited for him to introduce me but he never motioned me forward with a wave of his hand or gestured in my direction and the longer they talked the more uncomfortable I felt. It was like we hadn't bagged up the buns and the bread into two equal halves in the kitchen of the apartment. It was like we didn't ride over in the car together, or went back to get Lolly's sweatshirt halfway to the duck pond. It was like he didn't know who I was at all.

I overheard snippets of their conversation and pieced together their relationship. They were former co-workers. They talked about the phone company, who was still there, who was gone. They snickered at someone's ineptitude and joked about someone else's on-time record. I stayed on the park bench and watched the girls break up the bread into tiny morsels, their heads bowed low as they worked alongside one another. "I was real sorry to hear about your wife," I heard Darryl say a few feet away from me. "I read about it in the paper. I would have stopped by only for I was sick the night she was waked. I sent a card though. She was a beautiful woman, Ray. I'll always remember that Christmas party where she had a little too much to drink and Millie had to fish her out of the bathroom for you. You remember that?"

Ray nodded, but his face had changed from the grin he sported a few moments ago to a scowl. I felt myself deflate. For some reason I'd never pictured Ray's wife as anything other than a body in a casket, or a sickly woman in a hospital bed. That she was someone beautiful, someone who got drunk at office parties and had to be fished out of the bathroom, it just didn't fit into the image I'd stored away in my mind. I pictured a carefree woman with her arm slung across Ray's chest and her black hair the same colour as Lolly's draped over the pillow, and I felt such a sting of jealousy I had to hold my belly. It was ridiculous I knew. She was dead, tucked away underground and I was here feeding ducks with her husband and her child and still I felt the squeeze of insecurity around my heart. It made me cold and I shivered, zipped my jacket. I felt Ray's eyes finally rest on me. He could continue to ignore me. I wasn't going to get up from my seat and put an arm around him and he knew that. He waved me over anyway.

"This is Marie, my special friend," Ray said, placing a hand on the top of my shoulder. My special friend. Ray sounded awkward himself the way he said it, like he was a child introducing a new friend in the sandbox. There needed to be a new word to describe people like me. Friend was too insignificant. Girlfriend too juvenile. I could tell by the look on Darryl's face that the word he was thinking of was harlot, slut, opportunist. Ray could see it too because I felt his fingers dig into my shoulder right through the fleece.

I smiled weakly. "Pleased to meet you." I offered my hand and Darryl hesitated before taking it.

"Looks like you're doing all right there, Ray," Darryl commented.

"Yeah well she was sick a long time," Ray said defensively. "Just trying to get my life back together."

"How's your little girl holding up?"

Ray pointed to Lolly who was walking around the pond in search of a duckling. Floss wasn't being as discriminating, throwing bread crumbs to the ducks, gulls, even the pigeons. "She's grand, that's her over there. This one over here..." He pointed to Floss but stopped. If introducing me was difficult, introducing Floss was near impossible to Ray. *My special friend's daughter.*

"That's my daughter," I said, "the one in the blue sweatshirt," and Ray shot me a look of gratitude.

Darryl looked awkwardly at the both of us. "Good for you," he said and it sounded like it held a tinge of sarcasm along with tons of judgment. "Best be getting on. Good to see you again, Ray. Nice to meet you," he nodded at me.

"He always was an asshole," Ray said when Darryl was out of earshot.

"He was just uncomfortable," I said in his defence.

"So was I. We shouldn't have to keep explaining ourselves all the time."

Three days later Ray came out of the bathroom after he'd been in there for fifteen minutes.

"I s'pose we should get married," he said. "It'll make things easier. I got a pension. Won't have to keep explaining ourselves."

I nodded in agreement, like he'd just told me we should go to the supermarket because we were out of milk. A more romantic version of myself longed for a different sort of proposal, one where he got down on one knee and proclaimed his love for me and his desire to be together forever. The more practical side of me knew he'd already done that once for someone else.

lolly

Gabe brings my car back from the body shop, the dent gone and with a shine to it so brilliant I barely recognize it. It reminds me of the day we picked up the car for my mother's funeral, the day my father met Marie.

We took the bus from the mall straight to the garage that day. It was dark out by the time we got there, the snow had started to accumulate on the roads and Dad was in a rush to get home. We drove home in a car I didn't recognize. It was shiny, vacuumed, and all the clutter was gone. The empty Tim Horton's coffee cups had disappeared, along with the wad of Canadian Tire money that fell into your lap every time you turned the visor down. There was no sign of my mother's sunglasses that sat on the dashboard for an entire year or the soft blanket with the fringes on either end that she bought the day we spent together downtown. Everything of her was gone, even her scent. The car smelled like pine from the cardboard cut-out in the shape of a Christmas tree that hung from the rear-view mirror.

"I thought we were just getting the muffler fixed," I said to him as we pulled out onto the trafficked streets along with everyone else who was trying to make their way home before it got too bad. We snaked along so slowly it seemed like the wipers were moving faster than we were. He never answered the question directly, just prattled on about how nice the car looked.

"They did a good job on the interior. The windows are all clean too, although a lot of good it'll do now in this weather. Smells some nice, huh?"

He went on and on about the car because he didn't want to talk about my mother, or how he was scared to be alone now, and especially how he had Marie's business card in his jeans pocket. He was ashamed of that, couldn't believe he'd done it. I could tell by the way he kept rubbing his thighs as we inched along Kenmount Road, checking to see if it was really there. Administrative Assistant. I caught a glimpse of it before he slid it into his pocket. I knew it meant she made copies, phone calls, and coffee. She scheduled meetings she wasn't invited to, and made sure there was enough Scotch tape and staples in the supply closet.

The snow illuminated under the streetlights. It was falling faster now. I wondered if there would be school the next day. I wondered if we'd have to postpone the wake. I wanted to stave it off indefinitely.

"Do you think they'll have to cancel the wake?" I looked out the window when I asked this, assessing the wind and the snow.

"Nah," Dad said, shaking his head confidently. "Sure most of this will be gone by tomorrow evening." And it was.

The dent in my own car is gone now, buffed and shined along with the rest of the exterior. Even the tires are clean. I can't even see dirt or mud in the treads. The inside has been vacuumed, the Cheerios and Goldfish cracker crumbs strewn around Kenny's car seat are gone, as are the tiny rocks and pebbles left behind from winter boots. It smells like cherries and mint, like a cough drop. I clear my throat reflexively.

"What do you think?" Gabe asks me, and I shrug my shoulders at him.

"I thought you were just getting the dent fixed. I didn't ask you to do all this." I refrain from telling him I didn't ask him to take care of the dent either. "I don't know what you want me to say, Gabe." I say this quietly. I wish he wouldn't do things for me anymore. It makes me feel like I owe him something.

"You can say thank you," he responds sarcastically.

"What do I owe you?" I say instead.

"How about a thank you? How about an apology?"

"I'm sorry." My apology surprises him. I'm not usually one to apologize and he knows this about me. Everyone knows this about me. He'd been gearing up for a racket, waiting to go off on me with self-righteous indignation, but now that I've apologized he doesn't know what to do. He stands with his hands in his pockets, kicking a pebble from one shoe to the other.

"Yeah so like I told you, this guy gave me a real good deal. You can't even tell where the dent was. I did most of the cleaning myself. You're a bit of a slob, no offence," he jokes. "Cracker crumbs, chip wrappers, empty juice boxes…"

I smile a little at his observation. I've heard it a million times from Marie. Gabe mistakes my smile for playfulness because he dangles the keys in front of my face. "Want to go for a spin? We could go parking for old-time's sake. You could suck me off behind the school just like you used to when—"

"Oh my God, Gabe, can you grow up already?" My voice cracks with exasperation and desperation. He stands there with his mouth open and his eyes wide. He looks disappointed and I don't know whether it's because I've yelled at him or because I didn't jump at the opportunity to fool around with him in my newly cleaned car.

"All right then," he nods. "So where is the little squirt?" He asks like he's only now realizing the purpose of his visit is to pick up Kenny, not me. He follows me inside and immediately proceeds to wrestle with Kenny on the beige carpet in Marie's living room. He pretends to be defeated, his hands flailing in the air as Kenny jumps on his chest, digging his knees into Gabe's ribs and pummeling his little fists into Gabe's belly. Gabe must have bruises the length of his chest. Kenny is only a little thing, but it's got to hurt. He can't even crawl in the bed with me in the morning without a knee to the stomach. As is always the case, once Kenny defeats his father, Gabe holds him upside down by his ankles.

"Watch will you, he just had lunch." I can't understand Gabe's incessant need to dangle our child upside down.

"What's your problem?" Gabe releases Kenny on the floor and takes a seat on the sofa with his arms and legs splayed so far apart he takes up two full cushions. Kenny goes to jump in his lap and Gabe's limbs close instinctively and his hands protectively cover his privates. "We're just playing."

"I don't have a problem. I just don't feel like cleaning up vomit right now."

"You don't clean up much, judging from the state of your car," he shoots back. Gabe sits Kenny properly on his lap, pulls out Batman from the back pocket of his jeans and hands it over to him. "Look who I found in Grandpa's car."

"Batman!" Kenny grabs the toy and runs to his bedroom to retrieve his other Batman toy. "I have two now," he shouts to Gabe.

"Two Batmans? Let me see that." Gabe picks up the toy, examines it like he was appraising a precious heirloom at an antique shop. His eyes squint in confusion as he holds the cape between his thumb and index finger. "Did your grandmother get you this one? It's not the right colour or size. It doesn't even have a batarang. Your mother wouldn't have bought this piece of junk."

I feel my face grow hot as I pack the rest of Kenny's overnight bag. I feel the urge to defend the toy as much as the person who purchased it. "He likes it," I say. "Tell your dad that you want to keep that Batman here." Gabe and I have developed a habit of speaking to one another through our son since he was an infant, before he could even understand either one of us. At first it was endearing types of things. *Your daddy is going to run to the store and get you more milk. I think your mother could use a nap too so let's go for a drive.* Then it evolved into more testy conversations that spiraled into nasty exchanges. *Your father brought home the wrong diapers again. Your mother didn't tell me you wore a bigger size. Your father doesn't pay attention.*

"The policeman got it for me." Kenny's face is wide-eyed, smiling. He has no idea he's just unleashed a torrent of emotions between myself and Gabe. I shouldn't have said anything to Kenny at all. I should have just handed him the toy and been done with it, but I wanted Carson to get credit for the gesture. I wanted Kenny to like him, so I went on more than I should. I told him the policeman bought him the toy. I told him he was a friend of mine.

Gabe kneels down and looks intently at Kenny. "What policeman? The one that was here the other night?" Kenny nods. "What did he buy you a new toy for?" Gabe looks confused, keeps staring at the action figure like it was going to speak to him.

"Because he's Mommy's friend," Kenny answers as if this explains everything.

I feel my face grow red and flushed. Gabe stands upright now and pulls his sweatshirt over his head as if he were readying himself for a brawl. He's hot. His face is redder than mine and the colour goes all the way down to his neck in a mottled-looking rash. His undershirt has stiff yellow stains under the arms from his deodorant and a pink hue around the collar from the time I put it in the wash with one of Kenny's blankets, the one with the big fire engine. Maybe I'm just feeling guilty about the toy but the sight of the undershirt on Gabe leaves me almost breathless with sorrow. I was sorry that I ruined his undershirt, sorrier that he still wore it, and even sorrier that we were here in this place we could never have imagined. I pretend to sort through a stack of mail, although every envelope has Marie's name on it.

"What is he, your boyfriend now?"

"Of course not," I respond, perhaps too emphatically. I haven't even seen him since he dropped the toy off and that was nearly a week ago. But I think about him all the time, fantasize about the three of us living in the east end, a picture-perfect family, me and Carson and Kenny. It is in these moments I feel a shade of envy for Marie. She was lucky that her first husband abandoned her. She didn't have to listen to him ask her to suck him off when he came to pick up his kid for the night.

"You like him, don't you?" Gabe nods in understanding. I used to love that he always seemed to know what I was feeling. I never had to say anything, he just knew. He knows this now too and I feel uncomfortable under Gabe's watchful stare. He looks at me harshly and I have to shield my eyes from him like I was looking up into the sun. "I like him as a friend that's all."

"Bullshit." He enunciates every letter, his face so close to mine I can feel his hot breath like a slap on my cheek.

"And why is that bullshit?"

"Because you don't have any friends."

I feel tears pool in the corners of my eyes and swipe them away angrily. I watched my mother die without shedding a tear, and it was only when the rose was taken from the top of my father's coffin at the grave that I lost it. But Gabe shoots me an insult more suited to the playground and I break down like a school girl. He's right. I don't have any friends. I never wanted friends. All I wanted was a proper family. It was part of the reason why I loved Gabe. He came from a family where they had barbecues on the deck and spent weekends at the cabin and no one ever questioned why they were there.

"I'm sorry." He says it like Kenny after he's grabbed a toy from someone else on the playground and I tell him he has to apologize, with eyes downcast and arms folded. Gabe blows the hair out of his eyes, shoves his hands in his pockets and sighs. He's not good with tears. They leave him nearly paralyzed. He's like this even with Kenny, who cries about everything from having to wash his hands to having to wear socks. Gabe usually sits there and stares at his son like he was observing such behaviour for the very first time, even though it happens fifteen times a day.

Gabe turns away from me and tells Kenny to get his shoes, they are going to Nanny and Poppy Hillier's for the night and then he pulls out his phone and calls a cab to pick him up. He came in my car, my newly repaired, clean car.

"I'll drive you," I say digging in my purse for my keys.

"Don't fuckin' bother." Gabe is angry, angrier than I've ever seen him before but I can smell the fear in him. It's one thing for me to leave, but the thought of Kenny replacing him makes him queasy. His hands start to tremble, just the slightest as he's lacing up Kenny's shoes. He pries the new Batman toy from Kenny's grasp, his little fingers unable to hold on against his father's strength. "You're. Not. Taking. That." Gabe says it through gritted teeth and tosses the toy in the middle of the living-room floor where it lays face down in the same spot Gabe had wrestled Kenny a few moments earlier. Kenny begins to wail and scream, his fists pummelling Gabe's chest. Both their faces are red with anger, Kenny's filled with snot and tears and injustice, Gabe's with fear and betrayal. I feel as if I should say something to ease the tension but anything I could say would only make it worse. Finally Gabe just overpowers his child, scooping him up into his arms and out the door while Kenny kicks and punches and screams the word Batman over and over again.

I watch them through the window. Gabe kicks my car, leaving a bootprint in the middle of the door. Kenny is still crying but it's tapering off. Gabe must have promised him a trip to the toy store. I watch until the cab comes, and just as it drives away, I get the feeling that someone else is watching too.

marie

This place is a shithole," Lolly announced casually. She relieved her arms of a box, dropped it onto the living-room carpet, and then looked down at it with a measure of disgust, afraid my carpet might dirty up her box instead of the other way around.

The armload of coats and jackets I held over my arm felt heavier when I heard her say it. I knew it wasn't the nicest of places but I'd spent the past four days cleaning it up and making room for them. The apartment smelled like lemon Pledge. I'd even rented one of the carpet cleaners from the supermarket and it got nearly all the stains out, even the chocolate milk I was sure had set in.

"It's only temporary, honey," Ray said in a way that seemed to indicate he agreed with her assertion that the place was indeed a shithole. I looked around the room, assessing it as if for the first time even though it had been home to me and Floss for the past eight years. The walls needed a fresh coat of paint, the furniture was outdated, hand-me-downs from Dad and Doris, and the carpet was an ugly shade of light blue despite having just been cleaned.

"We talked about this," he reminded her. His face and neck were all sweaty from lugging a box up over the stairs and down the hall and he wiped the sweat off his face with the bottom of his shirt. I caught a glimpse of his belly, also moist with sweat. "We're going to buy a house, maybe next year. A nice place with plenty of rooms. They're building new houses in Mount Pearl every day," he assured her, but I knew we wouldn't be buying one of the new ones and I didn't care. "We just can't afford it right this second," he said more gently.

"This is a nice place," Floss said so quietly I had to repeat her words over inside my head to make certain I'd heard them right. While I appreciated the sentiment, I knew Floss thought it was a shithole too. She never invited friends over and always insisted she be dropped off down the road whenever she got a drive home from a friend's mom or dad, and then walked the rest of the way home.

I concentrated on hanging up the coats in the hall closet. I wished I had a brother or a cousin, or someone strong to help Ray with all the boxes. I had every window in the place wide open and still Ray was coated in sweat. The smell overshadowed the Pledge. His breathing was laboured too, but it might have had nothing to do with the physical exertion, but rather the explanation he had to keep giving Lolly on why they were moving in the first place. She knew why; she simply couldn't understand.

It made more sense for them to move in with me. Neither one of us thought it was a good idea for Floss and I to move in with them, even if they had more room than we did. I didn't want to lie in the same bed as he did with his first wife, cook supper over the same stove as she boiled milk on the nights she couldn't sleep. This was the only solution. He looked over at Lolly, looked like he might say something to that effect, but then thought better of it. She didn't need reminding.

"Lolly, why don't you go unpack your stuff," Ray suggested since she was sitting on her box in the middle of the living room. I felt bad for her sitting there on top of the only possessions she had left, looking like she didn't know what to do with them.

"I don't want to," she said flatly.

"Lolly, Jesus Christ," Ray pleaded. He sounded desperate. I kept straightening the coats even though they were already hung up since the tone of his voice was so pained I couldn't bear to look at his face. I felt the stirrings of anger at her for making Ray so upset. She knew his weakness and went straight for it every time, manipulating him whenever she could. "It's only temporary, Lollipop," he said again, this time more softly, like an apology.

I fixated on the word *temporary* in my head, knowing he meant the living arrangements, but wondering if he might also mean me. We hadn't talked that much about the future, just talked in general terms about getting a house big enough for all of us. He didn't mind a fixer-upper, he told me, because he could do most of the work himself. He could do basic plumbing, he was adept at electrical he assured me, and when he said it, there was no doubt in my mind it was something we were planning together. Now it sounded like something he and Lolly had plotted together and it made me feel like an outsider to the two of them. I felt uncomfortable listening to their strained voices and lengthy pauses and I felt an uneasiness settle in the room. They needed time alone, Ray and Lolly.

"Floss, come on and help me with the rest of the boxes," I said perhaps too loudly.

"My arms are tired," Floss protested, "and I'm already after moving half my own stuff to make room for all their stuff in the first place."

"Floss," I said sharply, noting that she didn't bother to

differentiate between Ray and Lolly. One was as big an inconvenience to her as the other. "Outside. Now."

The sun was so hot it was after heating up the hood of Ray's car like he'd just driven clear across the island. I sat on it anyway, enjoying the way the heat went through my jeans and warmed up the backs of my thighs. I lifted my face toward the sun, felt the wind caress my temples.

"I thought we were supposed to be getting more boxes."

"Oh Floss, sit down will you," I laughingly chastised her. I was in a good mood again despite Lolly's protestations. The sun was shining, I could smell fresh-cut grass in the air from the subdivision behind us, smelled steaks sizzling on barbecues. That would be us one day. Lolly would come around quickly once she unpacked her things.

It filled me with an unexpected giddiness to create a few drawers for Ray in the bedroom. I bought new sheets, striped ones with a hint of masculinity, instead of the floral patterned sheets that pilled and faded on the one half I occupied. I bought Ray and Lolly toothbrushes and put them in the holes next to mine and Floss' toothbrushes. I bought a new set of dishes that came with four bowls, four dinner plates, four salad plates, four mugs. We were a family of four and everything came in a package of four—four glasses, four spoons, four batteries, four pork chops to put on four dinner plates. I bought the Corel set since I couldn't bear the thought of a single piece breaking. That was how I imagined our new family. We were durable, unbreakable, and we fit neatly together.

I patted a spot next to me on the hood of Ray's car in invitation and Floss climbed up alongside me, holding her hand over her forehead and squinting in the bright sunlight.

"Ray and Lolly just need a few minutes that's all," I told her.

"What for? Do you think they changed their mind?" There was a hint of joyful excitement to Floss' voice that irritated the hell out of me, but I quelled the urge to act the least bit annoyed with her.

"Of course not," I said brightly, although Floss had already planted the seed of doubt in my mind. I wondered if it was foolish to leave the two of them alone like that. He shot me a look as I brushed past him that I thought was an apology for his daughter's behaviour, but now I wondered if it was a look of apology for something yet to come. I looked up at the open window and strained to hear what they were saying, but all I could hear was the traffic behind me. The sun went in behind the clouds at that moment and I shivered even though it was still warm out.

"I'm not that fussy about her you know." Floss stared up at our living-room window from the hood of the car. I wondered if she saw Lolly up there but I couldn't see anything, not even a shadow. "She called the place a shithole and even though it is, she shouldn't be saying stuff like that. What if I don't like her?" I should have told Floss to stop her bitching and complaining but it was Lolly who needed to hear it more than Floss, who was only telling the truth. I could picture Ray up there right now standing awkwardly against a stack of unstable boxes, their contents written in black marker, and pleading with her to just try. I wondered what would happen if Lolly said she couldn't. Ray would be gone, the same as I would have been gone if Floss told me she couldn't. It gave me an insecure feeling at odds with the optimism I had when I woke up this morning knowing Ray would lie with me that night. My whole future dangled precariously on the whim of a nine-year-old girl who couldn't have cared less about me. Ray would acquiesce to whatever Lolly wanted and it only made me love him more. My hands started to shake and I tucked them under the tops of my thighs to hide them from Floss.

What if I don't like her either? "You'll get along once you get to know her better," I said instead. "I think we all just need time to adjust." It was advice for me as much as it was for Floss. I twisted uncomfortably on the hood of the car, my hand on my side like I was having a bad cramp.

"She's really a sweet little girl. She's just been through a lot of changes and needs time to get used to things." I didn't know whether I was trying to convince Floss or myself but decided it didn't matter. I loved Ray and she was an extension of him. I would pick up after her just like I did with Floss. I'd match her socks up and fold them neatly, I'd take up her supper for her and lay the plate in front of her, I'd put flannel sheets on the bed in the winter and lay her wet mittens over the radiator when she came in out of the snow. I'd do everything for Lolly that I did for Floss because I loved Ray. One day I knew I would love her too.

lolly

There's a strange man sitting on the front steps when I get home from the grocery store. It's such an unexpected sight it takes me a few moments to comprehend. A delivery-man, maybe, but there is no package in his hands. Someone collecting money for the Heart and Stroke Foundation, but there's no clipboard resting on his lap, nor any pamphlets tucked under his elbow. His only purpose appears to be waiting for someone to come home and let him in, like he's locked himself out. He's a small man, although perhaps it's just an illusion brought about by baggy clothes. The sweatshirt falls to the tops of his thighs and the hood shades his gaunt face. He stands up when he sees me, makes his way down the steps and walks over to me like he was going to help me with the groceries.

"Do you live here?" he asks me. Yes seems like the wrong answer, as does no. I feel sweat pool on my lower back and I begin to fidget nervously with the zipper of my purse. I keep waiting for him to ask me to hand it over to him.

"Can I help you?" I sound far too polite under the circumstances. He stares intensely at me as if trying to discern something familiar about me. His eyes scan my face for what seems like a long time, although it's probably no more than a few seconds. I can see my image reflected in his eyes, two identical versions of myself looking small and terrified.

"You're not her," he declares sadly.

"Who?"

"I'm sorry, I was looking for someone else," he sighs with such ringing disappointment I almost feel bad to be the wrong person. He turns away slowly and saunters up the road, looking dejected with his hands in his pockets and his head down. A warm wind lifts the hair off the back of my neck as I watch him leave, reminding me of the first time I met Gabe.

He showed up on the doorstep looking for someone else too. It was the day we moved into the new house. I didn't know whether to be happy about it or not. On the one hand I was relieved to be out of the tiny apartment, but on the other hand I knew this arrangement was not temporary. I was going to be stuck with Marie and Floss forever. Dad must have grown accustomed to living in a shithole because the new house was exactly that. The carpet was old and dirty, the fixtures outdated and the paint was peeling off the walls. I told Marie it smelled like old people, and she just tsked at me saying there was no such smell as old people. She acknowledged it did have a distinct odour though, because she opened every window in the house to air it out and started scrubbing everything before we even had single a box unpacked. She was in the kitchen with her rubber gloves and her Comet when Gabe knocked at the door.

He had a big heavy bag slung over his shoulder filled with newspapers. He had a bottle of Pepsi in his hand with a thick layer of bubbles in it from shaking and going up and down so many sets of stairs. His hair was in his eyes but the wind kept lifting it up off his forehead and blowing it back. It was a warm wind though and he didn't seem bothered by it.

"Where's Mrs. Duffy?" He looked at me almost accusatory, like I'd gone and done something to her. Before I had a chance to tell him, he was smiling again, an infectious grin that made me smile back at him.

"Are you Mrs. Duffy's granddaughter?" He pointed a finger at me that was smudged with newsprint. "Up from Toronto are you? She told me you were coming but I didn't think it was for another couple of months. Talks about you all the time."

I shook my head at him. "Mrs. Duffy," I repeated woodenly.

"You calls her Nan, I s'pose. That's what I call my grandmothers, Nanny Hillier and Nanny Powers. So what have you been doing since you got here?"

"Unpacking."

He looked surprised. "Did you just get here then?"

"Yeah. This morning." I knew we were having two different conversations but I was grateful for the distraction of not having to stare at the box of my mother's things any longer. A jumbled mess of ingredients in her manic script written on the back of envelopes and grocery receipts. Dad told me to throw it away. It wasn't how I wanted to remember her but I kept them anyway. How did he know how I wanted to remember her?

Gabe gave me a broad smile. "First time here?" I nodded. "What do you think of it? It's nice right?"

It was bigger and brighter than Marie's apartment. I had my own bedroom. When I moved into the apartment Dad kept apologizing and saying it was temporary. He wasn't like that this time. He was proud of the house, thrilled he'd been able to get it so quickly and at such a good price. He talked about being in the right place at the right time. He talked about planting trees and painting the walls and laying new carpet. He was nearly dizzy from pointing out all the things he was going to work on. He was like a kid at a playground, moving from the swings to the slide to the monkey bars. At this very moment he was over to Kent Building Supplies to buy a lawnmower. I knew he'd come back with more than that, grass seed, trimmers, netting, whatever he could fit in the car.

"It's better than where I just came from."

"Anything's better than Toronto. No offence."

I smiled brightly back at him. "None taken."

"What are you going to see first? If I were you I'd go to Cape Spear right now. It's a warm southwesterly wind and we don't get too many of those, not this time of year anyway. Most of the time the wind is enough to freeze the arse right off ya. But on a day like today you can stand at the top of the cliff with them gulls, and let the warm wind blow on you. It's the closest you'll ever get to flying."

"Maybe I will," I said, knowing full well I wasn't going to Cape Spear that day. There was too much settling in to be done.

"So is your Nan here or what? She should be expecting me. It's the first of the month and I always collect on the first of every month. She makes these lemon cookies with icing sugar on them every time I comes. Do you know the ones I'm talking about? They taste like paper mâché or something. I can only eat four or five of them while she digs in her purse for my tip and I'm burping up lemon the rest of the day. She probably didn't make them this time in all the excitement of having you here. Thank God for that, right?" He gave me a conspiratorial wink.

Mrs. Duffy was the dead woman. Dad didn't tell us too much, just that he got a good deal from someone eager to sell, someone from the office whose mother had lived here until she fell down the basement steps, broke a hip, died three days later.

"The lady who lived here passed away. I'm sorry."

"Oh." He looked crestfallen. I knew by the expression on his face that he'd never known a single person who died. He'd never been inside a funeral home, never had to look at a body being waked. He unscrewed the cap from his Pepsi and brought it to his lips, but he didn't drink. He was just trying to hide. The wind blew his hair up and he looked over his shoulder to hide his face but not before I caught a glimpse of a tear that the wind blew in a zigzag pattern down the length of his cheek.

"Fucking wind," he mumbled wiping at his face. He probably felt foolish for being so upset over an old woman he delivered the paper to, but I wanted to reach out and put a comforting hand on his arm. It didn't matter if it was your mother or a woman you collected paper money from, grief was grief and I saw it in him.

"Lolly, who's at the door?" Marie came out of the kitchen, dripping soap from her rubber gloves all over the carpet. It didn't matter. Dad was going to rip it up anyway. She stood with her hands on her hips, the water soaking stains into her jeans.

"The paper boy," I said, although it made it sound like he was made of paper and I was afraid he was going to crumple up and blow away right in front of me.

"What's your name?" I asked him.

"Gabe," he said, turning to face me.

"I'm Lolly. We just moved in. Mrs. Duffy wasn't my grand-mother. I don't even have a grandmother. I don't have a mother either. She died a few years ago."

"Lolly!" Marie snapped at me in reprimand.

"It's true," I said, although I didn't look at her. I locked eyes with Gabe. Neither one of us could look away.

"You don't have to go telling everyone you meet that," Marie whined in exasperation. She sounded childlike, upset I was telling on her.

"I don't," I said, and this was true. Gabe was the first person I'd ever told who didn't already know it, and it had been three years.

I could hear Marie sigh and I felt a twinge of regret,

although not for telling Gabe the truth, but because I knew the truth hurt Marie.

"Are we going to get the paper delivered?" I already knew the answer. Marie and my dad read the paper every day, traded sections. They even did the crossword sometimes if there was nothing on television. I asked her because I was trying to give her something back, a little authority.

"Of course." She still sounded defeated.

He dug into his bag, folded the paper neatly in half and handed it to me. He came the next day and the day after that. I made him lemon cookies with icing sugar once and he told me they were nearly as bad as Mrs. Duffy's. I've seen him every single day of my life since I was twelve.

I know the man on the front steps wasn't looking for Mrs. Duffy the way Gabe was all those years ago, but I wonder for a moment if he was someone my father knew and chide myself for not asking him more questions. I was too scared at the time.

I clean Kenny's room, fuss over putting toys back in their proper places. I toss action figures in a bin alongside bad guys, blocks, dinosaurs, and trains. They hit the pile with such a dull thud it's as if they were protesting the injustice of being kept amongst such company. I make Kenny's bed, wishing all the while he was jumping on it or under my feet so I could bawl at him to go and play while I neatened up his room. I hate not having him underfoot, pleading with me to play a game with him. It's too quiet in the house, almost unnatural in its silence.

I keep thinking about the man out front, with his sad eyes and his perusal of me, slow and deliberate. I sit on the edge of Kenny's bed and find the new Batman toy tangled up in the pajamas he had on last night. I pick it up, hold it in the palm of my hand. Perhaps it's the quiet or the loneliness but I feel a sense of longing for the man who bought the toy on impulse. He didn't normally act on impulse, he told me. I convince myself that impulses are not always a thing to be denied. Surely Dad acted on impulse when he asked Marie where to find her that day on the bus. Call me if you need anything, Carson said. I pick up the phone knowing I need something but not sure what.

Carson comes quickly after my summons. He's not on duty because he's wearing sweatpants and a T-shirt. He has the tiniest growth of hair on his head, black dots that hug the back of his neck, and his beard needs trimming. Dad never shaved on his days off either. By Sunday night his neck would be covered with the beginnings of a beard, only to be shorn off by the time I went to school again on Monday morning.

"What happened?" He appears slightly out of breath, like he'd rushed to get here. I feel foolish now for having asked him to come. There is no crime. There was just a man who looked lost and forlorn but that was it. I was scared of him, not because I thought he was going to hurt me, but because of the way I looked in his eyes. I was going to end up like him, alone, waiting on someone else's front steps for people who didn't exist anymore.

"Nothing." He looks at me with enough impatience that I explain. "Well there was a man outside the house when I came home today. I think it might have been the same man was here the other night."

"Did you call the police?"

"I called you."

"You should have called the station."

"I'm sorry," I swallow, feeling foolish.

"It's okay. You can still fill out a report."

"I don't want to report it. He was just looking for someone else." I could say the same thing about myself, about my father all those years ago, about most people. "I think he had the wrong house, that's all. Every house on this block looks the same."

Carson nods in acknowledgement. "So what do you want to do? You want to report it? You want to leave it alone?"

"I just want to get out of here." I feel slightly claustrophobic, alone in the house with nothing but old memories.

"Are you okay?"

"Yeah," I nod, staring out the window at the tree my father planted all those years ago. The wind whips the branches around, and the wind chimes Marie hung on one of the branches makes a mystical sound. It's a warm southwesterly wind. I turn back to Carson. "I'm sorry you came all the way here for no reason. I didn't mean to disturb you on your day off."

"It's okay. I wasn't doing anything anyway."

"Me either." I was lonely. Kenny was at Gabe's until tomorrow, Floss was working, and Marie was off to lunch with Doris. "I'm going to Cape Spear." I'm surprised by what comes out of my mouth but not in a bad way. I should have gone all those years ago when Gabe first suggested it.

"Now? By yourself?"

It's not the sort of place people go to alone. They usually bring family members who are visiting from away, or pack a picnic lunch and sit with a partner overlooking the ocean and the rocks. "You can come with me if you want." I say it the same way I tell Kenny he can come to the store with me. "You said yourself you weren't doing anything."

He shakes his head, smiles at the absurdity of such a suggestion and shrugs his shoulders in defeat. "All right, let's go. I'm driving though. There's more than one traffic light on the way," he adds in a teasing manner that makes me feel lighter.

Even though it's a clear day in town, the road to Cape Spear is foggy. I look out the window but nothing passes me. There are no trees to watch speeding by, no houses nestled on the roadside, nothing save for the bank of fog that closes in on us. It feels like the kind of dream Floss might have, except she would find the fog disorienting or smothering, whereas I find it comforting to be shrouded.

A sheen of moisture covers the windshield as we get closer to the ocean, but it's not raining. It reminds me of past Sunday mornings, Marie's roast simmering in the oven, cabbage and salt beef boiling on top of the stove, and the windows all steamed up and dripping with condensation. I never thought I'd experience a nostalgic longing for those days but I do now. It feels like something is caught in my throat. It's cold, damp, grey and nearly deserted save for three other cars and one camper. Carson parks the car, stares out the windshield at the faint outline of the coast, looking like he expects the ocean to impart some sudden wisdom or truth.

"Take a walk with me."

Carson reaches for my hand until it's nestled safely and securely in his grasp. He holds my hand the way I hold Kenny's when we run across the parking lot of the grocery store to get to the car. He's different than Gabe, who intertwines every one of my fingers into his own when he reaches for me.

Carson and I walk silently along the path and in the spots where it's too narrow for both of us to fit, he doesn't loosen his grip, but goes first, gently tugging me behind. He leads me to the shelter of the World War Two barracks, ruins now covered in spray paint, graffiti, and the initials of lovers past, every combination of the alphabet it seems.

Somewhere in the men's bathroom of the Dairy Queen, my own initials are there. G.H. + L.S. Gabe told me he carved them into the door of the bathroom stall and I remember feeling incredibly pleased by this information. He was brave, I thought at the time, for committing such a daring act all in the name of professing his love for me. I look around at all the lovers' names now and wonder how many are still together.

Does Bill still love Lisa? Does Todd still think Donna has nice tits or have they gone all saggy? It's not just homages to love; there are trite sayings, hurtful accusations. James sucks dicks. Jackie is a slut. I wonder if Jackie is married now, has children, attends church every Sunday morning. I wonder if she even notices it's her name someone carved into the paint of an old cannon when she brings her family to Cape Spear for a picnic. I feel a wave of sympathy for her, whoever she is. Or was.

Carson does not seem to notice any of the graffiti. He moves along with his head held level, staring out into the ocean concealed by a bank of fog. We know it's there from the sound and the smell but the fog is disorienting, so much so I'm forced to look down to secure my footing.

We step inside the old barracks, the thick concrete affording instant shelter from the howl of the wind. The sudden quiet feels almost eerie. Carson stops abruptly, turns toward me. A few moments ago I could hardly hear anything save for the wind whipping by us and the crash of the ocean below us and now all I can hear is Carson's breath, the shuffle of his wet sneakers on the concrete. We are both covered in a shroud of mist, making the moment feel ethereal.

"I don't know what to make of you. I don't know what to make of this." He looks like a man who usually knows what to make of everything. He's different than me in that regard. I've never known what to make about anything. He swallows hard and I count the shadowed lines in his forehead. There are five of them, perfectly spaced apart, and I want to run each of my fingers across them and down his neck but his grip on my hand is still tight and I don't want to wrestle it away. "This is crazy."

I don't know whether he expects me to agree with him or to protest his assertion. "I know." I look away from him. Of course it's crazy. It's like an invisible hand is pushing us together. This is the third time we've met, and each time it's as if fate had put us there—a car wreck, a would-be intruder, a stranger on the front step. I know almost nothing about him and none of it seems to matter.

"What do you want to know?" he asks as if he were reading my mind. "You can ask me anything."

"How did you get your name?"

He looks at me in surprise, raising an eyebrow and curling his lips into a slow smile. "That's what you want to know?"

"Yes," I nod. I imagine someone asking Kenny this very question. Everyone thought I was going to name him Ray. Even Gabe was fairly certain I would insist on Ray if it was a boy, but I didn't want to look at my little boy and see my father. I picked Kenneth because my father told me that would have been my name if I was a boy.

"My parents named me after the boat. They met on the Carson," he clarifies. "It was a stormy crossing. My father was seasick and my mother took pity on him, at least that's the way she tells it. My father swears to this day he had food poisoning," Carson chuckles, reciprocates by asking me how my parents met.

I realize I don't know the answer, haven't the faintest clue. It's not like I was around to witness it and it's not like my parents talked about it. They had too many other things to talk about. "On the Metrobus," I say to my horror. I tell the story from when my dad got on the bus until Marie landed in his lap, mimicking the way Marie's arms reached out to him until I find myself reaching for Carson in the exact same manner.

Carson smiles at me, a genuine smile that reaches the corners of his eyes. "That's romantic," he says, chuckling at the silliness of it all, or more importantly his willingness to buy into it. "You told that story so well, it was almost like you were there."

I have to look to my feet so he won't know the truth. It hadn't occurred to me that it was romantic before now. Marie sat in his lap for a moment longer than was necessary and my father responded in a way that made my face burn with embarrassment. I knew I was witnessing something I wasn't supposed to. He gave her a broad smile when she tried to collect herself, the first time I'd seen him smile in months. He brushed her hair from her face and he stared at her with his lips parted and his breath almost laboured. It was the first time I felt invisible in my father's presence. Even now it was hard to think of my father and Marie in that way. I couldn't stand the thought of their naked bodies rubbing against one another. I used to wonder if he liked the waxy texture of her frosted pink lipstick or if she left the smell of onions on his skin after she'd touched him.

Carson leans in towards me, his eyes still laughing at the story of how my father met Marie. He looks almost mythical covered in mist, and surrounded by fog and I become aware of my own appearance. My hair is curling now with the dampness, turning dark and thick and heavy. Carson is looking at me the same way my father once looked at Marie. His hands lean against the cold stone on either side of my face. His lips are parted and they move closer to mine, his breath so hot I feel my skin melt away.

"I wanted to do that ever since I saw you shivering in the cold that day," he says after he kisses me.

It feels like fate brought us together, but the problem is I've already sealed my fate with Gabe and Kenny.

marie

Gabe told me he was going to give Lolly an engagement ring when he came to pick up Kenny for the night.

"Don't tell her," he said, hoisting the diaper bag over his shoulder. "I wants it to be a surprise. I was going to take her out to dinner maybe and ask her when they bring the dessert out. Do you think she'll be embarrassed? I don't want her to get mad with me. She doesn't like it when people stare at her."

He looked up at me, his hair falling in his eyes. He still looked like a kid to me. I didn't know why he was telling me. I wondered for a moment if he was asking for my permission the way he hesitated in the foyer. I was all Lolly had left in the way of a parent but the notion that I was supposed to grant my approval on their union was so ridiculous I almost laughed right then and there.

"I got the ring on layaway over to the mall," he explained. "I should be able to get it in time for her birthday but just in case something comes up, you know. I don't want her to be disappointed."

"I won't say anything," I assured him, stuffing a rattle that had fallen on the floor back inside the diaper bag. "Congratulations, I guess," I offered weakly and felt badly that I wasn't more enthusiastic for the two of them. I should have been hugging him or squeezing my hands tightly with excitement but I did neither.

"Sure she hasn't said yes yet," Gabe said jokingly, but he had just the slightest tremor of doubt in his voice.

I thought everything changed after Ray died, but it changed even more after Kenny was born. I watched Kenny on Tuesdays and Thursdays for a couple of hours, just to cover that window when Lolly had to leave for work and Gabe hadn't made it home yet. Lolly dropped him off to me, carting along a big bag of toys and diapers and bottles and a few things I didn't even know what they were. She was always tired and cranky, snapping at me whenever I asked a simple question like how long the bottle was supposed to go in the microwave for. *Thirty seconds. Same as the last time you asked me.* Gabe would come to pick him up after supper, nearly as exhausted as Lolly had been when she dropped him off. His laces were never tied properly, his eyes had dark circles under them, and his lips were always dry and chapped like he'd been licking them all day. It was from working in hot offices, fixing machines, and then going back out in the cold. He did it ten times a day. He had ink stains all over his fingers and I had to use Brasso on the doorknob at least once a week to wipe them off.

But it was Gabe and Lolly who changed the most. For years I'd never seen the two of them apart and now I never saw them together. I'd known Gabe almost as long as I'd known Lolly. From the day we moved in, back when he delivered the paper. Lolly would sit out on the step waiting for him and he'd sit down alongside her, the two of them never running out of things to say. I used to be afraid they were talking about me, that she told him all my secrets—that I coloured my hair or that I got my upper lip waxed once a month—but Ray told me I was just being foolish, they were only talking about their friends but it didn't seem like they had any friends, only each other. I used to tease Ray that Gabe was going to be his son-in-law one of these days and he'd laugh at how foolish I was being. *They're just kids, Marie,* he'd say. I wondered what he'd say if he knew the conversation Gabe and I were having.

I wandered around the mall looking for the right jewellery store. I should have asked him but I wanted it to be a surprise. Gabe was surprising Lolly, and I was surprising Gabe. I didn't like surprises, not after the surprise Ray left for me after he died. My heart couldn't take any more surprises.

I visited three separate jewellery shops, and I was beginning to wonder if I had the right mall when neither one of them had anything on layaway for Gabe. I was beginning to get a wary feeling, like maybe I should leave well enough alone, so I stopped into the food court for a cup of tea and to reconsider what I was doing. Lolly would be mad with me. She'd probably tell me to mind my own business. She was always telling me to mind my own business.

The lineup at Tim Horton's was long and my feet were too tired to stand in the back of it. It was only eleven o'clock in the morning and no one was interested yet in sampling the Chinese vegetables or the fried chicken. The only ones here were old people anyway, lining up for their tea and raisin biscuit because they couldn't eat anything heavy in the middle of the day anymore.

They all looked exactly the same to me, clones of one another with their wrinkled skin, their grey hairs and sunken watery eyes that looked as if they were receding from their own faces. The men were mostly bald, their speckled foreheads glistening under the fluorescent lights while the women sported identical hairstyles of short grey curls. They all had the same stains on the sleeves of their coats from resting their arms on dirty tables in food courts and coffee shops. They blew into their cups, the loose skin on their necks and cheeks flapping with the effort. They talked about their appointment to get their cataracts removed, they talked about the grandkids, most likely they wished Sobey's was still in the mall because they were low on tin milk.

I watched an old man take a bite of his biscuit and then a sip of tea as if he couldn't produce enough saliva to chew it up, and I watched the woman sitting across from him scold him for stuffing too much in his mouth like he was her child instead of her husband. I wondered if she still saw him the way he used to look, before he began to look like everyone else. I couldn't tell him apart from the man four tables away but when she looked at him she probably saw things no one else did. I couldn't sit there any longer and look at them.

I was washing my hands in the bathroom sink in the mall when I caught sight of my own reflection in the mirror. I barely recognized my own face. It was the makeup that made me look different. I used to put it on in front of the bedroom mirror and step back admiringly. Ray used to sit on the edge of the bed and watch, fascinated by the beauty routines of women. I would kiss him once, long and slow, before I applied my lipstick because he said he didn't like the taste of it. He used to make me wash it off before he'd kiss me.

The makeup used to soften my features and highlight my eyes and lips. But now all it did was emphasize the flaws. The foundation settled into the lines around my eyes and mouth, making them appear even more pronounced. The mascara and eye shadow made my eyes look smaller and darker, and the lipstick had a hint of shimmer, which might have complemented someone young, but which had the opposite effect on someone my age. I looked harsh. I looked, much to my own horror, like one of those women who'd been around the block a few times, as Doris would say. I ran the hot water, took a folded rectangle of brown paper and dabbed it in the sink, pumped the liquid soap onto it and spread it around the paper with a fingertip. I was going to wash it off, the eyeliner, the foundation makeup, the frosted pink lips, but then I stopped, turned off the water, and threw the paper into the garbage.

I looked like I'd been around the block a few times because I had. I was divorced once, widowed once. I'd been a single mom, a stepmother, now a grandmother, more or less. I struggled to make ends meet, I felt like every bit of affection and love I had in my life, I had to work for. I hoped Ray, if he could have seen me at that moment, would remember the way my face looked on the bus the day we met. I longed to go back out to the food court and find him waiting for me with a cup of tea in his hand.

I wanted the same thing for Lolly and Gabe. I wanted her to sit with Gabe in another fifty years and remember the kid with the bag of newspapers slung across his shoulder. I wanted Gabe to look at her and remember the girl with long hair who used to twirl it around her finger shyly whenever he looked at her.

It took me a trip to the other mall and two more stores, but I finally found the ring he'd put on layaway three months ago and I paid the balance. It was modest, a small diamond, but it was pretty. I fingered my own wedding band with my thumb, twirled it around and around my finger while the saleslady boxed the ring up for me. I never had an engagement ring. Ray and I just decided to get married and we picked up a pair of plain gold wedding bands the same day we applied for a marriage license. I wanted it to be different for Lolly and Gabe.

I gave the ring to Gabe when he stopped by to pick up Kenny the next night. He protested at first. "No my love, I can't take that from you," he said shaking his head and raising a hand in objection.

"Please, Gabe," I pleaded with him. "I never get to do anything for her anymore."

A few days later, Lolly stopped by with Kenny in her arms and the same bag, laden with all of the baby gear he travelled with. She popped the bottles of milk into the fridge, giving them a gentle shake first.

"He just ate so I wouldn't feed him anything for a couple hours. If he gets fussy, I packed some Cheerios. They're in here somewhere." She rooted through the bag in a frenzy as if Kenny was crying for them instead of asleep in his little car seat with a blanket thrown over him. She produced the small container and handed it to me, the ring shining in the light of the kitchen. I reached for the container and held her hand in mine, staring at the ring.

"What's this?" It was a foolish thing to say since it was apparent what it was, but I asked the question playfully.

She pulled her hand out of my grasp and looked back into the diaper bag. "It's nothing. You remember to heat up the bottle for thirty seconds, right? You gotta give it a shake then so the heat gets evenly distributed. I don't want him to burn his mouth."

"You're engaged?"

"Yes," she said quietly. "He asked me last night. We were going to go out to dinner but I was too tired so he gave it to me before I went to bed. I wish I knew what he was planning. I would have got dressed maybe."

"Congratulations, Lolly." I wanted to hug her but she stood stiffly over the kitchen table like a piece of plywood.

"Thanks." She smiled, a fake smile that never reached her eyes. She was feeling guilty. I didn't know if it was because she'd ruined his plan to surprise her, or because her feelings were changing. She wouldn't tell me either way.

"I'll help you plan the wedding. I'll go dress shopping with you, look at some places to have a party. I promise I won't pretend to be sick for your wedding." It was meant to be lighthearted, an affectionate tease, but it made Lolly wilt. She hung her head low, exhaled deeply and then brought it back up straight. Her eyes were moist the way Ray's sometimes got when he was getting a cold.

"I'm sorry about that," she said. "I really am."

"I got over it," I assured her.

"I have a four o'clock appointment." She flung her purse over her shoulder and turned and left. I knew she'd either forgotten the kid who delivered the newspaper to us, or it was all she saw when she looked at Gabe.

floss

"How's your toilet?"

Leo is leaning against his white van with the cell-phone cradled against his shoulder and he's wearing a hint of a smile, his perfectly white teeth barely visible. I don't know any of this for a fact, but I hear the whir of traffic in the background so I know he's outside somewhere, and his tone is so light that it's impossible to picture him asking the question without smiling.

I grip the phone tightly, wish my mother and Lolly weren't sitting there watching me with puzzled expressions.

"It's great," I utter with more enthusiasm than is probably warranted by such a question but I can't stop myself from elaborating all the same. "It flushes perfectly every time. I think it might even be quieter too." I don't feel as foolish as I probably should for gushing about the performance of the same toilet we'd had for years now.

"Good, I'm glad there aren't any problems," Leo says, but he sounds almost disappointed. I have the sudden desire to fabricate a plumbing emergency—frozen pipes, a broken thermostat, a leaky faucet. I shouldn't have said that about how wonderful the toilet worked. I probably should have said you have to jiggle the handle after every flush and the hot water tap in the sink gets stuck, but I was so used to that now I didn't even think about it anymore.

I feel Lolly's and Mom's eyes on me, regarding me with a mixture of curiosity and amusement as I prattle on about the toilet. Lolly looks up from Kenny's colouring book and Mom irons a neat crease in Kenny's pajamas at the dining-room table, but I don't look at either of them. I stare straight out the front window and watch the lone tree in the front yard, its branches finally starting to bud. Ray planted it a few weeks after we'd moved in and promised me and Lolly both that it would be bigger than the house one day. He said it with an exaggerated confidence that required him to stand on tiptoes with his arms stretched up to the sky. He lifted Lolly up over his head and she screamed in mock fright, and all I could think was that I wouldn't scream if he were to hoist me so high in the air, but he didn't. He never did. He let Lolly down gently, so gingerly her feet didn't even make a sound when they touched the grass and he looked at me like he was waiting for me to ask him for my turn but I kept my arms by my sides, so stiff I was afraid the muscles were going to cramp.

Ray was right, though. After years of it looking exactly the same to me, I notice now that the braches extend slightly longer, reaching almost to the edge of the driveway. For some reason this makes me feel sad for Ray, who would have pointed out the tree's growth to all of us during a lull in the conversation, the kind of lull I was having right now with Leo. I hear the traffic in the background fill the space, the sounds of people headed somewhere, and it makes me feel like the tree— rooted, immovable.

"How is your hand?"

"Good as new," Leo replies quickly. "You fixed me up nicely."

"Did you go to the doctor or anything? I told you it might need a stitch or two. It was pretty deep."

"Nah, it's fine. Might leave a tiny scar but that's nothing. Sure, it's just my finger." He says it like he was reptilian, capable of growing another limb if need be.

"Just be careful you don't get it infected."

"Yeah, I'm sure it's fine. So um...I was wondering if we could have that supper next time."

"Okay."

"Okay then," he repeats. "I'll call you."

I hang up like an awkward teenager. I think he's asked me for a date but he didn't say when or where. I don't know what next time means. Next time my toilet breaks? Next time I get hungry?

Lolly, who is sprawled out on the living-room floor colouring a picture, leans on an elbow and regards me curiously. "Who was that?"

"Leo."

"Who's Leo?"

"He's our plumber."

"Since when do we have a plumber?"

Since your father died, I want to say but I'm afraid it would upset Mom more than Lolly. Ray could fix the drip in the kitchen sink and she'd look at him like he'd just bought her home a dozen long-stemmed roses. "Since the other day," I shrug.

"And what, he's calling to ask how our toilet is?" Lolly snickers in a way that makes me feel insulted on Leo's behalf.

"Yes." I answer her emphatically as if all good plumbers were in the habit of calling up their customers to inquire about such things.

"What did we need a plumber for anyway?" Lolly asks.

"Because your son flushed a toy down the toilet," I snap at her like it was all her fault even though it was probably my fault since I wasn't watching him properly.

"Which toy?" Lolly wears a pained expression. "Was it the new Batman toy he got? The one with the blue cape?" Her voice trails off like she'd just realized how foolish she must sound. She lays on her stomach with her legs folded in the air behind her and her chin propped up against the palm of her hand. She was colouring a picture with Kenny. He'd long given up to go off and play in his room but Lolly had kept on colouring alone. She was unable to give up anything she'd started, and even now she was colouring in the trunk of a tree a deep brown, using long even strokes.

I couldn't differentiate one action figure from the other. "It was a bad guy with a green shirt," I offer. Lolly's shoulder blades drop in relief but she keeps colouring in the tree as if she hadn't been holding her breath a moment earlier. I have no idea why she should be so concerned with what specific toy Kenny chose to flush, but I know she won't tell me either.

"Well I don't think he's really calling about the toilet." My mother makes the statement as she irons more of Kenny's little clothes. It's a statement that seems to require some sort of response on my part, a protestation or a girlish giggle, but my silence provokes her to egg me on further. "Looked like he was more interested in you."

Lolly looks up at me from her colouring, a look of amusement on her face. "You seduced the plumber," she teases me, laughing. "What did you tell him? Your pipes needed thawing?" It feels strange to have Lolly respond in this way. There were only a handful of times we shared in this type of banter and I find myself smiling foolishly at her teasing nature.

My mother is smiling too, nostalgic for the handful of times we carried on like this. It makes her feel like we're a proper family when we act this way, makes her feel like it's all worth it even though most of the time she's wondering otherwise.

"He owns the company you know," I add in an effort to impress them both with Leo's vast accomplishments but I forget for a moment that mom is not impressed with entrepreneurs. Too risky, no pension, maybe even a little shady. "He does more than unclog toilets. He fixes the heat too, replaces pipes and stuff. I mean it's very precise work. He's probably good at measuring things, and calculating things."

I don't know why I feel the need to point out such qualities as if they were of utmost importance in a mate but it seems to impress my mother somewhat because the look on her face softens and the lines around her eyes become less pronounced. Her approval is important to me, and I suddenly understand why she wanted me to love Ray so much.

She should be impressed by Leo's area of expertise since she was so taken with Ray's knowledge of electrical and mechanical things. She hovered around him when he worked on something, passing him bolts, wrenches, washers, whether he was under the kitchen sink or up on the ladder. It was like it was the only time they weren't dragged in different directions.

I watch Lolly colour a squirrel brown. It's holding a brown acorn in its grasp, surrounded by green trees with brown trunks and branches. Lolly always was a painful realist. Would never occur to her to make the squirrel purple or the trees blue. It was just the way it was. To Lolly, her father was just fixing a leaky pipe, but to Mom, Ray was fixing her life.

"He has a daughter," I add tentatively. "Her name is Faith and she's eight. She likes purple. She's going through a purple phase. She only drinks grape juice now." I stop talking because I've already said everything I know about her. I wish I could offer more details, but I don't have anything else. "I haven't met her or anything. I haven't even gone out with him yet. He's divorced."

I can tell without looking that I've upset my mother. The

sound of the water sloshing about inside the iron stops abruptly and then resumes with even more vigour. Lolly keeps colouring, afraid now to stop. She fills in a bird a dark shade of blue, colours the sun yellow, waits for the tension to pass.

"I don't think it's a good idea, Floss," Mom says. "Better set your sights on someone else. Surely God there must be a young doctor at that hospital you work at to sink your teeth into instead of the goddamn plumber."

"I don't see what the big deal is."

"He has a child," Mom whispers the same way she might if he was a convicted rapist, with a measure of disbelief mingled with self-righteous judgment. "What are you thinking getting involved with a man like that?"

Lolly's hand slips and she colors outside the line, a big blue streak down the centre of the page. "Shit," Lolly sighs sadly at having gone out the line. I stop myself from reminding her it's one page in a colouring book from the dollar store that has nothing but scribbles on every other page in the first place. I watched Kenny this morning put one mark on at least a dozen pages without colouring in a single item.

"A man like what?" I ask her. *Like Ray?*

"Do you have any idea what it's like to be with a man who has a child? It will tear the two of you apart. No matter how much you thinks you love one another, it's always going to come between you. You're setting yourself up for heartbreak, Floss." Mom places a hand on her heart in a dramatic gesture. Her face, pale a few moments ago, is red now, filled with a burgeoning anger that she'd suppressed for years. "You think love is just going to grow wild in your backyard but it doesn't grow. It just gets divided into smaller pieces and at the end of the day you got the smallest piece of it and you're supposed to be grateful you got any bit at all."

My mother covers her mouth with the palm of her hand as if to prevent herself from saying anything further and blinks away tears. I steal a glance at the top of Lolly's head, wondering if she will say anything in response but she still lays on the floor, absorbed in her colouring. A drop of moisture falls onto the paper, diluting the blue and leaving a streak of indigo that bleeds down into the earth. She tears out the page, crumples it up and throws it on the floor.

Mom resumes her ironing, smoothing out the wrinkles very methodically. It reminds me of the day she came back from the funeral home after finding out what Ray had done to her. She ironed the suit he was going to be buried in, put creases in his slacks and pressed his collars. He'd upset her so much that day she couldn't stop. She ended up taking all his clothes out of the drawer and smoothed out the wrinkles, wrinkles she hadn't even known were there.

marie

"Lolly says she doesn't feel well. I'm sorry, honey." Ray looked at me apologetically and at the same time, with a measure of pleading. It was a look I'd become accustomed to seeing from him. Poor Ray, always in the middle. He spent our first few months together apologizing for his daughter's reprehensible behaviour. *Sorry Lolly didn't put her clothes in the hamper like you asked. Sorry Lolly said your shepherd's pie smelled like shit. Sorry Lolly said the new sheets you bought her made her itch. Sorry, sorry, sorry.* It was practically the first thing out of his mouth in the morning and the last before bed. It didn't matter, it just went on and on. *Maybe she ought to say sorry instead of you,* I would snap at him and he would look sternly back at me like I should be ashamed of myself. I was, after all, the adult and I was acting like a child the way I was fighting over Ray's affections. "She's been through a lot," he'd say, and I'd have to bite my tongue from shouting, *What about me? I've been through a lot too.*

And then I would overhear him speaking to Lolly at night in the same apologetic tone. *Sorry you don't like living here. Sorry Marie doesn't make shepherd's pie the way your mother used to.*

Sorry Marie doesn't use the same detergent as we used to. Sorry, sorry, sorry.

"What's wrong with her?" I pulled a strand of hair out of my bun and curled it with the iron, giving it that wispy look.

"I dunno," he answered, his fingers buttoning up a new shirt that still held the creases from the cardboard.

"Do you want me to iron that for you?"

"No, it's new," he replied as if it were foolish to even consider ironing something right out of the package.

"I know it's new but you can see the lines in it from where it was folded up."

"Sure I'm wearing a jacket over it. You won't even be able to see."

There wasn't much of an argument I could give for that and went back to curling my hair in front of the bedroom mirror. I was nervous about getting married again. Everything felt so perfect when we lay together. I loved the feeling of being wrapped up in his arms, giggling about something foolish. I loved the rise and fall of his chest as he drifted off to sleep. In those moments there was no doubt that marriage was the natural progression. But we had more things to consider than just ourselves.

"What did you say was wrong with Lolly?"

"I dunno. She just doesn't feel well."

"Does she have a fever? Is she throwing up? Did you give her anything for it?"

"No," he said shaking his head.

"Well you should give her something, Ray. You don't want her to be sick at the ceremony and we're going out to eat right after."

Ray concentrated on buttoning up the cuffs of his shirt. "I don't know. She says she doesn't want to come." He spoke in a whisper and I had to strain my ears to hear him.

"She's not coming? She has to come. You're not going to

let her ruin our wedding day."

Ray swallowed uncomfortably. "Come on now, Marie, it's not that big a deal if she don't come now, is it? We're getting married either way."

I walked past him without a word, the breeze from my robe lifted the bottom of his tie just the slightest, and walked into the room Floss and Lolly shared. There was Floss trying to zip the back of her dress, a beautiful blue sundress that made her eyes look more blue than the green I was used to seeing on her. I should have complimented her in some fashion but I was too angry with Lolly at that moment the way she laid under the covers of her bed eating a bag of potato chips and flipping through a magazine. At the very least she could have feigned an illness, pretended to be asleep or patted her stomach, perhaps even let out a cough of sorts but she wasn't even pretending.

"Get dressed," I said to her abruptly.

"I don't feel good." She looked defiantly at me and then licked the salt from her fingers like she was kissing each one goodnight. "I feel like I might throw up if I got to look at the two of you get married," she added, and I would have grabbed her by the hair and hauled her out of the bed except I didn't want to mess up my nails.

"This is my wedding day," I reminded her through gritted teeth, but Lolly stared at her magazine, ignored my warning tone and hoped I would go away. I hated Ray right then, who was at that very moment hiding in the bedroom like a goddamned coward. It should have been him in here having this fight with Lolly, not me. He didn't think it was a big deal at all, a formality, a piece of paper. He didn't even want to go out to eat afterwards to celebrate. *We still got that chicken in the fridge from Friday. I'll just have that this evening so you won't have to cook.*

What did I expect from a man who asked me to marry him after he spent twenty minutes in the bathroom? The whole idea had come to him while he was taking a shit. *We should probably get married I s'pose. I got a good pension.* I could barely hear him over the bathroom fan.

I wanted to go to the Hotel Newfoundland to eat because I'd never been, and they were always writing them up in the paper. I wanted to go somewhere where they had a real chef and not someone who'd been promoted from busboy or dishwasher. I wanted to eat somewhere where they put sprigs of parsley on top of the meat or the potatoes, where they had chives sticking out of the food like stalks of plants on the edges of rivers. I didn't want to come home and eat leftover chicken and I didn't want to get married unless we were all going.

"You're a spoiled little brat," I spat at her. "Always thinking about yourself." I breathed deeply then, filled my lungs up with air because I was about to start crying and I didn't want to mess up my makeup, nor did I want to give Lolly the satisfaction that her behaviour could reduce me to tears.

"Do you want to borrow my yellow skirt?" Floss offered tentatively. "It'll fit you."

Floss, my peacemaker, always eager to please. I felt the tears prick the corners of my eyes and I dabbed at them with a knuckle.

"I don't like yellow," Lolly sighed and tossed the magazine onto the floor. Even she couldn't deny Floss. "I'll go but if I pukes up just as you're saying your vows, don't say I didn't warn you."

Lolly donned the same outfit she wore to her mother's funeral. It was a different season though and the fabric was heavy and dark in contrast to my own lavender sundress and Floss' blue one. Lolly had outgrown the outfit and the sleeves hit above her wrist and the hem hit too high on her thighs. She kept yanking the fabric, pulling and straining to get it to reach her knees. I thought surely Lolly selected the outfit to purposefully annoy me and to signal this was a day of mourning for her.

Ray grinned stupidly at her when she announced she was ready and told her she looked beautiful. He didn't think anything of the fact that she was wearing her funeral clothes; he probably didn't even notice. If I dared say anything, he'd say I was making a fuss over nothing. We were on the Crosstown Arterial on the way downtown to meet with the judge before I realized he hadn't told me I looked beautiful.

Ray drove up and down Water Street and Duckworth Street and Harbour Drive so many times I was worried we wouldn't make it. He was looking for a meter that still had money on it but after driving around for fifteen minutes he would have settled for any spot. He cursed under his breath every time we passed the courthouse without finding a place to park.

"I can't stand coming downtown," he griped. "No fucking parking and they're always tearing up the goddamn streets." Ray started to sweat in his frustration. I could see his face getting red and beads of perspiration dripped down his forehead. I fished a napkin out of the glove box and blotted his temples and he grabbed my hand and held it so tightly the tips of my fingers went white. "I'm petrified," he said.

"Me too," I smiled encouragingly. "But we're going to make this work. I promise."

The service was quick, quiet, and understated. "I do. I do." Rings, kiss, signatures, done. The judge offered to take a picture but no one brought the camera. It was still on the coffee table, forgotten in all the rush and drama of the morning. Ray offered to go to one of the gift shops on Water Street to pick up a disposable camera but I shook my head like it was too much of a bother.

We ended up at the Swiss Chalet after the wedding because Lolly wanted to go there. I refrained from pointing out that she was allegedly not feeling well and probably shouldn't eat at all. Floss said she'd go wherever everyone else wanted to go and Ray sent me a pleading look and placed a reassuring hand on my lap. "We can go someplace fancy some other time, just you and me," he said. "Besides the Swiss Chalet has plenty of parking," he added as if that alone was going to win me over.

I felt resentment building inside me like blocks stacking higher and higher until the tower wavered precariously just before it all came crashing down. There was so much I wanted to say. *It's my wedding day so why can't I decide where to eat? Why does Lolly always get her own way? We're never going to go someplace fancy to eat some other time.* I'd only been married fifteen minutes and this was what I wanted to say to my new husband. I felt ashamed for myself and just as ashamed for Ray.

As my quarter chicken dinner was placed in front of me, I wondered if I'd made a terrible mistake. I thought we could be together forever because of the way he held me at night, squeezing me so tightly it was like I was the only thing stopping him from falling off the edge of a cliff. He made love to me with a fierceness borne of being denied the affection of a wife too fragile for too long. He told me I saved him in a way that evoked a religious connotation and in those moments I felt like I was the centre of his world.

But he was just a man with barbecue sauce on his chin; a man who forgot the camera on our wedding day, a man who circled around for twenty minutes because he couldn't find a parking spot he didn't have to pay for. He came part and parcel with a girl who cursed at me from the very time she laid eyes on me and hadn't warmed up to me yet. I hated to admit it but not only did I not love her, I didn't even like her. We had the same last name now. We were Sullivans, a sad ruse. My own daughter, who I loved with all my heart, had a different last name than me now. It separated her, made her different than the rest of us. She had the name of a stranger, a man who wouldn't even recognize her if she sat down in front of him. It didn't seem right. Nothing seemed right. I stared at the plate of chicken, fries, dipping sauce. There was no garnish, not a sprig of parsley to be found.

That night, in our bedroom with the door closed, Ray presented me with a small box with a ribbon tied in an awkward bow. Inside was a sprig of fresh parsley, the curly kind and only slightly wilted. He tucked it behind my ear and then retrieved the camera from the dresser, snapped a picture.

"You take the breath right out of me," he whispered. He unzipped my dress, peeled off the rest of my clothes, everything except the parsley and made love to me with the intensity I'd become accustomed to from him. He tasted the parsley afterwards, making a face. "Make no wonder it's a garnish," he grumbled, and we both laughed quietly under the covers. Then I knew that our life together was going to be hard, but it wasn't a mistake.

lolly

"What would you get him this year? Dad I mean," I clarify since I could be talking about anyone but I know it's unnecessary. Marie knows without any reminders that today is Dad's birthday. She tries to pretend it's any other day the way she stands over the sink soaping up the coffee pot but she moves slowly, like she has weights strapped around her ankles like the women on television leading the exercise programs. She shrugs her shoulders like it isn't worth the effort to think about, and it probably wasn't. Marie would have made him a cake, chocolate with vanilla frosting, predictable just like she was. Maybe she would have gotten him one of those foolish greeting cards with a husband and wife represented by cartoonish squirrels or raccoons with hearts swirling around the tops of their heads. Maybe Dad would have even laughed at it.

"I don't know, Lolly. He didn't need anything. He never wanted anything either. Hated for anyone to spend a cent on him. All he ever wanted was a bit of peace and quiet, I suppose, and that was the one thing we never gave him." I expect her to sound somewhat mournful at this revelation but instead she starts giggling, a surprisingly youthful sound to come from her chest.

"He was good at tuning it all out. How many times did you have to bawl out to him before he'd answer you? He pretended he didn't hear you, but he did."

I smile softly, knowingly, and she smiles back.

"Are you going to the cemetery?" I already know her answer.

The smile leaves her face instantly and I feel the blush of shame in my cheeks. I knew it would evoke such a reaction, but I couldn't bear the sweetness of the moment we were having. I could feel the tag of my shirt itch the back of my neck and the seams from my socks felt tighter around my calves. Marie only goes to the cemetery once a year, for the flower service, and even that is an ordeal for her. She's on edge the entire day, snipping at me like it's all my fault what Dad did to her even though I didn't have anything to do with it.

"No," she sighs, shaking her head. "I'll watch Kenny for you if you want to go by yourself though. Lord knows it's hard to take a child to a place like that. They wants to run around the stones and jump over everyone's grave like it was the playground." She licks her lips, then bites the bottom one. "I s'pose it's better than all the questions that's gonna come when he gets older and starts asking you who everyone is in the ground, and if they're all up there in heaven together."

It sounds more like her questions than Kenny's but I don't say so. Kenny doesn't have questions about anything of that nature. He asks me if worms sleep, and how water gets in the tap, but he never asks me why Marie isn't my mother even though he calls her Nanny. He doesn't ask about Poppy in heaven, maybe because he thinks that's the name of the cemetery. I know because he asks me to take him to the Dairy Queen by heaven like it was a building, no different than the

Village Mall or the supermarket. He never questions why he lives in two different houses, with two different beds and two different sets of toys, or why his mom and dad keep carting him back and forth.

I wonder if it would have been better if I was Kenny's age when my father met Marie. The same questions might not have plagued me. I wouldn't have to worry about betraying my mother's memory because I wouldn't have any memories, or at least nothing too overt. I might remember a tone or a scent, but that would fade over time, replaced by Marie's tone and all her smells.

It's different for Kenny. I think about the way he crawls into Marie's lap, not the least bit phased that her hands smell like onions or that she just spritzed herself with musk. Kenny can wrap his arms around her bony neck and lay his head on her shoulder while she plays with his hair. The combination of all her odours—the onions, the musk, the lemon Pledge— might even bring him comfort. One day he'll be standing behind someone at Tim Horton's and he'll breathe in a whiff of the musk and it will remind him of Nanny Sullivan in a nostalgic rush of thoughts and memories that I was glad he would have.

"I was going to go this afternoon and lay a few flowers there," I say quietly. "Gabe is taking Kenny to a movie so you don't need to watch him."

"That's nice," Marie replies absently, but I'm not sure if she's referring to the movie or my planned outing to the grave.

"It seems like a foolish thing to get him, don't you think? Flowers. I'd just as soon go and lay a screwdriver or a pair of pliers, even a bottle of cologne on his grave. I'd never get him flowers if he was alive. He doesn't even like flowers," I say quietly, aware that I've spoken of him in the present tense. It's a slip we both make from time to time.

The cloth in Marie's hand drips dirty water on the floor,

puddles of brown soapy liquid pool near her slippered feet. "That's not true."

"Sure it is," I argue. "The only time he ever bought flowers was to lay on my mother's grave." I wonder why it is we always seem to get to this place, how we could start the day out with good intentions and end up throwing hurtful comments around. I expect Marie to protest in some fashion but she looks distant with a smile plastered across her face.

"He brought me fresh parsley once." Marie is remembering something sweet. The corners of her lips stay lifted for too long and her gaze rests on a coffee cup left out on the kitchen counter.

"Parsley?"

"Yes. On our wedding day. You remember?"

I don't know if she's referring to the wedding day, which I recall in vivid detail right up to the sharp pain in my chest when they sealed their vows with a kiss, or to my father giving her parsley, which I don't remember at all. Dad didn't even like parsley. He liked salt. He liked pepper, and sometimes he liked a bit of ketchup, but I was certain he never liked parsley. He didn't like things that were green. He barely even ate cabbage in his jigg's dinner, although it was boiled for so long it looked more yellow by the time it came out of the pot.

"I want you to bring him some for me," Marie says like she's just had an epiphany, the perfect birthday gift for her deceased husband.

"Some what?"

"Parsley. To lay on his grave."

"Why?"

"I just told you why." She's impatient with me once again.

"Okay," I nod wondering how it is that my father and Marie's husband were ever the same man.

I can't find the parsley anywhere in the supermarket. I'm at the one by the lake, and I'm not familiar with the layout. It's too big, too crowded, and I wander aimlessly around the produce section wondering if I should just lay turnip greens on Dad's grave. At least I know he ate them and Marie would never know the difference. Whatever I leave there will be long dead by the time she's anywhere near the cemetery, but I keep looking anyway. Eventually I give up and grab a jar of parsley flakes from the spice aisle. I can't imagine sprinkling them on top of the grave but I promised Marie I would. I head back downstairs to the floral shop to get Dad the flowers, debate whether he'd like tulips or gerberas.

"What's the occasion?"

I turn suddenly at the sound of Carson's voice. He's wearing shorts and a T-shirt soaked with sweat. His face is red and beads of sweat drip along the side of his forehead. He looks almost like he did the day of the accident, when the snow melted on the warmth of his skin. He holds a bottle of water in his hand, although nothing else, no shopping cart, not even a basket for those who are only picking up one or two things. He's slightly out of breath.

"It's my father's birthday."

"Nice of you to bring him flowers," he smiles, and glances at my jar of parsley. "Are you cooking dinner for him too?"

"He's dead," I say flatly, cradling the bouquet in the crook of my arm like an infant. The cellophane crinkles loudly and a stem pokes my ribs. "I'm just going to lay these on his grave." I refrain from saying the parsley awaits the same fate.

"I'm sorry," he says taking a step back. "I didn't know."

For some reason I thought he would know this about me. I assumed everyone knew this about me, as if it were written in a black marker across my forehead. "That's okay. You were running?"

"Yeah, letting off some steam. I forgot to pack my water

so…thankfully this place is here or else I'd be drinking out of Quidi Vidi Lake. You should come with me sometime."

"I don't like to run."

"Why not?"

"It makes me tired." It feels like I'm running around all the time as it is with Kenny and work and dropping off and picking up.

He laughs at this revelation. "I find it just the opposite. Well maybe you could walk with me instead. Do you have time?"

I want to. I want him to take my hand again and have him lead me down the trail all around the lake, sit on one of the quiet park benches and rest my head on his shoulder.

"I have to pick up my sister."

"You used that excuse once already." He takes another long swig from his water bottle, smiles playfully back at me.

"From work," I smile. "She's covering a shift at the Miller Centre today."

"Did she just break up with another boyfriend?"

"No, but I think she has a crush on our plumber now."

"I confess I'm a little bit in love with my plumber too." His expression turns more serious. "Everything quiet now? At your house," he clarifies although he didn't need to.

"Yeah. I told you he was just looking for someone else. Haven't seen a sign of him since."

"You should still be careful." He takes another gulp of water, looks around me. "Where's your little boy?"

"Kenny?" I sound silly with the questioning tone, like I had more than one little boy. "He's with his father." *His father*, I repeat silently. When had Gabe been reduced to such a title? At what point had I stopped using his name, and had he done the same to me? I picture the words coming out of his mouth like he'd tasted something that was after going bad, *Kenny's with his mother.* "They went to see a movie."

The easiness between us seems forced now that I've mentioned Kenny and Gabe. I'm aware of the glare from the bright overhead lights, the hum of the escalator and the constant beep from the registers scanning products. It's so different from the roar of the ocean, the whip of the wind and the feel of the mist that it's almost as if we'd travelled through time. Carson is thinking about that day right now. He looks longingly at me, knowing he can't possibly hold me the way he'd held me on the coast, shrouded in fog. Not here in the lobby of the Dominion.

"I really want to see you again," he says but he doesn't elaborate or make any firm plans. It's almost as if he were making an appeal to the fates.

floss

Leo eats like Ray. There's nothing left in the brown and orange cardboard box bearing the Mary Brown's logo save for bones. They're picked clean—no skin, no fat, no cartilage, no blue veins—just bones. If you emptied out the box in the woods you'd think a wild animal had done with its prey, then scavengers had taken what they could get and insects had finished it off. It looks like you could send these bones off to a lab to be carbon dated. I stare in fascination at them, and then at the contents of my own cardboard box. I delicately peel the skin back from my chicken thigh like I see the doctors do when they're removing something from inside someone, remove strings of meat with my plastic fork, the tines bending and buckling under the pressure. I thought Ray was bad the way he sucked on the bone of a pork chop like he was trying to find the marrow, but Leo's bones are picked clean.

"Sorry I couldn't take you out someplace nicer," Leo apologizes again. He wipes a waxy sheen of grease from the top of his lip with a paper napkin, which he balls up, passing it back and forth from one hand to the other. I should eat faster

I think, feeling bad that he's nothing left to do except fidget with his garbage, the dirty napkin, an empty salt packet. "It's just I'm supposed to pick up Faith from her friend's house at seven and I wanted to see you."

"It's fine," I say reassuringly. "I don't get Mary Brown's that often and I wanted to see you too."

"So how did all your tests come back? Clean bill of health?"

"Oh yes," I answer. "Everything is good."

"And how is your dad?" A flicker of concern crosses Leo's face, probably more than I'd shown the last time I saw him, which was nearly a week ago now. My father had walked up to me in front of the house in plain sight, not that I could blame him since there weren't many places to hide in Mount Pearl, save for the tree Ray planted in the front yard. My only feeling at the time was relief that Mom wasn't home. He'd unnerved her enough already for her to call the police. If she'd have known it was him, I don't know what she would have done. He took a step toward me and I shrank back.

"Florence!" he shouted at me. "Is that you?"

"Go away," I bawled at him. "You're upsetting my mother." I glanced out across the street and hoped Mrs. Lush wasn't watching. She sat out on her step sometimes and watched us like we were a soap opera, there for her entertainment.

"I'm sorry," he said, coughing into the air between us. "I just want to talk to you. You took off flying last time. Do you know how long it took me to track you down here?"

I wanted to laugh right in his face at such a ridiculous claim, as if I was the one who walked out on him. "I don't want to talk to you. I don't want nothing to do with you. Fuck off." I'd never told anyone to fuck off in my whole life and I felt immediately guilty for it. I couldn't understand how people could say it so casually, even affectionately. It was almost like a term of endearment for some people but it felt wicked to me, like my soul was shriveling up inside, but he didn't seem to flinch. He was probably the sort who was told to fuck off all the time.

I followed his gaze over to the tree and it felt like Ray was there watching us, with his feet planted firmly on the grass and his hands on his hips. Ray would have told him to fuck off in a heartbeat. He told lots of people to fuck off—telemarketers, meter maids, people who honked the horn at him if he wasn't fast enough at a light. It was like Ray was there, standing next to me, proud of me that I'd said what I did.

"But you told me who you were," my father adds with a look of confusion. "You're the one who came to see me."

"So?"

He shrugged his shoulders. "So, I thought you wanted…." His voice trailed off. He was feeling foolish now. "I'm trying to tie up some loose ends, I guess. I just want to look at you."

I was nothing but a loose end to him. Something he wanted to take care of before he died. He was only here for himself and it made me feel even sorrier for him. "You saw me. Now go. Go on." I made a shooing motion with my hand like I was trying to get away from a dog that followed me home. "I don't want my Mom to find out you were here."

He coughed, almost for effect, it seemed to me, and I felt a little bit like a bully.

I sighed. "You can't come around here. If you want to talk to me again meet me after work or something. I'm at The Health Sciences now."

I haven't seen him since and I can't help but feel duped in some fashion.

"Floss?" Leo's voice sounds far away until I realize it was me who'd drifted, not him.

"What?"

"I was just asking how your father was."

"He's the same." My tone is measured, conveys the fact I don't want to discuss him any further.

Leo looks like he's about to say something else but his

phone vibrates, a soft hum coming from his pants pocket. It's a text and he holds the phone at arm's length, squints to read the message. I stare out the window to the parking lot while he texts back. It's nearly dark out now and his white van glows fluorescent under the street lamp. The smell of industrial strength sealant inside was so overpowering, I felt the beginnings of a dull ache behind my ears that lifted as soon as I stepped out of the van. I wonder if that's something you get used to the same way I couldn't smell shit or vomit anymore after working in the hospital and being around it all day. He lays the phone down next to his tray and it buzzes again almost immediately. This time he sighs with annoyance, his patience clearly gone.

"Work?" I shoot him a sympathetic look. "Some other kid flush a toy down the toilet?" I smile at him but his good humour is gone.

"No, my ex. She thinks I'm a fuckin' moron who doesn't know what time it is or where Cowan Avenue is. Amazing I can make it out of bed in the morning."

"You're texting your wife? While you're on a date with me?" My voice is shaky and carries further than I want it to. I'm vaguely aware of another customer's eyes on me. I'm the type of person who thinks a snackaroo on twenty minutes notice is a date, the type whose heart is paralyzed with jealousy by a text message reminding Leo to make a left onto Cowan Avenue.

"I'm sorry, that was rude." Leo places a hand over mine, squeezes it gently. His palm is damp and I pull my hand away and wipe the moisture off on my jeans underneath the table. Everything had been so easy up to this point. There was a comfort between us that took both of us by surprise. There were no awkward silences. In fact the only time Leo didn't talk was when he was eating and that was only all of five minutes. I thought we'd never run out of things to talk about. We wouldn't be like the old married couples I watched at the food court in the mall or in the hospital cafeteria. They sit and chew and stare off into space and the only time they talk to each other is to ask about how the food is. *How's your sandwich? My soup is not hot enough.*

But we sit cloaked in silence now, each of us staring at our own individual brown and orange boxes. I look at my watch. It's only taken us a little over an hour to run out of things to say. All it took for things to fall apart was a simple text message.

He has a whole other family, an ex-wife he loved at some point in the past, and a daughter who is a product of their love. I picture the three of them walking together, the little girl in the middle tugging on her parents' hands and asking them to swing her. And I don't picture his ex-wife with a round waist and big hips and a stern demeanour anymore—now I picture someone much slighter, with smiling lips and neatly plucked eyebrows. She wears clear nail polish that make the half-moons of her fingernails shiny and her hands elegant, befitting the ring Leo slipped on her finger at some point in the past. I can feel her presence so acutely she may as well be sitting at the table next to us.

"Floss," Leo says, and I look up from my lap. "Are you okay?"

"I'm fine." I say it casually, like it would be completely absurd to think otherwise. "Why?"

"You seem upset."

"Well I'm not." I sound abrupt. "I like the taters," I say more softly, picking one up with my fingers and taking a bite. "I like the thinner ones. More crispy," I elaborate.

"Yeah," he nods. "The coleslaw is good too. I don't usually like coleslaw, but I like it here."

I try to think of something else to say.

"They have a Mary Brown's in Calgary but it's not the same."

"Really?" He sounds far too interested in what I've just told him.

"Yeah, I was there for the past three years."

"What were you doing out in Calgary?"

"Screwing up my life."

"You didn't have to go to Calgary to do that. I screwed up mine just fine right here in St. John's." The tension between us eases. "Come on, let's get out of here."

We're stopped at a red light on Topsail Road the next time he speaks. "Do you want to do this again sometime? I mean like a proper date." He drums the steering wheel with the tips of his fingers while he waits for my response. The same tight knot that I felt in the restaurant still sits in the pit of my belly and the dull ache behind my ears is coming back. I tell myself it's the sealant.

"Yes."

"Why?"

"Why," I repeat dumbly. "What kind of a question is that?" If I didn't know better I'd say he was fishing for compliments the way Mom used to do with Ray. *My hair is a mess today. This colour is awful on me.* Leo reminds me of Ray, the way he seems slightly lost, a man with half a family who just wants to feel whole again. I see Ray in everything he does and for some reason it doesn't scare me at all.

"My life is complicated right now."

I give him a warm smile, then lean my head against the window and watch all the lights speed by. He thinks his life is complicated. "My life has always been complicated." It's almost patronizing the way I say it, as if no one could be more fucked up than I was.

When we are parked outside my house under a pink sky slowly turning dark, Leo kisses me. It's not a long, lingering kiss brimming with unbridled passion, although I am definitely aware of my racing heart. It's more the feeling of being wanted and needed. It's the same feeling I'm certain my mother had when she fell into Ray's arms, heady that she had the power to fix someone, even at the risk of becoming broken herself.

marie

"Why do we have to go to Doris' for supper anyway?" Lolly asked the question from the back seat of the car just to annoy me, I think. We'd already had the conversation that morning, and again as we were getting ready to go.

"Because she's family," I said.

"She's not my family."

"You're lucky she isn't," Floss quipped, causing Ray to chuckle a little too loudly. I shot him a stern look but then smiled at him all the same. I rested the brownies the girls made on my lap. The pan was still warm and even though it was wrapped tightly in foil, the fragrant smell of cocoa and chocolate filled the inside of the car.

I couldn't blame Lolly for not wanting to go. It had always been uncomfortable after the first time, which was Boxing Day the first Christmas I spent with Ray. It felt like ages ago. I blamed Doris at the time but it was probably my fault for not explaining better. Doris presented Floss with a big box all wrapped up in reindeer paper and then looked guiltily at Lolly while she dug in her purse until she found a twenty dollar bill.

"I keeps forgetting," Doris apologized. "I'm not used to Marie bringing company around." It was an uncomfortable choice of words, made it seem like Ray and Lolly were just visiting me. She folded the money and held it at arm's length toward Lolly who was looking at her in confusion. She wasn't sure what to do. "Go on take it," Doris urged her. "Go and get yourself something for Christmas. They'll have good Boxing Day sales now."

Ray gripped the glass of rye he was holding so tightly that the ice cubes started to rattle against the glass, and the other hand he balled into a fist and rested in his lap. Doris bit her bottom lip and glanced desperately around the room as if she were trying to find something she could take in the back bedroom and wrap up.

I knew Lolly had a mouth on her and I was petrified she was going to make a scene and tell Doris to shove her money up her ass, but she shook her head and politely refused the cash. Floss sat cross-legged in front of the box tracing the reindeers on the paper.

"You can open it," Lolly told Floss.

"I don't feel like it," Floss whispered.

Doris was red in the face, angry with me. "You could have told me they were coming." I had just assumed she knew.

That was ages ago. They were teenagers now and neither one of them wanted to be at Doris' for supper. I was surprised when Lolly suggested they bake brownies to bring over for dessert and I listened to the two of them in the kitchen from my living-room chair. They were cooking up more than brownies from the sound of it. I pretended to be reading the paper but I focused on the sounds coming from the kitchen, imagining the two of them stirring and mixing and licking the bowl, their faces covered in chocolate. It filled me with such euphoria to hear them cracking eggs and whispering like real sisters that it took every ounce of concentration to sit still.

"I don't know why I have to go," Lolly whined. "I mean it's not like your aunt wants to see me, or my dad for that matter. I don't think she likes either one of us."

"Yes she does. Doris is just protective of my mom," I heard Floss say in response. "She used to think your dad was using her, at least at first. I used to overhear Mom on the phone talking to Aunt Doris about Ray."

"You mean for sex," Lolly said casually.

"Eww, no," Floss responded emphatically. "I mean Doris thought he was using her so that she'd look after you."

"She doesn't look after me," Lolly protested.

Yes she does. I knew Floss, and I knew that was exactly what she said in her head.

"That's the same as saying she married my dad so you could have a father."

"That's stupid," Floss retorted. "I didn't have a father for years. What would I need one for all of a sudden? Maybe they just fell in love."

Lolly was uncomfortable with the notion that Ray could actually be in love with me. I think she'd have rathered Ray married me to give her a mother. At least she could make sense out of that.

"Don't take any offence. Doris didn't like my real father either," Floss added. "She didn't care too much for her own husband, for that matter. They got divorced when Ted was just a little baby. I don't think she likes men, period. Except for her precious boy, Ted."

Lolly giggled, a genuinely happy sound that spilled out from the kitchen into the living room and tickled my own lips. I wished I could talk to her the way Floss was, wished I could make her laugh like that.

"What do you think she's going to bring up first?" Lolly's voice was filled with mirth and mischief. "Ted or her collection of spoons?"

"Definitely Ted," Floss replied. "I already heard her talking to mom on the phone about his marks in university, how he's tutoring high school kids because he's so smart."

"I bet she talks about her spoons. It's right after Christmas and I bet she got a new one. If she brings up spoons first then you have to shout out the name of the boy you likes in front of everyone."

"And if she brings up Ted first?"

"I'll shout out the name of the boy I like."

"But everyone knows it's Gabe," Floss said dismissively. "What's the fun in that? If she brings up Ted first you have to curse—the F word."

Doris took the pan of brownies from me as soon as we arrived. She peeked inside the foil, sniffed in the chocolate smell. "This looks some delicious," she said. "Did you make it?"

"The girls made it," I responded proudly. "They've been cooking up quite a bit today."

"Well come on in. Let me get you a drink. A rye and seven for you, Ray?" She went off into the kitchen, clinking glasses and mixing drinks. The girls sat together looking nervous, kept whispering to one another and giggling. I didn't think either one of them would actually do it, no matter what Doris said. She handed them both envelopes stuffed with equal denominations of twenty dollar bills and told them to buy something for themselves at the mall. Even when she handed over the envelopes, I could tell she was still thinking about the year she forgot, still feeling just as bad about it as she did right in the moment. Lolly had a way of doing that to you, and she wasn't even aware of it.

If I didn't know better, I'd say Doris was onto them. She talked about the neighbour's cat having a litter of kittens. She was thinking about taking one. She talked about the rain and how much we were after having already this year. She was sad we were having a green Christmas but grateful at the same time, since it was hard to get around in the snow. She asked Ray about work. It was a long wait before the brownie pan was placed on the table and she went to get a knife to cut the brownies, only to come back with a new spoon.

"Look at what Ted got me for Christmas." She held it up in her hand for all of us to see. Lolly and Floss were gaping at one another. There was no clear winner or loser. "He bought it for me into the university to add to my collection. He's doing some good in there. Got high marks in everything, even in the math."

Floss' eyes darted back and forth and she smiled nervously, clasped her hands out in front of her. "Andrew Wheeler!" Floss shouted it at the top of her lungs and stared down at Lolly. Before anyone could ask what she was talking about, Lolly shouted, "Fuck!" just as loudly.

Doris' mouth dropped to the table. She looked at me, expecting me to yell at the two of them. Ray looked at me too. He was waiting for me to shoot him a look, a look that meant he should have a talk with Lolly about her foul mouth. I laughed instead. Then Floss started and then Lolly too. There were peals of laughter, so much we couldn't stop, couldn't even catch our breath. I had a pain in my back and another one in my side from laughing so much. Doris looked quizzically at the three of us laughing so hard there were tears. Tears that didn't even taste the least bit salty. It was like the sweetness from the brownies had glazed them in sugar. Poor Ray looked on at us in confusion. He didn't know what had just happened but he got caught up in the moment enough to laugh too.

"I love you, Doris," I said, gasping for air between fits of laughter. She was my sister and this was the kind of thing sisters did. I couldn't stop laughing. The same way I couldn't stop crying some nights. *I love you, Ray. I love you, Floss. And I love you too, Lolly.*

lolly

arie approaches Kenny's birthday with much more fanfare than she does my father's. She has chips and cheezies and pretzels all laid out in bowls on the dining-room table. The pizza is ordered and the ice cream cake is on the bottom shelf of the refrigerator, defrosting just enough that she can slide a knife through it when it's time for dessert. She has Floss blow up balloons that sink to the floor as soon as she ties them up, like they were mocking her celebratory mood. She places a pile of paper plates and napkins emblazoned with Batman's masked face on the dining-room table.

It seems a bit overboard for the four of us, who are together most days. Marie's effort seems sad to me, a feeble effort to create the kind of family she dreams of having rather than the one she ended up with. I start to say something to that effect but it comes out as an assault on what's on the table instead.

"Kenny is going to get sick as a dog this evening," I state flatly, noticing that he is already on his third plate of cheezies. His fingers are orange and his jeans are streaked with orange crumbs. He hasn't even eaten the pizza or ice cream yet. "You bought too much junk food. He's going to be complaining his stomach hurts when it's time for bed. And I don't know why you had to go out and buy Batman napkins and plates. The plain ones are just as good considering they're all just going to end up in the garbage."

"You are your father's daughter," Marie says this like she was paying me a compliment. She's right of course. This was exactly the type of thing my father would say and I feel a prickle of annoyance with her that she tolerates the comment with such good nature. If my father were here she would tell him not to be such a crooked old sonofabitch, but she has a nostalgic smile plastered on her face. She roots around in the junk drawer of the kitchen, moving around batteries and receipts and a warranty for the toaster. Marie gives up her search and closes the drawer with her hip. "Can you call Gabe and ask him to pick up some matches when he goes to pick up the pizza? I thought I had some," she says, opening the drawer again and looking deflated when they haven't made a sudden appearance.

"Why is Gabe coming here?" It sounds like an accusation. "Me and Floss can pick up the pizza. For that matter, they deliver. Why is Gabe bringing it? Why didn't you tell me? Why can't you ever just mind your own business?" Marie is still bent over the drawer. She shuffles around spools of thread and an expired coupon.

"Because he's Kenny's father, and Kenny would like to spend his birthday with his family," Marie says, standing up slowly and turning to face me. I hear her knees crack although she doesn't seem to be bothered. "I didn't tell you because I didn't want to argue with you about it. But today isn't about you, Lolly. It's about Kenny."

"What's that supposed to mean?"

"Every day since I met you, it's always been about you. Your father was always worried about how everything was going to affect you, no one else but you. Even from the grave he made it about you. Now stop complaining and put on your Batman mask."

Marie hasn't spoken to me like this in years, not since before Dad died and it takes a minute to gather my composure. To me, it was always the other way around. I could argue the point but it didn't matter anymore. Dad was gone and sometimes it felt like we were still vying for his affections. Fighting for my share of love was the only way I knew how.

It's the same with Kenny. I don't want Gabe here because somewhere in the back of my mind I think Kenny loves Gabe better than me. I see the way Kenny laughs when Gabe dangles him by his ankles, and the squeals of delight when Gabe wrestles with him on the floor make me feel like I'm stepping on a rusty nail. It's the same way I felt when I heard my dad crack up laughing at something Marie said. I put the Batman mask on, a cheap cardboard cutout with elastic along the back of my head. At least it affords me some security from Marie's knowing gaze.

Gabe gives me a slow perusal when I open the door for him in my Batman mask. "Is it my birthday, or Kenny's? Because I had a fantasy just like this once."

I slide the mask on the top of my head, shoot him a look. "Did you bring the matches?" I know immediately he's forgotten them by the way he looks at me, like he's trying to discern my reaction.

"Jaysus, I knew I was after forgetin' something," Gabe replies. He hands me the pizza box, warm and fragrant with cheese and spices and relieves his other hand of a box wrapped neatly in paper printed with colourful balloons. His mother wrapped it for him. I can tell by the neat folds in the paper, the Scotch tape perfectly centred.

"I figured you'd forget."

"What's that supposed to mean? I got the pizza didn't I?"

"Lord knows, Gabe, you never could remember two things at the same time."

"You don't even need matches anyway."

"Then how am I supposed to light the candles?"

"Kenny don't even know how to blow his nose. You think he's going to be able to blow out candles?"

"You can't have a birthday cake without candles," I protest.

"Okay, don't go getting worked up over a pack of goddamn matches. I'll run back out and get them. You want to tell me what this is all about?"

It's about you being here, I want to say but I hear it in my head first and stop it from coming out. I anticipate Gabe's response too. *I'm not allowed to visit my son on his birthday?* I can't win the argument. Maybe I'm not supposed to. Maybe Marie is right, although I hate to admit it. "Nothing."

"Daddy!" Kenny screams at Gabe and the two of them wrestle on the living-room floor. I slide the Batman mask back over my eyes but it isn't necessary. I already feel invisible.

"Get up now, let's play some games," Marie says. "Does anyone want to play pin the tail on the donkey?"

"That's just what we need," Floss says dryly, echoing the sentiment of the rest of us. "To blindfold a four-year-old and give him something sharp. They had a kid in the ER in the Janeway not too long ago because his brother stuck a pin right up his nose playing that game. You see all kinds of crazy stuff with kids you know. They end up in the ER from the most ordinary sorts of things."

"Can I open up my presents?" Kenny stacks them all up neatly in front of him and starts tearing away at the paper.

The afternoon is long and exhausting. Kenny is tired from the excitement and all the new toys. By the time birthday cake rolls around, it feels like a chore. Nobody wants it. We're all too full with pizza and cheezies and chips and dip. Floss dims the lights and Marie lights the candles with the matches Gabe ran out for two hours earlier. Everyone looks younger in the candlelight. Marie's features soften, and she smiles deeply at Kenny's beaming face, her lips curling into a broad smile. I don't think I'd ever seen her look so happy, not even when Dad was alive. Even Gabe looks different to me in the candlelight, relaxed with his hands in his pockets and a contented smile on his face. He's not thinking about office equipment or putting gas in the car. He joins the rest of us in singing Happy Birthday to Kenny. When the song is over, he stands upright, removes his hands from his pocket and claps in encouragement. Kenny's cheeks inflate and he blows hard on the cake in an effort to extinguish the flames but, as Gabe predicted, spit flies everywhere, on top of the icing, on Floss' arm, on the bowl of cheezies left out on the table. Still the flames burn and Kenny begins to cry in frustration until Gabe comes up from behind him and blows them out in one single puff.

"Now my wish won't come true," Kenny bawls, punching Gabe in the arm.

"He's just tired," Marie insists.

"It's been a long day," Floss chimes in, wiping a piece of chewed up cheezie and spit from her forearm. "Sure I can barely keep my eyes open."

No one asks Kenny what his wish was. It's bad luck. It won't come true. It might break my heart to hear it. I think Gabe might have forgotten the matches on purpose.

"Happy Birthday, squirt," Gabe says rubbing a hand through Kenny's hair and kissing the top of his head.

Squirt. It's the first thing Gabe said to him after he was born. Kenny was just moments old with his eyes closed and swaddled up in blankets. I wanted to coo over the baby alongside Gabe, smile in wonder at our happy accident, but I couldn't. I already had my doubts we were going to make it but

I pushed the thoughts aside, attributed it to the stress of the birth. I wished I had someone to talk to about it, but the only person I'd ever confided in was Gabe. I shot Gabe a half-smile and asked him to call Marie and let her know I'd had the baby. My legs were still numb from the epidural and I pinched my thigh under the blanket but I couldn't feel it. I just wanted Marie there.

marie

Floss and I went to see Lolly in the hospital just a few hours after she had Kenny. They'd moved her up to a room and brought the baby to her once they'd done their examination and deemed him healthy. It was different when I had Floss. At least they gave you a couple of days to recover. I didn't know what the nurses did all day on their shifts if all the babies were being sent to their mothers to be looked after right away. There was another woman up in the ward with her. Maybe it was just because Lolly was so young, but the woman looked old, too old to have a baby. She had crow's feet nearly as pronounced as my own, a severe looking haircut and long, bony fingers. It was hard to imagine her, naked and laying underneath someone, out of breath with her head thrown back in passionate abandon.

If Ray and I had had a baby I'd have been just like her, the old woman up on the maternity ward, all the young mothers staring at me since it didn't seem right to them to have a baby at such an age. It didn't seem right that Lolly had one either, but at least she had youth as an excuse. Everyone would look at her and think she didn't know any better, whereas they'd look at me and wonder what I'd been thinking. Ray said as much to me the night I asked him if we could try for our own child.

Lolly was trying to feed the baby when Floss and I got there. She held him awkwardly trying to get him to latch onto her breast. I felt self-conscious walking in on Lolly in her state of undress. There was something vulnerable about the way she was lying in the bed, with her hospital gown on that was too big for her. I could tell Floss felt the same way. She stood in the doorway with a bunch of balloons that were already wilting with old helium as if they were exhausted from stretching up to the tile ceiling.

"We can come back," I said, but Lolly waved us in from the doorway half-heartedly, like her arm was too tired to give a more enthusiastic gesture. Floss placed the balloons weighted down with a pot of plastic flowers on the window sill. They were ugly but it was all they had in the hospital gift shop and I wanted to come right away. I didn't have time to stop at the florist. I had a sense of urgency to see her, and my grandson, as soon as I could.

"Congratulations," Floss said. "You look radiant." She tried to hug Lolly, which turned into such a series of awkward missteps that I refrained from doing the same. Floss was wary of crushing the baby, brushing against Lolly's exposed breast and bumping into the medical equipment. I wanted to say something along the same lines but the truth was Lolly looked far from radiant or glowing. I'd never seen her look worse. She looked exhausted with dark circles under eyes that were red and glassy, and she sported a dark bruise on the top of her hand where an IV needle had been taped. The bruise would yellow in a few days and would take a couple of weeks to heal. There was something else about her though, like something inside her had changed.

I regretted getting dressed up then, telling Floss to put on something decent and put a little colour on her face. It seemed ridiculous now that people got dressed up to visit patients in hospitals, almost like a taunt. I'd done the same thing. I'd curled my hair with the iron, put on eyeliner and lipstick and wore black slacks and a blue sweater and high-heeled boots. As if I didn't learn my lesson from Ray the time I saw him in the hospital. But I wasn't the only one. I passed them in the corridors and the elevators of St. Clare's in their Sunday best and their made-up faces as they went about visiting people who were shrunken, who writhed in the bed like the letter S to give shape to their discomfort—people who ate and breathed through tubes. They visited these poor people as if it were a dress rehearsal for the funeral. I remember the way Ray bawled at me when I did the same thing. I thought it was just his nerves talking but I couldn't see it then.

"How are you doing?" I asked her and her lip quivered the same way it did the first time I saw her on that bus.

"They gave me stitches down there," Lolly whined, pointing with a finger at her privates. "They sewed me up like a fuckin' Christmas turkey." Her voice was high-pitched, it cracked and trembled. I hadn't expected that from Lolly. She was always so hard, so taciturn.

"You only gave birth a few hours ago. Give it time," I assured her. I should have talked to her about the birth beforehand, but I'd been too shell-shocked by Ray's death to think about much else. Not for the first time, I felt misgivings that I'd somehow failed Lolly. I should have told her what to expect. I should have described what a contraction felt like, told her how to time it, but I didn't know. All I remembered from Floss' birth was being in the bed and being scared to death.

It seemed like a million years ago since I'd given birth. Danny didn't even come in the room with me when Floss was born. He could have, but he didn't want to. *That's the last thing I needs to see. Sure I'll never get a hard-on again.* He sat in the waiting room, watched a hockey game and ate a bag of cookies from a vending machine.

They did things different nowadays. I didn't understand any of these young mothers. They went to pregnant yoga, refused to eat soft cheese, talked about drug-free births. They wanted a midwife instead of a doctor, like they were back one hundred and fifty years ago. They wanted to feed the babies their own milk and pointed their nose down at people who used formula, like they were just a bunch of ignorant people. It used to be the other way around.

And it wasn't just young mothers. I didn't understand young people at all anymore. They didn't wear watches, they didn't separate their laundry, their tampons were half the size they used to be, their underwear was half the size it used to be. I wasn't supposed to end up this way but I was clearly going to end up like every other old person, crooked and confused. It didn't seem so long ago that I looked upon older people with a mixture of haughty superiority and pity. I wished Ray was here because he'd feel just as lost as me.

"You decided to breastfeed the baby?" It was said as a question but it hardly seemed necessary since she was still struggling to get his mouth wrapped around her nipple.

"It's better for the baby," Lolly explained.

I wouldn't get to feed the baby and I wanted to so badly. I wanted to cradle him in my arms, watch the tiny bubbles of air rush to the top of the bottle. Lolly would be the only one who could feed him. I know she didn't do it on purpose just to spite me, but it felt that way. I watched as she winced in pain, shifted the baby slightly to the side.

"It bothers you, does it? Having him suck on you like that?" It couldn't be very comfortable. I didn't even like a lace bra, the way it itched. I couldn't imagine what it was like to nurse a child.

"My tits hurt," Lolly admitted in the same way she used to tell Ray her throat hurt. Ray would look down her throat too, shine a flashlight down there like he knew what he was looking for. He'd be mortified if he were here now. He'd be down to the cafeteria looking for a cup of tea, anything but talk about her sore nipples. Lolly looked down and stole a glance at herself. Her nipples were bruised and cracked. "Gabe is never going to want to touch me again. Not after this!"

Floss made a pitiful sound in her throat. "The drugs must not be worn off yet for you to say something so foolish. Where is Gabe anyway?"

It seemed like only a few moments earlier, he'd called us, his voice brimming with excitement and adrenaline. "You're a grandmother!" he shouted into the phone and I wanted to weep right then and there because I knew I wasn't really a grandmother. Ray was a grandfather but Ray was dead. My silence on the other end of the phone must have jarred Gabe into awareness because he stopped talking about me being a grandmother and went on to recite facts like the baby's weight, his height, the time of his birth and the size of his lungs, the size of his balls.

I feigned happiness, offered up the word congratulations, but I could have said anything my tone was so empty. I was happy for her, I was, but I felt her slipping away from me all the same. She wouldn't come to me for child-rearing advice, wouldn't call me exhausted in the morning and tell me the baby was teething or that he started to blow bubbles or sit up on his own, things every daughter talked about with their mother. Even now with the baby no more than a few hours old, we were already butting heads. It made me feel heavy, lethargic and I leaned against the radiator underneath the window sill for a little support. It was hot in the hospital room, or maybe it was because I was leaning on the heater, but I felt the sweat pooling down the centre of my back. My waistband was damp with sweat and cut into my stomach. When I took my pants off later I would see the imprint of my underwear splayed across my belly. I shouldn't have come here.

"I sent Gabe down to the cafeteria," Lolly replied, "to get me a bag of chips and a bar."

"I could have picked you up something on the way."

"Oh, Marie, I don't really want it. I just wanted him to leave me alone for a little while. He was getting on my nerves."

This was so uncharacteristic of Lolly both me and Floss exchanged a wary glance.

"What happened?" Floss asked.

"Gabe told the doctor all about how I got pregnant when I was in labour," Lolly explained, her eyes pooling with tears. "I think he was just trying to explain that we weren't trying to get pregnant because they were giving us looks. But God, I'm having all these contractions and it hurt so bad and he's telling the doctor and the nurses about the broken condom and how his sperm shot a hole through the rubber. I'm laying on a bed, legs spread apart and naked from the waist down in a room full of people and he's what makes me embarrassed. That's the first time I've ever been embarrassed by him. I wanted to shout at him to get out or to shut the fuck up but if I did everyone would laugh and say every other woman in labour says the same thing. So I didn't say a word. I just laid there and pretended I didn't hear him."

Ray used to embarrass me sometimes too. I used to pretend I wasn't with him at the supermarket. He'd pile all the no name brands in the cart and I refused to push it around the store. I'd go and pick out bananas while he was filling up on canned soups. Floss used to tell people she lived in the subdivision behind the old apartment when they dropped her off. She went in someone else's backyard and hopped the fence home. She might have been embarrassed by where we lived but I was more ashamed of her than anything that she couldn't tell people the truth. It seemed to me that part of loving someone meant being ashamed of them sometimes too. If you didn't have that feeling every now and then, you couldn't be proud of them either.

"You can always come home, you know," I told Lolly. "Even though Dad is gone, you'll always have a room there. And me and Floss can help you with the baby."

"I can't," Lolly said in a voice thick with resignation that sounded familiar and strangely comforting. She handed the baby to me like she'd just had enough of him and his sucking and pulling at her. I held his tiny body next to my chest. His face was scrunched up, his pale lips a small circle under a tiny nose. He had blue eyes. They say every baby is born with blue eyes but I didn't think that was true. They were the same colour as Lolly's, and it had to come from her mother's side since Ray's eyes were a soft brown.

I thought of Floss, when she was only a few hours old. I didn't feel much of anything at the time. I was hungry, sore, and uncomfortable. I had maxi pads on the size of bricks and nearly the same weight, and the astringent smell of witch hazel blocked out every other odour in the hospital—babies, bleach, vomit, shit, coffee, and despair. Danny came and I handed Floss off to him, although she was Florence then. She hadn't grown into Floss yet. He held her awkwardly, didn't support the head right like the nurses told us to and I snatched her right back from him. I'd never felt so protective toward anything or anybody in my whole life.

I felt the same fierce protectiveness stir inside my chest for this child, who felt every bit my grandson even though we shared no blood. "Can he call me Nanny?" I asked Lolly, but I didn't look at her when I asked the question. I was afraid she was going to look at me like I was gone cracked.

"I don't care what he calls you," Lolly answered finally. I let go a breath that I didn't know I'd been holding.

lolly

My mother took me downtown when she was sick, although I didn't know it at the time. She wasn't even sure herself how bad it was going to be, but she must have had a feeling for her to do what she did that day. I was shoving a spoonful of cereal in my mouth at the breakfast table when she asked me to spend the day with her.

"Do you want to play hooky today?"

"For real?"

"Uh-huh," she laughed at my shocked expression, twisting the hair until it was in a pile on top of her head and then letting it go again. "We'll call in sick," she said, her fingers curling around the handle of her coffee cup. "We'll go to the waterfront and look at the boats," she said in a voice that tried to tempt me. She knew I loved to look at the boats and see the flags from all the different countries displayed on their masts. "And we'll get something to eat at one of those nice restaurants down there. A hot turkey sandwich maybe. It's been ages since I had a hot turkey sandwich."

"It's Friday. I have a spelling test."

"Oh, who cares?" There was an edge to her I didn't recognize. "You'd rather take a spelling test than spend the day with me?" This was so uncharacteristic of my mother, who normally would be sitting at the breakfast table with my spelling words in her lap while she sipped her coffee. Spell *prompt*, she would say, enunciating every letter until it didn't even sound like the same word.

"No," I shook my head.

"You're so little," she said with a twinge of nostalgia. "You thinks a spelling test is the most important thing in the world."

"No I don't," I protested.

"Cynthia, what the hell are you doing?" It was Dad and it was a warning. He'd just gotten out of the shower. A towel was wrapped around his waist but the top of him was still soaking wet. The steam emanated from the top of his head like he was furious even though it was just the heat from the shower escaping him.

"Nothing. Just planning a day with my daughter."

"You're jumping the gun again. You're always jumping the gun. You don't know anything yet. Don't you dare—" He stopped abruptly, like he didn't know what it was he was daring her not to do.

"I'm not going to say anything," she shot back. They talked a lot like that lately, like I was an infant who didn't understand what they were saying. It was like they'd forgotten I was in the room. They stayed up late, talking, and flipping through the wall calendar circling dates like they were suddenly so important they had to be in two places at once. I wondered if they were getting divorced, settling out their visitation schedules. "Ray, I don't know when I'm going to be able to do this again."

"Cyn!" He shouted at her and he sounded almost evangelical, like a preacher pointing an accusatory finger at her. *Sin!*

"Why don't you come with us?"

"I don't want no part of it," he spat.

I didn't care why they were fighting or why my mother let me stay home from school that day. I was just grateful for it, whatever her reasons were. We walked along the harbourfront, looking at boats and pointing at gulls. Mom bought me a new woolen hat from one of the souvenir shops and even though it itched more than the one she bought from Sears I didn't complain because it seemed to make her happy. She picked out a blanket that was soft and fleecy and had fringes, and a silk scarf dyed the most vibrant shade of blue I'd ever seen that she wrapped around her shoulders in front of a mirror.

"What do you think?" She framed her head with her hands and smiled brightly at me. I wanted to tell her that it matched her eyes perfectly, that it was the colour of the ocean, but I had never seen ocean that colour before. The harbour water was more of a murky green and her eyes were like the sapphires in the display case in the jewellery store. We ate lunch at a tiny restaurant and ordered hot turkey sandwiches, but she didn't eat hers. She seemed content to watch me eat.

"I have to have an operation," she said, and then she bit into a crispy fry to prevent herself from speaking again.

"What kind of an operation?"

"They have to take out one of my kidneys. But I have two so I'll just use the other one for now, and then later I might be able to borrow another one from someone else." I knew it wasn't as simple as she said but she wouldn't tell me anything else, not until she talked to dad first.

Later that afternoon she laid out all the groceries we had in the fridge and put them out on the counter.

"Do you want to learn how to cook?" She started writing things down on a piece of scrap paper by the telephone. She scribbled recipes for beef stew, meatloaf, pork chops and rice, just about everything we ever ate. She ran out of paper and started looking for more.

"What are we cooking?" I was confused. She had everything laid out. She had one onion peeled but she left it on the cutting board without chopping it up while she wrote something down. Quarter cup of ketchup, two tablespoons brown sugar, half cup vinegar.

"I don't know," she whispered. "You should know how to do some of this for Dad."

It was like she summoned him because he stood there in the doorway of the kitchen, his eyes darting around at all the food. His bad mood was gone from this morning and he leaned wearily against the doorway like he needed it to hold him up. He still had on his work uniform, a blue button-down shirt with an ID slung around his neck. It had a picture of him in a hard hat.

"Cyn," he said quietly. "What are you doing?"

But she couldn't answer him. She just sat there with a pen in her hand with her words written on the envelopes of bills and on the backs of receipts.

"She's showing me how to look after you," I said, smoothing the skin of a green pepper that was past its freshness.

"Cyn," he said again, but this time it wasn't angry or filled with fire and brimstone. It was more of a heavy sigh. "I'm not the one needs looking after," he said, but I didn't believe him. I knew my mother was always right.

"Can you play hooky?" When Carson shows up unexpectedly to ask me this, I get the feeling that something bad is going to befall me, that taking a day of indulgence can only be repaid with something awful. If I give in to the temptation, I'm afraid he'll disappear from my life, the same way my mother did. Of course, I know this isn't really true and that my mother was going to die whether we took a day together or not.

"I don't like to do that." I can still picture my father, the bewildered look on his face after coming out of the shower and picking up on what my mother was saying.

Carson shifts his weight onto his other foot. He doesn't know quite what to say now. He'd asked me the question playfully, told me there was something he wanted to show me, but it had to be today. I remember the way he told me he rarely acted on impulse save for recently. This was clearly another impulsive act by a man rarely given to impulse. "All right, it's probably silly anyway. I just wanted to show you something," he says again. "I thought you'd get a kick out of it."

"What is it?"

"It's downtown, at the waterfront."

I feel the hairs on the back of my neck stand up. I hear my father's voice, the evangelical tone of judgment. "As long as I'm back for four o'clock," I relent. "I can juggle a few appointments. It doesn't get really busy until after supper anyway."

Carson smiles at me. "That's perfect. You won't even need to get out of the car." He can barely contain his excitement. It's nearly infectious and I allow myself to be swept into the mystery of what awaits me downtown.

Carson drives to the waterfront just like Mom did all those years ago. He parks in front of the waterfront, rolls the window down to afford me a better view. I inhale the smell of fish and salt water, a vague whiff of gasoline. A breeze lifts my hair and tickles the side of my neck.

The air feels colder here by the water but Carson seems oblivious to it. He wasn't the least bit cold the day of the accident, with snow falling on his head. He's one of those men who probably wears short sleeves all year long, shovels snow in his shorts, sleeps with the window open just a crack even in the dead of winter. I stare at his face instead of out the window.

Whatever it is he wants to show me, I only want to look at him. His nose is wide, his jaw broad and his ears lie so close to his scalp it's as if he went bald on purpose, just to show them off. He has a scar that runs perpendicular to his right eyebrow, cutting it almost in half. It's such a neat line, not at all jagged like most scars. I want to know how it got there. I imagine it being a battle scar, something incurred in the line of duty but most likely it was something more mundane, like he fell down the stairs when he was a toddler, or he wiped out on his bike on the way to school one day. I trace the scar with my thumb and he smiles contentedly at my ministrations.

"Don't you have any scars?"

"No," I shake my head. The only stitches I ever had was after I had Kenny.

"You must have one somewhere. C'mere," he says invitingly, and I lean into him, feel his lips on mine. The cold dissipates almost instantly, replaced by warmth that travels to my centre and then on to my limbs and to my fingers and toes, almost as if I'd had a shot of rum.

"Look," he points to a fishing boat directly in front of us, a big rusty black trawler. "This is what I wanted to show you."

"A fishing boat?" I suppress a giggle. "Why would I want to see that smelly old thing?"

"Look at the name," he urges. "Miss Laura. I saw it the other night on patrol and I couldn't stop thinking about you. It's shipping out this afternoon and I wanted you to see it before it goes. So you'd see we're both named after ships."

"It's a pretty ugly boat."

"This is true. You are deserving of a much grander boat, but at least it's still sailing. The Carson sunk, remember?"

I laugh in response and his hand squeezes mine. "There are signs of you everywhere I go, Miss Laura." He whispers it in my ear and I feel his breath on the back of my neck, hot and even. I feel him tense, he squeezes my hand tighter and it's almost as if everything around us shakes. The wind picks up and the gulls take off, and then there's nothing but calm.

"I'm going up to my cabin on Saturday. It's in Salmonier so it's pretty close. Do you want to come with me? It's quiet and peaceful and I keep picturing you there, in front of the fire. Just for the day," he adds convincingly. "It's supposed to go up to 17 degrees on Saturday."

I sense he's nervous about asking me something so forward, thinks I might be insulted. I look over at the trawler bearing my name. It's not as ugly as I first thought. It's not a big vessel but it has a sort of unrefined elegance to it. It's braved the sea with all its rough waves but now it bobs gently up and down in the harbour, protected from all the elements. Carson makes me feel like that, calm, sedate, protected. It's almost like my mom is there with me, pointing to the trawler, her lips curling up in delight at how the boat has the same name as me. I can almost see the dark blue of the ocean in the harbour, instead of the murky green.

floss

Leo's ex-wife has short hair. This fact jars me for reasons I can't really fathom. It wasn't how I pictured her, and I pictured her several different ways, but none like this. I imagined her hair would be shoulder length, sensible and yet still feminine and soft, grazing the collarbone when she tilted her head off to the side. It's too short to pull back, twist on top of her head, or put in a ponytail. Her hair will always look the same whether she's going to the grocery store on a Saturday morning, or out to dinner on a Saturday night. I'd feel bad for her if I didn't already feel bad for myself. I give her a half smile in the doorway of Leo's apartment but I don't invite her in, nor do I introduce myself. I wait for her to speak first but she's just as taken aback at me as I am at her, maybe even more. She smoothes her hair along the tip of her ear although it doesn't look any different when she's done. There are no errant hairs allowed with such a style.

It's strawberry blond with golden highlights that were painted on with a brush and then wrapped in foil for fifteen minutes. It's the type of style that you need to get cut every six

weeks and no one notices when you've just gotten back from
the salon because it looks exactly the same all the time. I
imagine her ordering her hairstyle the way I order Chinese food
at the food court. *I'll have the number three with extra highlights
please.*

She smiles awkwardly back at me, shifts her weight
thrusting her hip to the left. I wait for her to say something,
for Leo to get out of the bathroom. The silence feels painful,
like a tight grip around my wrist. She moves her hand up to her
ears this time, pushes the back of an earring into her thumb
until I'm sure it's left a tiny mark. The earrings are diamond
studs. I know Leo bought them for her, maybe for Christmas or
on her birthday. I wonder if he had them gift wrapped at the
jewellery store in the mall and if he surprised her, or if she'd
dropped enough hints that the unveiling was anticlimactic. I
wonder if she kissed him after he presented them to her and if
so was it a kiss filled with lust that she felt it all the way down
to her knees, or more of an obligatory peck before she went to
retrieve the clothes out of the dryer.

She wears a pair of charcoal dress pants that are too short
and hit just above the ankle. Her pointy toed black pumps are
dull and speckled with a brown residue. She must have hopped
over a mud puddle but didn't clear it all the way. The most
striking thing about her is that she looks like a mother, sensible
and stern, capable of sending a child to her room with a
disapproving glare. I think of Lolly, also a mother, but with
a thick cascade of dark hair down her back. She wears sweatpants
with words like Angel and Princess sewn onto the backside. Leo's
ex-wife would never wear a pair of sweatpants with writing on
the butt.

She probably wouldn't wear sweatpants at all. She might
wear loungewear that she got from Sears, in an expensive
fabric that's allegedly breathable. I'm not even sure what the
term means but it makes me think of a miniature set of healthy

pink lungs tucked in the front pocket. I picture her sitting on a chenille sofa, wearing her loungewear in a pale pink almost iridescent fabric, with a cup of coffee that she held like a bowl to warm her hands, with the bottom three fingers slipping around the handle.

"Um," she says finally, testing her voice to see if it still works. "Hello?" It's a question, two distinct syllables, the way she might answer the telephone. It sounds mildly offensive, like she's questioning my presence here in the first place. She glances up at the number on the door in case she's rung the wrong bell. I shouldn't have answered the door at all. I hope Leo won't be angry with me, think I'm too comfortable in his apartment. I thought it would be the pizza delivery man and I didn't want to miss him while Leo was in the shower. In fairness, I did call out that someone was at the door twice. It wasn't my fault he didn't hear me.

"Hello?" I repeat in the same questioning tone.

"Where's Leo?" I hate the way she asks the question, just throws his name out there like I was in possession of something that belonged to her—a wallet, cellphone, a husband.

"He's in the bathroom," I reply and she nods knowingly in an expression of familiarity that makes me squirm with discomfort. She gives me a conspiratorial smile that indicates she is not at all surprised. *Oh Leo, yes that one is always in the bathroom. Makes you crazy doesn't it?* "I'm Cathy."

She smiles again, but this time it's more awkward like there was nothing else to do with her mouth. The remnants of a rust-coloured lipstick, applied several hours earlier, settle into the cracks of her lips, putting me in mind of oxidized metal. I fidget nervously with the doorknob, locking and unlocking it with a twist of my wrist.

"Floss."

She steps inside the foyer although I haven't asked her in. She scans the room as if searching for something. The apartment is sparse. The walls are off-white and bare, the carpet an industrial greyish blue. The sofa is typically male, the kind of furniture purveyors of good taste balk at. It doesn't have clean lines. Rather, it's oversized with puffy arms and a built-in recliner. It's microfibre, a colour somewhere between beige and brown, and it clashes with the carpet. The next biggest thing in the room is the television, a 50-inch flat screen that takes up an entire television stand made of pressboard. There's no coffee table, no lamps, no end tables, no plants. I wish I'd brought some throw pillows over, a scented candle maybe, or a vase, something to make it less cold besides the stuffed animal and the Barbie doll on the floor. I think about picking them up in a feeble effort to tidy, but there isn't anywhere to put them save for Faith's lavender room and it seems intrusive for me to go in there and start tidying when I haven't even met her yet.

The toilet flushes and Leo emerges from the bathroom. He's just shaved because he's left a small patch of shaving cream on his jaw and his face is red from the razor. He's cut himself again. I see blood ooze from his neck but not enough to pool and drip. I can feel his discomfort in the back of my throat, or perhaps it's just my own. I feel myself shrinking, feel the walls edging closer toward me. He eyes us both warily as if we'd been comparing notes on his sexual repertoire. His face is red, humid from his recent shower.

"What are you doing here, Cathy? Where's Faith?"

"She's waiting in the car." There's a sigh conveying relief that comes from both of them, in perfect unison. "You forgot to bring her backpack and she has homework. I thought it was done but she says you played Monopoly instead." She hasn't accused him of anything but she may as well have called him irresponsible. I feel embarrassed for him. He scans the sparse apartment but there is no backpack anywhere.

"She must have left it in the van," Leo says, reaching in his jeans pocket for his keys. Cathy follows him to the van and I watch from the window, not caring if they can see me. Leo retrieves a backpack from the back seat. It's pink and has kittens or puppies on it, I can't tell because Leo rests it on one shoulder, obscuring it from my vision. I see him shake his head and put his hands in the air.

They're talking about me in whispered tones and I imagine the exchange. Cathy is asking who I am, if we're dating, how long we've been dating. She's being sarcastic too, I can tell she has a sarcastic streak. I'm younger than she is, younger than Leo and she's probably asking him if he's helping me with my homework too. She hopes he does a better job with my homework than he did with Faith's. She's telling him she doesn't want him to start parading his girlfriends around their daughter. She prefaces it with the phrase, You can go ahead and screw whoever you want but....

Leo, I suspect, is trying to downplay my prominence. *I fixed her toilet a few weeks ago that's all. She's just a friend, we're not serious, we're not dating, she's no one.*

I feel more distraught than I should over a conversation that's purely imagined. I feel like an outsider, observer to the love story of Leo and Cathy. I want to know about them so much that it aches. I want to know how they met. Did he fix her toilet too? Where did they go on their first date? Did he pick her up in his plumbing van and take her to Mary Brown's too, and if so, did the fumes give her a headache? Of course they probably had a first date before he even became a plumber, a speculation that somehow stings even more. I want to know how he proposed. Did he hide the ring in some romantic fashion, or did he mention it after he'd come out of the bathroom, the way Ray did? I wanted to know what her wedding dress looked like, and how many times they stood up and kissed for all those guests who tapped their forks against their glasses.

My head hurts with all the questions and my stomach feels

like a tight ball. It seems to be taking Leo a long time to hand over a backpack. They must still be talking about me. I want to leave, put my shoes and coat on and slip out the back but there is no back door in the apartment and I'd have to walk right past the three of them, the mom and dad and their little girl, their eyes burning a hole in my back.

"I'm sorry," Leo says when he finally comes back inside. "I thought Faith remembered her backpack." It sounds as if he's still talking to Cathy. I didn't give a damn about the backpack but Leo seemed to have trouble switching gears, forgetting the context of the conversation he was supposed to have with me.

Leo comes to me and wraps his arms around me. "I know that was probably uncomfortable for you. You shouldn't have to...."

His voice trails off like I know what he's about to say but I don't. The only thing I know is that his arms feel good. Leo has a way of making all the insecurities go away even though he's responsible for bringing them to the surface in the first place.

"So that's your ex-wife?" I say it even though it's obvious. I can't help the need to verbalize it.

"Yup," he says, playing along.

"How long were you married?"

"Few years," he says evasively. He's uncomfortable having the conversation, as am I, but I'm unable to stop the barrage of questions.

"Where did you meet?"

"We went to the same high school." I note the way he purposefully avoids saying they are high school sweethearts. I try to imagine a young Leo in high school, with a backpack that does not have puppies or kittens on it but I can't picture him young.

Cathy would know what he looked like back then and I would never have such a memory. I feel a jealous rush of air through my lungs that makes me bolder and more wicked.

"How long did you date her before you had sex with her?" We'd been dating nearly a month already and hadn't.

"Floss." He says my name sharply, a touch of exasperation and warning. I wonder if he says Faith's name the same way when she asks him something inappropriate.

"I just want to know about your marriage."

"Why?" He doesn't seem angry with me so much as puzzled.

"Because I want to get to know you better." I'm not sure that's necessarily true since I'm not asking a single question about him. If I wanted to get to know Leo, I would ask him what his favourite television program was or if he put ketchup or mustard, or both, on a hot dog. I could find out those answers simply enough. It doesn't seem necessary to ask since the answers will reveal themselves to me eventually. It will be a discovery of sorts and less an interview, like the kind of conversation we are having now.

The truth is I don't want to know about Leo, I want to know about Cathy. I want desperately for Leo to say something mean about her, like she wears control top pantyhose but he stands before me, silent.

"Do you still love her?"

"God no," Leo says emphatically.

Do you love me? I ask the question silently in my head but his arms tighten around my waist and he looks down at me, kisses the top of my head. I feel a moment of panic that I might have asked the question out loud. I hadn't asked anyone that question since I posed it to Ray that time we all went away on vacation. I swore I'd never ask anyone again.

marie

We needed a vacation. Ray hadn't taken any time off from the phone company in more than a year and he often pulled a double shift or got called in on the weekends. He never said no to overtime, even if we had something else planned, or if he wasn't feeling well. He was exhausted, cranky and complained of sore muscles and a stiff neck when he did come home. I massaged his back and his neck, kneading the knots in his shoulder blades while he grunted with relief. I was worried about him, afraid he was going to keel over one day and that would be the end of him. I broached the subject of a vacation to him one evening after the girls had gone to bed. He sat with his feet up on the coffee table, a beer in his hand. I wasn't going to get a better time to bring it up.

"Maybe we should go away for a few days. All of us. It might bring us closer together if we had some family time. The weather is getting warmer. Sure I didn't even need a jacket this afternoon."

"We can't afford to go anywhere right now, Marie," Ray

said decisively, and he crossed his feet up on the coffee table. He had a hole in his sock and his big toe poked through.

"I wasn't talking any place fancy. I thought we could go camping. We could all go swimming and have bonfires and hike some trails." Ray looked at me, amused, when I said this since I wasn't much of an outdoors type.

"You wants to go camping do ya? You must be some desperate to get away."

I was desperate. No one was getting along. Lolly blamed me for most things and had recently accused me of trying to turn her father against her because I'd told Ray she didn't finish her homework. As absurd as it sounded, Lolly accused me of marrying Ray for the sole purpose of destroying her life. I told her such a comment was self-centred, that there were more people in the world than her. This made her cry and caused Ray to turn on me like the savage.

"Do you have to start as soon as I walk in the door? I don't even have time to take my goddamn shoes off and I can't wait to go back out the door."

But if Lolly and I had a volatile relationship, Floss and Ray had no relationship at all. They barely spoke to one another, unless it was absolutely necessary. I saw the way he kidded around with Lolly, tugged on her ponytail when she was bent over her homework at the kitchen table, or horsed around with her out in the yard, turning the hose on her or showing her the bird's nest in the tree he planted out front. To Floss, he gave a wide berth. It was almost as if he bent over backwards not to be left alone with her. Floss pretended not to notice but she did. I saw the way her face fell whenever Ray made a deliberate effort to avoid brushing against her, watched the look on her face when he joked around with Lolly.

"I just thought a vacation might relax all of us. Maybe it'll bring you and Floss closer together. You could stand to be a little bit more affectionate with her, Ray." It sounded critical, like I was chastising him for doing something wrong, when all I meant was to encourage him to be more loving.

I waited for him to accuse me of being antagonistic towards Lolly but he just wore a pained expression. "She's fourteen years old, Marie."

"So?" I couldn't understand what that had to do with anything.

"So I'm not her father. Every time I thought about putting an arm around her, or giving her a hug, it just felt wrong. It's like I'm not supposed to be pawing away at a teenage girl."

"Oh, Ray, please," I said dismissively. "You're being ridiculous. A little fatherly affection every now and then is all right."

Ray took a mouthful of beer, started picking at the label. His cheeks were flushed, even his neck was red. "It's true, Marie. I don't want her to take it the wrong way and I don't want other people to think that way. I've held Lolly in my arms since she was a baby but I'm frightened half to death to touch Floss. It don't mean I don't care about her, Marie. I just don't know how to show her."

It hadn't occurred to me before, this explanation. It might have been different if we'd met years ago, when Floss was a little thing who would crawl up in your lap or who needed a hand to hold in the parking lot. Ray looked at his bottle of beer, bit the bottom of his lip. He was afraid I might judge him for speaking the truth about it. I could tell he'd never verbalized it before and he wouldn't again.

"Maybe a vacation isn't a bad idea," he said

The cabin smelled musty so I opened up the windows as soon as we got there. It had been a long drive out to Terra Nova, four hours cooped up in the car, but it was made longer by the silence. I gave up trying to engage everyone in conversation before we even got on the highway. Lolly pretended to be asleep but I knew she just didn't want to talk. Floss asked once if we could stop to eat at the Irving Restaurant but Ray sped past it. I wasn't sure if he'd done it on purpose or if he just didn't hear her. He had the window open just a crack, which made a racket inside the car. He probably just wanted to make good time, I assured myself, check in before it got dark.

"I'm hungry," Floss announced as soon as she was inside the cabin. She flopped down on one of the beds in the room. The bedspread was blue and floral and decidedly feminine for a rustic, almost sparse cabin. There was a dresser, a lamp, a green oval rug, and a small kitchenette all in the one room. I was hungry too. We'd left as soon as Ray got home from work and we hadn't even stopped to pee. There was a restaurant in the main cabin, where we picked up the keys, that would probably close soon if it hadn't already since it was nearly nine o'clock. Darkness had descended, seemingly out of nowhere. It was a pink sky and then suddenly it was black, dotted with stars that went on forever.

Ray needed the flashlight to unload the car and it took him four trips. He piled it all in the doorway of the cabin. A duffel bag for the two of us, Dominion shopping bags for the girls. We didn't have luggage and when it was time to pack we just stuffed jackets and changes of clothes into the plastic bags until they stretched out to the limit. His last trip was for the cooler I'd packed earlier in the day. He hoisted it in front of him, his hands on the handles, and balanced it on a knee before he laid it down gently on the floor.

"The girls are getting hungry," I said to him. "Is that the last of it?"

"Yup, that's all she wrote." He looked happy, more relaxed than I'd seen him in ages. He stood upright with his hands on his hips and surveyed the surroundings. "Nice cabin," he said with pride as if he'd built it himself from wood he'd cut down with an axe. "You know what, I'm a little hungry myself." He opened the cooler, sifted through a few items. "Let's make some sandwiches." He pulled out bread, mustard, butter, sliced turkey, and peanut butter. Lolly would only eat peanut butter.

"I don't know why we couldn't stop on the way here and get a proper meal," Floss protested, which shocked the both of us since Floss never really complained about anything. She saw the two of us looking at her, and even Lolly looked up and stared at her. If anything, the attention seemed to make her bolder. "We must have passed one hundred restaurants on the way, and sure there's one right there in the main cabin." She gestured with her hand in the opposite direction from the main cabin but it didn't matter. She was making her point. "You're just too cheap to take us out to eat."

Ray was angry and getting angrier by the second. He clasped and unclasped his hands, his breathing became louder and more laboured and he clenched his jaw. He was fighting a battle inside himself, trying to keep control over his emotions but in the end, reason lost out to rage. He lifted a leg, placed the sole of his boot on top of the cooler and kicked it over, spilling the contents out onto the floor. Bread, tins of Pepsi, hot dogs, a carton of eggs, ice cubes all scattered across the floor. It made such a loud thud that my hands flew reflexively up to my ears. I wanted to start cleaning up the mess, check for broken eggs and put the ice back in the cooler before it melted and the food spoiled but I was paralyzed by the look on Ray's face.

"Do I need to remind you that I paid for this cabin, this food, the clothes on your back, not to mention your goddamn braces that I had to work overtime for?" He was pointing his finger at Floss and a spray of spittle landed on the collar of his jacket, a white bubble that burst and left a wet stain behind. "You don't appreciate anything. I work like a dog to support you and your mother. I sat through your school play, which was boring as hell. I drove all the way out to Kelligrews to pick you up from the basketball game you wanted to see and you didn't even say thank you. This," he said, gesturing toward Floss and me and Lolly who hung back by the door of the cabin as if she were plotting her own escape, "is the single most thankless fucking thing I've ever done."

Floss' lips quivered and her eyes welled up. So much for making an effort. It made me want to slap Ray, hard, right across the face. I couldn't believe he'd said such things to my child. Not that it wasn't all true. Things had gotten tighter for us financially after we bought the house, and Ray did work overtime, for three weeks straight, to pay for Floss' orthodontia, and it was true that her school concert was tedious, and that he dropped her off and picked her up whenever I asked him to without complaint.

But that wasn't the point. I could fill a book with all the things I did for Lolly that not only went unappreciated but were met with outright hostility. I ran out and bought her a new winter coat and boots when they forecast the first big storm of the season and she told me the boots gave her blisters. I made her grilled cheese when she didn't like what I was making for dinner and she told me I used the wrong kind of cheese. I helped her do her social studies project, bought the poster board, and drew the map of Newfoundland for her and she complained I made the Northern Peninsula too big.

I let everything go because I wanted her to like me and because Ray and I lived by an unwritten rule that we would each be responsible for disciplining our own children. We never spoke about it. It was just assumed. I treated Lolly better than my own child and she still hated me. She'd always hate me. It didn't matter whether I was kind or mean or indifferent. It seemed so hopeless all of a sudden that I sank down on the bed next to Floss in defeat. I didn't care anymore if the ice melted all over the floor or the meat spoiled and went bad. It seemed inevitable.

"Do you even love me?"

Floss asked the question so softly I could have imagined it. Ray heard it though, I knew he did. He stood in the middle of the cabin, surveying the damage he was after doing. He was ashamed by his outburst and his lack of self-control. His breath came in rapid puffs like he'd just been running at full speed. I knew he couldn't answer Floss. He wasn't the type to say that he loved you. He could show you but he couldn't tell you. He showed me in the darkness of our bedroom in the way he held me. He showed Lolly with the playful tug on her ponytail and I guess he showed Floss by paying for her braces and going to her school play. She didn't understand him but in that moment I did. I understood both of them. I just couldn't figure out how to make them understand one another. I put an arm around Floss and she wept quietly into my neck.

"Fuck," Ray said so softly it could have been an endearment—sweetheart, honey, duckie. "Fuck!" Louder this time. He was either going to break down and bawl or heave the cooler out into the woods altogether. He pulled at his moustache with his thumb and forefinger and then he turned and left. I heard the car start up and drive away. I thought he was being childish for running off like he did but I envied him all the same. I wanted to leave sometimes too, especially when things were so tense I felt my muscles seize up.

"He'll be back in a little bit," Lolly said reassuringly, although I think she was trying to reassure herself. She was mad with him too because he didn't take her with him. We were all mad at him, all three of us.

"Of course, he'll be back."

"He wouldn't have gotten so upset if Floss hadn't been so mean to him," Lolly insisted. "Why did you have to go and make him so mad?" Lolly's voice was shrill, went right through me. "Are you so high and mighty you can't eat a sandwich for supper?"

"Lolly!" I snapped at her but then stopped. I didn't have anything else to say save for her name.

"I hope he never comes back," Floss spat at her. "I hate him."

"Don't speak like that, Floss. He's my husband," I said defensively, as if the title afforded him some respect. Other mothers could say, *Don't talk to your father that way*, but, *He's my husband* was the best line I had.

I got up from the bed and started cleaning up the floor like I was trying to wipe away the entire incident. Four of the dozen eggs had broken. I held the egg carton aloft in one hand like I was protecting the good eggs and sopped up the broken ones with a paper towel. They were cold and slick in my palm.

"I do, Mom. I hate him."

"Why? Because he said your school play was boring. Because he wanted to have a sandwich for supper?" I was tired and frustrated and taking things out on Floss. Later, I would take it out on Ray. I was already thinking about all the things I was going to say to him to make him feel bad. It wasn't right the way he left me alone with the girls to clean up the mess he was after making.

"Because I'm the only one in this family he doesn't love."

I dropped the rest of the eggs after she said it, breaking the whole lot of them.

"Fuck," I whispered softly, just like Ray had said it. "Fuck." I longed to be in that car with him heading somewhere, anywhere but where we'd ended up.

Ray came back at the first sign of daylight. The sky was pink again and he was loading up the car all over, throwing bags in the trunk that didn't even get opened. Me and Lolly and Floss stood in the doorway and watched him pack up everything.

"We're going back home," he announced. "Get your shoes on."

Ray pulled into one of the Irving restaurants for breakfast about a half hour into the drive. He was trying to tell Floss he was sorry for bawling at her but he couldn't say that. He just wanted to buy her eggs and sausage but she didn't have an appetite for it. None of us did.

lolly

"Well, what do you think?" Carson gestures around the room with a sweep of his hand. The interior of the cabin is rustic. Everything in it is purely functional. Nothing on the walls save for two hooks to hang jackets and lanterns, no decorative throws for cold nights, not even a mat to wipe your feet. It's different than Gabe's parents' cabin, which is done up almost better than their house. Carson's cabin is more like the one my father dragged us to all those years ago, only to drag us back the next morning.

"It reminds me of a family vacation a long time ago," I answer. "We rented a cabin for a weekend, but we all got into a fight and left the morning after we arrived." I can almost picture a younger version of myself hanging back behind the door, upset that Dad went and ran off without taking me with him.

"What were you fighting about?" Carson unpacks a small bag of groceries, laying the contents on the counter—two steaks, three potatoes, garlic salt, a small bag of onions, and a tin of mushrooms.

"What to have for supper."

Carson laughs aloud at this explanation. "Well I was going to grill up some steaks on the barbecue later but I don't want you storming off or anything about it."

"It wasn't really about what to eat."

"It never is," he says soberly, wrapping his arms around me. He doesn't ask what it was really about. I would have been at a loss to explain it anyway. I'd felt so miserable that night, sitting on the bed with Floss and Marie, listening for the sound of Dad's car, waiting to see the headlights light up the wall behind me. I was afraid he was never going to come back for me but Marie kept rubbing my hair and whispering that he just needed to cool off. I didn't know if she was comforting me or herself. The anger had worn off her by then and she seemed more scared than anything.

The next day I watched Floss put away her swimsuit that still had the tags on it, sweatshirts and folded socks. She slammed drawers like she was mad but I knew she wasn't. She was feeling guilty about ruining our vacation.

"I s'pose you hate me now too," she said.

"You did me a favour. I didn't want to go to that stupid cabin to begin with."

Floss shook her head at me disapprovingly. I watched her unpack her pajamas, shorts, a hairbrush, sunscreen even though her skin never got to see the light of day, a camera with twenty-four shots and not a single one taken. I felt bad that she didn't get to take pictures but at the same time I was relieved there would be no mementos of the disastrous trip. I'd never get the image of my father kicking the cooler out of my mind. It didn't seem like him at all. It was like he'd been possessed by someone else. I didn't need to be reminded of it.

"Well I wanted to go," she whined. That much was apparent by all the things she'd packed up in the grocery bags. I'd only taken a change of clothes but Floss had taken everything you could think of. "Vacations are supposed to be a break, but this was just like every other day," Floss sighed as she folded a T-shirt and put it back inside her drawer.

I wanted to protest. It wasn't like every other day. Every other day we muddled along, each of us caught up in our own business—work, homework, supper. This was worse than every other day because it highlighted everything that was wrong with us, brought it out into broad daylight.

I could hear Dad puttering around in the yard and I looked out the window at him. He was setting up the tent. I groaned and Floss joined me at the window.

"What's he doing?"

"It's for us," I told Floss. "He feels bad."

"I don't want to sleep out in the yard," Floss protested. "There's bugs and teenagers, and it's going to be cold out when the sun goes down."

"Neither do I but we're going to do it anyway." I expected her to argue. I wouldn't have done it if I was her but Floss seemed resigned to it. It was like she knew it was the only thing that would make everything go back to normal, and as bad as normal was, it was better than this.

We slept out in the yard that night with Dad watching over us from the deck the whole time, and by morning, we were all grateful for normal.

Carson is different from Gabe. His chest is broader, his arms more muscular, even his body hair darker and more coarse. I make note of these comparisons as I slip a hand under Carson's T-shirt and run it up over his chest until it finds the back of his neck. I'm bold in my exploration of his body, taking more liberties than I ever did with Gabe. Gabe was the only one I'd ever had sex with and I always followed his lead, touched him the way he told me to, tentative that I might be doing it all wrong. There doesn't seem to be any wrong way to touch Carson. With every movement I make, his breathing becomes more excited. I can feel the heat coming from him, his skin feverish. I can't tell if it's the passion or the sunburn. We both got burnt today even though it didn't feel that hot by the water. My skin feels tight, tender, and scorched. The sun is setting now, the sky glows with streaks of tangerine. The last remnants of the sun filter through the green curtains of the cabin, casting shadows over Carson's face. I can feel his erection through his jeans, feel the shape of him outlined against the worn fabric. He groans in response to my touch, kisses my neck. Everything about the day has been perfect, and I shudder with anticipation of what might be next.

"Are you on the pill?" The question reverberates in my ear, takes a few moments for me to process.

"What?" My head is swimming now, murky images of Gabe, Gabe with his broken condom, the look of panic all over his face.

"It was an accident," I say defensively. "Gabe used a condom. It just broke. We were always careful." Carson shifts onto his side, rubs his thumb over my knuckles. I regretted a lot of things but I never regretted becoming a mother. "I wouldn't change a thing."

"What's this about, Laura? I never meant to suggest...." Carson's voice trails off, unsure of what it was he's suggested in the first place, trying to make sense of how we transitioned from would-be lovers to this, whatever this was. My insides twist painfully at the sudden realization that Carson won't love Kenny the way me and Gabe do. It's not his fault. Marie thought my father could love Floss, and she could love me. They were in love with one another and they had the best of intentions but it wasn't enough. I picture Carson kicking over a cooler of food while Kenny watches, his big eyes as sad and desperate as Floss' were that day.

I think of how Kenny might react to the sudden appearance of Carson in our lives. He would be jealous, I was sure of it. I was jealous of Marie, of the way my father stood behind her at the kitchen table and rubbed her shoulders while she sipped her morning coffee. I was jealous of the way she curled up next to him on the couch and by the way they shut the bedroom door at night. Dad never shut his door until then and the sound always startled me, created a boundary that was never there before.

It would be hard for Kenny. He crawls into the bed with me in the middle of the night all the time and I'd have to tell him he couldn't do it anymore. He'd blame Carson, act out and on and on it would go. I picture Kenny trying to tell me something. It would take him ages to spit it out, as it takes him forever to form a coherent thought. It takes Kenny twenty minutes to tell me he has to go to the bathroom. Gabe and I find this amusing, endearing even. I've seen Gabe leave ten minutes later for work because Kenny hasn't finished telling him about a commercial he just saw on television. Carson would likely find this habit more irritating than entertaining. He'd tune him out after a while, oblivious to Kenny's fervent excitement over a new flavour of cereal.

I can hear my ears crack as if I were descending somewhere too rapidly.

"Laura, what's wrong?"

"I keep thinking about Kenny."

"What about him?"

"What if he doesn't like you? What if you don't like him?"

"One step at a time, Laura. You're jumping the gun aren't you?"

I picture my father standing in the doorway with the towel wrapped around his waist, bawling at my mother, "You're jumping the gun again. You're always jumping the gun." I feel a rush of satisfaction at having at least that much in common with her.

"My father used to say that to my mother all the time."

"Your father was a very smart man then." Carson smiles at me, brings my lips to his.

I had a lot of regrets, more than most people accrued in a lifetime. I didn't want any more. This time Carson's hands begin an exploration of me. With each touch it's like he's erasing every single one of my regrets. He gives me a clean slate and then he makes love to me with the same range and mix of emotions I've come to expect of him, hot and intense, sweet and playful. I've never been with anyone but Gabe and it feels strange to lie with someone else, someone who doesn't have a mole on his right shoulder, or a smattering of freckles on his arm that resembles a crown. It feels strange to have Carson with his muscular legs wrapped around mine, to smooth my fingers over his wiry chest hair. I lay my head on his chest until it grows damp with sweat and I feel stuck, my cheek molded to his shoulder.

I'm just drifting off to sleep when it occurs to me that my mother wasn't really jumping the gun at all. She was dying and she seemed to know it. It was my father who jumped the gun when he took up with Marie, and I didn't know if that made him smart or foolish.

marie

"I'm going up I tell ya. This time I'm going up." Ray slapped the cologne on his neck just like they did in the commercials. It was a gesture filled with sex appeal made even more heady by the smell of leather and sandalwood that filled the room. I thought better of going out at all, thought about making a night of it at home. Doris had the girls overnight for our anniversary, and it was probably the only time we'd ever have the house to ourselves. I wanted to hop in the bed with him right then and there, stay with my arms around him without interruption until the sun came up.

"Go on, Ray. You are not getting up there on that stage and embarrassing yourself like that. Not to mention how mortified I'd be."

"I just want to see if I can be hypnotized."

"And if Raveen puts you in some trance you're going to go making a fool out of yourself in front of the whole Arts and Culture Centre. I might have to disown you. Either that or I'll have to ask Raveen to put you under long enough to show you how to put your socks in the hamper."

I pulled on my stockings and walked into my dress. It had been so long since we went out like this, which we almost never did. The girls and no money was the perfect combination for nights spent at home in front of the television. I was surprised when Ray showed up with the tickets to see The Man They Call Raveen. It seemed too indulgent for someone like Ray. I didn't think he believed in all of that, at least not enough to throw so much of his money at it.

"They say smart people, and people with a real good imagination, are the easiest ones to hypnotize. And if I do get hypnotized, they give you free tickets to the next night's show."

"Surely God you're not going to go strutting around stage like a rooster so you can get free tickets." That was my Ray, cheap in a way that was downright entertaining. "You don't really believe in all that do you, Ray?"

"What, being hypnotized?"

"Hypnosis, mysticism, all that foolishness. I'd have figured you'd think all those people running across the stage were planted there. It just seems sort of gullible to me."

Ray looked hurt, mildly insulted. "I believe in a lot of things you can't necessarily explain or put your finger on."

"Like what?"

"I don't know, just things. Fate, life, the afterlife," he said as he knotted his tie. It was the same one he wore to our wedding, and before that to his wife's funeral. This was the third time he put it on.

"Like heaven? Do you believe in heaven?" I don't know why we hadn't had this conversation before. We'd been married three years and hadn't ever had such a philosophical conversation. We'd been too preoccupied with talking about more pressing matters—work schedules and car insurance rates. We talked about what to make for dinner and what colour to paint the fence and what time the Shoppers Drug Mart closed on a Sunday. I'd never seen this side to Ray before. He'd always been so practical. Everything he did was functional.

"Of course I believe in heaven. You don't?" He looked at me, his brow furrowed in confusion. It was his turn to wonder about me. What kind of person didn't believe in heaven? It seemed impossible to comprehend.

I shrugged, dabbed perfume behind my ear even though I'd already applied it after I got out of the shower. "Do you think your first wife is in heaven?" I hated to call her his first wife. It made me sound like a runner-up, a consolation prize.

"I suppose so."

"So when you die, are you going to spend all eternity with her or me?" It was accusatory the way I asked the question, like I caught him running around with her. All he'd really done was to profess his faith.

"Well what kind of a question is that, Marie?"

"It's a perfectly valid question. If you believe in heaven, what comes to mind when you think about it? Do you see you and her reunited, floating about with your goddamn haloes and angel wings while you wait for your daughter?" I was shouting, trying not to cry but the effort drove my voice higher. I was grateful Floss and Lolly weren't home even though they'd witnessed enough of our arguments. "And where do I fit in your precious afterlife? Are we all one big happy extended family up there, or do you just end up with the one you loved the most on earth? Who is it, Ray? Me or her?"

I knew it was crazy. Surely we weren't at a loss for things to fight about that I had to go picking an argument with him over which wife he wanted to spend all eternity with. I was tired of having the kinds of arguments we had and wanted desperately to fight over the kinds of things everyone else fought about—dirty dishes left on the counter, too much money spent at the mall, toenail clippings left on the coffee table. Our fights were always about not being loved enough, or not loving one another's kids enough. They were exhausting and destructive.

"You're out of your fucking mind, woman." Ray shut the dresser drawer with so much force the bottles of cologne and perfume teetered on their edges and the mirror shook and vibrated against the bedroom wall. We looked at one another in the mirror then, our reflections showed things we couldn't see when we looked each other in the face.

Ray ended up being dismissed from the stage by Raveen along with a throng of others who couldn't seem to focus enough to shut everything else out. Ray came back to his seat, looking dejected. I felt guilty, that maybe it was my fault he couldn't be hypnotized. I'd distracted him by picking a fight.

"You were right I suppose," he said sheepishly during the intermission to the show. "Probably all just a crock." I felt bad for him since he seemed to want to believe in something other than the rut of everything we lived through day after day.

By the time we got home, the phone was ringing off the hook. It was Lolly of course, looking to come home. I could hear Ray whispering to her on the phone like he didn't want me to hear.

"What's the matter, sweetheart? Did you try watching television? How about a cup of hot chocolate? No my love, I didn't get hypnotized. I suppose so. All right, I'll come and get you."

Ray walked into the bedroom where I was changing, peeling off my pantyhose and debating whether or not to wrap up in my everyday bathrobe, or to slide under the sheets in my underwear. One was intended to deny him, the other a blatant invitation. Ray had turned down the heat before we left and it was cold in the house, especially without my clothes on. He stared at my discarded pantyhose with his hands stuffed in his pockets. He bit the top of his lip and cleared his throat. He didn't have to say anything since I already knew what was going to happen but I didn't want to let him off easy.

"Lolly wants to come home. She's having a rough night.

Can't sleep." He looked up at me for something, maybe encouragement, maybe understanding, but I didn't give it. "I'm going to go get her. Doris said Floss was asleep, but I can bring her home too if you wants. Or I can get her in the morning."

I stood and wrapped myself up in my bathrobe, pulled it tightly around my neck. I didn't want him to see me naked, wanted to deny him a glimpse of my breasts, nipples erect from the cold. I was punishing him, I realized, although it felt silly, even petty. I picked my pantyhose off the floor and balled them up in my palm and threw them in the garbage by the bedroom door. They didn't even have a run in them and it felt sinful to throw them out like that. I realized I was picking a fight in that one gesture, daring him to argue with me.

"And you says you can't be hypnotized? She's got the wool pulled right over your eyes. You spend most of the day walking around in the trance she's after putting over on you."

Ray sighed in frustration. I could hear it all escape in one breath and I knew there was more of it inside him. That it filled him up. "She says pretty much the same thing about you."

floss

My father is after getting worse. He looks even thinner and slighter than he did the last time I saw him in front of the house. He takes me by surprise not just in his sickly appearance but by the fact he's here in front of The Health Sciences looking for me in the first place. I thought he'd gone back to Calgary and I was relieved to be done with him.

He's only wearing short sleeves and his arms are bony, covered in goosebumps. He blows on his hands at the doors in front of the hospital and tucks them under his armpits. For the life of me I can't imagine him and my mother together, living in the same house, sleeping in the same bed. The very thought of it covers my own arms in goosebumps.

"Florence." He puts a hand on my arm to stop me from blowing past him. It feels cold, and the muscles in my arm contract in protest. I shake his hand off me, rub the spot where he touched like I was erasing the feel of him. "I need to talk to you," he says.

"I thought all you wanted to do was look at me. You never said anything about talking to me. I don't want to talk to you."

"I need you to do something for me."

I think he must be crazy with the illness, or maybe he'd always been that way. What did I know about him? I can't believe he has the nerve to come up to me and ask me for something. I don't know what he wants from me but I already know I'm going to say no. Even if all he wants is for me to buy him a cup of coffee, I'm not going to do it on principle alone.

"I'm on my way to work so I don't have time right now." A gust of wind blows from behind me, scattering an empty Tim Horton's coffee cup across the parking lot. "Don't you have a jacket?" My tone is accusatory, the way Lolly sometimes speaks to Kenny. *What are you after doing with your socks? Did you take them off outside?*

"I don't need a jacket. Don't need much of anything anymore. Summer's coming and I ain't planning on being around much longer anyway." The wind blows in our faces now. His eyes tear up with the force of it.

"Do you need money?"

"No." He shakes his head.

"Then what do you want from me?" I wish the cancer would spread faster. It seemed like years since I saw him in Calgary. I wish he'd get on with it already. It's too late for him to try to be a part of my life at this stage.

"I'm dying, Florence," he says. "I'm too far gone now for them to make any difference."

I pull my hood up over my head. Sections of my hair are already blowing out of my ponytail and curling around the sides of my face. I'm afraid he can read my mind, hear me wishing his cancer would hurry up. "I know," I say impatiently.

"I stopped the treatment. I'm done with doctors."

"You should probably get something to make you comfortable."

"I'm comfortable enough. Besides, I got a plan for all that." He doesn't strike me as the type of person who makes plans and I almost laugh at how ridiculous the thought is. That and the fact he's just sworn off doctors in front of the biggest hospital in St. John's. He blows again on his hands, red and raw with the skin peeling off of them.

"Can you to do something for me?"

I feel a sense of trepidation. "What do you want?" I sound frustrated when I say it, just the way Lolly asks Kenny the same question when he says he's hungry but he doesn't want peanut butter crackers, or grapes, or cereal, or a tin of noodle soup.

"I'm going to be cremated," he tells me. "I already took care of it. I prearranged it with Barrett's."

I'm taken aback again at this version of Danny Donovan, a man who threw away years of his life only to plan for the future when there was none to be had. "Lots of people are doing that now," I say approvingly.

"I want you to have the ashes. You can scatter them around some place if you want." He says this as if he were bestowing a rare honour upon me. "Barrett's will call you when they're ready."

"No thanks, I don't want them," I say politely as if I were declining a cup of tea. I wish I could be angrier. I wish I could tell him to fuck off again like I did that time I saw him outside the house in front of Ray's tree but I can't. I try to dig up some deep-seated anger but the best I have is mild annoyance.

"I'm not scared," he says reassuringly, like I'd asked him to comfort me.

"Me either." I don't know why I say it since it isn't me who is sick. I'm not afraid of losing him. I never had him to begin with.

It wasn't like the time Ray had his heart attack. I was terrified at the sight of him in the hospital, big, strong, and quiet Ray with a bag of his own piss filling up alongside of him. He was why I wanted to look after sick people, why I wanted to work at a hospital. I didn't care about all the anatomy and the technical things, although it was good to know. I remember wanting to look after Ray so bad, hold his hand and tell him everything was fine even though I'd never held it before.

marie

The day Ray got out of intensive care, we all went to the hospital to see him. I expected him to be in a good mood. After all, he'd survived a heart attack, he'd had a blockage removed from his artery, his prognosis was excellent. He hadn't seen the girls since the morning he wouldn't let me call an ambulance until I'd got them off to school. They were anxious to see him again.

He sat up in the bed when we came in and I expected him to give us a welcoming smile, hugs all around, introduce us to the two other men on the ward. I was ready for a celebration. I did my hair, applied lipstick, and wore a ruffled skirt.

"Hi sweetheart," I said brightly with Floss and Lolly trailing behind me. Ray looked better than he did when he was in intensive care, but he still had that sickly look to him. He had bags under his eyes despite the fact he'd slept more over the past three days than he did in the past month. His skin seemed looser, sagged around his neck and exposed moles and freckles I hadn't noticed before. The skin on his hands was thin and bruised up from all the needles and IV's they had going into him.

I kissed him on the cheek and rubbed the lipstick off with my thumb. Someone had given him a shave since yesterday. I traced a finger over a purple vein that protruded on the back of his hand.

"Jesus, Marie," he said, pulling his hand back. "I fucking told you not to bring them in here."

It was all bad enough Ray bawled at me in front of the girls, but there were two other patients in the room, and a nurse who was checking temperatures. My face burned with embarrassment. He didn't even speak so harshly to me when it was just the two of us all alone.

"The girls wanted to see you, Ray," I defended myself. "They missed you and you're nearly good as new now." Other than yelling at me for bringing Floss and Lolly into the hospital, Ray refused to acknowledge them. They hung back along the side of the bed, watching him and waiting for him to wave them over. "How are you feeling?" I asked him

"How do you think I'm feeling?"

"The doctors say you're going to be fine. You just have to look after yourself a bit better." I wondered if the doctors had told same thing to the other two men on the ward. One of them had a tin of Pepsi opened up and the other one had his hand in a bag of cheezies.

"Hey there, Ray. Is that your family?" The old man in the bed across from Ray sat up and stared at the four of us.

"Yes, Walter," Ray conceded like he'd been caught having the audacity to have a family that cared about him. "This is my wife, and my daughters." He didn't bother to introduce us all by name. He didn't plan on being there long enough to bother. It didn't matter. "They're not staying."

"You look good, Ray," I lied. He looked thinner every-where, even his skin looked paper thin, especially in the places where it hugged the bones. I was afraid to touch it. It looked like it might crack and tear.

"Yeah well I don't feel good. I feel like I got run over by a truck. What the hell you got done to your hair?"

I self-consciously smoothed the back of my neck, tucked a lock of hair behind my ear and began rooting around in my purse, pretending to look for something. "Nothing," I said shrugging. "I just got it blown out."

"While I'm laid up here you're off to the beauty parlor are you?" He spat it at me in an angry accusation. I could see the spit gather in the corner of his mouth, his face got redder and I was afraid the machines were going to start up beeping dangerously. I didn't know what was wrong with him. He looked like he was going to have another heart attack and all because I'd done my hair. "What? Are you getting ready to find another man to look after you in case I don't walk out of here? Jesus, you looks like you're off to my funeral already."

"Ray," I whispered. My eyes watered up and I sniffed in response. I could feel Lolly's and Floss' eyes on me. I shouldn't have brought them. "What's wrong with you?" I choked out the question, put a hand over my mouth, and started to bawl quietly. Ray looked down at his bruised hands, flexed them like he was trying to regain the feeling in them.

Floss pointed to the bag of urine on the side of Ray's bed. "Is there a bag for your shit too?" Floss asked. "I think you're going to need one because you're full of shit, Ray."

I wanted to reprimand her but I couldn't find my voice. "Get out," Ray said quietly. "Both of you," he said waving his hand at the two of them. "Just go outside and wait for a little bit. I got to talk to Marie and your mother for a few minutes." It sounded like I was two separate people the way he said it.

When they were gone he said, "I've just been thinking about what's going to happen if I die."

"You're not going to die for a very long time," I said reassuringly, like I knew something nobody else did.

"Lolly." I waited for him to say more but he needed a few

minutes to say it in his head first. "Can you look after Lolly for me? You're the only family she's got left. I got a sister in Halifax but she don't know Lolly and I wouldn't want her to have to move."

"Stop it, Ray, you're being crazy."

"Just…will you?"

"Of course I would. Of course I'll look after Lolly." I thought about what I would do if it were me in the hospital bed. Would I ask Ray to look after Floss? It seemed more of a symbolic gesture at this point anyway. They were both nearly grown now, and some days I thought it was a wonder that our marriage had held up. It didn't seem fair that our health had to go right when we were done raising the girls. I prayed in my head for a few more good years.

"I did something that's going to hurt you." I felt Ray look at me and I followed suit reluctantly, looked up into his face. The whites of his eyes were yellowed, jaundiced looking. I couldn't imagine what Ray had done to hurt me. He didn't have time to fool around, and besides, he was too cheap to keep a woman. "It was a long time ago." I wished he'd shut up. I didn't want to hear it, whatever it was. "It's about when I die."

"Stop it. Stop talking like that." He was talking in circles and I wanted him to stop.

"I been thinking a lot about it here in the hospital and I thought about changing things to make it easier for you but then I'd end up hurting Lolly. That's kind of the story of my life, Marie. Who am I going to piss off today, my wife or my daughter? Sometimes it's both of you in one shot."

I couldn't seem to stop crying even though I didn't know what he was trying to tell me. Perhaps it was just to say he wished we could have done some things differently.

Ray coughed into his fist and sat himself upright, reached for my hand. "You asked me one time who I was going to meet in heaven and I just wanted to tell you now, before it's too late, that it's you. I'll be waiting for you even if it don't seem like it all the time."

I got cold shivers along the tops of my arms and on the back of my neck. I didn't know what he'd done but I knew I'd forgive him anything after he said that. Anyway, I figured whatever he'd done would go to the grave with him. I didn't know how I would ever find out what he'd done if he wasn't ever going to tell me.

floss

Leo is making bacon and eggs. I can smell it circulating from the kitchen and into the bedroom. I can hear it too, the sizzle from the frying pan, the spit of grease that used to make my mother jump back from the stove and curse at it, like it was deliberately trying to hurt her. *Ow! Sonofabitch*, she'd yell at it, rubbing her arm protectively where the grease smacked her. I don't imagine Leo would even flinch. His cut was deep that day and he sat at the kitchen table talking about superheroes with Kenny like he didn't even feel it. Leo is the type of person who saves all his hurt up for the inside.

I wonder if he's making pancakes too. He says pancakes are Faith's favourite food, that she even likes it when he makes them for supper. *I'm pretty good at it now. I'll make them for you one time*, he said and I pictured me and the little girl sitting at the small table in the kitchen passing the bottle of syrup back and forth until our fingers got sticky from the way it oozed out over the sides.

I think about hunting around Leo's dresser drawers for one of his undershirts or a T-shirt to wear, maybe finding the

233

one he wore to the doctor's office that day, with his last name on the back. Lolly was always wearing Gabe's clothes, his hoodies and his sweatshirts, and Mom was always complaining it was all bad enough she had to wash Lolly's clothes but did she have to wash Gabe's too? It wasn't like Lolly didn't have plenty of her own clothes. I asked her once why she was always wearing his hockey jerseys with Hillier on the back and she shrugged at me. "So everyone knows he's mine." I didn't quite understand her then, but I get it now. I don't do it though. It feels too presumptive to go through his dresser drawers and start putting his clothes on.

I lay in his bed listening to the coffee dripping in the glass pot, and to Leo's movements in the kitchen. He's either clumsy, or just loud. He's dropped one utensil or another on the kitchen floor four times. He sets the glasses of juice on the table with more force than necessary and he mixes the eggs with such vigour I imagine they might be meringue before he gets them into the pan.

I close my eyes, remembering the previous night, how Leo had lain above me, the light from the bathroom lending him a ghostly quality. His skin was pale, his lips translucent, and his hair glowed from both the clock radio and the phone charging on his nightstand. *Are you sure?* he whispered to me although he didn't wait for an answer, just shifted his weight and began making love to me. I was certain the question was intended more for himself.

It's quiet in the kitchen now, eerily so. When I first heard Leo in the kitchen I thought he might be bringing me break-fast in bed. I didn't want to ruin his surprise by getting up, but I can tell now that he's waiting for me at the kitchen table. He'll think I don't want to be with him, that I'm ashamed about the previous night. The eggs must be growing cold and no one can eat cold eggs, so I throw on my clothes from the previous evening—jeans, a wrinkled pink T-shirt that still has a stain of oil from the salad dressing. It's set in now. Even Mom won't be able to get it out. I again contemplate putting on one of his shirts but think better of it. I can only find one sock so I venture out into the hallway barefoot. I smooth a hand over my hair before I enter the kitchen. It must look wild. It always does in the morning but there was no mirror in Leo's bedroom.

"Good morning. I made breakfast," Leo says awkwardly, stating the obvious. He fidgets nervously with a napkin.

"It looks delicious," I lie. The eggs look undercooked, jiggle on the plate as if they might get up and make a run for it. The bacon is undercooked too, the meaty parts curling up around the translucent fatty parts. There's no pancakes.

"You have a good time last night?" Leo takes a sip of coffee and looks expectantly at me.

"Oh yes," I nod. "It was a nice night." I'm not sure if he's referring to the restaurant or to what happened when we came back here.

"That's the first time I've been with anyone else since I got married." He looks at his coffee when he says this and his fingers drum on the kitchen table in a rapid tempo. His fingernails are chewed past the skin so the effect is hollow and loud, like a bass drum.

"Oh." I don't know how to process the information. I don't know whether to feel special that it was me who broke his streak of celibacy or insulted that he refers to having sex with me in the same breath as getting married. His eyes dart up from his coffee cup but then dart down again so quickly I might have imagined his glance. He's looking for a compliment, or more likely, reassurance. Insecurity is a familiar feeling, one that I'd never thought of as endearing until I see this brief display by Leo.

"Well, you did great," I offer and then cringe. I sound like Lolly congratulating Kenny on wiping his own arse or putting his own socks on. Perhaps I should have been more enthusiastic last night, moaned louder, cried out his name, ran my fingernails down his back or simply wept when it was over from the sheer power of his lovemaking.

Leo coughs into his fist, takes another sip of coffee.

"It was nice," I tell him. "Amazing. Earth shattering." I grip my hands on the edge of the table in dramatic fashion and he wads a paper towel up into a ball and tosses it across the table. I giggle back at him and take a bite of toast, the least offensive thing he's cooked. "So what would you like to do today?"

"I have plans," Leo says checking his watch as if he had to leave any minute.

Plans. The very word is ominous, shrouded in mystery with an air of exclusion. I wonder what sort of plans he has that he would refer to them as plans. If they weren't ominous he would just say what he was doing, like that he had to get the oil changed in the van or he was going fishing with a cousin.

"Oh, okay," I say quietly. I'm relieved now I'm not wearing one of his shirts. I would feel foolish about that now.

"Floss..." he starts out gently. "It's my weekend with Faith. We're going to the park. And to the movies later. I picked up the tickets for the two thirty showing last night. It gets sold out fast. We're playing cards tonight, and I bought cheesy popcorn. She likes that."

By the time he's finished telling me all of this, his face is flush with excitement. It wouldn't bother me so much save for the fact he doesn't put in near this much effort in planning our outings. We watch television, order in food. Sometimes we go out to eat but nothing fancy. I get the sense I'm around to fill the space between visits with Faith. Leo might have time for only one relationship right now, and it isn't with me. Of course saying any of this will make me seem petty and jealous. It was the way my mother must have felt, smiling at the door and waving to Ray and Lolly as they traipsed off to the cemetery on

Mother's Day. As soon as they pulled out of the driveway she went back to her room to lie down, told me she had a headache.

"We'll get together next week," Leo says, laying a warm hand on top of mine. It feels like I've been dismissed, sent away until he has use for me again.

"I'd like to meet her. Your daughter. When do I get to meet her? Maybe I could go to the park with you guys sometime."

"Not yet." He shakes his head as if I'd suggested something outlandish.

"When then? Why not? I mean at what point…." They are all the same questions, just a different way of asking. Leo is silent. I've made him uncomfortable and I don't care. In fact, I'm glad I've made him feel this way since he didn't think much of making me feel awkward.

It's stuffy in the small kitchen now. It smelled of bacon and coffee a few moments ago but now all I can smell is the stench of grease and burnt toast. The beads of fat from the bacon have congealed into tiny iridescent pearls.

"I'll have to ask Cathy if it's okay. See what she says."

"Why do you have to ask Cathy?"

"Because she's Faith's mother. I'd like to know, if it was the other way around."

"You're so considerate." My sarcasm is lost on him. "What if she says no?" I feel powerless and the feeling is awful. I get a terrible thought then, a wicked thought that makes me lower my gaze to rest on my lap. My mother was lucky Lolly's mother was dead. Ray never had to ask anyone's permission to bring Lolly around. He might have left her on Mother's Day, but it was only one day.

marie

Mother's Day loomed over our heads. It was our first and we didn't know how we were supposed to celebrate, if at all. There were commercials on the television for flowers and ads all over *The Telegram* for Mother's Day lunches and brunches. Jewellery stores advertised charms and rings with birthstones set in white gold. Neither Ray nor I talked about it but it was hard to escape. Even the weather forecasters talked about whether or not the sun was going to shine on Mother's Day, as if Mother Nature could have it any other way. Every time it was mentioned on the TV, Ray would stare straight ahead, making a concerted effort not to look at me. I looked at him though, almost dared him with my stare but his gaze remained transfixed, the only sign he was aware of my eyes on him was the redness that crept up from his neck to his cheeks.

There was no doubt it was going to be an awkward holiday. I was a wife and a mother, although not the mother of his child. There was no precedent and even though I knew we should discuss it beforehand, I also knew he didn't want to have the conversation, would roll over and pretend to be asleep if it were at night, rush off to work if it were morning, or run out on an errand if it were the weekend. Avoidance was Ray's favourite coping mechanism. He always waited until the last minute to tell you something bad.

He announced his and Lolly's plans before I even made it out of the bed to relieve myself. Then I couldn't make it out of bed if I tried. I couldn't move and not because I had no feeling in my extremities. Rather, they felt oversensitive. I could feel every drop of blood coursing through my veins, every pathway to and from my heart was on fire.

Ray put a hand on my shoulder and I flinched. His hand was rough, calloused and hot. My flesh singed. I could swear I smelled the tiny hairs on my arm burn. Floss would tell me later she burned toast trying to make me breakfast in bed.

"You okay?" Ray asked. He rubbed his hand up and down my arm to comfort me but I pulled it away, rolled over to look at the nightstand. I could hear Ray sigh behind me, felt the weight of him the way he threw himself back down onto the mattress. I knew he rested his arm across his forehead. It was the position he found most comfortable. I liked tugging on the hairs under his arm when he lay like that, giggled at the way his arm sprung protectively back down. He had reflexes like a cat. I'm going to end up clocking you in the head one of these days if you don't be careful, he'd warn, but he'd be laughing too.

"I'm fine," I mumbled.

"Tell me that you understand, sweetheart." He never called me sweetheart. He was feeling guilty, although it wouldn't make him change his mind.

"I understand."

"No you don't."

"What do you want me to say, Ray?" I turned around to face him. "It's just a stupid holiday so you can spend it however you like."

"Okay then. Good." He looked relieved. He was so stupid sometimes. Didn't even know when I was mad, and sometimes didn't even know we were fighting until we were halfway through an argument.

"Fuck off, Ray," I spat at him. I got out of bed, wrapped my bathrobe so tightly around my waist I felt the air leave me. I still had to pee but I wanted to finish our argument. I wanted him to know how deeply he'd wounded me. I wanted him to hurt as much as I did. He just lay there in the bed, bare-chested and stone-faced, waiting for what was going to come out of my mouth. It didn't matter what I said, or how loud I said it. It wouldn't change a thing. Ray would still go about his day exactly as he had planned it.

He wanted to spend Mother's Day with Lolly, just Lolly. They planned it together, a secret outing that no one told me about. I couldn't imagine when they had time to discuss it. They would get flowers and go to the cemetery and lay them on Ray's wife's grave to wither and die and be blown about. Then they would go out to eat, just the two of them. They'd probably talk about her, how pretty and nice and sweet she was and how sad they both were to have lost her. Lolly would say how much she missed her mother and how much she hated me.

I did not give birth to Lolly, but I did all the things a mother was supposed to do. It was only a few weeks ago I took her to the doctor when she woke up with a high fever, and I checked on her every few hours, feeling her forehead and refilling her juice. I was even beginning to love her a little bit. And that, I thought, deserved more recognition on Mother's Day than anything. I couldn't believe the day could pass without either of them showing me a little bit of gratitude. I tasted the bitterness in the back of my throat. It felt thick, dark, and poisonous.

I sat back down on the edge of the bed, my back to Ray

with my hands in my lap. My fingers were cold, the tips nearly white. I'd never felt so helpless in my entire life. I couldn't argue. How could I get upset for a little girl wanting to lay flowers on her mother's grave on Mother's Day? It would make me everything Lolly already thought I was. I felt defeated, exhausted, out of breath. I didn't know if I had the strength to keep going. No matter what I did, she'd never feel anything for me that came close to the feelings she had for her mother.

"It's okay, Ray," I sighed.

"Okay," he echoed. "That's it?" He seemed almost disappointed. "So you're not mad?"

"No." This was true. I was many things—hurt, sad, empty—but angry wasn't one of them.

"So you understand then?" This was half of Ray's problem. He never wanted to talk about anything, but once he started he didn't know when to leave well enough alone.

"Yes, Ray. I understand." *It doesn't mean I have to like it.*

He kneeled up on the bed, pressed his chest against my back. I could feel the hairs on his chest prick me through the thin fabric of the robe, felt his erection in the small of my back. I closed my eyes while he lifted the hair from my back and kissed the side of my neck. I wanted to deny him just a little, but I responded anyway.

Floss walked in on us at that moment. Ray moved quickly to cover himself with a towel left on the bottom of the bed from his shower the night before.

"Jesus Christ, can't you fuckin' knock!" Ray shouted. The plate of eggs and toast and coffee slid off the tray Floss was holding in her hands, soiling the carpet with jam, and soaking it with coffee.

"I'm sorry," Floss said, although we didn't know if it was for walking in on us or for making such a mess. Probably both. She stood there staring at Ray's half-naked body, not knowing whether she should run out or bend down to pick the food up off the floor. "I just wanted to make you breakfast for Mother's Day," she said softly, shielding her eyes from Ray like the sun was in them. She kneeled down, turned the mug right side up and surveyed the damage.

"Just leave it," Ray snapped and Floss bolted from the room, crying.

"Oh for Christ's sake, Ray. Why do you have to be yelling at her like that?"

"She saw me thing!" He said this with a certain measure of indignation, as if it justified his tone of voice. I would have laughed under any other circumstances. Ray and I would have both laughed but these weren't any ordinary circumstances.

"She didn't see anything. Now put it away." I got up and started piling the food back onto the plate. I took the towel Ray had hidden himself behind earlier and kneeled over the coffee stain, dabbing at it until the towel was beige and saturated with the bitterness of the coffee. I kept my back to him but I could still feel him watching me. He was sorry but he didn't know what to say. It didn't matter because I wouldn't have known what to say back to him anyway. "I s'pose you should get going to the florist now. It'll probably be crowded today."

It wasn't the first time I felt that our family was truly divided. But it was the first time I felt Ray and I weren't even on the same team.

lolly

I know something is wrong by the way Gabe's mom keeps rubbing her hands together, like she's applying hand cream except there is no cream. Her hands are dry and red and they make a sandpapery sound when she rubs them against one another. She's doing lunch dishes, a wet tea towel draped over her shoulder from where I interrupted her. I can see a handful of bubbles on her wrist she didn't wipe off when I knocked on the door.

"Lolly, what are you doing here?" There's surprise but there's also a sharpness to her voice. It feels strange given that I practically grew up in this house, called it home a year earlier.

"I just came to pick up Kenny a little early." I try to sound confident and assured, but I already feel like I'm in the wrong being here.

"A little? Sure it's only one o'clock. Gabe said you weren't coming till five. That's four hours from now." She points out this fact like she was speaking to Kenny, even going so far as to hold up four fingers in front of me. Her eyes dart up the road every now and then and squint at every approaching

243

car. Normally she would invite me in, offer me a bowl of her ambrosia while I waited. Four hours used to be nothing. *Stay for a snack. Stay for dinner. Mr. Hillier will bring you home later.*

"I know. I just wanted to come by and see Kenny." I feel an unexpected rush of anger at Gabe's mother for having to explain my presence.

"Gabe took Kenny out for a bit. You can come back later, or Gabe can drop him off. Why don't we do that, let Gabe drop him off. No need for you to be going out again." She speaks faster than normal, fidgets nervously with the tea towel, no longer on her shoulder but out in front of her, concealing her chapped hands.

"Where did they go?"

"I don't know. Perhaps out for a drive." She's a bad liar. It's starting to drizzle outside and no one goes out for a drive in the rain. No one goes out for a drive at all anymore, not without a destination. Kenny especially doesn't like drives. He gets bored. He complains he's hungry and thirsty and has to go to the bathroom. He thinks it's a long drive to the supermarket and we're only in the car for five minutes. There's no way Gabe would take him out for a casual drive. Mrs. Hillier massages her lower back, as if the strain of lying to me were giving her a body ache. Gabe could never lie either.

"He said he might take him to Tim Horton's for a doughnut, but he didn't say which one. They're all over the place now, sure you'll never find him." She says this as if I was contemplating getting back in my car and driving from one Tim Horton's to the other.

"Can I wait?"

"Oh Lolly," Mrs. Hillier sighs deeply and I think she's about to reveal something to me. "You should have called first."

"I guess," I say quietly, but it's not near what I want to say. *Who are you to tell me that I have to call and make an appointment to see my own child?* But there's too much history to say such a thing. There were too many afternoons spent in meek acquiescence to the kind of authority she wielded as Gabe's mother. *Thank you, Mrs. Hillier. That was delicious, Mrs. Hillier. How are you feeling today, Mrs. Hillier?* Marie would have had a stroke if she saw the polite respect I afforded Gabe's mom. I saved up all my rebellion for Marie. I wanted Gabe's mother to like me. I wanted Marie to love me. *Fuck you, Mrs. Hillier.*

Gabe pulls into the driveway, startling both of us. Mrs. Hillier jumps a little at the sound of the tires on the driveway and swallows hard. Gabe doesn't notice me standing on his front porch because if he did he wouldn't have pulled in the driveway. He would have circled around the block a few times and waited until it was safe. He would have told Kenny to be quiet while they drove around the neighbourhood, because he needed to concentrate on finding a route I wouldn't drive near. But he didn't drive away because he was too preoccupied to notice me.

I see his face through the car window. He has the visor down like it's a blinding sun even though a fine mist has already settled on the windshield. He's smiling, laughing, having a grand old time. I can hardly remember the last time I'd seen him smile like that. A woman sits next to him in the passenger seat. She wears the same stupid grin and turns her head behind her to say something to Kenny. She gets out of the car, shuts the door closed with a swing of her hip. She has short dark hair, a pixie cut that frames her delicate features. She holds a black sweatshirt in her hands but it's cold outside the car and she wraps it around her without putting her arms in the sleeves. It's Gabe's sweatshirt. It smelled of fabric softener and Right Guard this morning but now it smells like her, which for some reason or another I imagine must be like spices.

She has a tattoo on her shoulder of angel wings. I can hear Gabe in my head right now. *If you're looking for an angel, my name is Gabriel so look no further.* It would be just the kind of corny line he would use too, even though he hated the name Gabriel. I once saw him drop his backpack in the schoolyard and tackle Randy Gosse to the ground because he had the balls to call him Gabriel in front of his friends. This girl calls him Gabriel. She likes the sound of the three syllables on her tongue. It makes him sound more dignified to her.

She holds a Tim Horton's cup, but it's not the paper kind, it's a plastic cup, the kind of cup you get if you order coffee with ice cubes and drink it out of a straw. Her straw is chewed slightly and is stained with a bright berry lipstick. She opens the back door and unbuckles Kenny, helps him out while Gabe steadies a box of timbits in one hand and a tray of coffee in the other.

Neither one of them have seen me yet and they move as if in slow motion, in time with my own slow dawning of what I'm witnessing. Gabe's mother puts a hand on my shoulder. I barely feel it but I shake it off anyway. I don't feel anything else yet. I'm still trying to comprehend what's happening. Kenny takes the girl's hand willingly and even though he sees me he doesn't let go but instead tugs at her hand and points me out to her. *That's my mommy.* I can see him mouth the words.

I feel my son's betrayal, a deep and mortal wound that makes my knees buckle. I can feel the woman's stare, at me first with my hair piled on the top of my head, stained jeans and blue shirt streaked with deodorant from where I pulled it over my arms, and then her stare shifts to Gabe who only notices me now when he follows his girlfriend's concerned gaze.

"You're early," he says awkwardly, looking up at me from the bottom step.

"What's going on, Gabe? Who's your friend?" I sound calmer than I feel, which seems to make Gabe nervous.

"You're not supposed to be here yet." He sounds confused. He looks at his watch. I can see him thinking. Gabe does that, his lips move when he thinks aloud. He's playing out our last conversation. *I'll get him around five. He'll have supper with me.*

"What is happening, Gabe?" My voice gets louder but Gabe stares at me like he can't hear me. To my complete mortification, I realize I'm about to cry.

"Not in front of the baby," Gabe's mother whispers in my ear, her breath hot along the side of my neck. "Go on home, Lolly. Gabe will drop him off in a couple of hours, when everyone is feeling a little bit calmer."

This girl has everything that belongs to me. She has Mrs. Hillier's ambrosia, she has my spot in the passenger seat of Gabe's car, she has Gabe, she has my son and he doesn't even seem upset by it. He looks downright thrilled to be holding her hand. I feel all the rage that my mother would have felt if she could look down and see Dad walking hand in hand with Marie, me trailing behind. Marie took everything that belonged to her and I wasn't going to let it happen to me. It's blind rage that makes me do it.

"No," I say shaking my head, racing down the front steps, the sting of tears in my throat. Gabe reaches for me when I run past him and that throws off his balance. He drops the tray of coffee and it spills out of the cups and runs down the driveway in a neat path out into the street. I have every intention of grabbing Kenny's hand and pulling him away, but he comes willingly, takes my hand and follows me to the car. *How could you do this to me!* I want to shout out loud as I buckle Kenny in his car seat but I'm not sure if it's intended for Gabe or Kenny, probably the both of them.

I'm about to drive off when I hear Gabe's knuckles rap against the window. I feel like snubbing him, driving away and leaving him standing in the driveway with his hands in his pockets and his girlfriend staring at the circus she'd wandered into. But I open the window anyway and he bends at the knees, his face inches from my own.

"I'm sorry. I didn't have any of this planned for today. It just sort of happened."

"How could you do this to me, Gabe?" It sounds melodramatic. What did he do, save for get on with his life.

"I didn't do anything to you, Lolly. You did this to yourself."

marie

"I'm moving."

Floss stood in the hallway with a duffel bag that belonged to Ray. He used to carry his tools around in it, screwdrivers of varying sizes and hammers, a crowbar. I put his old photo ID from the phone company in a zippered compartment after he died. I was saving it all for Kenny. Her clothes took up more room than the tools, and I realized how big the bag actually was now.

"What did you do with all his things?" I tried to hide the accusation from my tone but I heard it all the same.

"That's it? That's all you got to say? I'm moving out and all you care about are his stupid tools?" Her face was red with anger and she dropped the duffel bag on the floor so she could cross her arms at me. It didn't make near as loud a sound if it had been filled up with all of Ray's tools. In fact, it hardly made a sound at all, just a soft scrape against the carpet. Her clothes probably smelled like grease now. I wouldn't even be surprised if there were stains on her jeans and her T-shirts. She looked like a little girl to me with her hair tied up in a ponytail on the top of her head and her freckles looking darker without all the makeup she usually wore to hide them.

"Where are you going?" I had the feeling I was speaking to a younger version of Floss, a child whose rebellion was late in coming. She looked like a kid threatening to run away and I decided to humour her. She could act out with the best of them when she wanted attention and this was no different.

"Calgary."

"Calgary," I repeated with a smile on my face. She could have said China, the moon, Mars. She was being fanciful. "That's exciting now isn't it? What are you going to do in Calgary?"

Floss regarded me curiously. She thought I'd pull a fit. Forbid it. Tell her to straighten herself up, but here I was going along with it because I knew she'd never leave me. Danny had left me, Ray, Lolly. Floss wouldn't dare.

"I'm going to look for a job in one of the hospitals out there. They're always hiring." The further into the announcement she got, the more nervous she became. Her bravado, so pronounced when she dropped Ray's duffel bag on the carpet, all but disappeared. Her breathing became louder, more laboured. It struck me that she was afraid of me, not physically afraid, but afraid of my reaction all the same. "Lolly is giving me a ride to the airport on Friday. My flight leaves early so you don't need to come. Probably better if you don't actually."

"Where are you staying?" We didn't have any relatives in Calgary. I was probably the only Newfoundlander who didn't know a single person who lived in the province of Alberta— not Calgary, not Edmonton, not even Fort McMurray. I didn't want to belong to that club, another aging person whose family was off chasing money across the country. They didn't even have to do it anymore. The economy was good here now and still they left like it was a bad habit they couldn't get out of, like biting their fingernails. I thought I'd dodged it. It was too late for her to be leaving now. She was out of school, she finished the program she was in, we even threw a little celebration for her. Lolly bought her a card and a bowl of Mrs. Hillier's ambrosia, and Floss bounced Kenny on her knee and cooed at him all evening. She announced she might get on at the nursing home where she did one of those work study rotations. She was twenty-one, too old to be chasing down dreams out west. When I was her age, I was smart enough to know there wasn't anything out there worth chasing. Lolly had figured it out too. She never once talked about going to Calgary or Toronto or anywhere else. She only talked about going to work or running to the supermarket and asking me if I needed a loaf of bread while she was there. That was how it was supposed to be. She wasn't supposed to be running away from me.

"I have some friends who went out there a couple of years ago," Floss said so gently it was like the words were caressing the tops of my arms. "They said I could stay with them."

I was starting to actually believe her. I rubbed the tips of my fingers over my lips as if I were trying to coax them into talking her out of it. "Why?" My voice sounded small and weak. I couldn't imagine what I had done to her to make her hate me so much. I'd sacrificed everything for her, finally settled down with a good man who supported us in every way he was asked. I never asked for much. I always did without so Floss and Lolly could have what they wanted. I didn't expect a party. I didn't even expect a thank you but I did expect to be looked after, not abandoned. It wasn't supposed to be Floss who was running away at this stage. I wished it was Lolly, that their lives were switched, and it was Lolly who was announcing her departure. I felt guilty for thinking it, but I couldn't help it.

"Mom," she asked uncertainly. "Are you all right? Doris is

going to check in on you, and Lolly promised she'd do things for you too. She said she'd do your hair once a month and pick up your groceries every two weeks. She said Gabe can drop you off milk if you need it in between, when he comes to pick up Kenny."

They'd all had a meeting about me behind my back, set a schedule to look after me based on the shelf life of a litre of milk.

"Are you okay?" Floss asked again.

I nodded but I wanted to tell her that she'd taken the wind right out of my sails. I wanted to ask Ray what I should do but he was gone. I imagined he might tell me to stop smothering her, let her come into her own. *She'll come back to us when she's ready.* His voice seemed to echo inside my head. Floss was silent, but I heard her voice too, her soft whisper tickling the inside of my ear. She was looking for something but didn't know what it was yet. I was glad she was taking Ray's duffel bag with her. It could hold a lot, whatever it was she was trying to find.

floss

Faith needs braces. Her teeth look too big for her mouth. One of her front teeth hangs lower than the other and there's not enough space for all of them to come in. I wonder if Leo knows this, knows he'll have to work overtime to pay for them. I wonder how many toilets he'll have to take apart or how many furnaces he'll have to fix. I run my tongue over my teeth, straight and even thanks to Ray getting out of bed at six o'clock on a Sunday morning to climb up telephone poles in the dead of winter. Ray said I would thank him some day but he was dead and I never did get around to it.

Faith smiles sweetly at me, asks me if I think the sprinkler park is open. She looks excited about the prospect, skips in a circle around Leo, who warns her to watch out for cars since they're still in a parking lot.

Leo is nervous about the meeting. He jingles change in his jeans pocket, scuffs an arc in the gravel lot with the sole of his boot. He was reluctant for us to meet, discussed the terms and conditions of our meeting as if he were drawing up a contract.

"We'll meet at Bowring Park. We'll arrive separately. There won't be any outward displays of affection in Faith's presence. No hand holding, no kissing, no putting our arms around one another. We're just going to take it slow. I'll say you're a friend of mine and invite you to come to the park with us."

A friend. The night before he'd held me so tightly I could hardly breathe. "Oh God, Floss," he whispered to me in the dark so hoarsely I thought he might weep in the moment of it. "You saved my life."

"It's too early in the year for sprinklers," I answer, and her face falls a little. She stomps a sneaker into the ground. The sole lights up from the force, a bright red flashing light emanates from the bottom of her shoe. I should have said I didn't know.

"But I'm hot," Faith whines. "Daddy, I'm so hot." Leo actually looks pleased to hear the whining. He smiles at her, offers a juice box from a small insulated cooler he carries over his shoulder. He's pleased to provide a solution. Parenting by hydration. Lolly subscribes to the same approach. She is never without a bag or box of juice, hybrids of apple, berries, mangoes, even a smattering of vegetable juice concealed for good measure. It seems deceptive and unnecessary. I don't remember my mother ever carrying around water or juice in her pockets or her purse or in insulated coolers. I remember her telling me I was only going to have to go to the bathroom if I drank too much, and she wasn't going to go out of her way to find one for me.

"We'll have to wait and see," Leo says when Faith is finished with her box of juice, handing Leo her garbage. Of course the sprinkler park isn't open yet. It's only May and while it's relatively mild, you need a jacket. There are a few fools around, the ones that put on their shorts at the first day the temperature gets into the teens, but the clouds are already getting lower in the sky.

Faith seems to have forgotten the sprinkler park once she spies the playground. She tackles various climbing apparatuses, slides down and does it all over again. Leo laughs heartily every time she comes down the slide with her hair standing up on end from the static.

Look at us everyone, his laughter seems to proclaim. *Look at how clever and funny my child is. Look at how happy she makes me.* Other children at the park are being reprimanded by at least one parent. *Take turns. No pushing. Watch your mouth, you're like the savage. That's enough junk, you're going to spoil your supper.* No other parents are laughing. They are tired, thinking about their next shift, paying the electric bill. They hope the run in the fresh air will make the kids go to bed early. All of them take their kids for granted, all of them except Leo. He knows what it's like to wake up in a different house than his daughter, to get up and have a cup of coffee and miss the sound of her in the bedroom talking to her stuffed animals. Maybe a few years ago he was just like all those other parents, but divorce has made him revere his child in a way that marriage can't.

"Can we go feed the ducks now?" Faith is breathless. Her hair is a tangled mess. I imagine Cathy trying to comb it out later tonight, cursing Leo for not putting it in a ponytail. She has dried snot from her nose to her ear where she wiped it with the sleeve of her sweatshirt. The remnants of something chocolate gather in the corner of her mouth.

Leo carries her on his shoulders all the way from the playground to the duck pond. She's big for that and Leo sweats under the weight of her. I resist the urge to wipe his brow and offer instead to relieve him of the cooler full of drinks and the bag of bread. I hope the gesture carries no romantic undertones. I watch other couples hold hands, or walk arm in arm along the trail, and bemoan the fact we aren't one of them, at least not in the light of day. He would balk if I reached for his hand now, as if it were a perverse gesture guaranteed to cause Faith emotional trauma by witnessing it.

The ducks are hungry and Faith feeds them quickly. She tosses the bread in high arcs overhead, then spins quickly around before the bread lands in the pond. Leo watches, a look of contentment settles into the lines of his face.

"Aren't you having a good time? You're quiet."

"Oh yes," I nod fervently. "Faith seems like such a happy little girl."

Leo smiles. I've pleased him, I can tell by the way he lifts his own hand up, and then drops it back in his lap. He was going to reach for me but remembered his self-imposed restrictions. He adores her. He watches her the same way Ray looked at Lolly and I feel the familiar sting of jealousy in my veins.

"Do you think she likes me?" I ask the question uncertainly.

Leo shrugs, making me wonder what sort of response I was hoping for. That I would be a wonderful stepmother? It hardly seems like something to aspire to. It hardly seems like such a thing exists. It's an oxymoron. "We're just going to have to take it slow," Leo offers with a smile. "Let it evolve."

I watch Faith toss the bread into the air and onto water. It doesn't look like she's feeding the ducks at all, only scattering a bag filled with bread crumbs. I imagine myself tossing my father's ashes, throwing handfuls of them in the air and turning around before they reach the ground. I tug on a loose thread from the cuff of my sweatshirt, wind my finger around it and tear it off. It's getting colder, the sun is all but gone for the day and I feel a light mist touch the tip of my nose. It might stay this way for hours, or the sky might open up.

I want to tell him about the ashes and about my father but I haven't said anything about it yet. Sometimes Leo asks how my father is and I just respond that he is the same in a curt manner that puts an end to the conversation right then and there. He doesn't push. He has too much going on in his own life to be overly concerned about what's going on in mine. I feel guilty for not agreeing to take the ashes. I haven't seen my father since that day and I wonder every day if he's already dead. I scan the pages of the obituaries looking for him but he hasn't turned up yet.

"I'm bored," Faith announces, jumping into Leo's arms. "Did you bring any snacks? I'm getting hungry."

Leo's brow is furrowed in concentration as he rummages through the cooler and tosses Faith something in a shiny foil wrapper. His phone rings and he sighs deeply in annoyance at the display. It's obviously Cathy. I only hear one half of the conversation but it's not difficult to fill in the blanks.

"Hey. We just finished feeding the ducks and now Faith is having a snack." Leo clears his throat. He's uncomfortable speaking to her in front of me. He knows I'm hanging on to every word.

"Just a couple of cookies…I don't know, chocolate chip I think," Leo says, smoothing out the wrapper Faith balled up a moment earlier. "It's a granola bar. It's not going to spoil her lunch. It's only eleven-thirty." He looks awkwardly at his watch to make sure. Cathy frightens him. Every call and text, it seems, holds a lingering doubt about Leo's ability to adequately carry out the simplest of tasks.

By the time he puts his phone away, I no longer care about the conditions of our meeting. Surely it's better for Faith to see her father loved by a stranger than ridiculed by her mother. I reach for him, place one hand on his arm, the other on his shoulder.

"Floss." He states my name in warning but doesn't back away from me either.

"We shouldn't lie," I whisper.

Faith stares at the two of us in wide-eyed wonderment. I don't understand the point of lying. My mother certainly never shielded her intentions with Ray from me. If I remember correctly the first night Ray came over, I walked in on the two of them making out on the living-room chesterfield. His hand was up her shirt and her bra was hanging off. It was black lace and I knew she bought it special for him since my mother only ever owned white or beige bras and panties. She had one pair of polka dot underwear but they were stained with bleach and she only wore them when she cleaned out the bathroom tub or coloured her hair. I didn't want to sneak around with Leo. It made me feel as if we're doing something inappropriate.

"Your father is a very good friend of mine," I say to Faith. "I like him a lot."

"I know," she shrugs and then something seems to register. She regards me in another light, looks me over methodically.

"Like a boyfriend? Like someone you kiss?"

"Yes."

"Jesus Christ," Leo says, balling his fists by the sides of him. He's angry. His face is red, his teeth are clenched. "Floss, what the hell are you doing?"

He may as well have slapped me hard across the face, I'm so stunned.

"Well I have to go home now," I say to Faith as if it were just she and I at the park and my mother had called me home for supper. I turn and walk away from them, slowly at first but then my pace quickens until I'm all out sprinting.

lolly

olly, honey, now what's the matter with you?" Marie sits on the couch next to Floss, who is cross-legged with a box of tissues in front of her. I stand in the foyer like the youngsters selling raffle tickets to send their hockey team away for a tournament, invited in long enough for Marie to find a few dollars to buy a booklet. Kenny charges in though, as he always does after a night spent with Gabe, and runs to the bedroom to check on his toys. He's making sure they're all there in their right places, hoping none of them ran off in the middle of the night to find him.

I don't remember how I got here. It's all automatic anyway, the route between Gabe's house and mine. I've done it a million times, maybe more. I've never actually counted. The second left after the gas station, merge. I try to think of what comes next but it eludes me. If I got back in the car I'd get there without thinking. I'm sometimes halfway to Gabe's before I realize I'm supposed to be going to work, or to the supermarket.

I can't stop shivering. I can hear the wind blowing dirt and gravel and an empty tin of Pepsi down the street. I can feel the

draft from the front door. Dad would have been to the hard-
ware store by now to purchase weather stripping and caulking.
Save a few dollars on the oil bill. It all adds up you know. I can
hear my teeth chattering and I wish I could stop shaking.

"Lolly? What's going on? Are you all right?" Marie pats the
cushion of the sofa next to her in invitation. "The two of you
today. One coming home more upset than the other." I look at
Floss. Her eyes are red, her nose drips and she sniffs it all back
up and then wipes whatever residue is left with a tissue.

"Gabe just called," Marie says. "He said you should call
him. Did something happen to Kenny?"

"Gabe." It comes out as a hoarse sounding whisper. It
doesn't even sound like my voice. It sounds like I have a bad
cold or a sinus infection. "Gabe has a girlfriend."

"Oh Lolly," Marie sighs wistfully, almost patronizingly so.
It's like she already knew it and was sad for me that I found
out about it. It was the same way you'd speak to a child after
they found out the tooth fairy wasn't real. But it isn't just about
Gabe having a girlfriend, it's more explosive than that.

"She held his hand, my son's hand, like he belonged to her.
She unbuckled him, got him out of the car. Kenny took her
hand too like he was used to it. They were at Tim Horton's and
the girl who served them probably thought they were one big
happy family." I picture them going out to eat. She'd sit next to
Kenny, take the pickle off his hamburger and squeeze the
ketchup on his plate. Other people in the restaurant would
look at them and smile sweetly. Old people would walk up to
them and say, "God Bless his little heart." They might even say
he looked just like her and she would giggle because she knew
something they didn't.

People used to think Marie was my mother all the time and
each time the effect would be less and less until I didn't notice
it anymore. The lady in the bank would tell me to wait with my
mother and I would comply without even flinching after a few

short months of hearing the same mistake made over and over again.

"What would you like us to say, Lolly?" Floss asks me the question, stares at me with her own glassy eyes. "That we feel bad for you? Just imagine how she feels?"

I didn't give a shit how she felt. "I am Kenny's mother," I say shrilly. "How do you think I feel?" It's my only argument but it's a big one. I cut his sandwich with a dinosaur cookie cutter. I wash the same cup three times a day because it's the only one he'll drink milk out of. I read *Green Eggs and Ham* ten times a day because he laughs every single time. I wipe his nose. I wipe his arse. I pick the sleep out of the corner of his eyes and none of that is remotely gross to me. I can't stand the thought of anyone else doing it.

Floss shrugs at me and her eyes water with fresh tears. She sighs, like she was annoyed with herself for starting up again. She thought she was done. I feel the fight go right out of me at the sight of her and in its place is a weary resignation. Floss was meeting Leo's daughter today. She talked about it for three days straight. She mulled over outfits, moaned that she didn't have anything purple except for a pair of gloves and a pair of shorts and it was too warm out for gloves and too cold for shorts. She watched YTV after supper and wandered off with Kenny to the toy department at Walmart when we went to pick up detergent and toilet paper.

Floss was the girl in the car to someone else. Right now another mother was hating her, seething with anger at her for spending the day with their kid. It seemed so unfair that anyone could hate Floss. Nothing was fair. I thought of the girl with her angel wings, branded on her shoulder as if she knew something about them. There were no such things as angels. I wanted to tell her that, but not in a malicious way. Maybe the way I would tell Kenny there was no such thing as monsters or ghosts.

I still stand in the foyer in the midst of a pile of everyone's shoes, Kenny's sneakers, Floss' ballet flats, and Marie's rain boots. Kenny comes running from the bedroom, his cheeks flush with excitement. Children have a way of diffusing tense situations, as if they had some type of built-in sensor that they eventually grow out of, the same way their legs get too long for their pants and their feet keep getting squished into bigger and bigger shoes.

Kenny's was sharp in infancy, when he'd cry at just the moment I was about to yell at Gabe for something. It was honed in toddlerhood when he knew just how to ask for a drink, or a snack, or a toy at the moment Gabe and I were contemplating how we'd gotten where we did. Then we'd forget about it while we retrieved crackers, or poured apple juice, or got on our hands and knees looking for a missing toy. They were the best distractions. We'd move beds away from the walls, look under the sofa, take all the cushions off, look behind dressers. It was hard to remember what Gabe had done wrong when he'd gone out in the rain or the snow to find a missing toy under a car mat. The interruptions were less now, but they seemed expertly timed. It's hard to imagine one day he'll be the one to start causing trouble, creating tension where it shouldn't be.

Kenny waves a piece of paper over his head, presents it to me with great fanfare. It's a crude drawing, as all of Kenny's drawings are, of a bird I think, which immediately fills me with unease. Kenny draws robots and superheroes and T-Rex's. He might even draw the occasional farm animal but never a bird. I see it then, the haloed circle over the head, the draped body. It's not a bird at all.

"It's for Vanessa," he says. "She likes angels. Do you think she'll like it?"

Vanessa. I didn't want to give her a name. I just wanted her to be the girl. "I like it, Kenny. In fact, I'd like to keep it. Can

I?" His little mouth frowns in confusion and his eyes, dark blue like my own, grow darker now. I sense Marie's disappointment in me, Floss' anger. I have so many of Kenny's pictures already. They cover the fridge, they weigh down my purse, they litter the floor of my bedroom, I even use them for coasters and placemats. I throw some of them out, the ugly ones drawn hurriedly in the waiting room of the doctor's office, or the bank, scribbles on the back of a deposit slip.

Kenny smiles broadly up at me, his face lit up with the kind of pure joy that only a four-year-old can display. The look humbles me, makes me feel weak. "I'll make you a different one," he says, pulling the sheet from my hands and running back to his bedroom.

"Why don't you make one for Auntie Floss instead?"

"Okay."

"That one is an angel," Marie says. "God bless his little heart."

marie

wanted to have a baby. I wanted one with a desperation that
made me ashamed. I turned into one of those women who
cooed at babies in their strollers in the mall. I watched their
little hands shovelling timbits in their mouths, drool mixed
in with the sugar until their hands and face were a sticky mess.
I thought about it while I poured my coffee just after Ray left
for work and it stuck with me throughout the day, when I was
typing letters or making copies in the office, when I sat at the
kitchen table helping Floss do her homework assignments,
and when I stood over the counter peeling potatoes in the late
afternoon.

It didn't make any sense. I had a child of my own. I had
Lolly. I was over forty years old. My joints ached late at night, my
gums bled sometimes when I brushed my teeth, onions started
giving me heartburn and I had to wear a sweater around the
house in the evenings. I was having a midlife crisis, mourning
the chipping away of my youth.

"I wish we had a baby together," I said to Ray one night
when we were getting ready for bed. It came across as wistful

rather than serious and he smiled a little bit, imaging the kind of child we'd make together. It would have Ray's dark hair, my complexion, Ray's build and my eyes—a perfect hybrid of the two of us.

"That's all right now," he said, placing a hand on my shoulder in comfort. He rubbed his palm across my shoulder like he might a child who was being consoled they didn't get what they wanted for Christmas.

"I'm serious, Ray." I looked up at him, wide-eyed.

"You're off your rocker," he said, standing up now dressed only in his underwear. It looked like he wanted to pace but there was nowhere really to go save for his side of the bed. "Sure we can't handle the two we got right now."

"It would be a relief to have a child we both felt the same about," I said and it shocked me to hear me acknowledge it, even as we both knew it was true. Lolly was his and Floss was mine and as much as we pretended otherwise, it was always going to be that way.

We were polarized, Ray and I, forced to choose sides in every facet of our lives. If the girls argued, so did we. If Lolly was upset about something, so was Ray. If Floss felt that something was unfair, so did I. They were extensions of ourselves no matter how much we tried to make it different. We needed a referee, an unbiased third party in the form of a baby. Ray and I would feel the exact same way about the baby. Lolly and Floss would love it too, I knew they would. Everything would be better. Meals would be smoother, errands a team effort, homework would get done without complaint, if only we had someone we could all love together.

Ray understood what I was trying to say because he sat back down on the edge of the bed and reached for my hand. "That's not going to happen, Marie. We're past the making babies part of life. We got our hands full as it is, and besides, we can't afford a baby."

"Can't we just try, see what happens?" We weren't using any reliable method of birth control. I was past the recommended age for the pill and Ray didn't like condoms so he always just pulled out, his hand cupping himself to prevent it from getting on the sheets. All he would have to do was not pull out.

"No," he said firmly. "We can't try."

This stung more than it should have. He made perfect sense. We had no business becoming new parents at our age. We'd be the oldest ones around. Other kids would make fun of ours because his mom and dad were so old. We'd buy the wrong clothes and sneakers and we'd talk about things like our blood sugar or our cholesterol when he had friends over and he'd be so embarrassed he'd never ask them back.

Still it left a gaping wound in my chest. I was jealous that Ray had a child with someone else. I pictured the two of them going to doctor visits and buying baby clothes and picking out names. I pictured Ray changing diapers and pacing the floor back and forth with a sleeping infant slung over his shoulder while his wife caught up on her sleep. It didn't matter that it probably wasn't that way at all. I'd not done any of those things with Danny. It was my father who bought me the crib and then assembled it at the foot of my bed. Danny wasn't home for any nighttime feedings. He was mostly out carousing and if he was home, he was passed out drunk on the living-room sofa.

Ray ran a hand through his hair. It was so thick and dark his fingers disappeared save for the glint of his gold wedding band. "I know things have been a little rough around here but we need to give it time. They're good kids."

"You're right," I said softly. "I just didn't think it would be this hard." I chided myself for my foolishness at wanting another child.

"You know when the girls are grown, it'll just be you and

me," Ray said. "Most couples get that in the beginning of their relationship. We'll just get it later and when we do, it'll be better because we'll have waited for it."

When Ray made love to me that night he didn't pull out. His hands, instead of cupping himself, held my face afterwards. I didn't get pregnant that night and Ray never indulged me again. I think he was just too heartbroken to try.

floss

Faith cheats at Go Fish. I asked her straight out if she had an eight a split second earlier and she responded Go Fish and then turned around and asked me for the eight. I stole a sideways glance at Leo to see if he was aware of what was going on but he sat cross-legged on the floor staring at his burgeoning hand of cards. He had to have at least one pair in all of that but he claimed he had not a single match.

He was letting her win. I saw Lolly sometimes do the same thing with Kenny in Candyland, flip through the cards until she found the gingerbread man and then act deflated she had to go back to the gingerbread forest. The days of bawling over losing a game were over now because losing was over. The youngsters today must think their parents are inept, simpletons, always losing and seemingly thrilled by it.

Even now Faith is pumping her first in the air in victory and jumping up and down like she just won the Lotto 6-49 and Leo reacts to this display with shocked disbelief. He makes an O with his mouth as if he can't believe the miracle he's just witnessed. He smiles at her, gushes, "Again! You little stinker, that's four in a row," he says in mock disappointment and Faith giggles and squeals with delight. "I'm going to get you next time," he warns. Leo looks genuine, like he might actually enjoy playing this monotonous card game over and over again. I'm bored with it already. Four games have taken only a half hour and we have her for three and a half more. I'm counting down the time like a babysitter waiting for the parents to show up. *She was no trouble at all, Mrs. LeDrew.* I smile awkwardly back at them but it feels like I'm pretending to be in on a private joke.

Faith's hair is in two neat braids that graze the top of each shoulder. It's thick and blond and prettier than I remember it being at the park, but then it was just a tangled nest. I picture Faith sitting patiently while her mother combed and separated her hair. My mother used to brush Lolly's hair and Lolly would howl and scream the entire time, tilting her head back and accusing mom of trying to rip the hair right out of her head. *You'd know if I was trying,* my mother would say. The other day I watched Lolly apply my mother's hair colour at the kitchen table, and Mom complaining the whole time that it itched her, that Lolly was after forgetting to set the timer. It was odd how quickly things changed, how suddenly roles could be reversed.

I wonder if I'll be combing Faith's hair one of these days. I can't do braids as evenly as Cathy has done them and Faith seems like the kind of kid who would be quick to point it out. I wonder if Cathy might even allow it, or if hair combing would be another one of her restrictions.

I suppose I should be thankful I'm here at all after the debacle that was Bowring Park. Leo was mad with me but I wouldn't apologize. I didn't have anything to be sorry about. "I was only being honest," I told him. "Why would you lie to Faith?"

"I'm not lying," he protested.

"So I'm just your friend? Do you have sex with all your friends?"

"No." He sighed at me, the way I crossed my arms at him. "Floss, you're so much more than a friend, which is why I wanted Faith to meet you in the first place. I don't bring just anyone around my daughter." He brought me into his arms then. He wasn't mad at me anymore, but he was still upset at the way things were. "This is hard for me," he whispered.

"It's not easy for me either."

It was harder after Cathy passed on all her rules and regulations that were supposed to govern our relationship. There were several of them she passed on to Leo. I was not to sleep over on the nights Faith slept over. I was not to give her baths or accompany her in public restrooms. I was not to dispense medication. I cried at the sheer insult of the last one. It sounded like Leo was taking Cathy's side.

"I'm not taking her side," Leo said firmly.

"She thinks I'm a child molester," I sniffed.

"No she doesn't," Leo assured me. "She's just being cautious."

Stop defending her, I wanted to shout at him. That's what it sounded like to me.

"I work in a hospital," I said meekly. "I give medicine all the time."

He just shrugged. He was relieved he'd had the conversation with Cathy done and over with. He had no desire to debate it.

I wonder if it would have been different if Gabe told Lolly about his outing with his girlfriend and Kenny beforehand. I doubt Lolly would have been amenable either way. She was still mad at Gabe and still insecure about Kenny. She paid more attention to him now, followed him into his room and helped him build big block towers instead of telling him to go find something to do because she was busy.

"This is a really big step for me, Floss." He said this as if I ought to be honoured, but I didn't feel that way at all. I felt like I'd just come in last in a race, but grateful that at least I'd crossed the finish line.

Leo wants to take Faith to Swiss Chalet for supper. I haven't been since my mother married Ray. Ray didn't like to go out to eat. It was too expensive. He said he didn't like people watching him eat. He was worried about food poisoning and cleanliness. He had trouble figuring out how much to tip.

Swiss Chalet looks nearly the same as it did the last time I was here. Faith complains her menu is sticky, her chair is wobbly and she can't reach the salt, none of which should matter since Leo has already told her what she's going to order and she's practically sitting on his lap now anyway. I offer to switch seats with her but she shakes her head. Leo tugs on a braid and the gesture puts me in mind of Ray and Lolly. I can picture them sitting at the table on the day of the wedding, her sullen in her funeral garb and him tugging on her hair in a feeble attempt to placate her.

"My mother took us here the day she got married." I say it like it was something she did all on her own. "It looks the same."

"You weren't even born yet," Faith says smugly.

"I was too," I shoot back as if I were speaking to Lolly ten years ago. "My mother got married twice." Faith looks at me dubiously, like she didn't know you could do that. "I was a bridesmaid. I got to wear a beautiful dress and hold a bouquet of pink roses." My dress wasn't really all that beautiful, although I thought it was at the time, and it was mom who held the bouquet not me, although I held them afterwards in front of the mirror.

"Oh," Faith looks reflective. "I wish I could be a bridesmaid."

"I'm sure you will one day. Maybe if your Dad ever gets married again." As soon as I say it I know I've made a terrible mistake. It was supposed to be a flippant comment but it was anything but. It was the first conversation Faith and I were having that was not arbitrated by Leo and I was encouraged by it. I thought we'd talk about dresses and ribbons and flowers, things Leo couldn't talk about with her, but the conversation had veered off into uncomfortable territory. I think about a way to salvage it but all I can see is Cathy's angry face confronting Leo. *You're going to get married? To that woman?*

"To you?" Faith asks me, with a quivering lip. "Are you going to marry my Dad?"

"No," I say it so quickly that the mere idea of it comes across not just as absurd but downright abhorrent. Poor Leo. I've insulted him. "I mean, I don't know," I say, hoping to backtrack. "He hasn't asked me or anything. We're just friends," I add quietly.

"Christ," Leo whispers so softly it sounds like a prayer more than a curse. "No one is marrying anyone." He gestures to the waitress and gives his and Faith's order. "What do you want, Floss?"

I want to stop saying foolish things. I want it to be easy with Leo the way it was before I met Faith. We stayed up late into the night talking. I fell asleep in his arms. He said things that were so funny I laughed and hiccupped and even lost my breath for a second. I want to care about Faith as much as Leo does, but I'm scared to death of her.

lolly

I was scared to death of Marie, not when we first met, not even when I knew Dad was smitten with her. It wasn't until we spent the night there that it occurred to me I ought to fear her. I wonder if maybe this is the same thing Kenny is feeling, why he doesn't seem bothered by the fact his father is spending company in the presence of someone else. The fear would come to him, I was sure of it, the same way it came to me.

We weren't planning on staying the night but Dad and Marie got caught up in talking and whispering until Marie stifled a yawn and looked at her watch in surprise. Floss and I were curled up in a blanket on the floor watching television but Floss was asleep and I was preoccupied with straining my ears to hear all their whispers. I was waiting for them to talk about something important but they kept talking about silly things—foods they liked, shops they frequented, people they worked with. My father draped an arm around Marie and she laid her head against his chest. Her head bobbed up and down with his breath and she had the silliest smile plastered on her face, but Dad couldn't see it from his vantage point. He kept staring at the top of her head, sporting his own grin.

"We better get going," Dad said after Marie started to drift off in his arm.

"Don't go, Ray," Marie said sleepily, burrowing her head further into his chest as if to keep him there, hold him in place. "Sure it's freezing out and it's after getting too late to be on the road now. Floss honey, get up and go to bed. Make some room in there for your guest."

"She's not my guest, she's yours," Floss murmured although she complied all the same, handing me a pillow and a quilt while she scooted across the bed in her room. I couldn't sleep. Floss was awake too although neither one of us said a word. It was unlike any sleepover I'd ever had. There was no television, no conniving to stay up late, no popcorn. The two of us just disappeared into the bedroom as soon as we were asked.

"Do you think they're doing it now?" Floss whispered to me in the dark. It was more than an hour after we shut the light, more than an hour since either of us spoke. It was a whisper but it sounded so loud to me I thought Dad could hear her all the way in the back bedroom with the door closed.

"Doing what?"

"Having sex, dummy," Floss said. "I bet he has a small dick. My Aunt Doris said so. She said he was a little dick but when my mother argued with her, Doris took it back and said he was a big dick which made Mom even more mad."

I felt my face grow hot at the mere mention of my father's privates. I pictured my father holding Marie in bed, smoothing her hair and kissing her goodnight. I remembered walking in on them that first night with her hair all messy and her bra hanging brazenly from her arm. I had the taste of metal in my mouth when I saw that, like I had just run my tongue along the handlebars of my bike. I felt the same taste in my mouth. I could tell Floss felt it too.

"Want to get a drink?" She threw off the covers and cracked

open the bedroom door. It was quiet and dark in the house. I followed her into the kitchen, saw mine and Dad's shoes neatly lined up next to one another on the mat in the hallway. I let out a breath of relief that he was still there somewhere in the apartment, hadn't left me here altogether. Floss handed me the milk out of the fridge and retrieved two glasses from the cabinet. They were coated in a fine layer of dust that Floss blew off and then wiped with her pajama top.

"We don't get to use these ones that much," she apologized. "Our regular glasses are still in the sink."

I gulped down the milk. I was thirsty and I still had a bad taste in my mouth but Floss sipped hers slowly, eyebrows raised inquisitively like she'd never tasted milk before. It was awkward standing in the kitchen with her without either my father or Marie around.

"This is weird," Floss said, mimicking my own discomfort. "She's never had a boyfriend before, not since my father, but I can't remember him. Mom thought he died but he just left. He might be dead by now though. Mom said he was on borrowed time. I think he was an alcoholic. Is your dad an alcoholic too?"

"No," I replied emphatically.

"He drinks though. He had three beers this evening," she said pointing to the empty bottles on the kitchen counter. "That's probably why he had to sleep over. Too drunk to drive I suppose. Does he get drunk a lot?"

"No! I've never seen him drunk once before in my whole life," I lied but it was a white lie. He got drunk the night of my mother's funeral, after everyone went home. He sat down on the couch, opened a bottle and drank glass after glass. He didn't act the way I thought a drunk person would act. He didn't laugh or yell or even slur his words. He just curled up with my mother's blanket and fell asleep.

"How much does he make an hour?"

"I don't know," I shrugged. It wasn't the type of thing a

parent talked about with their child. "He has a good job. He's in a union."

"That doesn't mean anything. All that means is that he hasn't made manager yet."

Floss had a way of twisting things around and I took offence. "He has a lot of responsibility," I said, but I wasn't necessarily referring to his work. "He works at the phone company. He spends a lot of time outdoors, climbing up telephone poles."

Floss looked like she was picturing him in her mind shimmying up the pole outside. She made a face like she was unimpressed but I knew she was.

"What religion is he?"

"Catholic."

"Mom doesn't like the Catholics." Floss blew on the milk in her glass like she was about to take a sip of tea. "I mean she's not prejudiced against them or anything. She just thinks they have too many silly rules. The church won't let her marry your father because she's divorced. They probably didn't talk about that yet so that might be the end of it." We both looked at one another, relieved to have found an out for them. Floss even shook her head like she felt sad for them.

"My father is a good Catholic," I said even though he wasn't. He never went to church, except near the end of my mother's sickness and by that time all that was left to pray for was her soul. "That stuff is important to him. It's too bad your mom doesn't believe in it," I added with relief.

Floss shrugged. "I knew he wasn't good enough for her. Aunt Doris said that too."

I felt the prick of something behind my eye. I blinked at her. It was one thing to point out their differences, but quite another to put him on a level beneath the likes of Marie.

"He's too good for her," I said, slamming down my glass on the kitchen table. It was still cluttered with supper dishes my father had urged her to ignore until later. There was dried up barbecue sauce on the plates and the forks and it would be that much harder to clean later. I resisted the urge to put them in the sink to soak them in hot soapy water. My mother never would have gone to bed with a mess like this in the kitchen. "I don't even know what he's doing with her. She's got a face on her like a dog."

That was when Marie walked into the kitchen. She was wearing a pink fleece bathrobe that she self-consciously adjusted. I could see her collarbone and wondered if she was naked underneath it, wondered if my father had seen her without her clothes on.

"What are the two of you doing up?"

"Making an effort," Floss said, using her fingers to make quotation marks. It was obviously something Marie had spoken to Floss about.

I thought Marie might get mad at me for saying bad things about her but she walked around me silently. She belted the robe tighter around her waist, rolled the sleeves up and started filling the sink with hot water. She scraped the plates over the garbage can and slipped them in the water, submerged her own hands in the sink, kept her back to us.

"Get back to bed now," she said quietly. That's when I started to fear her. Anyone else would have said something back, or spoke to my father about my behaviour the next day but she stood there in dignified silence like she wasn't going to lower herself to my level, like it was her who was too good for me.

"The Constable is on the phone." Marie creeps into my bedroom and hands me my cellphone. "You left it in the kitchen last night," she whispers. She's trying to cover the part that you speak in but she holds it upside down. "I was just putting on the kettle when it started going off. I only answered cause I didn't want it to wake Floss. I was trying to mind my own business," she says defensively even though I haven't accused her of anything. "Don't be getting mad with me, I didn't mean to say anything."

I take the phone from her, confused and somewhat wary by her quick retreat from the bedroom. "Hey," I whisper into the phone.

"Are you awake? Or should I just mind my own business?" Carson's teasing voice rings in my ear.

"No and no." I yawn sleepily but I'm smiling when I do, squint at the clock, five thirty in the morning. I curl up with the cellphone under the blanket wishing he was actually here with me instead of out in the city.

"I thought that boy of yours got you up around now."

"He's at Gabe's. He'll probably sleep in till ten today."

"Are you in the mood for breakfast?"

"At this hour?"

"What do you mean at this hour? I know plenty of people are thinking about lunch by now. I want to see you." His voice grows husky with passion.

"I want to see you too."

"I'm picking you up in an hour," he says authoritatively. He sounds nearly manic, high on adrenaline from patrolling the city all night.

Carson smells like the waterfront, salt water, and diesel. I smell it off his skin even though I'm sitting across from him at Tim Horton's where the smell of coffee and sugar flood the room.

"What kind of night did you have?"

"The usual," he shrugs. "Few drunks, few fights. We had a break-in at a pharmacy, prescription drugs were stolen but we got his picture on the security camera so we should be able to get him. We'll put it on the news, and someone will recognize him. Most criminals aren't very bright."

"Why did you want to be a cop for anyway?" The hours seemed bad. It was dangerous. Everybody hated you, even the people who never did anything wrong.

Carson smiles at the question. "My bike got stolen when I was a kid and I swore right then and there I was going to be a police officer so I could find the guy and arrest him. Silly, isn't it?"

"No." I didn't think it was silly at all. It made more sense than fixing copy machines because your father knew someone who owned the repair company. Gabe had been thrilled to get the job. He strutted around his parents' living room with his chest puffed out, like he really believed his father had nothing to do with it, that Mr. Hillier didn't have to explain that Gabe had a baby on the way and needed the work.

"What about you. Did you always want to do people's hair?"

The question makes me squirm with discomfort even though I know it's not his intention. I became a hairdresser because my mother predicted it. She was right about most things, had a knack for knowing what was going to happen next. She knew she was going to die, even before the doctors did, and it wasn't because she was a pessimist. She just knew. I used to spend hours doing my dolls' hair, putting them in braids and ponytails and curls, giving them fancy updos for evening parties. My mother always used to say, "I believe you're going to be a hairdresser one day." I couldn't fathom doing anything else after she died. I was afraid of disappointing her, as foolish as that seems. "It was my mom's idea."

"She's seems worried about you."

"Who?" My heart practically jumps out of my chest.

"Your mother."

"My mother?" I blink at him dumbly. "Who are you talking about?"

"Your mother," he repeats. He laughs at my reaction. "You do know who your mother is, don't you?"

"Yes, of course. I just thought you were talking about someone else for a second."

"Well how many mothers do you have?"

One, two, none. None of those seems quite right.

"What did she say?"

"Who?" he jokes playfully and I kick him under the table but he anticipates my move. His reflexes are quick and he catches my foot and rests it on his lap, squeezes my calf.

"Your mom just said you were upset at your ex for something when I called you this morning," he says, turning serious. "Is everything okay?"

I sip my coffee, resent Marie's intrusion. This is what she meant when she said she was minding her own business this morning. "Gabe is seeing someone and he brought her around Kenny. It just took me by surprise is all."

Carson releases his grip on my leg. I let it linger for a moment and then cross my legs, turn to the side. Gabe's new girlfriend, I realize, is only part of the problem. The bigger part of the problem is my reluctance to bring Carson and Kenny together. We don't do the types of things Floss and Leo do with Faith. We don't play games, or go to the park, or get doughnuts from Tim Horton's. I've deliberately put them in different compartments. There's time for Kenny and time for Carson but they don't overlap.

"Why do you think we don't do things with Kenny?" I pose the question to both of us, although it's more intended for me.

He sighs heavily at the shift in mood. We'd been playful all morning and now we're both keenly aware of having to evaluate our relationship and make a decision. It doesn't feel fair that we should have to think about such things at this stage of our relationship. It felt like my father moved too quickly. All of a sudden Marie and I were thrust together, vying for our share of my father. I was in no rush to do the same thing to Kenny and Carson.

"It's not that I don't want to," Carson coughs into his fist. "Believe me, I'd like nothing better." He yawns. He's coming down off his high of chasing criminals and now he just looks tired.

"I'd like that too," I say reaching for his hand.

I feel the anger at Gabe dissipate, and in its place is gratitude. He'd taken the first step and, whether it was intentional or not, he was telling me it was okay to move on, for both of us to keep going.

marie

"That sonofabitch is fucking my daughter." Ray had his back to me when he said it so I couldn't see his face but I could tell he was madder than I'd ever seen him. I walked up behind him in the kitchen where he stood in front of the sink, looking out the window past the lawn and out to the bank of fog that was slowly creeping in from off the water. It hovered a little bit out there like it was trying to make up its mind, but it would soon descend on us, darkening the pink sky and smothering the cars and the grass and the trees. It was like Ray's anger, slow and powerful and determined.

"Who?" I asked stupidly since it was fairly obvious who Ray was talking about. I'd just left Lolly and Gabe in the living room. Floss was there too, sitting cross-legged in Ray's recliner. It didn't make sense the way she opened up the chair with its resting spot for your feet and then curled her legs underneath her. Lolly had her head resting on Gabe's shoulder and he had an arm draped possessively across her back. They were watching television, all three of them quiet as could be save for a loud yawn coming from Gabe.

I'd just invited Gabe to stay for supper, which was probably why Ray was upset in the first place. Gabe had eaten over with us three times already this week and Ray was losing his patience. He was insulted the Hilliers didn't think twice about him feeding their teenage son. It was true Gabe ate like a horse and I ended up putting more food on than I normally would. I peeled extra potatoes and took an extra pork chop out of the freezer. Last going off Ray sighed that the Hilliers ought to pay for part of our grocery bill but he was half joking. I think he was as fond of Gabe as I was.

"You knows who I'm talking about, Marie."

"What makes you say that?" That's when I noticed the package in Ray's hand, the shiny plastic square with a condom inside it. He gripped the package so hard the tops of his fingers were white. "Where did you get that?" I felt something like nervous excitement in my fingertips, although I tried to suppress it so he wouldn't fly off the handle.

"It was in his jacket pocket."

"You went through his pockets?" I was nearly breathless.

"His car was blocking me in, as usual. I didn't get the bread yet for supper and I was going to run to the store and pick it up. I was just going to move his car. I thought his keys were in his pocket."

"You didn't get the bread yet? Jesus, Ray, I asked you to get that this morning." I don't know why I said it other than habit. He wasn't himself and I wanted to bring him back. He glared at me and I stood back on my heels. "What are you going to do?"

"I'm going to fuckin' kill him that's what I'm going to do," Ray said through clenched teeth. He banged a fist on the countertop, sending a nearby butter knife up in the air a few inches. It came down hard, a loud metal clang that echoed across the room. I'd never seen Ray mad with Lolly, never seen either one of them say two bad words to each other, and I felt the anticipation build. I was going to see something I'd never seen before and I didn't know if I should try to stop it or let it take its course. Part of me couldn't wait to see it, wanted to pull up a chair, make some popcorn, watch the show, and I felt an overwhelming sense of guilt about it too.

"She's nearly sixteen, Ray," I said quietly, wondering why I was defending her. "They've been together forever. You know he's not some fly-by-night boyfriend. He loves her." I put a hand on his forearm and felt his muscles pulsate under my touch. He brushed past me then, the swish of air lifted the hair on the back of my neck and I felt a chill. I followed him from the kitchen and watched as he tossed the package at Gabe. The condom smacked him in the chest and fell into his lap.

"This belong to you?" Ray asked him. "You planning on using it later?"

Gabe and Lolly looked up at Ray and then down at the condom. We all stared at it, the black foil with the Trojan label in white letters. It was ribbed, it said, for her stimulation and pleasure. I was struck by the sudden urge to laugh. A condom never provided anyone with an ounce of pleasure. It burned and chafed and made your privates smell like a fresh pack of rubber gloves. Just the look of it made me think of the green container of Comet and bright yellow rubber gloves that were under the sink. All the colour seemed to drain from Gabe's face and go straight to Lolly's, whose cheeks were an unnatural shade of crimson. Gabe licked his lips. He was nervous. We all were.

"Uh...I..." Gabe stammered and my heart went out to him. He kept looking down into his lap at the square package. Ray wouldn't put him out of his misery. He just stood there looking down on him, waiting for Gabe to say something but what could he say? That is was true, he was fucking Ray's daughter? And then what? I shivered to think about it.

"It's mine," Floss said, after a pause, folding the recliner upright and snatching it from Gabe's lap. She crinkled the wrapper in her fingertips, daring Ray to say something. I didn't know if it was an act of defiance on her part, the way she stood up to Ray with such a bold look on her face, or if it was an act of mercy, sacrificing herself to save her sister.

"It's not yours," Ray bawled at her. His face started to get red with irritation. It started with his cheeks and crept all the way down his neck in a blotchy sort of heat rash. "It was in his pocket."

"I asked him to hold on to it for me," Floss said smugly. Poor Ray was the only person in the world Floss would stand up to like that and I couldn't understand it for the life of me. She was so quiet in school, all the teachers used to say that Floss needed to assert herself more, she needed to speak up in class, she needed to work on her confidence, and here she was right in Ray's face when the rest of us were scared to death of him.

I watched her face, my Floss, her jaw firm, her eyes determined as she stood up to him. It wasn't at all the way I thought the altercation would happen. Ray was supposed to be angry with Lolly, not Floss. He was supposed to be bawling at Lolly about being irresponsible, sneaking around behind his back and doing things she wasn't supposed to do. He was not supposed to be staring down my daughter. I couldn't figure out what had gone wrong.

"Ray," I said in warning, "Leave it."

"I don't want him to leave it," Floss screamed. She looked like every other teenage girl on the outside. She dressed the same as everyone else, bought her clothes at the same stores in the mall and watched the same television programs but she wasn't like everyone else. She wanted Ray to be angry with her, as angry as he'd been with Lolly when he first walked in the room. She wanted to evoke that same reaction, wanted the same protectiveness directed toward her. It was why she was trying to start something with him. It was what she always wanted. I knew she wouldn't get it. I think she knew she wasn't going to get it either. I wondered if Lolly did the same thing with me.

"I'm going out to get some bread now," Ray said, his voice quieter and calmer. He looked somewhat confused, like he'd awoken from a dream and was still trying to discern what was real and what he'd imagined. He looked away from Floss and his eyes locked on Gabe's. "You'd better be gone by the time I gets back."

Once Ray was gone Lolly walked Gabe to the door, wrapped her arms around his neck. "I'm coming with you," she said. I couldn't imagine Ray's reaction if he came home and Lolly wasn't here. It wasn't about seeing them argue anymore. It was about her breaking his heart. I wanted to tell her to stay put. Ray wasn't above driving over to the Hillier's and forcing her back home. She wouldn't listen to me though. Even if she agreed with me she wouldn't do it.

"You better not," Gabe said and just like that she was nodding her head at the wisdom of it. He was the only one she'd listen to.

floss

Leo is in a bad mood. He paces around the small space in the living room of his apartment, looking at his watch and his phone every few seconds, stopping only to stare out the window, craning his neck to the side in search of Cathy. She is nearly twenty minutes late dropping Faith off.

"She always does this," he mutters. "Insists she drop her off like she's doing me a favour and then takes her sweet time getting here."

Since we have no pressing plans other than another thrilling round of Go Fish, I don't understand why he's so agitated. "Relax, Leo. Why don't you come sit down on the couch with me?" He glances at me as if he was surprised to see me here. I look around the small room and wonder if I'm in the wrong place.

It wasn't like this the night before when he reached for me in the night, pulled me closer, whispered that he needed me. His breath tickled the side of my neck, which made goosebumps appear all down my arms. He is a different person when he is awaiting Faith's arrival. He's on edge, nervous, uncertain. He's doing a mental calculation of how many minutes Cathy is late and he vows to be just as late in bringing her back this evening.

He's not normally petty, but he gets all worked up on the days Faith comes over. He straightens up the apartment, lines up her stuffed animals on the bottom of her bed just so, stocks up on arts and crafts supplies, and makes sure he has all her favourite snacks in the cupboard—Goldfish, Fruit Roll-ups, salt and vinegar chips. I don't think Gabe and Lolly do it this way. It's far less regimented. Lolly gives Gabe broad guidelines. *Around three o'clock. After dinner. Did he eat yet?* I can't imagine Leo and Cathy ever getting to that place. They are precise in their directions for dropping off and picking up. They recite the itinerary for the day. *We are going to my mother's this afternoon and then I promised her I'd take her to the store to get new shoes.* At first when I overheard the hushed conversations I thought it was just small talk, but it wasn't. Leo actually did want to know what Faith was doing at any given minute throughout the day. He'd look at his watch sometimes and murmur something. *The movie is letting out about now. She's probably on her way back from that birthday party.* It seemed his mind was constantly so focused on Faith that I was surprised he was able to concentrate on anything else.

"I'm sure there was traffic," I offer as an excuse, wondering whether I'm defending Cathy or calming Leo. "They're painting new lines on a lot of the streets now. Old Placentia Road was down to one lane yesterday."

"Finally," Leo says, squinting down the street as Cathy pulls up to the curb. Leo races down the steps, a huge smile on his face to welcome Faith. You wouldn't know he'd been cracking his knuckles in agitation seconds earlier.

I know right away something is wrong. Faith does not bound out of the car, an eager bundle of energy, but I can make out her form in the back seat. Cathy has the window down but

Leo doesn't crouch down the way Gabe does with Lolly. They are having words, Leo and Cathy. His face is like stone. There is not a single trace of Leo's good humour or his easy-going nature in his face or in his stance. He's so still, the only evidence he is not a statue is the way his clothes blow in the wind, outlining every detail of his body, the broad chest and muscular calves.

Faith is crying now, I can see that from the window. She sits in the back seat, her shoulders shaking, but neither Leo nor Cathy pay any attention. Either she has been sobbing too long for either of them to pay any notice, or they are too engaged in whatever conversation they're having to stop and offer comfort. I suspect it's a bit of both. At one point Leo kicks a rock out into the street, chews on a thumbnail, watching its path. It goes far, all the way through the intersection and past the bus stop sign before it stops rolling.

Cathy looks tired, stares vacantly ahead at her hands, which are still in a perfect ten and two position on the steering wheel despite the fact her car has been idling in park for more than ten minutes now. Leo cracks his knuckles again, intertwines his fingers and flexes his arms overhead. The veins on his forearm are raised and purple. He looks up as if I'd summoned him and our eyes meet. I can tell from his expression that he's angry, apologetic and filled with such helplessness that I have to look away, shut the mini-blinds with a firm twist.

When Leo finally trudges in, Faith trails behind him carrying her backpack in her arms like she might carry a doll or a teddy bear. Her eyes are red, her face is stained with tears. She runs into her bedroom as soon as she steps inside, seeking solace in her lavender oasis. I stand because it seems as if it's warranted.

"Is everything okay?" I know it's a foolish question but I don't know what else to say. I know right away we won't be playing Go Fish, or video games, or going for an ice cream later. We won't be doing anything together today. "What happened?"

"She didn't want to come today." His voice trembles when he says it. She's hurt his feelings terribly and I feel a surge of anger toward Faith along with a fierce protectiveness toward Leo. She should know how hard he tries to please her. She should know that he knows the name of every single stuffed animal and doll that she owns. She should know that he looks at his watch in the middle of the day to think about what she's doing. She should know that he lets her win all of those ridiculous games of Go Fish.

"Why not?"

He shrugs, sighs deeply. He knows why. I know why too. It's the same reason I didn't want Ray around. "We should probably talk."

"Okay," I reply woodenly. I brace myself for impact, tighten my muscles and clench my jaw.

"Look, Floss, we've been spending a lot of time together, as a couple and with Faith more as a family, and I love the effort you've been putting in."

It sounds rehearsed, like he practiced in front of the mirror the night before, but he couldn't have because the night before he was on top of me grunting and moaning and collapsing into my arms.

"I guess what I'm saying is that it's important for me and Faith to have alone time too. We might need to slow things down for a little while." He sighs.

"You're breaking up with me," I say flatly, and he shakes his head in protest. I feel sorry for him. He'll let me walk out the door this afternoon and he'll put a smile on his face, pretend he's enjoying all those hands of Go Fish. It's probably easier with two people anyway. The game goes faster, you don't lose track of who has the seven and who has the nine.

Leo is saying something to me but I'm not listening

anymore. I know exactly how to solve the problem but I don't say it. All Leo has to do is say the same thing my mother said to me all those years ago. She handed me the power, laid it right in my lap, and told me if I didn't want her to be with Ray she wouldn't. How could I have said no then? Leo won't put that kind of pressure on Faith though. He'd rather settle her down and play cards, problem averted, not solved. Never solved really. He tells me he hates to see me upset, but in the end, I know I'm the one leaving today, and I know exactly where I'm going.

lolly

"Kenny's sick and he wants blue Gatorade." Gabe's voice is flat and even, no expression or inflection. He gets that way when he's tired, talks like he's reading. "Can you pick some up? Mom and Dad went up to the cabin yesterday so I can't get out."

"What's wrong with him?" It's easy for Gabe to be laid back about such things, but I immediately think the worst. It's what happens when both your parents die before their time. I can't help being a hypochondriac as far as Kenny is concerned. I take him to the doctor at the first sign of sniffles and coughs and fevers. Gabe is far too laid back in such matters. *He's fine, Lolly, Jesus, you're going to turn him into a fuckin' pussy running off to the doctor every time he sneezes.*

"Stomach virus. Been puking all night. He ate bacon and eggs for supper and something red. I think it might be jam but it could be a red smartie. It was pretty fuckin' gross. I mean eggs are bad enough going down, right? Just imagine them coming back up. Actually I take that back. You probably couldn't even tell the difference, 'cept for the smell."

"Was it blood? The red stuff. Could it have been blood?"

"What the fuck kind of question is that? If he was throwing up blood do you really think I'd be calling you for blue Gatorade? Jesus Christ, Lolly, it's a fuckin' stomach virus. It's going around. I think it was jam," he adds when he's finished his little rant.

"Does he have a temperature?" I mentally tally Floss' work schedule over the past week. I think she might be off. I'll ask her if she can stop by Gabe's and take a look at him, make sure he isn't dehydrated.

"I don't think so."

"Did you even take it?" There's judgment in my voice, bordering on a full scale accusation.

"No, he's not hot, relax."

"Do you think I should send Floss over to take a look at him?"

"Not unless she's got blue Gatorade."

I'm there in twenty minutes with two big bottles of blue Gatorade, more than he'll drink in a month. Gabe is wearing an old pair of grey sweatpants and a faded blue T-shirt. His hair is a dishevelled mop on the top of his head and he has at least two days growth of beard. The smell of vomit clings to his skin.

"You look like shit," I say to him.

"Yeah I know. I was waiting for you to get here before I got in the shower."

"Where's Kenny?"

"He's asleep now. I think the worst of it is over."

I put the Gatorade in the fridge, on the door where the drinks go. The familiarity of the house jars me, as it does every time I come here. Sometimes it still feels like my house and other times it's as if I'd never been here before. Each time I step inside waiting for Kenny to get his shoes on, I notice a subtle difference about the house, a new picture on the wall, the lamp moved to the other side of the couch, a new rug to wipe your boots on. Right now in the kitchen, I notice a new set of tea towels folded neatly over the handle of the oven. I almost think Mrs. Hillier does it deliberately, tries to alter the house a little at a time until eventually it becomes unrecognizable to me.

"You're probably going to get it now, you know," I say to Gabe. He picks up all of Kenny's ailments. He had pink eye a few months ago, strep throat before then.

Gabe shrugs. "Yeah well what are you going to do? It's going around."

"Yeah. Floss says she's seen a bunch of it at the hospital."

Small talk. It feels weird to be with Gabe and be this uncomfortable. There's something not quite right about it, the tension between us lingering. The last time I was here I was making a scene in front of his house, ripping our child away from his new girlfriend.

"Are you calling in sick today? I have to go in at eleven, but Marie, she might be able to watch Kenny for you." I sound like it's more Gabe's problem than mine.

Gabe shakes his head. "No need to be getting Marie sick. I already called in. I couldn't wake him up this morning after he was up all night. Poor thing threw up all over his bed and then he came into mine and threw up all over my pillow. I don't think he made it to the toilet once. I got a load of fucking wash to do now."

I open my purse and hand Gabe Kenny's drawing. Gabe unfolds it curiously, a subtle smile on his face like I was giving him a love letter. I used to do such foolish things.

"Kenny made it for your friend," I explain. "It's supposed to be an angel."

Gabe smiles at the drawing, folds it back up. "Are you okay, Loll?"

I nod my head. "I guess so."

"C'mere," Gabe says, holding out his arms and I fall into them, sob into his chest. I can smell the sickness off him, take in the scent of his toothpaste from his breath. We haven't been like this since my father died and it feels almost exactly the same, knowing I'd lost something and not sure how.

"I'm sorry about the other day," Gabe says, taking a step back and leaning his palms on the back of Mr. Hillier's recliner. The warmth from his body leaves mine instantly, making the embrace seem as if it happened long ago. I shiver with the cold, cross my arms in front of my chest. "I should have told you first. Next time, I'll give you a heads up."

Next time. Of course there would be a next time. And a time after that. It will never end.

"I should go," I say finally. "I'll call later to check on him."

floss

Ray taught me how to drive. Lolly was mad about it, jealous that I was the one Ray was taking out every evening after supper. "It's not fair," she protested. It wasn't so much that Ray was teaching me how to drive, it was that he hadn't taught her yet. It was a new experience and he was having it with me instead of her.

"You're not old enough yet, honey," Ray said. "When you're older I'll teach you too."

"It won't be the same then," she sighed loudly.

My mother sighed with impatience and shot Ray a look. I offered to take a course at Young Drivers instead but Ray said it was too expensive and the instructors weren't any good. "You get a little break on the insurance but not enough. They get you coming and going."

I was nervous about being cooped up inside the car with Ray. He parked in front of a warehouse in Donovan's Industrial Park and we switched places. It was the only time I ever saw him not behind the wheel. Ray pushed the seat back, stretched out his legs and turned the radio on, started singing along. It was one of the songs on the countdown and I was surprised he seemed to know all the words. I'd never seen him more relaxed in his life. He spent so much time and effort being pulled in so many different directions by Lolly and my mother that he looked relieved to be away from them for a little while.

"Which way should I go?"

"Wherever you want," he shrugged, smiling lazily back at me.

I passed buildings I'd never seen before. I was afraid I was going to end up on the highway. I was going to end up in a turn lane and I didn't want to turn. Nothing was familiar to me. "I think I'm lost," I said nervously. Ray put his hand over mine on the steering wheel. It was one of the only times he ever reached out to touch me.

"I'll get you back home," he said reassuringly, and it sounded almost protective when he said it.

My father slips into the booth across from me at Tim Horton's, startling me so much I spill a little coffee on the table even though I'd expected him. There aren't any napkins but I'm afraid if I get up again he'll be gone, disappeared like a figment of my imagination.

"I didn't know if you would come," I say.

"Why wouldn't I?" I could think of a million reasons but he says it in such a way that I'd be shocked to assume otherwise. He confused me. There were so many different blanks I didn't know what to ask him.

The man at Barrett's was reluctant to give out the phone number written in the manila folder bearing my father's name. They had strict privacy policies with all their clients, he insisted, but I carried on enough for him to finally relent when I told him my father had already asked me to take the ashes.

"All right, I'll do it," I say to him when he looks settled. "I'll take your ashes. What do you want me to do with them? Do you have some special spot you want me to leave them?" I realize how very little I know about him. I don't know where he grew up, or if he had a favourite place he liked to go when he was a little boy. "You can bury them now," I suggest in case it hadn't occurred to him before. I'd only heard of it myself recently. "I mean in a cemetery. You can get a nice case and bury them. I've heard of people doing that."

He shakes his head, smiles slowly at me. "I never got that far. I just want you to have them."

"Mom won't be letting me take them in the house," I answer. "Or out in the yard either. She'll be mad I even talked to you."

He sighed. "How is your mother? She always was too good for me. Never could figure out what she was doing with the likes of me." He takes a long swig of coffee. I watch his Adam's apple bob up and down as he swallows. It seems to jut right out of his throat like a tumor. I massage my throat to stop myself from touching his. "I always thought she'd be fat by now. Her sister was fat, Doris, a ball busting man hater."

"Mom is good. She had a rough patch after what happened to Ray a few years ago." The lines on my father's face crinkle in confusion. "Ray's mom's second husband," I explain.

"Oh," he says in shocked surprise like she'd just left him for another man. "What's he like?" He asks it in a way that Ray might be competition for him. It's funny the way you can leave someone and still think you hold some title over them.

"He's okay. He's been dead this past four years, nearly five now," I say but it's like I'm hearing it for the first time. Ray is dead. How can he be dead? He tells lame jokes at the dinner table, he leaves his cereal bowl in the sink but he never dumps out the milk and at least one wayward Cheerio is floating and bobbing on the top. He surprises you by knowing all the words to the songs on the radio. He hasn't sat at the dinner table in nearly five years, he hasn't bought the yellow box of Toasted Oats cereal either, and he's never heard any of the songs on the countdown because they were all recorded after he died. The knowledge is swift and harsh. My throat gets tighter and my eyes moisten and tear up. Ray is dead.

My father grabs a pile of napkins and pushes them forward in my direction. It may be the only fatherly act he'll ever perform for me. My hand reaches for them and I cover his hand with mine, leave it there slightly longer than necessary. His fingers are long and cold, like he's got one foot already in the grave.

"Are you scared yet?" I ask him.

"Nah," he says. "It's going to be peaceful." He gets up to leave.

"Where are you going?" I ask him.

"Hell, I suspect."

"Oh," I nod as if he'd given me a more tangible destination. Port aux Basques, Toronto, Atlantic Place. I know for certain it's the last time I'll see him but it's the realization that I won't see Ray again that moves me to tears.

marie

I was anxious about Ray's body. It wasn't here at the funeral home yet and the wake was scheduled for tomorrow afternoon, between two and four. I felt like I should make a joke about Ray being late for his own funeral but Ray was never late for anything a day in his life. He was someone you could rely on, someone who got up at six o'clock every morning, ate a bowl of cereal and drank a cup of tea at a quarter to seven. If he was going to pick you up at five, he'd be there at ten minutes before. The funeral director didn't know any of this about Ray, but he did know one thing about Ray I didn't.

I sat in his office while we talked about the arrangements. I sniffed garlic in the air, it mingled with the smell of fresh flowers in the lobby and cedar that might have been from the caskets, but might have also been from the funeral director's aftershave. I was certain he'd eaten his lunch at his desk, scarfed it down before his one-thirty appointment. It was just another day at the office for him. His desk was neat and organized, a tidy pile of papers in manila folders were pushed off to the outer corner, opposite the phone. There was a filing cabinet behind him, and I wondered if they kept a file on each of the dead people they were after waking here, and if so what sorts of things would be in it. I supposed it was financials, invoices for caskets and flowers and funeral fees, all neatly stamped with PAID in red ink up in the corner.

"Mrs. Sullivan, your husband prearranged his funeral. Everything is already taken care of," the funeral director told me, folding his fat fingers together on the desk in front of him.

I was surprised by this revelation since Ray hadn't mentioned any of this but I didn't want the funeral director to know that Ray kept secrets from me so I smiled vacantly back at him. "Of course," I said assuredly, but I felt my cheeks grow hot.

He looked uncomfortable sitting there behind his own desk. His shirt was too tight around the neck, leaving a loose fold of skin to hang over the collar. "He must have got a deal then," I said thinking out loud. "Ray was awful cheap. He loved a good deal."

"That's certainly one of the advantages of prearranging your own funeral. You can protect yourself from inflationary costs, but primarily people do this to make it easier for their loved ones after they're gone."

Lolly, of course. He did it for Lolly. She wasn't even here with me, although I asked if she wanted to tag along with me to pick out a casket. I said it like we were buying new shoes but Lolly said she didn't want to come. Ray would have wanted to shield her from this. He was always thinking about her feelings. He'd have been mad with me for even asking her. I felt bad for saying how cheap Ray was and I wanted to tell the funeral director about a time when Ray splurged on something, even if it was something little, but I couldn't think of a single thing. He was cheap. He probably picked himself out the cheapest shittiest casket there was.

"Well that was certainly smart of him," I said instead. "Ray was a very smart man. He knew the final jeopardy question a lot, and not just on the teen week. He even knew the right answer on the tournament of champions once. Carbon and radon was the answer," I babbled. "You had to get both of them and he did." I was feeling more and more foolish and I didn't imagine the conversation could turn any worse. "Well I hope he picked out something nice," I added quietly.

"Of course," the funeral director replied, but it wasn't really a proper answer. I thought maybe he'd try to sell me some add-ons, an embroidered pillow, upgraded fabric in the lining, perhaps even a gold plaque on the side, but he just sat there staring at me. There was something else he wanted to say but he looked more and more uncomfortable, bending a paper clip out of shape and turning it around in his fingers.

"Were you aware that your husband prearranged his burial too?"

"Of course," I lied.

"Then you know he purchased a double plot. It was quite some time ago."

"You mean he bought one for me too?" I sounded almost hopeful, like a child waiting for a present from their mom and dad. I couldn't believe Ray didn't discuss any of this with me earlier.

"No ma'am," he answered shaking his head. "He pre-arranged his own funeral and purchased the double plot at the time of his first wife's passing."

I was thankful I was sitting because I knew for certain I would probably have fallen over with the shock and the hurt of it. I thought I knew what I was being told but I needed to know for certain. "He wants to be buried alongside his first wife, then?"

"That's what he requested at that time, yes."

I didn't want to cry in front of this fat, balding man with a smear of olive oil on his tie. I knew how to get the stain out but I wasn't going to tell him. I hated him, I hated Ray, and I hated the first Mrs. Sullivan more than all of them because she got to lay with my husband for all eternity and they were going to put me way out on the edge, all by myself, maybe even by the entrance where all the cars drove in, right up against the chain link fence. They'd drive right over the side of my grave, park right on top of it during the flower service. They'd throw their cigarette butts and their Tim Horton's cups out the window. They'd scrape their car doors off my headstone as they got out, and then bend down to inspect the paint on their car. They'd walk right over my grave in a shortcut to get to the person they'd come to see.

It was blurry. My eyes filled up so fast I couldn't see a single thing. I remembered seeing Ray in the hospital the time he had his heart attack. The slick eyes, all yellow and sad as he told me he'd done something to hurt me. This was it. This was what he was talking about, the thing he thought about changing but couldn't.

"Mrs. Sullivan…" The funeral director proffered a wad a tissues toward me, which I gripped tightly in my hand but didn't bring to my face, "this was all done a very long time ago. Please don't think it's a reflection on his feelings for you. Try to remember your husband and the love you shared together."

I wanted to tell him to fuck off but I didn't, not because it wasn't proper but because I couldn't speak.

lolly

Carson shields his eyes with his hand, squints into the sunshine reflecting off the ocean. He's left his sunglasses in the car and we're too far along the trail to go back. We sit on a rock somewhere between Signal Hill and the Quidi Vidi Battery. He's fidgety today, picks up a handful of pebbles and shakes them in the palm of his hand, the sand falling through his fingers. After a few moments of rattling them against one another, he flings them over the side of a crevice and then begins the process anew. It's the first truly hot day of the season and beads of sweat appear on his forehead and glisten in the sunshine. They look like jewels, hundreds of tiny diamonds adorning the top of his head.

"You're sweating," I say unnecessarily, and he dabs at his forehead with the bottom of his T-shirt. The sparkling effect is instantly gone, transformed now into a dark blue spot on the bottom of his T-shirt.

"Sorry," he apologizes, as if he'd done something wrong.

"Don't be. I like it."

"You like sweat?" He laughs then, a quiet chuckle which

either means he's amused by my confession, or he doesn't believe me.

My face grows red with the admission. I remember my father coming in after a day out in the yard. His T-shirt was nearly soaked though, his cuticles were covered in dirt and he had bits of grass that stuck to his neck, glued to the skin by the perspiration.

"I'm soaked," he said to Marie. "Sure just feel my shirt." Marie laughed at him, insisted she wasn't interested in touching his sweaty clothes but in that moment she looked at him with what I knew to be desire. I didn't understand it then. She was always bawling at me and Floss to wash our hands or soak in the tub if we were out playing in the grass, but she looked at my father like she could scarce breathe, and he was filthy. I feel the same way right now about Carson, overcome with desire to breathe in his scent, feel his sweat against my skin, watch it evaporate as if our bodies were being fused together.

"We should probably talk," he says but then he grows silent. His gaze out to the ocean is intense and I find myself picking up a handful of pebbles and repeating the same process of sifting and shaking them as he has just done. He invited me out to talk about something but he hasn't done any talking at all.

"What do you want to talk about?"

"I don't know," he says shaking his head even though he'd been the one to bring it up in the first place. "Us," I guess. Carson tucks my hair behind an ear, lifts it out of the way so he can kiss my neck. "I think about you nearly every second of the day and I don't get to see you near as much as I want to. I just wish things were different between us."

My heart beats rapidly with the admission. I understand his concern, his restlessness, and I don't blame him. I'm sure he's waiting for me to come around, waiting for me to incorporate

Kenny into our outings, but I'm still hesitant. It's like Floss' relationship with Leo got harder the minute she started spending time with his daughter. I was afraid the same thing would happen to us.

We sit quietly for a long time listening to the sound of the ocean underneath us, the gulls squawking above us, the wind all around us and shouts of other hikers along the trail behind us. The beads of sweat are coming back on his forehead. I lean into Carson and he places an arm around my shoulder. The smell of clover lingers in the air and settles around us. I could stay this way forever, staring off into the ocean with Carson, buoyed by possibility, but I know better than anyone that nothing is forever. There would be a time when Kenny and Carson would have to meet, and I wanted it to be soon. First I would tell him the truth about my relationship with Marie and Floss, and he'd understand better why I haven't brought Kenny around him yet.

"I have to tell you something," I say, rubbing the sweat from my palms on my thighs.

But then something makes an awful sound, a high, sharp ringing in my ear. Carson is on his cellphone, nodding, pacing. He's filled with adrenaline, so completely at odds with the lazy afternoon we'd been enjoying.

"Come on," he says, extending his hand out to me. He jumps without his feet leaving the ground the way the boxers do on television before a fight. "I got to go. They found a body."

marie

olly knew about the double plot. She had to. They went to the flower service together every year, she and Ray. And the two of them went every Mother's Day and on her birthday, August the twelfth. I stayed away on every single one of those sojourns over to the Holy Sepulcher cemetery, so I couldn't know. The day of Ray's funeral, I refused to go to the burial.

"I'm not going," I said, sitting on the floral couch in the funeral home with my arms folded, just like Lolly did all the times I told her she had to come to the supermarket with me, or over to Doris' for Thanksgiving dinner.

We were in the room where Ray was waked and they'd just closed the coffin on him. That was hard, watching them seal it all up, knowing I'd never lay my eyes on him again. The only ones left were me and Floss, Lolly and Gabe, and Ray's awful sister who said the rosary over him just before they closed the lid. She was the last one to touch him and I wanted to run over and tag him once before they shut the top just so my touch would be his last, but I didn't. She had to get Gabe to help her to her feet since she'd been kneeling there for so long. People were already moving the flowers out of the room and bringing them over to the church and already it was looking empty, like an apartment people were moving out of. The new occupants would be here soon, carrying their own heartache with them.

No one knew what to say to me, sitting there with a petulant look on my face. Ray was always the one to placate me, put a convincing hand on my shoulder or follow me into the bedroom where I was sulking about something. I thought it would be Floss to say something but she didn't look like she wanted to go to the burial either. In fact, for the past three days she looked like she didn't want to be there at all, standing off to the side with her lips pressed into a thin line. But it was Lolly who spoke up.

"You can't do this to him," she said softly, but she meant that I couldn't do it to her. "I can't be doing this alone."

I stood straight and smoothed the wrinkles from my skirt. "Fine then," I said as if she'd been carrying on for hours trying to convince me. I didn't go to the cemetery for Ray, though. He was dead and gone. He couldn't feel anything anymore. I went for Lolly because she looked like she might break.

Gabe drove the whole lot of us to the cemetery, following slowly behind the hearse with his hazard lights on the way everyone belonged to the funeral did. We were holding up traffic on Topsail Road and Blackmarsh Road. The line of cars seemed to snake on forever, and inside them the people complained what bad luck they had to run into a funeral procession. They were cursing themselves for not taking a different route, and calling ahead on their cell phones to say they were stuck behind a funeral, like Ray's death was a huge inconvenience for them.

I watched Gabe the whole time he drove. He'd cleaned up a bit, wore a pair of khakis with a crease down the front but he had on the same sneakers he always wore and a blue wind-breaker. He kept on the gloves they gave him at the funeral home to hoist the casket into the hearse and he put me in mind of a chauffeur. I didn't know what he was to me anymore. My future son-in-law. The father of my grandchild. A pall-bearer at my husband's funeral. Last week, he was just my stepdaughter's boyfriend, slipping his sneakers off in the front porch to sit with Ray and watch the hockey game while Lolly picked out a shirt to wear.

I wondered if he was relieved Ray was dead. It wasn't everyone who could knock up their girlfriend and not have to answer to either one of her parents. I felt the weight of responsibility and wondered if maybe I should say something but I didn't know what to say. I tried to think of what Ray would say but I didn't know what his reaction would be. I remembered his unbridled anger the time he found a condom in Gabe's jacket pocket but then the next day it was all forgotten. Ray could baffle you that way. You'd think you knew everything about him and then all of a sudden he'd pull something completely unexpected, like prearranging his own funeral.

It was hard to get out of the car. I wanted to stay in the back seat and feign a bad leg, or joint pain, but if Ray's sister could still stand after all that time kneeling and saying the rosary, I didn't have much of an excuse. I looked at the stone for Ray's first wife. Cynthia Sullivan, Beloved Wife and Mother. Ray's wasn't there yet. It was being etched, all the blanks were being filled in. I couldn't look at them all lifting Ray's casket from the hearse over the grave because I kept staring at hers. There they were, The Sullivans, Ray and Cynthia, alongside one another for all eternity.

At first I felt the bitter stab of jealousy. She was nothing but a box of bones and decomposing cells but I envied her. I wanted to be there, firmly planted in the ground alongside my husband but in the end she got him. I felt embarrassed then. People felt sorry for me and not just because my husband had died, but because it was like he'd chosen her over me, flaunted it in front of everyone to see, his old co-workers, his sister, people I didn't even recognize, people I'd never seen before and would never see again. I was sure they were all feeling sorry for me. I felt myself sway a little, saw darkness in my peripheral vision. I was petrified I was going to faint, fall headfirst on top of the coffin.

I kept thinking about Ray in the hospital telling me he was going to be waiting for me in heaven. I wanted to shout out to everyone that it was okay because Ray chose me. I wanted to tell every single person who looked at me that Ray had only done this for Lolly's sake, but that seemed almost as bad to me, that he cared more for her feelings than mine. It was like Lolly knew what I was thinking because she squeezed my hand at that very moment.

"I'm sorry," she sobbed in my ear. "He really did love you."

I breathed deeply and focused on the other emotion that was coursing through my blood, anger. I was livid with Ray. How dare he do this to me? I couldn't wait until the part where they started throwing dirt on top of the coffin. I wanted to take a shovel full and throw it at him and then turn around and walk away. I imagined him chasing after me. He did that when I was angry or hurt about something. He was predictable in that way. I pictured him rubbing my shoulder and kissing the back of my neck until I gave in. He'd never chase after me again. *I hope you're happy now.* I said it silently but it sounded loud to me, echoed in my brain and rattled around my skull until I covered my ears with the palms of my hands. Floss must have thought I was doing it because I was cold. The wind was blowing, causing Gabe's jacket to inflate and flap loudly. He was like a flagpole and we all hovered near him, our bodies bent over in mourning at half-mast.

The priest presented me with a rose from the top of Ray's coffin and I wept. My tears were tainted with jealousy, self-pity, rage. Then he gave one to Lolly and she wept too but her tears were pure. They were for the loss of a father's love, the deprivation of a mother, and the grief of being left behind. I cried harder then, harder than I ever had before because my tears were filled with shame.

lolly

"What are you doing home?" Marie is surprised to see me sitting on the sofa with a cup of tea. "Where's Kenny?" She looks around the room like she'd misplaced him. Marie is filled with nervous anticipation. She arranges all the coats in the front porch by size, makes sure the hangers are all facing the same way. She gets like this every year around this time.

"He's still sick. He's not throwing up anymore but he's tired, still fighting it off, I guess."

"Jesus, I s'pose we're all going to get that now. He must have picked it up at the mall. I told you not to let him touch those candy machines. They're crawling with other people's germs." She makes it sound like our germs are of superior quality than everyone else's. "And now with Floss spending all that time with that girl belongs to Leo, we're going to be sick right through the summer, all of us. The stomach virus, the cough, the cold, the sore throats. May as well put an X on the front door right now." Her frenzied movements come to an abrupt stop and she turns to look at me. "You're going to be able to make it tomorrow aren't you? Lolly, you knows I can't be going there myself."

I feel sorry for her. She hates going to the flower service and visiting the graves. Every year I tell her she doesn't have to go, but she insists every time, and by the end she's a sobbing mess of self-pity.

"I'm going, yes," I assure her and she goes back to straightening until she eventually runs out of things to put away. I plop my teacup on the table, spilling some of it over the top and onto the wood. It wasn't intentional but Marie looks almost relieved to have something else to do. She gets up and dabs at it with a paper towel. She folds the paper towel, concealing the stained parts with even square folds. Most people would just crumple it up into a ball and throw it out but she likes to fold and unfold it. She tucks it up her sleeve, keeping it at the ready for the moment she'll need it again.

She swallows a big gulp of air. "Did you see the paper yesterday?"

"I don't think so."

"Floss didn't either," Marie says, an announcement not at all shocking. Floss doesn't read the paper any day. Floss would be hard-pressed to name the premier. She never even watches the news. She says watching the news is like watching a soap opera. You can miss an entire year of the CBC news and still pick up exactly where you left off. One union or another will be threatening to go out on strike, someone will be complaining about health care, someone else will say the bad roads caused a collision. The news anchors will still look exactly the same.

Marie swallows. "I'm going to show you something but you can't tell Floss."

"Okay," I say warily. Marie and I have never had a secret before and the notion that we're about to have one now leaves me baffled. She brings me the paper from her bedroom. The newsprint smell mixes with baby powder. She's kept it hidden under her mattress, folded to the relevant article.

Police Seek Suspect in Pharmacy Theft. It's the robbery Carson told me about a few days ago. It's the same man I'd seen sitting on the front steps that time. "It's her father," Marie tells me. "It's Floss' dad, the same man was out in the back skulking about the night I called the police. Back to his old ways again," she says, like he'd been a good man for years, suddenly falling from grace.

He was looking for Floss when I saw him, although I didn't know it at the time. Carson's suspect is Floss' father. It's the only picture I've ever seen of him. She has his colouring, fair and lightly freckled but that's where the resemblance stops. He has a small frame and a slight build that lend him an almost adolescent appearance, save for his face with lines so harsh it looks like someone took a pencil and scribbled all over him. He could easily be a drawing in one of Kenny's colouring books. He looks unfinished, not quite coloured in all the way, but I tell myself it's because the picture is out of focus and slightly grainy on the newsprint. That it's taken from a surveillance camera only adds to the poor quality.

He looks so different from my father that it's clear Marie has no discernible type. My father's hair was dark and thick, he was broad-chested and wider all over, but I guess the same could be said for me, since Gabe and Carson are also worlds apart. Gabe is also of a slighter build with sandy hair and hazel eyes. He has a boyish quality that I can't imagine him without. I wonder if it's simply because I've known him since he was a boy. If I were to meet him for the first time, would I see the man he'd become? Carson has no hair at all and that lends him an ageless quality. It makes it hard for me to discern what he was like as a boy, and even harder to imagine what he might look like as an old man.

"So what?" I try to downplay it but Marie keeps rubbing

her forehead. She started out gently but now she rubs vigorously the same way she scrubs the sink or the toilet, like she was trying to rub the mildew off the grout and tile. "Marie, stop it," I shout, slapping her hand away from her head. The skin is all red and pink. "You're going to hurt yourself."

We both hear Floss climbing up the front steps. She has a certain way of climbing up the stairs that's different from anyone else, which is how we know it's Floss and not the mailman or Mrs. Lush looking to borrow an egg or a cup of sugar for her cookies. Floss skips the bottom step and always walks up holding the handrail on the left side when everyone else walks up to the right.

Marie bawls at me to get rid of the paper but there's not enough time to shove it back under Marie's mattress so I crumple it up and toss it in the trash just as Floss opens the door. I throw the coffee grinds on top of the paper. Normally Floss jumps on me for throwing recycled materials in the garbage. She roots cereal boxes and pasta containers out of the garbage, breaks the packaging down and places the cardboard in the recycle pile. I imagine she thinks the old packages must have feelings or something the way she tsks at me. *Lolly that's a sin*, she reprimands me in a harsh tone. *You're some wasteful.* It's like she's channelling my father when she says it, assuming his stance even with her arms folded and legs spread wide apart. It's the same way Dad acted if he caught you throwing away leftovers or stale crackers. I don't think Floss is driven by the value of a dollar though so much as she feels sorry for the garbage. She doesn't flinch though at my latest violation against the environment.

"What's going on?" Floss has always been intuitive, able to walk into a room and not only sense but absorb the tension in the air, suck it into her own body like a black hole.

"What are you doing home? I thought you were going to Leo's after work."

"We broke up a few days ago. I mean we decided to slow things down. Honestly, I don't know what happened. Faith was having a hard time sharing her father with me so then I decided to look for my own, find out what the big deal was." Marie drops a pile of magazines she was in the process of straightening. Floss has said it so flippantly it could be a joke.

Carson knocks on the door. He looks businesslike. His coat is slick with rain and drips into a puddle at his feet in the foyer, dirtying up the spot Marie had tidied earlier in the evening. I don't know when it started to rain. He's brought the dampness in with him. It feels colder; he even brings the smell of the ocean in with him although I don't know if it's the way the wind is blowing, or if I've just come to associate the salty smell with him.

He stares at Marie and Floss, addresses them as if I weren't in the room at all. He knows now. He knows everything, I can tell. I get a feeling of dread, a state reminiscent of the time Marie sat us down to tell us that dad was dead. I knew as soon as I sat down alongside Floss that day that something awful had happened. The house was spotless. It smelled of lemon cleaner and lilac spray. The magazines were in a neat pile on the coffee table, but none of that was the giveaway. It was the way Marie sat, with the edge of her behind on the recliner and her back so straight I could have laid a ruler along her spine. It was as if she couldn't decide whether she should stand or sit and decided instead to merge both stances. She'd folded her hands in her lap but they shook so much she'd tucked them underneath her thighs but that only made her whole body tremble. I'd noticed my father's absence and my heart slowed to the bare minimum. It was loud though. I thought Floss could hear it but she didn't look over at me at all to tell me to stop making such a racket. Maybe she just couldn't move because I couldn't either. I remember being jealous that at least Marie's hands could still shake. Mine wouldn't budge.

Carson talks to Marie and Floss about the body of Daniel Donovan, found in some hotel room on Kenmount Road. He says something about pharmaceuticals, an autopsy, arrangements. He delivers it all in an easy, professional manner. He could be reciting his shopping list, naming all the cousins on his father's side, he is so devoid of emotion. He probably does this sort of thing every day, is trained in how to deliver such news. I'm quite certain though, his audience has never reacted in this way.

Marie breathes a sigh of relief.

"He was very sick," Floss says. "He could have gotten a prescription for the drugs, but he doesn't like going to doctors."

The only person more surprised than me by this revelation is Marie, whose eyes are so wide the wrinkles disappear temporarily from the corners of her eyes.

"He wants me to take his ashes," Floss adds, "and spread them somewhere special. Do you know where I can get them?" She poses the question to Carson directly. She could be asking him where to buy electrical tape.

"Don't you dare go bringing them ashes in this house," Marie says shrilly. "And don't you dare go putting them in the yard either. That is Ray's yard and I don't want you to go dirtying it up with the likes of him."

"I'm sorry for your loss," Carson says, turning to leave. Carson knows who I am now, or at least he knows who I am not. I feel exposed and ashamed in a way that makes my heart slow to the point that I feel sluggish, almost disoriented. My legs move of their own volition, slowly at first as I make my way across the living-room floor and then down the front steps and across the lawn. It's still drizzling and I feel the dampness from the grass seep into the bottoms of my feet from my socks. Carson is waiting for me at the curb. He knew I'd come after him to try and explain. Regret reflects in his eyes and I start to panic.

"I was going to tell you today," I stammer. "But then your phone went off and I didn't get a chance."

"Laura," he says, cutting me off and shaking his head. His voice is soft the way he whispers my name. He pulls me into his chest and wraps his arms tightly around my waist. "Everybody has secrets."

marie

only thought about saying goodbye to Ray once, and it was early on. We were going to the movies, when I heard a flicker of doubt in his voice.

"Have you told anyone about us yet?"

Ray asked me the question while he dug around in his pants pocket for his car keys. There was something sketchy about him that evening, the way he hauled out the keys even though we'd just gotten in line for movie tickets. It was like he was thinking about bolting, running up over the stairs to the exit to find his car in the parking lot and drive away. It was packed at the mall since it was Tuesday, half-price night, and the line snaked down the corridor. The crowd in the lineup next to us moved quickly while our line seemed to come to a virtual standstill.

"Christ, I always gets in the wrong fuckin' line," Ray bitched.

I didn't know which to respond to, the question he'd posed about us dating, or the slowness of our line. The latter felt safer. "I know. I always get in the line where they got to change the paper in the register, or they're changing shifts. I hates moving this slow," I reiterated although it could have been a metaphor for our own relationship. It started as a whirlwind but I sensed Ray was pulling back now. It was eating away at me, this change in his demeanour. I was starting to respond in kind, sniping at him, giving him terse responses where before I would have elaborated on a point instead.

This seemed to jar his memory to the original question. "Have you then? Told anyone about us?"

I'd told everyone. The girls in the office, my father, Doris, Floss of course, my hairdresser, Floss' dentist, and the girl down to the bank. I'd even told the teller that I'd probably be opening up a joint account at the Royal Bank with Ray soon enough, but that I'd be keeping my own account separate here at the Bank of Montreal. I said it like I was assuring her I was still going to be a good customer when she couldn't have cared less.

I had to tread carefully here. I didn't know what to say but I knew there was a wrong answer by the way he studied my face so intently.

We'd been dating for nearly three months, although it wasn't always easy to get away together. He didn't bring Lolly around anymore, not after the first time she ran from Floss' room and caught Ray with his hand up my shirt. He kept her separate from me, leaving her with a neighbour on the nights we went out. Part of me was offended and the other part of me was relieved. I'd blocked out that he even had a youngster and when he'd mention her I'd have to think for a second about who he was talking about before it would come back again.

"Well, did you? Tell anyone?" He repeated the question. He was growing impatient with my silence.

"I might have mentioned it to a handful of people," I replied. This was most certainly true and did not, I thought, reveal anything that might make me seem overeager.

"Did you explain the circumstances?"

"What circumstances?"

"About my wife's death, and Lolly." He practically whispered this, made it seem like he was harbouring a dark secret.

"I said you were a widower and that you had a child. What is this about, Ray?"

He shoved his keys back inside his pockets, coughed into his fist. "I got a sister in Halifax. I was talking to her on the phone a couple of weeks ago and I told her about us. She seemed to think it was a bad idea."

I tried not to be insulted but I felt as if I'd been kicked in the ribs. His sister hadn't even met me and she'd already decided I was no good for Ray. Until that moment I didn't even know Ray had a sister and yet she'd judged me or, at the very least, my relationship with Ray to be inappropriate. I hated her. She would not be welcome for Christmas dinner or Easter, and if she ever invited us over to visit her in Halifax, I would come up with some sort of excuse. I'd say I was afraid to fly. I'd say I was afraid of boats.

"Why does she think it's a bad idea?" I asked him calmly. I struggled for control, bit down hard on the inside of my cheek. I wanted to rail at his sister. What business did she have passing judgment on us? I wanted to rail at Ray. Why did he give a shit what his sister thought anyway?

"She thinks it might be too soon. She's worried I might be looking for a mother for Lolly instead of a…" His voice trailed off, left the blank for me to fill in. I struggled thinking about how I might define myself. Girlfriend just felt silly, lover was hokey. Wife was too committal, mate too primal. It didn't matter. His point was that he was concerned he was running around with me so he could have someone to look after his child, which made no sense whatsoever since I'd only seen her a handful of times.

I'd had this same conversation with Doris just the other

day. "He's using you," she said. "Using me for what?" I'd laughed when I'd asked the question since it seemed ludicrous that I had anything anyone would want to use.

"So you can look after his youngster," Doris said flatly. "My God, Marie, open your eyes."

"Oh," I answered Ray because I didn't quite know what else to say. I didn't lash out at him with Doris' accusation since I was afraid it would only add credence to his concern. I had wrapped my legs around him the other night while he made love to me so the assertion that we were anything other than lovers stung. It seemed so far-fetched I would have laughed if I didn't have such a sinking feeling. Whatever his sister had said, it struck a chord with him. He was different, distant, preoccupied.

I shifted my weight around. It was getting hot inside the mall, standing in a lineup that wasn't going anywhere. My wool coat was heavy and weighed me down to the point I didn't think I could move even if the congestion in the line were to suddenly ease. I felt hot and cold, that queasy feeling that precipitated getting sick. I felt my feet sweat inside my high-heeled boots. They would smell when I finally got home and peeled off my pantyhose, a sour odour that would stink up the whole living room.

"It's probably foolish," he said when I failed to muster any sort of response.

"Yeah, probably," I echoed his sentiment but it was too late. He'd already expressed doubt about us and we were unravelling right there in between a young couple holding hands in front of us, taunting us with their assuredness, and three girls who worked in the same office behind us. I wondered if they could hear snippets of our conversation as I heard bits and pieces of theirs. The new billing system didn't make any sense. Cheryl was after losing some weight. One of them needed a new pair of shoes. If I could pick up on all this, how much could they hear of our own conversation? I was mortified, glad my back was to them. They would talk about me at the office the next morning. *That poor woman,* they'd say. *Her boyfriend practically dumped her in the lineup to the movies.*

"I have to go to the restroom," I said and I left him right there, walked down the corridor, disappeared from sight and ended up at the food court. I could have made a more dramatic exit but I would have embarrassed myself more than Ray. I got a coffee and sat down at a hard table, thinking about what I had done. Ray was probably inching closer to the ticket booth, looking at his watch and growing increasingly annoyed with me. He wouldn't know yet. He'd think I was just re-freshing my makeup. The girls behind him though, they'd know. Maybe one of them would even tell him after they noticed him standing outside the entrance with the tickets in his hand searching the crowd for my face.

I stayed there for a long time. The crowd cleared and the noise dissipated to a gentle murmur. My coffee was cold and it still wasn't touched. I'd call a cab in a few minutes. I saw Ray coming out of the corner of my eye and looked down at the table, folded my hands together in my lap. He looked angry, which irked me since I was the one who was supposed to be angry. He sat down heavily on the chair, irritated that it was bolted into the ground and he couldn't jerk it out first. The two tickets he flicked onto the table like he had just folded in a card game.

"I waited a half hour outside the theatre. I might as well have wiped my ass with the money it cost me to buy these." He gestured to the tickets.

"It was half-price night," I pointed out.

"What the hell are you doing, Marie?"

I shrugged. "I wanted a coffee," I said petulantly.

"I'm out of patience, Marie, and I'm a very patient man."

Ray's voice was so quiet it bordered on a whisper.

"You were going to break up with me anyway."

"What are you talking about? I didn't say anything about breaking up."

"You said we were a bad idea," I shot back defensively.

"I didn't say that. My sister said that. And she didn't even say that, not exactly. She just said it might be too much too soon for my kid." Ray ran his fingers through his hair, pulling the ends. "My daughter has been through a lot. More than any kid ought to go through and I was just saying maybe we could slow it down, wait a bit before we dove headfirst into a relationship."

It sounded like breaking up to me. It sounded no different than when I left him in the movie lineup. "I've been waiting for you for nine years, Ray." My voice trembled just a little. "I don't want to take it slow. I can't take it slow. I can't wait any longer for you to make up your mind about us." I thought he might leave me right then and there. I'd thrown down an ultimatum and I didn't know if it was fair or not, but it was how I felt. I was getting older. It felt like I'd been alone my whole life and I couldn't wait on the sidelines for Ray to make up his mind about something I was so certain about.

"I love you, Ray." That's the way I told him. Not after we'd made love, or enjoyed a romantic dinner together, but in the food court at the Avalon Mall when I thought we were about to part ways.

floss

My father's ashes won't be ready until tomorrow evening. I wonder what they're doing to him to get him ready. I don't think they go through the same rituals they do in a burial. There's not much of a point to embalming him or making him up but I keep wondering how they arrange his hands, if they lie loosely by the side of him, or if they fold them together like he was in prayer. People always felt the need to comment about the way a person's hands were laid out in the casket. Either it was done perfect, in which case they told the closest relative how it was exactly the way such and such used to sit. Or it was done all wrong and it was up to the closest relative to say they wished his hands were different. They had Ray's hands resting on him like he'd just fallen asleep on the couch and it was so real I thought he might start to snore.

My father was nothing to me and yet I can't stop thinking about him, the way he heaved into the bowl, the way his eyes seemed to recede into the back of his head when I told him my name, the sad look on his face when I told him I didn't want his ashes. He was filled with regrets but he seemed resigned to them.

When I see Leo's van outside the house, it only irritates me. The last time we'd spoken, he'd practically thrown me out, told me we needed to slow things down. He sits in the driver seat with the window rolled halfway down. He has his eyes closed and his lips move silently. He must sense my eyes on him because he jumps in his seat, startled at having been watched.

"Hi," he waves like we were old friends who accidently bumped into one another. He climbs down from his van and runs up the front steps. "I was just going to ring the bell. I was thinking about what to say to you first."

The van is empty. Faith must be with her mother. "What are you doing here, Leo? I thought we broke up."

He shrugs in response. "Faith got a goldfish."

The response is so off topic, I have to wonder if he's drunk, or high, or something. Maybe the sealant has finally got to him. My look of confusion amuses him because he smiles broadly at me.

"She wants to show it to you. She specifically said, 'Can I show Floss?' She named it Goldie." His smile broadens further and he looks expectantly at me, searching my face for some sign I might delight in the cuteness of the name but my expression is blank. I can't be in a relationship that thrives and dies on the moods of an eight-year-old girl. I won't. It didn't matter that Ray and I kept our distance or that Lolly and Mom bickered back and forth. Mom and Ray loved one another and Lolly and I both knew there was nothing either one of us could do to change that fact, nor did we even want to after a while.

"Don't you think it's funny? Goldie the goldfish?" The smile fades on Leo's face. He's getting nervous now, senses I'm not so easily swayed. I feel a little bit sorry for him and very nearly agree to go see the fish just to make him happy. My pathetic need to please is habitual. I've been doing it forever and in the end I haven't made anyone happy, not my mother, not Lolly, certainly not me. I meet Leo's gaze, make a conscientious effort to resist.

Kenny has a black teddy bear he calls Blackie, a brown one with a fire hat he calls Fire Bear. I wonder if Leo really thinks Faith is so clever because of the name of her goldfish. "I don't like fish."

"That's all I'm allowed to have in the apartment. I'll get a dog one day, when I'm ready to buy again."

"Look I can't come over to see your fish right now. I have to go to Ray's flower service tonight and then pick up my father's ashes. He died."

"Oh shit. Are you okay?" He reaches for me but I back away.

"I'm fine, yes."

"What can I do?" He looks expectantly at me like I was going to start giving him instructions. I know his type, he's just like Ray, always wanting to do something so he can avoid feeling anything.

"You can leave me alone for now, until you're ready to offer me more than a visit with your daughter's pet fish." I'd like to explain my request to Leo but it's something he's going to have to figure out on his own and I have no doubt he will eventually. "Go on now," I say shooing him away the same way I shooed my own father away a few months earlier.

"Floss." My name sounds like a question, hazy and dream-like as if he were just regaining consciousness and I was the first person he saw. He was confused. I feel sorry for Leo. I know he thought I'd be happy, thrilled even at this apparent breakthrough with Faith. He expected me to hop in the van alongside him, delight in Goldie the goldfish, and later lay with him in the darkness. "You're just upset about your father right now."

I shift my weight, stare at my slippers. I wasn't upset about my father at all. I was more upset with Leo, and a little sad for him too. He has a ways to go and I hope he doesn't take too long. I give him a smile of encouragement, to let him know I'm pulling for us. "I love you, Leo."

I shut the door on him, not a slam or anything, but it makes a statement all the same.

I hear Leo's car door slam, hear him hit the front of the steering wheel with the palm of his hand because he inadvertently sets off the horn, a short but loud sound that I feel in the centre of my forehead, in the place just above and between my eyes. I don't know what it is with men and their incessant desire to hit inanimate objects in a show of frustration—countertops, walls, kitchen tables, stair railings. They make it seem like an act of chivalry the way they take out their aggression on a piece of furniture instead of pummelling the wives or lovers they really wanted to hit. *Look at me*, the act seemed to proclaim. *I'm angry and frustrated but I still love you enough not to break your jaw.*

Ray once hit a tree right in the middle of Bowring Park after a spat he had with my mother that had something to do with heaven, although I don't know what they would have to fight about over something that seemed so beautiful. The tree, of course, didn't budge, although the leaves on one branch trembled just a little, causing a bird to flee from one of the branches. Ray's knuckles turned purple and bloody and my mother rolled her eyes at him disapprovingly, even as she retrieved a wad of snotty tissues from her purse and dabbed at the cut.

Leo's van peels away in the opposite direction, the screech of tires on gravel louder than the sound of the horn a few moments earlier. That was the other thing men did when they were angry, they drove faster and more reckless. Instead of hitting something they leaned into the accelerator and took the corners so fast you could feel the seatbelt tighten around your neck like a vise. Ray did it every time he got mad with me, up at that cabin when he drove off. He drove off again when I claimed a condom was mine instead of Gabe and Lolly's. Ray came back with a loaf of bread tucked under his arm and a red mark on his neck from where the seatbelt bit in. I wanted to think I had something to do with it, got him all worked up, but he seemed composed when he got back home, laid the bread on the counter and tried to massage it back into shape since it got squished from the way he carried it up under his arm.

Ray's face got red and he started slicing the bread in thick even slices, the only time he ever sliced it perfectly. Most of the time the bread was thick on the top and tapered into a thin, almost transparent slice on the bottom, but I suppose he never concentrated on a task more than he did at that moment. He asked me if there was anything I wanted to talk about and I almost laughed aloud at the image of me and Ray sitting down to chat.

I look at his tree, realize I want to talk to Ray now with a desperation that makes me look to the sky. I half expect to see his image in a cloud but there is only grey, all the clouds are mixed together in one system, all the souls of heaven fused into one. I want to ask him if he'd do it all over again, or if he'd have just taken the next bus home.

marie

The day we buried Ray, we ended up back at the house wondering what to do with ourselves. Lolly had always been an extension of Ray to me, and it was hard for me to realize that she existed separate from him. I was scared, the same way I was scared the day I brought Floss home from the hospital and didn't know what to do with her. I was certain Lolly felt the same way about me. We were only brought together because of Ray and with him gone, I didn't know where it left us. It had been a hard day. I could still feel all the stares on the back of my neck and all of the indecipherable whispers that blew past me and tickled the side of my face like the warm southwesterly wind that was forecast. Everyone knew what Ray had done to me and I wanted to die myself.

Lolly and Gabe sat together on the couch alongside Ray's sister. Lolly's eyes were still glassy, red-rimmed and smaller like she was already starting to disappear. She leaned her head into Gabe's chest and he splayed his arms wide along the top of the couch to accommodate her. He'd taken off his dress shirt and wore his plain white undershirt. I could see the hair on his armpits, damp with sweat and flakes of deodorant. He was going to leave a stain on the fabric and I didn't care.

Floss was in the kitchen making tea, standing in the same spot Ray had been keeled over a few days earlier. It was the first time I'd ever met Ray's sister and I already hated her. I kept thinking about the way she came between us, convincing Ray he was only interested in me because he was looking for someone to look after Lolly. She thought we moved too fast and too soon but what did she know? She was a spinster, childless. She sat cross-legged in Ray's chair as if he'd already willed it to her and accepted the teacup from Floss, taking several small dainty sips.

"You should go to the doctor. Both of you," she said gesturing towards Lolly and me with her teacup. "You'll need something to make you sleep." I hadn't pegged Ray's sister as someone who would advocate drugs to relax. Ray himself had to be dying before he'd take a little something for a headache, and he never took anything no matter how bad he had a cold. "It'll just be temporary," she insisted, "to get you through the next few weeks."

Lolly's hand instinctively went to her midsection. "I can't," she insisted. "It wouldn't be good for the baby." She hadn't mentioned the pregnancy since I first told her about Ray's death and truth be told, I sometimes forgot about it. When she said it then, it sounded only vaguely familiar, like the knowledge was supposed to remind me to do something but I didn't know what.

"You're having a baby?" Ray's sister was clearly shocked by the pronouncement. Her eyes seemed to get bigger the same way Lolly's looked smaller.

"Yes," Lolly replied with a hint of a smile although I didn't know why. To be young, pregnant, and without a mother or a father, hardly seemed like a cause for celebration. "We didn't plan it or anything," Lolly added as if it were an excuse for appearing happy.

"Jesus, no," Gabe said emphatically. "We were always careful but the condom broke and I got pretty potent stuff."

"Dad didn't know about it before he died," Lolly said. "I never got the chance to tell him. I was going to tell him this week, maybe even today, after the news was over. I was going to ask him to go for a walk with me. He liked to walk in the evening and it would have been such a nice night for a walk. I hoped he wouldn't be too mad about it. I wish I'd said something earlier." Lolly's voice, which had been cracking ever since she opened her mouth, now sounded breathless. She fought to keep speaking and it came out in a series of half whispers and half shouts. She sounded like the television when one of the stations had some sort of technical problem, the sound coming in and out in an uneven pattern. It made me tear up just trying to listen to her but Ray's sister set her cup of tea on the coffee table and sat back. She didn't look anything like Ray, or Lolly. Her nose wasn't wide like his. I couldn't tell about the mouth since Ray always wore a moustache, but the way she folded her hands together reminded me of Lolly. That they shared some genetic bond made me scoff aloud. She was a stranger. I knew more about Lolly than she ever would and no one would ever notice anything similar about us. The only thing we ever had in common was Ray.

"Sometimes when God gives us a new soul, he has to take away one too," she says soberly. I wanted to stand up and throw her out of my house. It was all bad enough Lolly had just buried her father, now her aunt had to think it was all her fault because she'd lain with Gabe. The Catholics were always looking for deeper meaning when there was none to be had.

"The same thing happened to my cousin," Gabe says. "She went into labour three weeks early and her husband's uncle got into a car accident that very same night." I wanted to throw Gabe out too. All day I thought how proud Ray would have been of him, the way he acted like a man throughout the funeral, but now here he was sitting on the couch talking about his sperm and buying into this foolishness.

"One don't have anything to do with the other," I insisted sharply, but I already knew that if Ray were alive, he'd probably ponder it too. He had more faith than me. "It's just a silly coincidence," I thought aloud. "It doesn't mean anything." But I was thinking about all the other coincidences in life—a chance encounter on the bus, a broken muffler, a dead wife, an ill-fitting suit, a forecasted snowstorm that moved slower than expected. Coincidence, I thought, was the only thing that kept us moving forward.

lolly

Marie is ready to go the cemetery a full two hours before I want to. She sits on the couch, nervous energy coursing through her. She can't keep her hands still, her fingertips drumming on the two-litre bottle of Pepsi, rinsed out and filled with water. She bounces a bunch of flowers up and down on her lap like she used to do with Kenny when he was small.

"Do you think I need a heavier jacket?" she asks me, stealing a glance out the window. "I hope the weather holds out. Is it supposed to rain later? It looks like the fog is coming in."

"I don't think it's supposed to rain," I say. "Why don't you turn on the weather channel."

She looks at her watch, her brows crossing into a V. "Where the hell is Floss? If she's not here in the next ten minutes we're going to have to go without her," she says with a trace of annoyance.

"My God, Marie, it's only four o'clock. The flower service doesn't start until seven."

"You got to get a good spot," she protests. "You knows how

crowded it gets."

This much is true. It does get congested but no one is going to be there before six. Marie was like this last year, having all of us there by five, standing around looking at one another. She kept saying the same things over and over again, that she hoped the rain would hold off, the priest would keep it short, that Dad's stone came out nice. It didn't matter the headstone was there for nearly four years already. She said the same thing every time we got there like she was seeing it for the first time.

"You don't have to go you know. Dad wouldn't mind if you went another time, maybe when it's quieter." The flower service is part religious ceremony, part family reunion but most of all it's a spectacle that seems to get worse every year. I hate going myself and then feel guilty for the dread. I suppose that's why everyone comes, the guilt they carry just for being alive. They bring flowers, framed photographs and their statues of the Virgin. Some of them bring lawn chairs and set them up alongside the graves of their loved ones like they were having a picnic in the park. They drape blankets over their laps, rest their canes against their feet and wait for their nephews and nieces and people who never come to visit them anymore. The people that are too old to get out of the cars park as close as they can, roll the windows down, and strain to hear the priest drone on from a passage in the Bible. There's usually a poor sound system and you can't hear much of anything anyway except the feedback from the microphone so most people just flip through the pages of their programs and wonder what part they're at.

"Well of course I'm going, Lolly," Marie insists. "What would your father think if I didn't come?"

She still talks about him like he's alive, ready to pass judgment. I stop short of telling her that he's dead, incapable of thinking or feeling anything, but it seems harsh even to me. "He'd understand," I say instead, and she stops bouncing the flowers on her lap.

"I know," she says quietly. "I just wish I could understand."

We still get there early, me and Marie, Kenny and Floss. The service won't start for another forty-five minutes. Marie gets to work right away. She wants to be ready when the service starts. She lays flowers on my mother's grave first, places the lupins in an empty glass jar and fills it with water from her two-litre Pepsi bottle. She does the same thing for my father's grave and then steps back to admire her arrangement. It's a gesture we don't talk about, this inclusion of my mother in Marie's ministrations. It makes my heart break for her.

"Looks pretty, doesn't it?" Marie speaks to my father's headstone and then looks to me and Floss. "These are the flowers he planted in the yard. Hard to believe they've outlived him."

Floss nods in approval, unscrews the Pepsi bottle and hands it over to Marie. There's something different about Floss this evening that I can't quite put my finger on. She says the same things she always says when we go to the flower service, that we're leaving too early, that the hymns are going to be too long, that traffic is going to be a nightmare, but something is definitely different about her.

"The stone came out nice, didn't it?" Marie says.

"Mom," Floss says wearily, "The stone was there before I left to go to Calgary."

"It was?" Marie asks uncertainly.

"Yes, and every time you come here you says the same thing."

"It's still a shock to the system every time I see it," Marie offers by way of explanation. "It's built up quite a bit since we were here for Ray's burial," she says like it's one of the new subdivisions they're building behind Blackmarsh Road. "Going to run out of room altogether." She gives a half smile and wrings her hands together. She has nothing left to do with them anymore now that she's decorated the graves. Kenny starts running around both headstones, weaving in and out of them.

"Watch out for the flowers, Kenny." Marie's voice is different than the gentle tone she usually reserves for Kenny and he stops for a moment to look at her in confusion. He is not used to being reprimanded by her; she usually intervenes if I speak to him harshly. It's just nerves. She must have gone to the bathroom a half dozen times before she put on her shoes. After a pause Kenny resumes his running.

"I knows he's going to knock them over," Marie says, stealing a sideways glance at me. She wants me to say something but I don't know what she expects. He's only four years old and has forty-five minutes to kill, and that's until the service starts. I'm saving my snacks for when he starts to get fussy and tells me he wants to go home. I can't imagine what else a youngster is supposed to do outdoors except for run around. Marie is always telling me he needs to run around more instead of watching television.

"I don't have any more flowers and I don't have any more water either," Marie continues. "If he knocks them down that's it. This will be the only grave without a flower on it. I s'pose it would be easier to get the plastic flowers like everyone else but they're so ugly. Hardly anyone brings the plastic ones to the Anglican cemeteries, but that's the Catholics for you," she adds and shrugs her shoulders dismissively. "The plastic flowers, the solar lights, the gaudy statues," she says shaking her head in disapproval. "I might not even decide to get buried here, you know," she says as if she were threatening me. "I might just go up to the one on Kenmount Road. That's where my father is."

Kenny begins climbing on top of the stones and jumping off. I get a warning glance from Marie and another one from a middle-aged lady in the row behind me standing watch over the grave of someone named Murphy.

"Kenny, honey, don't go jumping off the headstones. You're

going to hurt yourself."

"I'll be careful, Mom," he says before taking another leap. He thinks he's Batman.

"It's disrespectful," Marie whispers at me.

"Kenny come here," I motion and sit him down on the grass in front of me, offer him a juice box. I hope he'll sit long enough to satisfy Marie. People begin piling into the cemetery, so many they are a blur of sizes, ages and different coloured jackets. Eventually a familiar figure emerges from the crowd to step in front of me.

"Sorry I'm late," Gabe says like we'd been waiting on him, like the whole service can begin now that he's here. "Jesus, it looks like they're giving shit away. They even ran out of programs. You wouldn't know but they were going to resurrect everybody here this evening." Kenny, still sulking at being told not to play amongst the headstones, moves quickly to his father and Gabe hoists him up onto his shoulders in one easy motion.

"What are you doing here?"

"I'm paying my respects," Gabe replies. "Jesus, it's after getting some cold around here." He rubs his hands together, blows on them. "You bring an extra jacket for Kenny?"

The fog bank creeps closer and you can see people start shivering, rubbing the tops of their arms to keep warm. Marie, who is always cold, doesn't seem to feel it at all. She just stands there stoically.

"No, it was a lot warmer when we left the house," I say defensively. It seems like hours ago when we loaded up the car. "Besides, he's after leaving all his jackets at your mother's house. The only one he got left at my house is too small for him."

The priest's voice coming through the speakers puts an end to our conversation and I settle into the service. I don't pay any attention to the mass. The priest's voice is background noise to me. He could be saying the weather forecast or giving directions to Argentia. It doesn't matter. All the anticipation that surrounds the day and once I'm here I can't wait for it to be over another year. I listen to the people around me.

The crowd behind me are starved to death. They came straight from work and are thinking about where to eat after. A pair of brothers are wondering if the Tom Fitzgerald in the grave two rows ahead was the same Tom Fitzgerald who worked at the stadium years ago. A woman behind us sings along to a hymn but her voice is high-pitched.

"I wish they didn't have to sing so many hymns," Floss complains. "Nobody knows the words anyway. The traffic is going to be bad getting back and I have to get to Barrett's before it closes."

Marie bristles in response. "The ashes aren't going anywhere, Floss." Floss quiets but Marie turns on her anyway. "Ray went to every single one of your music festivals at the Arts and Culture Centre and he never complained one time that he had to sit through fourteen other school choirs sing "Greensleeves" before you got to go on. And that man you calls your father never sat through a single one. So if you got to sit through ten, twenty, one hundred more hymns, you'll do it."

Floss bursts into tears. It's the first time she's ever cried at my father's grave. "I never told him, Mom. I never got to tell him one time. I didn't even get to thank him for my braces and he said I'd thank him one day." People near us stop singing to stare. O'Reilly, Murphy, Fitzgerald, Walsh. They'll all be talking about us tonight. That Sullivan crowd.

"Oh Floss," Marie sighs. "He knew all that."

Kenny is restless again, squirms down from Gabe's shoulders and starts weaving in and out of my parents' graves.

"Will you control that child," Marie says sternly. I instinctively reach for him but it puts him off balance and he trips over the vase just like Marie predicted. The flowers spill out, the water seeps into the ground and Kenny falls, his head comes down on the corner of the stone.

I don't see the blood right away. I only see the water being absorbed into the ground and disappearing. Kenny starts screeching, big loud wails that make everyone turn to look. Gabe picks him up and starts dabbing at the gash with his sleeve.

"Oh Jesus," Marie screams, her hands covering her mouth. "He's after splitting his head open. What are we going to do?" Her voice is panicked.

Floss takes a look at him. She's still sniffly but she composes herself enough to pry Kenny's hands away from the wound and then bites her lip in concern. "Oh Lolly, he's going to need stitches. Maybe three or four. Five at the most." Kenny bawls even more at this news, although he doesn't know what it means.

A crowd gathers now. Someone offers a tissue. Someone else digs Neosporin out of her bag. A woman across the row from us has a baby wipe, someone else has a band-aid. All the eyes are staring at us, and at my bleeding child who I couldn't control long enough to get through a flower service.

"Come on, we got to get him to the Janeway before this is over and we get stuck in traffic," Gabe says. He hoists Kenny over his shoulder and starts walking toward the exit. I follow him but I have to run to keep them in my sight. I lose them about halfway to the gate. I feel disoriented, uncertain what way is out, where my car is, where my father's stone is.

I scan the crowd for Gabe but my eyes lock on Carson, making me wonder for a moment if I possess a secret ability to summon people when I most need them. I feel such a flood of relief at seeing him that I stop and take a step toward him. He wears a look of concern on his face, knowing something is wrong with me. I want to run into his arms and tell him to bring me to the Janeway, Kenny is hurt. I've lost Gabe altogether but I'll meet them there.

I begin moving towards him and as I get closer his expression changes from one of concern to one of fear. Whereas before I fixated only on him, my gaze takes in his surroundings, a bored-looking woman with brown hair and caramel-coloured highlights and two little girls in matching blue fleeces. They're sweet little girls with ponytails and sneakers. They're too big to jump off headstones and chase one another in between rows of graves, but they're bored nonetheless. They look to the sky and then down at their feet and pretend to follow along with the program. His hands are on his head now, anxiety emanating from his body. I can sense his panic over one row of the dead, and then another. The woman with the brown hair and caramel highlights leans into him and says something. It could be anything. She could have asked him what time it was or if he wouldn't mind staying for a few minutes after to chat with her aunt. It didn't matter because there was only one thing I heard. Everyone has a secret.

Carson belonged to someone else. He'd never belong to me. He tried to tell me in the beginning. "Ask me anything you want," he said and I asked him how he got his name. I'd let him off easy.

I feel so hot my skin burns. The grass is fragrant, freshly mowed by the grounds crew in anticipation of the evening, or maybe it's just all the fresh flowers people have brought to lay at the graves but something smells unbearably sweet. I can taste it on the back of my tongue just as sure as I've pulled it from the earth and chewed it up. I close my eyes to shut it out but the scent envelops me, the warm scent of musk. I feel Marie's arms wrap around me, hold me steady. I think for a moment that maybe I do have the ability to summon people when I need them, wonder if maybe it was me who summoned her that day on the bus, and not my father.

"I'm sorry," she whispers in my ear, the same thing I said to her in nearly the same spot, when we buried my father. I hold on to her like my life depends on it, and in many ways it does. I dig my nails into her shoulders and bury my face in her neck, take deep breaths while I wait for the earth to stop spinning.

"Are you coming or what, Lolly? Once you hear the words Go in Peace, we're fucked. We'll never get out of here." Gabe's voice startles me, shakes me from my reverie. He probably made it halfway to the car before he realized I wasn't behind him.

I blink, expect Carson to be gone, disappeared in a puff of smoke, but he's still there staring at me with such a look of fear and longing on his face I feel an ache in my chest. "Go on and look after your child," Marie says. Gabe reaches for my hand, each of his fingers interlace perfectly with mine, before giving me a gentle tug. Together we take flight, bolt like rabbits over to the car.

floss

The ashes are in such a tiny box. It can't be all of him. My father must have divvied himself up, gave some to me, some to a few other people, but I couldn't imagine who else would want him. I didn't even want him and I was his own flesh and blood. The man at Barrett's assured me this was everything. It was all that was left to him. He wasn't a big man but I still can't believe he could be condensed into this little tiny box.

I don't know what to do with him. I end up driving around town with the box in the front seat of the car like I'm taking him on a tour of the city—east end, west end, downtown. I thought I would know what to do, that it would come to me in some moment of clarity, but it doesn't. I don't know the first thing about him, haven't the faintest clue what mattered to him, or where I should put him. Even he didn't know. He just seemed to possess some blind faith in me that I would know. I don't.

I probably need a permit to scatter the ashes and I regret not asking the man at Barrett's if he knew where I could get one. I want to be rid of them now. I feel my stomach turn every time

I look at the box and I break out in a cold sweat. My stomach starts to feel queasy. I wonder if they're toxic, if maybe that's why you need a permit to scatter them. They're probably not allowed to be scattered near parks, lakes or schools. Cathy would include it in her list of things I wasn't allowed to do with Faith. Disposing of a body would be right up there with giving her Tylenol.

I pass the dumpster behind our old apartment building and resist the urge to toss the box in on top of someone's folded up rug with the stain in the centre. I wonder if I could just flush the ashes down the toilet. It's small enough. I could do it in two batches. People have bigger bowel movements than what's left of him. But Leo would probably say it would corrode the pipes, or offer some other plumbing explanation.

After an hour of driving aimlessly from one area of town to the other, I end up back home. Mom is sitting on the couch waiting for me.

"Did you get him?" she asks me nervously.

"Yes."

"Where is he? What did you do with him?"

"He's out in the car," I say like he's sitting in the passenger seat waiting for me to change my shoes.

"What are you going to do with him?"

"I don't know, Mom." I wipe the sweat from my forehead but my hands are damp now as well. "Did he have a favourite place that he liked to go?"

"Down to the pubs," Mom replies.

"Well I can't leave him there."

"Why not? Drunk crowd down there probably get a kick out of it. Throw the ashes out the window of a cab. A fitting burial for Danny. He'd probably like it, being carried away on the wind with little pieces of him scattered everywhere. No one would ever be able to find him." She makes it sound almost romantic, getting tossed out the window of a cab that's filled with drunks.

I sink down on the sofa, put my head in my hands. "I saw him in Calgary," I confess. "He was sick then. I could tell by looking at him he wouldn't be alive by the end of the year. I don't know why I told him who I was. I didn't think he'd try to find me. I just wanted to see what he'd say."

Mom sinks down next to me, expels a deep breath. "Is that why you came home?" I nod. "Then I'm glad you saw him."

"I didn't feel anything," I insist, shaking my head. "I swear."

"It would be okay if you did."

I fumble with a magazine, fold the corners like I was dog-earing every page. I wasn't telling the truth. I did feel something when I saw him but it wasn't longing or sadness that my father was about to die and I didn't even know him. I felt hollowed out because Ray was already dead and I wished I'd known him better. I knew bits and pieces of him but I didn't know the whole person, not the way Mom knew him, or Lolly. I wished I laughed harder at his jokes or asked him if he could spin me around the yard the way he spun Lolly around. He would have done it if I had asked him. I take a ragged breath and Mom rubs the space between my shoulders.

"Come on," she says getting up. "Let's get the ashes."

We scatter him together, Mom and I, spread his ashes around Ray's tree. The two of us kneel on the grass, heads down like it was a shrine. The sun is nearly gone now, just a faint pink hue left in the sky.

"The tree will probably die now," Mom says and we both laugh and then burst into tears. It's almost as if we timed it, our emotions seem so in synch. Neither one of us could bear it if Ray's tree died.

"Are you sure Ray won't be mad?" I wonder if Mom has thought this through, if she'll wake up in the middle of the night and start going through the dirt with her bare hands trying to dispel my father from Ray's tree.

"Ray won't care. He'd just be glad that he got to do this for you. All he ever wanted was to look after us, be happy." Mom reaches for me then, and we hold hands. I think it's the strangest thing that my father's final resting place is here, on my mother's property. It's almost as strange to me that Ray's final resting place is not with Mom, but with someone neither one of us ever met. It's hard to believe that Ray existed before us since it seems like Mom only came to life after she met him. I guess it doesn't matter where we end up on this earth. I know without a doubt that there are some souls that would always find one another eventually.

lolly

The doctor asks Kenny what happened. He'd stopped crying for the longest while but now that the doctor is here, he's started up all over again.

"His grandpa clocked him one," Gabe jokes.

"Gabe, I don't want to have to sit down with social services tonight," I sigh, rubbing my forehead with the tips of my fingers. "He hit his head on my father's headstone at the flower service," I say and then laugh at how ridiculous it sounds. Gabe laughs too, the culmination of a long, stressful day that finds the two of us making our first visit to the Janeway.

Kenny needs four stitches, just as Floss predicted. Kenny wails while Gabe holds him down. He promises him ice cream, anything he wants, so long he's a brave boy. A Blizzard, a sundae, a banana split, dilly bar. Gabe methodically starts reciting the entire menu. He does it more for himself than for Kenny, gives himself something to concentrate on instead of his son's tears. I'm glad Gabe is here because I don't think I could hold him down. It would take all my strength and I didn't have any left. I watch Gabe bent over Kenny, the sweatshirt lifting to expose

the curve of his back. When it's over Gabe looks worse than
Kenny. He has dark shadows under his eyes and smears
of Kenny's blood on the sleeve of his shirt. The blood is under
his fingers, dried up and crimson. He looks like he'd been to war
instead of to a flower service. I feel the same way, still reeling
with the shock.

At Dairy Queen, Gabe wipes a dribble of ice cream from
Kenny's mouth, inspects his head for the hundredth time. He
traces the perimeter of the bandage gently, circling around it with
a thumb, one full pass no more. He'll do the same repeatedly
this evening, ask him if it hurts, kiss the top of the bandage with
his lips. He rescues Kenny's ice cream, holds it in his hand and
licks all around it, consuming all of his snot and spit in one easy
lick, before he hands Kenny back the cone.

I used to wonder if Kenny was the only reason Gabe and I
were together and then later I'd wonder if he was the only
reason we were apart, but sitting here now in the booth, I
realize it doesn't matter. None of it matters. One way or the other,
Gabe and I will grow old together. There will be more nights like
this one, maybe not visits to the emergency room, God willing,
but there will be more nights spent conferring over illnesses.
There will be soccer games and hockey tournaments and parent
teacher conferences. There will be school functions and
birthdays and graduations, a wedding, a daughter-in-law, maybe
even grandchildren. I would get to see the lines form in the
corners of Gabe's eyes, get to see his hair thin, the paunch of
middle age set in. There was no one I wanted to grow old with
more than Gabe.

For the first time since my father died, I feel that all is right
in the world. I picture our initials somewhere in the men's room,
G.H + L.S. It's painted over now, been painted over a long time
but they would always be there, just under the surface professing
a truth that was pure and absolute. I was grateful that Gabe
would always be a part of my life. I was no longer bitter for all

the people who were gone, but grateful for the people who I had with me, Gabe, Kenny, Marie, and Floss.

I feel my eyes water and under normal circumstances I'd be ashamed to show tears, especially here in the middle of Dairy Queen, but there's nothing about them that makes me feel awkward or ashamed. I reach for Gabe's hands, hold them in my own. The same hands that just traced the outline of our son's scar are the same hands that held mine during my father's funeral. Gabe, who let me practice on him by putting highlights in his hair even though his friends teased him and called him a fag. He never cared what anyone thought except me.

"What's the matter?" Gabe asks me, alarmed at the tears that are only just coming now. He thinks they're a delayed reaction. Maybe they are but not to what he thinks.

"I love you, Gabe."

The hands that only a few hours ago wiped the tears from our son's, wipe the tears now from my own eyes. He blots at my face with a Dairy Queen tissue. It feels rough and slightly abrasive, the way love has always felt to me.

"I love you too, Lolly."

acknowledgements

My gratitude goes out first and foremost to Leslie Vryenhoek for getting to know my characters so well, and for all of her superb suggestions and words of wisdom. You are a wonderful, supportive and encouraging editor.

Thank-you to my husband, Roberto, for giving me the opportunity to do what I love every day.

Thanks also to my friend, Jane, who is always willing to talk through my story and discuss my characters over a drink. I am also grateful your camera is better than mine, and appreciate you taking all those author photos.

Thanks to the entire team at Breakwater Books for all the work that goes into creating the finished product. It's been a wonderful experience getting to know all of you. I am forever indebted to Breakwater Books for taking my stories to audiences I never imagined.

To everyone who took the time to e-mail me and tell me how much you enjoyed *The Widows of Paradise Bay*, I can't begin to tell you how much your words of encouragement meant.